The Art
of Inheriting
Secrets

PREVIOUS BOOKS BY THIS AUTHOR

The Lost Recipe for Happiness
The Secret of Everything
How to Bake a Perfect Life
The Garden of Happy Endings
The All You Can Dream Buffet
No Place Like Home
A Piece of Heaven
The Goddesses of Kitchen Avenue
Lady Luck's Map of Vegas
The Scent of Hours

The Art of Inheriting Secrets

BARBARA O'NEAL

LAKE UNION PUBLISHING

Published by Lake Union Publishing, Seattle
www.apub.com

Amazon, the Amazon logo, and Lake Union Publishing are trademarks of Amazon.com, Inc., or its affiliates.

ISBN-13: 9781503901391
ISBN-10: 1503901394

Cover design by Rachel Adam Rogers

Printed in the United States of America

For my uncle Tony, who loved good books and good food and India. You are always in my heart.

Spring

Sharing food with another human being is an intimate act that should not be indulged in lightly.

—M. F. K. Fisher

Chapter One

My first glimpse of Rosemere Priory came just before dusk, when the last of the day's sunlight fingered the old stones a rosy gold. It was vast and rambling, bay upon bay of Elizabethan windows, with two crenellated towers pointing into an eggplant sky.

Everything I knew about my mother shattered in that instant. I recognized it, of course, from her fantastical paintings. I recognized the woods, too, and the owl that flapped its wings and flew out of an upper window and probably even the fox that dashed across the rutted road, its fat tail sailing behind it.

I simply believed that she'd made it all up.

My grief, still so raw only a month after her death, dug its fingers into my lungs. I peered through the window of the hired car as if she might appear.

My tidy, reserved English mother. She never spoke of her life before arriving in San Francisco in her twenties, where she met and married my father. Once I was born, she settled in to illustrate children's books and create a series of exquisitely detailed paintings of a wild English wood, alternately seductive and threatening.

As the car slowed over a potholed, neglected drive, I saw where those paintings had been born. All these years, I believed that she'd fled some backward town in search of a better life, though now I didn't know why I made that up.

"This is the house?" I asked the driver, a sixtysomething man in a black uniform, complete with a cap and a neat tie, who'd been hired by the solicitor to meet me at the airport.

"No mistaking it, is there?" he said and stopped the car.

We both stared at the vast mansion. Vines covered her face, wantonly crawling through the broken windowpanes. "How long since anyone lived here?"

He rubbed his chin. "Forty years or better, I'd say. When I was a boy, there were festivals and picnics on the grounds. All very grand."

"What happened?"

"Now that's the thing everybody'd like to know, miss. One day, it was all thriving and busy, and the next, the lot of them disappeared."

"The lot of them?"

"The old lady died, as I recall. But her son and daughter went abroad and never came back."

Son? I knew nothing about an uncle. A flutter of wings moved in my throat. "Do you remember them?"

"'Course. Lord Shaw, the Earl of Rosemere, was my age, though we had no dealings to speak of. Lady Caroline was a great beauty, but she kept to herself."

Caroline. That would have been my mother.

Lady Caroline.

"We can head to town," I said. "They'll be expecting me."

"Right."

I found myself watching the house recede in the side mirror, imposing and impossibly huge. Ruined.

Mother, I thought, heart aching. *Why did you hide from me all these years?*

My mother's solicitor had arranged for accommodations in the local village, Saint Ives Cross, which was locked up tight when we arrived at six p.m. Full dark had already engulfed it. In my jet-lagged, disconnected state, my only impression was of half-timbered second stories leaning over narrow lanes and pools of light falling on the pavement from the streetlights. A central square held an ancient stone marker, the indication of a medieval market town. I knew from an article that I'd written on the history of markets that it was called a butter cross, and something about knowing that grounded me a bit. The evening was damp and cold, but even so, I could smell earth and growth, even this early in the year, February.

The driver carried my bag into the hotel, and I followed behind him in a daze, trying to control the limp that sometimes still plagued me.

I found myself in a tiny lobby with an unmanned desk. The counter flowed directly into a pub, where a scattering of patrons stared at me openly, hands gripped around their pints. I gave a nod, but only one woman acknowledged it.

My driver gave me his card. "You give me a call if you need anything, Lady Shaw."

I shook my head, wanting to protest the title. Behind me, a little rustle told me the people at the bar, three men and two women, had heard plainly enough. Flustered, I said, "Thank you. You've been very helpful."

He tipped his hat. I focused on sliding the card firmly into my wallet, willing someone to appear at the desk to check me in before I fell over from exhaustion.

At last, a stout woman with short white hair shot through with steely streaks appeared. "Help you?"

"Yes. My name is Olivia Shaw. I believe Jonathan Haver made a reservation for me?"

She gave me a glare, took a key from a hook, and slapped it down on the counter. "Third floor. Up the stairs to the back there."

I gripped my cane tightly. "Is there an elevator? I'm not able to navigate stairs easily."

"Should have said in the reservation."

"I'm sorry. I didn't think to—"

"Humph." It was an actual word. In my dizzy state, I had to bite my lip to avoid breaking into exhausted laughter. "Already the countess, are you?"

In my capacity as editor of a highly respected food magazine, I was used to travel and curt manners, but her rudeness seemed over the top. Taking a breath, I said, "Look, I've been traveling for nearly twenty-four hours, and stairs are a challenge for me at the moment." Follow conciliatory with steel: that was my motto. "Do you have a room I can reach more easily, or shall I call my driver back and have him take me somewhere else?"

For a moment, she stared at me. Hostile. Furious, even.

What the hell?

Finally, she snatched the key from the counter, hung it back on its hook, and took another. "You'll hear the pub, but no one'll be singing until Friday." She leaned over the bar. "Allen! Come show the lady to her room."

A youth, no more than twenty, rushed from the back of the bar, graceful as a cheetah. "Hello," he said, grabbing my bag. "This way."

We wound down a corridor beneath the stairs and across a tidy dining room furnished in chintz. "Breakfast here, miss, starting at seven. She quits at nine sharp."

"Thank you."

We walked down another corridor to the end, where a wide door opened into a very pretty room. I sighed in relief, offering him a pound coin. "Wonderful."

He pocketed the tip with a smile. "No trouble."

"Does the pub serve food?"

"Best fish-and-chips in town. I could bring you a plate if you like? Or a glass of wine?"

"A pint of ale," I said, eyeing the wingback chair that stood by the grate. "And the fish-and-chips sound perfect."

He gave a nod. "Right back, my lady."

"You don't have to—" I began.

But he was already gone.

When Allen returned with the food, he showed me how to light the gas fire, handed me a scrap of paper with the Wi-Fi password, and said he'd send someone round in an hour for the tray.

Eating the hot, flaky fish, seasoned liberally with malt vinegar the way my mother served it, I sank into the relief of being here, away from the craziness of my life the past few months.

My mother's sudden and crushing death had been the final blow in a series of disasters that plagued my thirty-eighth year. It had begun with a car accident that shattered my right tibia, which meant I could not manage the stairs in the San Francisco loft I'd shared with my fiancé, Grant, for six years, so I'd temporarily moved into my mother's ranch house in Menlo Park to recover. It was the house I'd grown up in, and although my mother wasn't the sentimental type and had done over my childhood bedroom with clean green lines, there were enough echoes of my teenaged self in the kitchen and bathroom to depress me, even without the fact that I felt wretched about imposing on my sixty-four-year-old mother, who'd suffered from bad health for two decades. And I was furious with Grant, who'd barely made the trip from our apartment—originally my apartment—once or twice a week.

I was still furious with him, honestly. I'd told him almost nothing about what I was doing on this trip, only that I needed to settle some of my mother's affairs. It was probably time to break it off, something else I had to think about while I was away.

But that was the other point of worry—the time, or rather lack of time, I had to wrap this up. The injury and resulting surgery had forced me to take a leave of absence from my position as editor at the *Egg and Hen*, one of the premier food magazines in the country. It had started as an eight-week leave. Now the count was fifteen weeks and growing.

A month ago, I'd gone back to writing and some editing, remotely, and I really wanted to get back before I lost my position entirely. I loved the magazine, the beauty of food and the industry, and I'd worked my ass off to get the position. Breathing down my neck, some kindly and some not so much, were a string of others just as ambitious, all of whom would be deliriously thrilled to take my place. I had to get back to it soon or lose it.

The final blow in this string of misfortune had been the death of my mother. She fell ill, pneumonia, just after Christmas. Not a surprise after a decade of lung issues. What was a surprise was that she died of it, simply and swiftly, in two weeks' time.

Leading to my discovery of the increasingly more urgent letters in her study from a solicitor in England, asking what to do about a legal matter he seemed to understand but I did not.

Which led to the phone call that led me to this moment, eating fish-and-chips in a damp English hotel room, with the locals calling me "lady."

It was a lot to absorb.

So instead, I did what I'd done since I was a child—I took comfort in food. Not in a binge-eating sort of way, which wasn't focusing at all, but grounding myself in the here and now by noticing exactly what I ate.

Right now, in this hotel room in front of a gas fire, the fish was fresh and sturdy beneath its crisp breading, the chips thick and expertly salted. My pint of ale was the color of walnuts, with flavor that had been developed over centuries. Salt eddied through my mouth, grounding me, and I thought of an essay M. F. K. Fisher had written about a meal she'd eaten in Paris after getting stuck on a train. It made me feel cosmopolitan rather than lonely. For the first moment since my mother died, I felt something akin to peace. Maybe I'd write about it in the morning.

But for now, it was a relief to be far away from the drama of my life, with a full belly and a sense of quiet stealing over me.

As I was falling asleep, my brain fancifully tried to write limericks with fish-and-chips at the center. They were incredibly clever in my compromised state, and I told myself to remember them in the morning.

It was probably just as well that I didn't.

Chapter Two

"I'm so sorry," the solicitor, Jonathan Haver, said in his modulated voice over the phone the next morning. "I'm well and truly stuck out here."

Taking a breath to keep my voice calm, I said, "I see. When do you think you'll be back?"

"I'm afraid it could be a couple of days. The roads are flooded from all the rain. I'm dreadfully sorry."

I looked out the window to the gray morning. "Things happen. I did have the driver take me out to the house yesterday when I arrived, just to get a feeling for what's going on."

"I see. I assumed you'd be fatigued after such a long trip."

"Yes, well, I'm very anxious to get things going, Mr. Haver. I'm in the middle of selling my mother's house in California, and I've been away from my job for much too long. I really need to get back. What can we do to settle this?"

"Well," he said cautiously, "you've seen the state of the house."

"Where I come from, no one cares about the building on a piece of land."

"Oh, my dear. I'm afraid Rosemere Priory is a Grade I–listed building, which means that not only can it not be torn down, but it can't even be upgraded without approval from the listing committee."

"It didn't look as if it could be repaired."

"I suppose anything is repairable with enough time and money."

"But you don't think it's worth it."

"Frankly, no. It has been neglected for forty years, and even if it could be shored up, these houses are dreadfully difficult to keep. There are more than thirty-five rooms—thirty-seven, to be exact. Imagine heating all of that. The roof alone will devour pounds like tea cakes. Then there's trying to stave off damp and rot and—"

"So what can be done?"

"Sooner or later, I expect it will simply fall down."

A visual of those golden walls tumbling into ruin gave me a sharp, unexpected pang. "How long did my mother's family live there?"

"Three or four hundred years, I expect."

Centuries. The shimmer of time prickled the edges of my skull, but before I could come up with anything to say, a murmuring in the background came through, and he said, "Look, I'll give you all the details when we meet. In the meantime, I'm going to send a friend of mine over. Rebecca Poole and her husband own the acreage bordering Rosemere. She'll be able to answer some of your questions."

I'd had my breakfast—eggs and beans and tomatoes—before taking the call from Mr. Haver. The skies outside threatened rain, but I needed to walk a little to shake the tightness from my leg.

A younger woman watched the pub and front desk this morning, a pretty girl with bright-blue eyes in a Snow White face. She smiled as I approached the desk. "Good morning, Lady Shaw," she said. "I'm Sarah. Did you have a good sleep?"

I waved my hand, wincing in embarrassment. "Oh, please don't call me that. Just Olivia is fine."

Her smile was crooked. "How about Ms. Shaw?"

"That's fine."

"What else may I help you with?"

"I'm going to take a walk, but the solicitor is sending someone over to speak with me. If anyone comes, will you ask them to wait? I won't be long."

"Of course. Take your time." She glanced over her shoulder through a mullioned window. "The rain might chase you back. Do you have a brolly?"

I lifted the long, sturdy umbrella I'd brought with me. One thing England and San Francisco shared was a tendency toward rain. "Covered."

Out on the sidewalk, I was one of only a handful of humans. A man in a fishing cap and a sweater vest walked a little dog who wore a knitted coat, the dog's short legs flying. A pair of middle-aged women in raincoats hurried between shops.

The fresh air eased my mood, as always. I'd been a walker all my life, trained at my mother's side from the time I was a small child. She had walked miles every day, and before I injured my leg, so had I. A scent of water and fertile earth filled the air. In the near distance, picturesque hills undulated behind Elizabethan buildings, looking as if they might fall over under their thatch roofs. The actual thatch surprised me, as I'd read an article on the expense and trouble of the material, and it looked surprisingly heavy.

The short, narrow lane opened to the square, a wide-open parkway with the butter cross in the middle. The narrow streets on all four sides were cobblestone, worn to slippery pale gray, and there was a fair amount of car traffic moving through, particularly on one side. Shops lined the street level—a handful of restaurants, a chemist, a sewing shop with a dusty-looking machine in the window. A bookshop stood at one corner, its mullioned window stacked with multicolored volumes, luring me closer. It wasn't open yet, but I promised myself I could come back later and browse. My spirits lifted.

A medieval church stood on a rise at the opposite end of the square, and I aimed for it, peering in the rest of the windows I passed:

the ubiquitous wool shop that looked as if it had been established in the thirties, a kitchen shop with bright-turquoise bowls and small appliances on display, a bakery that let the smell of coffee into the air, and a currently closed Indian restaurant with white-covered tables that made me suddenly homesick for my San Francisco neighborhood.

At the church, I paused to admire blackened headstones, unable to read more than a couple, then rounded the corner and walked up a slight rise to see beyond.

And there, rising from a nest of forest, flaws erased by distance, was Rosemere Priory. My breath caught at the splendor of it, the even rows of windows, the towers, the lands spreading around it with embroidered green skirts. Thirty-seven rooms! I'd never lived in a house with more than eight. What did you even *do* with so many rooms?

A light drizzle began to fall, and I opened the umbrella, unable to tear myself away just yet. Even if I'd had no connection to the mansion, I would have been enraptured. My mind struggled to encompass that it was the house of my ancestors. Ancient. Brooding. Beautiful.

And holder of my mother's secrets.

As I returned to the hotel, the rain picked up. The hems of my jeans were soggy by the time I came in, shaking off the wet.

Out of the corner of my eye, I caught sight of something coming toward me and braced myself in time to turn and see a giant dog suddenly screeching to a halt.

"Bernard!" a woman cried, racing behind the furry, well-tended Saint Bernard. "Oh, good, he stopped. He doesn't always yet."

The woman was as well tended as the dog, a slim-hipped blonde in a thick wool tunic and leggings tucked into whimsically flowered rain boots. "Hello," she said. "You must be Olivia. Jonathan is a friend of mine, and he sent me to rescue you—he feels wretched about the missed appointment. I'm Rebecca Poole."

I took her outstretched hand. Her fingers were cold. "Hello."

"Oh, my goodness, you have the lightning bolt!"

"*The* lightning bolt?" Self-consciously, I touched my right eye. My blue iris was marked with a diagonal yellow zigzag I'd hated with a passion as a child.

"It's famous in your family. It's not always a lightning bolt. Sometimes it's a sun around the pupil, sometimes something else. A lot of the villagers have it too." Her sideways smile gave her a knowing expression. "Lords will wander, don't you know."

Blinking, I asked, "It's a family trait?"

"Yes! Didn't your mother tell you?"

I took a breath. "Do you mind if we sit? My leg—"

She finally noticed my cane, and her hands flew in the air. "Sorry! Of course. Though I was planning to whisk you away to luncheon if you like. I'd love to welcome you to the neighborhood."

"That would be wonderful, thank you." I raised a finger. "Just give me one minute—"

"Of course!"

I sat down on the chair in the tiny lobby and rubbed the tight spot just below my knee. "I'll want to grab my purse," I said. "And my phone."

"Let's have Sarah fetch them, shall we?"

As I rubbed my knee, the dog eased closer and gave me a hopeful look. His eyes were the color of whiskey, and he snuffled over my wrist, very politely. He didn't slobber, which so many Saint Bernards did. "You're a pretty boy, aren't you?" His fur was silky. I touched his ears, scrubbed under his chin, found the magic spot on his chest. He groaned, leaning closer.

"Good dog, Bernard," Rebecca cooed. "He's only two. I have to keep bringing him with me everywhere because he was so impolite as a pup, and we can't have a dog this size knocking people down, can we? Are you a dog person?"

A Technicolor picture of my dog, Arrow, glossy and healthy, flashed in my brain, ears flying as he raced down the beach, back when he'd still been young and strong. "I am," I said simply.

Sarah arrived with my purse and phone. "It rang as I was coming along, though of course I didn't answer it."

"Thanks." I glanced at the screen. Grant, my fiancé. "I should return this call before we leave."

"Take your time; take your time." Rebecca leapt up and whistled for Bernard, who agreeably trotted behind her, leaving me alone in the pub to dial home.

Grant picked up on the third ring. "Olivia! I thought I'd missed you. How's it going?"

I imagined him in our top-floor San Francisco apartment—a tall, solid man with artfully shaggy hair and paint-stained fingers. We'd met at a showing of my mother's work eight years ago, and he'd pursued me with a single-minded focus that had flattered me deeply. A big man with clear gold-green eyes, he painted abstracts that were well received in some circles. I didn't ordinarily attract that kind of attention, and I had allowed him to take me to dinner. His knowledge of food and art, his general amiability, had won me over. Within months, he'd moved into my apartment, a jewel I'd snagged only by being in the right place at the right time.

His studio in that apartment was on the airy top level. It was a room filled with light and plants and artwork—my mother's and his and a few pieces I had bought before I met him, mostly whimsical renditions of food.

It seemed far, far away. I said, "The lawyer is stuck out of town somewhere, so I still don't have any details."

"Well, there's no rush. Take your time and figure it out. I'll manage the sale of your mom's house."

I hadn't told him everything, only that my mother had affairs that needed to be settled here. Since I'd already hired the Realtor when this business had come up, the obvious way to manage it for a week or two seemed to be to let Grant loosely oversee everything. "Did the Realtor give you a date yet?"

"The house could go up for sale as soon as next week. She expects to get three mil." His voice was this side of a chortle. "And she expects at least a couple of offers within hours."

Even after taxes, that was a lot of money. It was also not surprising. California real estate was stratospheric, and anything in the Bay Area was even more ridiculous. West Menlo Park was adjacent to Stanford and a plethora of tech campuses. "We knew it would go like that."

"We might really be able to *buy* this apartment, Olivia. That would be so awesome."

It was something we'd never had a prayer of pulling off before this. Even renting it had been a massive stroke of luck. It belonged to friends of mine from the magazine who'd adopted a baby and wanted to move out of the city. It was a gorgeous space on the top floor of a good building, but the killer was an outdoor space as large as the apartment itself with views of the bay in one direction and the city center in another. The couple had been making noises about selling it over the past year, but until now, there'd been no way we could have raised the funds to even consider it.

Now, everything was happening at once. I'd trade it all for one more hour with my mother, drinking tea and talking about . . . anything. Rubbing a finger over my eyebrow to keep my emotions in check, I said, "Yeah, maybe."

"Nancy is sending you an email," he said, "but basically, she wants to clear out the house. No one will keep it"—the lot would be scraped in order to build something new—"so you might as well go ahead and get rid of everything."

"No." It pained me to think of all my mother's things being handled by other people. Strangers. "I need to be the one to go through everything. I'll only be here for a week or two, and when I get back, I can sort through it."

"Would it really hurt anything to move it all to a storage facility?"

"What's the rush? It's only been a month."

"Okay, sweetheart. Your call." He was using the voice I'd come to know too well—the patient voice. The she'll-feel-better-soon voice. There were times lately I didn't even like this man, much less want to marry him. Many times. Sometimes I thought I'd never really loved him much at all. "I'll let her know."

"I'll get everything here sorted out, and then I can deal with everything there. One thing at a time."

"All right." I could hear him take a deep breath. "But I want to point out that you've been in a holding pattern for months. Don't you want to get back to your real life?"

The lake of grief in my chest sloshed a little. Maybe I wasn't really angry with him but at the way events in the past eight months had overturned my life. A flash of my mother's hands, splattered with paint as she stood before a canvas, washed over me, along with an image of those same fine, thin hands resting on her torso in the hospital.

Really, how could she possibly be gone? I kept waiting for someone to pop up and say it was all a mistake.

"I guess. I'm just not sure about anything right now."

"I know, sweetheart. Why don't you think about it for a day or two? Maybe the best thing would be to start the next chapter of your life as soon as possible. Nothing has been the same since the accident."

In the lobby, the dog gave a short woof, as if to emphasize the point. "Look, someone is waiting for me right now. I've gotta go."

"It's all good. Love you."

I almost said the words back, but they stuck in my throat, either a half truth or an untruth; I didn't know which. Instead, I simply hung up. He probably didn't even notice.

Rebecca drove a champagne-colored Range Rover, which carried us over the narrow roads between fields into a thick forest. "This is all part of the estate," she said, waving a hand. "Almost two thousand hectares, most of it forest and farmland."

I blinked. "Estate?"

"Rosemere." She gave me a quizzical look. "*Your* estate."

My grasp of land measurements was nonexistent, but it seemed like a lot. "Two thousand? That's like a whole park or something, isn't it?"

"Yes. It's enormous. Didn't you know?"

"I don't know anything," I admitted. "About any of it."

"Your mother never told you?"

"Not even on her deathbed."

We bumped onto a smaller lane, and she shot me another measuring glance I couldn't quite interpret. Had I said something wrong?

"All right, then," she said at last. "That gives us a place to start."

The lane swerved downward, and a house came into view. "This is the beginning of our acreage, Dovecote," she said, gesturing. "The boundary between Rosemere and us is this bank of trees." The house, rambling and whitewashed with a thatched roof, sat at the edge of a lush paddock where a trio of horses grazed.

"Gorgeous horses," I commented.

"Do you ride?"

"No, not really." I smiled. "I'm guessing you do."

She laughed, and again I noticed how unlike it was from everything else about her, loud and hooting. "I do," she said. "But mainly I breed racehorses. Point-to-point, amateur steeplechase, not the big leagues. The big gray is my champion," she said. "Pewter."

Pewter's tail swished, and he lifted his head in our direction. All three horses wore blankets, and I liked the look of the horse with a red coat and black mane. Steeplechase. I didn't want to confess that I didn't know what steeplechase was but tucked the word away for later on a growing list of things I needed to research. It felt as if I'd fallen down a rabbit hole, and everything that served me back in my own world was useless here.

As we pulled into the drive, I admired the house, which was long and rambling, two stories of sturdy walls beneath the thick thatch roof. Two men were at work on it, one high against the gray sky, weaving a pattern along the roofline, and the other carrying a bundle of thatch up a ladder.

"I noticed all the thatch in the village this morning," I said. "I had the impression that real thatch was on its way out."

"It is," she said, "but we are lucky in Saint Ives Cross, because Tony there—on the top—is a master thatcher from one of the oldest families on record. Handed down from father to son since the sixteenth century." She dropped her keys in her purse. "See how he's weaving the pattern? It's his signature. Every thatcher has one."

Both men were dark haired and tall, with long limbs. "Is that his son, then?"

"Oh, no. Tony's a wild one, never married. The other fellow is Sam, his journeyman."

The one carrying thatch slung it against the roof and climbed sideways on a thin wooden shelf. It made me dizzy.

As I swung my legs around to get out, I realized that my whole leg was getting stiff in the damp, cold day. Beneath my feet, the ground was muddy, and I took a moment to balance carefully—it was amazing how fast your balance went off!—hearing my mother remind me to put my best face forward. In her memory, I methodically measured out one solid step and then another.

In front of me, Rebecca called up to the thatchers, "You must come in and have some venison stew, boys. It's going to rain again any moment."

Venison. My heart sank.

"Come on, then," Rebecca said, sweeping me inside. "Let's get you settled. Cup of tea?"

A friendly fire burned low on the hearth, and I sank into a big, soft chair nearby, looking around: two rooms with wide-paneled wood floors, a sitting room with the fireplace, and a kitchen with mullioned windows looking out toward a garden.

Bernard flopped down on the rug in front of me, and a yellow cat came running from another room to swirl up to him. He gave it a lick, and it settled down next to his furry body. "That's adorable," I commented.

"They're the best of friends." Rebecca bustled around the kitchen, filling a kettle. "Jimmy's mother rejected him when he was about four or five weeks old, and Bernard was in love."

"You'd get a million hits on YouTube."

"Mmm." She shrugged. "Who has time for that?"

Her attitude was vaguely startling, another reminder that I'd left my world behind. In the arty, techy Bay Area, everyone used all social media all the time. I had to admit I was enjoying the break. "Right." My leg loosened next to the fire, and I stretched it out a little. "Have you lived here a long time?"

"Not terribly, just five years. My husband, Philip, and I met in London, and we both wanted to find an old property to renovate, one where I could raise my horses. Dovecote is perfect." Grabbing a shawl from the back of the sofa, she sat down in front of me. "It took us nearly a year to make it livable. I'll give you a tour after lunch if you like."

"I'd love it."

"Philip's in banking, so he stays in the city during the week, then comes up on weekends. I rattle around a little on my own, but it's been my dream since I was a child, so I'm very pleased to be here."

"I can see why."

The kettle began to whistle, and she hopped up. "Sugar, milk?"

"Both, please." I watched her pour water into the pot, her figure slim and elegant, her long blonde hair cut ruler straight just below her shoulder blades. "Did you work in the city too?"

"Oh, yes. I was a banker as well, though one of us had to step away when we got married—we both worked for the same company. It grew . . . complicated." She carried a tray over. "The house and stables are my project now—and the racing is an absolute delight."

"You do the racing yourself?"

"Yes."

"Impressive." I accepted a cup of tea on a saucer.

"So you really don't know anything about the Rosemere estate?" she asked.

"Nothing. My mother died a month ago, and when I was going through her things, I found the papers from Jonathan Haver. When I called him a week ago, that was the first I'd heard of any of it."

"Papers?" she asked.

A little bit too much blandness in her tone alerted me to keep details to myself. "I haven't made full sense of it, but there's evidently been some interest in buying the property."

"Ah, of course." Rain began to spatter the windows, and Rebecca looked up at the ceiling, as if she could see through to the thatcher. "Tony will be along now. He's crotchety, so don't mind his manners."

I shrugged.

"What kind of interest—have you heard?" She sipped her tea. "The house is a wreck. I mean, a falling-down *disaster* of a house, but it's listed, so you can't touch a bloody thing without permission."

"Mr. Haver mentioned that the house was listed, too, but I don't know what that is exactly. Historically protected or something?"

"It's a headache is what it is. Dovecote's only a Grade II, and we had to practically turn ourselves inside out to get a proper sink in the powder room. The local council is overseen by Mrs. Stonebridge—"

I laughed. It was the kind of name a battle-ax in an old cozy mystery might have. "Not really?"

"I swear. Hortense Stonebridge, and she guards the listed buildings like a general." She settled her cup on its saucer. "And listed means historical. A Grade I building means it's valuable or significant to the history of the country. Or a few other designations, but mainly it just means you have to get approval for every step of renovation. Grade II is a step below that, but she put us through our paces."

"Sounds daunting."

A knock sounded at the door, and Rebecca jumped up. "Come in, come in," she said, offering a towel hung by the door.

Two big dogs ran in, dashing directly for Bernard until their master halted them with a no-nonsense "Sit!" They screeched to a halt. The cat bolted.

Crotchety had made me think of someone old, but the man who ducked under the threshold was my age or a little older, maybe forty, tall and fit in a long-worn brown leather jacket and jeans. He gave me a dismissive glance and shook himself out of the jacket. "If it rains for long, I'll just come back tomorrow. Can't work with wet thatch."

"Olivia Shaw, this is Tony Willow. Olivia is the new Countess of Rosemere."

"How do you do," he said without inflection. His accent was less plummy than hers.

"Nice to meet you," I returned as blandly.

The other man stomped his feet on the mat outside. He was as tall as Tony but younger by a decade. Black curls, wild with rain, tumbled around a face drawn with no small drama—large dark eyes beneath black brows, a wide mouth. As he came inside, he caught sight of me, and I had the sense that I'd startled him.

"Hello," he said after a moment and gave me a grin. "You must be the new countess. The whole village is on fire with your arrival."

Heat burned along my neck up to my ears. I shook my head. "Yes, but please call me Olivia."

"Olivia it is." He crossed to offer his hand. "Samir Malakar. Most people call me Sam."

"Which do you prefer?"

"Samir, actually."

I smiled. "All right, Samir. It's nice to meet you."

"Come, everyone. Come sit. You, too, Olivia." Rebecca spread cloth mats on the old wooden table. I stood and carried my tea, but the cold, damp day had caught up with me, and my limp was irredeemably pronounced.

Embarrassing. The younger thatcher reached for my cup silently, and I allowed him to take it as I leaned on the wall and navigated up the single step. He placed the cup in front of me.

"Thanks."

Rebecca, dishing up stew, said, "We were just discussing Rosemere. Olivia had no idea it even existed until a week ago."

Samir shook out his napkin and inclined his head my direction. "That must have been a strange day."

"To say the least."

Rebecca laughed. "You're so American!" She placed a bowl of rich brown stew in front of me, full of chunks of carrots and meat and potatoes. It smelled exactly the way you'd want stew to smell on a rainy day in February.

But I remembered she'd said venison, which I'd eaten only once or twice and never enjoyed. It was always so gamey and tough, and I couldn't help thinking of the deer that wandered through my mother's neighborhood, with their big dark eyes and long eyelashes. They had nibbled all the roses until my mother had wanted to kill them.

A story I might not want to share right that moment.

"American how?" I asked, my hands in my lap.

She handed Tony a bowl, and he took it, and in the gesture, I saw a flash of something intimate. Were they lovers?

Rebecca brought her own bowl to the table. "American because you don't seem to realize that you've inherited an entire estate and a title to go with it." Her *t*'s were crisp, each one enunciated. "The average Englishwoman would kill for that."

I said, "It's just . . . kind of ridiculous."

"It's the lottery!" Tony said.

"Not if there's no money to go with it," Samir said.

"As if *you'd* know," Rebecca said. "Please, everyone, let's begin."

Samir shrugged but didn't seem put out by her sharpness.

I picked up my spoon—clearly real silver, recently polished, but not so recently that it hadn't been used since. The other three dug in with clear enjoyment, so I gingerly took a small spoonful.

Oh. I touched my lips.

Time halted.

Every now and then, a mouthful of food tilted the world on its axis. This was one of them. The stew was dark and rich, meaty, herby. Thick broth and tender carrots and cubes of potato, hints of spice and aromatic vegetables. I moved my spoon through the opaque lake of gravy, imagining words that might describe it in an essay. I'd use the setting of the room, the AGA cooker in the corner, and the mullioned windows and the thatchers in their jeans.

"This is venison?" I asked and took a larger spoonful. "It's amazing."

"Thank you," Rebecca said mildly. "Have you never had it?"

"Not like this. We don't really eat it in the US." I tasted again, mulled the flavors: red wine, garlic, bacon, and something I couldn't quite put my finger on. "There's a hint of sweetness. Not honey, I don't think, or brown sugar."

Tony chuckled. "She'll never tell you her secrets."

"Of course I will. Red currant jam." She inclined her head. "Well done, actually. Are you a chef?"

"Food writer. Until I broke my leg, I was the editor at a food magazine. I mean, I still am, just on a leave of absence."

"Editor," Samir echoed. "Would we know it?"

"I don't know." He didn't strike me as the foodie type, not to mention it was an American magazine. "*Egg and Hen?*"

His lips turned down in a quizzical expression. "Really."

"Do you know it?"

"I do. My sister has a stack of them. She's really into all that," he said. "She runs the Indian restaurant in town."

"Oh! I saw it this morning. It looks like a nice place. Upscale."

"Yeah. She's worked very hard. And she'll be dying to meet you when I tell her."

"I'll have to check out her food. North Indian, South?"

"She's created something new. She should tell you about it herself." He returned his focus to the stew, eating with the gusto of a man who'd been doing hard physical work all morning. When he'd taken a sip of tea, he looked at me again. His lashes were remarkably thick, giving his eyes the same softness as the deer in my mother's neighborhood. "It must be pretty exciting, a job like that."

"Yeah." My chest ached a little. "It's a great job. I miss it."

"But now," Rebecca said, "you have this amazing new adventure, and you won't *have* to work, will you?" Before I could say I couldn't imagine a world without working, she said, "Go back, though. Why is it ridiculous to inherit?"

"I don't know." I paused, trying to bring my discomfort into focus. "The woman I knew as my mother was a painter, not an heiress. She lived in the same house my entire life. And"—I paused, my hands in my lap—"she never told me about any of this. There must have been a reason. But . . ."

"But what?"

"I don't know. I guess maybe that's what I need to find out before I make any decisions."

Tony said, "It's cursed, you know."

"Of course it is," Rebecca said. "All old English houses are cursed."

"This is worse. Real. The Rosemere men die violent deaths," Tony said, glowering from below heavy brows. "Murder, war, suicide. Hard to deny it."

I thought of my mother running to America. "What about the women?"

"They're fine. Just the men."

"Why the curse?" I asked.

Samir said, "It was the curse of a village girl who fell in love with a monk when it was a priory. She's said to haunt the ruins of the church. Or the well, depending on who tells it."

Rebecca said, "I've never heard that. How did you know it?"

"My grandmother was part of the household there when the old countess came back from India." Samir looked at me. "Your grandmother."

My grandmother. The sense of my life as a box of puzzle pieces struck me again. I met his open, somehow cheerful gaze. "What else do you know?"

"A bit. My father knows more." He broke a hearty chunk of bread and dipped it in his bowl, holding it in long fingers as he added, "If the rain stops, I'll drive you up to the house after lunch, and you can look around. If you like."

"Sam, you surprise me!" Rebecca said. "A man of hidden depths."

He gave her a half shrug, and I thought there was something droll in a slight lift of his eyebrows as he stirred the stew. "You see what you wanna see," he said.

It made me think of a cartoon I'd loved as a child, *The Point*. "In the Pointless Forest," I said without thinking and tried to whistle the song "Me and My Arrow."

He looked at me, something new in his expression. "This is the town, and these are the people."

I wanted to give him a high five. "My dog's name was Arrow."

"Bit obvious, isn't it?"

I laughed. "I suppose. It's just easier than Oblio. And he did have a very pointed nose."

"Point made," he said without smiling but shot me a sideways look to see if I got it.

I laughed.

"Sam," Rebecca said. "More stew?"

"Yes, please."

Chapter Three

As if it wanted to accommodate me, the rain did stop after lunch. Rebecca and I drove up in her Range Rover while Tony and Samir followed in Tony's work truck. Under other circumstances, the distance would have been walkable, if a little steep, on a road that wound along the fields and climbed the hill. Today it was too muddy.

Our approach this time was from the rear. The house appeared as we turned the corner. Under the low clouds, it shone bright gold and looked considerably less tattered than it had yesterday from the taxi. I recognized the roofline, the trees marching away from the rise, from my mother's paintings. I thought of her, all these years, painting the place she'd left long ago, and it made me ache a little.

"Beautiful, isn't it?" Rebecca said. "It gives me a thrill every time."

I nodded.

"On the left are what remain of the gardens." She pointed at a series of walls and terraces, tumbling down the hill. "They were created in the eighteenth century and were really quite famous. The old countess—I supposed that's your grandmother—brought them back to life, but you see what time does."

I nodded. Everything was overgrown, the bare lines visible here and there.

"On the right are the farms, which as you see are fully functional. The family never participated in the enclosures, so some of the tenants' families have been here since the estate was created."

The fields were winter empty, but they rolled out in tidy rows, broken here and there with cottages and hedgerows. "How many people are farming here?"

Rebecca frowned. "I don't actually know. That would be a question for Jonathan. Enough to at least keep the taxes paid on the place."

"What do they grow?"

"Rape, mostly, some barley. Obviously sheep." She gestured toward a field of white bodies grazing in the distance. "A few other things, but the canola oil is the main thing." She braked and let me look out across the fields for a minute. "It's beautiful when it's in bloom—bright-yellow flowers across the whole countryside."

At the top of the hill, she parked, and we climbed out, waiting for Tony and Samir to pull in beside us. I took the chance to turn in a slow circle, trying to take it in—the farms and cottages, as quaint as a calendar picture. The ruined garden tumbled down the hill like an exhausted courtesan, and nearby crouched a wreck of a conservatory, glowing greenish blue in the cool light. I knew I would have to explore inside. Impulsively, I took my phone out and shot a series of photos. My fingers itched to sketch it all, but I'd left my sketchbook in the hotel room.

When I'd looked at the estate from the front the first day, the whole estate had appeared deserted. From this side, there were plenty of signs of life. A dormant garden waited for spring at the foot of what I assumed were the kitchen steps. "Who lives here?" I asked.

Rebecca answered, "The caretakers. There's been someone here since your mother and her brother disappeared—forty years? Fifty?—although I believe they're on holiday at the moment."

Again, the brother. I needed to find out more about him. Why was I inheriting, when surely the brother or his heirs would have claim? "Not very much caretaking. Why didn't they keep the house up?"

Samir stood beside me. "They've done what they could. It was already falling apart before everyone left. Your grandmother hated it and wanted it to fall down."

"Why?"

He glanced down at me, and I realized that he really was quite tall. "That's a long story. Come; let's go inside."

"Don't you need a key?"

"No. Lock's broken."

"I've been living down the hill for years and never knew I could get inside!" Rebecca made a soft noise of excitement. "Are you coming, Tony?"

He lit a cigarette and shook his head. "I'll wait."

She hesitated, glancing first at the house, looming over us, and back to him. "I'm just dying to see it."

A nod. He exhaled a cloud of blue smoke.

We three headed for the back door.

As Samir opened the door and stepped in, I found my heart pounding at what we might find. He turned, holding out a hand. "Countess," he said, ever-so-faintly ironic.

Twisting my lips at the title, I took his hand, navigated the battered steps, and found myself in a big plain room, clean enough. Shelves and cupboards lined the entire space, mostly empty.

"This must be part of the pantry," Rebecca said.

It was very cold inside, though without the bite we'd felt exiting the car, and utterly still. I followed Samir into the next room, which turned out to be a big kitchen, circa 1960. Yellowed sheet linoleum covered the floor, and stacks of boxes were piled on the counters, willy-nilly, as if the room had become a dumping ground.

But the windows were enormous, letting in great swaths of light even through the decades of dirt that had collected. A monstrous turquoise stove crouched beneath a hood. "An AGA!" Rebecca exclaimed, running fingers through the dust. "This was very top of the line at the time. I wonder if it still works?"

I'd done a feature on the British stoves. "Not sure they ever really die, do they?"

"We used to sneak in here and play when I was a child," Samir said. "Dare each other to see who could go the farthest alone."

"It's really not that terrible," I said. "I imagined much worse."

"Just wait." He waved a hand for us to follow. We picked our way through the maze of boxes, exiting through a more formal pantry, lined with shelves and cupboards. I wanted to peek inside and see if any dishes were left, dishes my mother might have eaten on as a child, maybe, or just something beautiful and old. I resisted the exploration and trailed Samir into another room.

"This is a little creepier," I admitted. Vines grew over and through the windows, creating a green interior. A dining room table with sixteen or twenty chairs was littered with chunks of fallen plaster, with more debris on the floor. Wallpaper hung in strips. A great crawling black stain marked one wall and half the remaining ceiling, but I also noticed a lighter rectangle on another wall. "Where's the art? Wouldn't there be portraits or something?"

"I dunno." He tucked his hands into the pockets of his hoodie, mouth turning downward. "There're some paintings upstairs in one of the bedrooms, but they're not portraits. Kind of fantastical."

I thought of my mother's work. "Are they forests?"

He swung around to look at me. "No. Gardens and things."

Behind me, Rebecca squeaked. "Mouse!" she cried and bolted, right back out the way we'd come.

I turned, looking, but if there had been a mouse, it had fled in terror. I shook my head, and Samir led the way through a pile of debris in the doorway into another room that must have been a sitting room or the like. Wooden panel doors hung at an angle, and the ceiling-high mullioned windows were almost entirely covered with growth.

"Look at that." He pointed, and I saw a blooming rose, white or pink, like a nightlight in the darkness. "It must be warmer in here than outside."

"It makes me think of *Beauty and the Beast*," I said, and I couldn't help picking my way over to the rose to touch it. "A house under a long curse."

"What did it take to break it? The curse?"

"The beast has to learn to love and accept love in return." I bent my head to the rose and was pleased to discover it smelled of lemons.

"Yeah, yeah. Women always like those brooding beastly types."

I smiled, coming back to his side. "You are not in that category, are you?"

"No." He sighed.

"Don't lose hope. Women eventually learn that beasts are only beastly."

He raised one thick brow. "Do they?"

"Mmm."

"Good to know." He offered a hand to help me over a rotted ottoman. "All right?"

"I'm good. Lead the way."

"This is the best part of whole house." He paused in the doorway, his eyes glittering. "Ready?"

"Yes."

He pushed at the door with a shoulder, pretty hard, and the door gave with a groan, dust flying into the air. We tumbled into a vast hallway with a wide carved staircase. Light filled the room.

"Oh, wow." I made my way into the center and looked up.

The area was enormous, three stories high, and every inch was paneled with elaborately detailed squares of golden wood. It glowed with the light coming in through an enormous stained glass window made of three broad arches, each showing a saint in what I imagined were acts of miraculousness. I knew the deep reds and clear blues were signs of early stained glass. Not a single pane was broken. I pressed a fist to my chest. "It must be eleventh or twelfth century. How in the world has it survived?"

"Crazy, right?" He was looking upward, too, black hair tumbling backward away from the strong bones of his face, high cheekbones, carved jaw. "They say it's the window from the abbey."

"Where's the abbey?"

"Just south. It's only a ruin now, but it's on an old pagan site, they say. There's a spring, and some of the local witches tend the herb garden."

I laughed. "Really?"

"Really. It's been there since medieval times, and it's supposed to be full of all sorts of blessed plants and healing herbs." He pronounced the *h* in *herbs*. "It's meant to be one of the best gardens of its kind."

"Medieval," I echoed. "So much time." Looking upward, I thought of my mother, once upon a time, coming down the steps and before her, my grandmother and her mother, stretching back to the Elizabethans who'd moved the window and even further back to the monks who'd lived in the abbey. I moved around the space, looking at the carvings in the paneling. "It's amazing that this is still in such good shape."

"So random," he said from behind me. "Some rooms are completely wrecked, and others look as if someone just stepped out."

I nodded.

"This is one of the spots that is supposed to be haunted."

"It *is* really cold," I commented, half-flippantly. "Who's the ghost?"

"A girl who jumped from the gallery." He pointed to an opening three stories up.

"These must be the towers then, right?"

"Yeah."

"Why did she jump?"

"It's always love, isn't it?"

"Hmm. I guess it is." I stared upward at the shadowed gallery, where once minstrels might have played. I imagined a girl so distraught that she would jump to her death on these tiles, and a shiver walked up my spine.

My leg was starting to ache in the cold, and I wished suddenly that my mother was here to tell these stories, share her history with me. "How do you know so much about it?"

"If you grow up in the village, you know all the stories." He moved, circling a pile of what looked like rotted magazines, and looked upward. "It's drawn me since I was a child. It just seems sad, doesn't it? Like it wants to be set free." He gave me a quick smile. "Uncursed."

That sore spot in my chest ached again. "I thought my mother was from a small, awful place. Industrial. She didn't like to talk about her life in England, and I—" I sighed. "I thought it was because she'd run away from some grimy place." I shook my head. "I can't believe she never said a word about this."

"You should come talk to my dad. There were some things that happened here, back when everyone left, but I don't know all of it. He was around then."

"How old is he?"

His mouth turned down, and again he touched the hair on his chin. "Sixty-seven?"

My mother had been sixty-six when she died. "I wonder if they knew each other."

He gave a soft chuckle. "Of course they did. Have you seen the size of the town?"

"Good point. But they would have been in—different circles, right?"

"Of course, but remember, our grandmothers were great friends."

"Were they?"

"Yes. They were girls together in India."

A vast well of sadness came over me. "I don't even know her name."

He only looked at me with his great dark eyes, his mouth sober. It was somehow comforting.

From the corner of my eye, I caught some movement, which raised the hair on my neck until I whirled to see a cat sitting on a stair about halfway down. He was a big, very furry black and white, with one torn ear.

"Hullo there," Samir said. "Shouldn't you be chasing mice?"

The cat only stared down at us with big gold eyes. "My mother painted a cat like him into all of her paintings," I said, and the words came out on a rough note.

His hand touched my shoulder kindly. "There's a whole troop of them. Barn cats."

"I think this one would call himself a house cat."

The cat didn't seem at all afraid. His big fluffy tail flicked up and down, up and down. Suddenly winded, I leaned on the newel post, which was carved to a height well over my head. "Maybe we should save the rest of the exploration for another day. I need to get somewhere warm and prop my leg up."

"Absolutely." He offered his arm. For a minute, I hesitated, feeling elderly and foolish in my doddering almost-forty-ness. But his ease gave me ease, and I stepped up to take his elbow. We made our way back the way we'd come, speaking little.

"Overwhelming, is it?" he asked.

"Yes."

We were in the kitchen and could see Tony and Rebecca standing by the truck. Samir paused. "Be careful with those two."

"What do you mean?"

He paused. "Just beware. Not everyone is happy about your arrival."

I gave a short laugh. "By 'not everyone' you mean no one."

"Mostly." He gave a rueful little grin. "May as well know it."

"Thanks."

He faced me, hand spread across his chest. His eyes glittered. "I, however, am as trustworthy as a Boy Scout, as loyal as a dove."

Was he flirting with me? He stood ever so slightly closer than he might have. Close enough I could smell the rain in his hair and realized how very broad shouldered he was.

I bowed, hands together in prayer. "Thank you, young sir."

"Not so young," he said, and I looked up in surprise, but he was already ambling out.

Silly, but it lifted my spirits. It had been ages since anyone flirted with me at all, much less a man with eyes like a night sea.

Hearing myself, I rolled my eyes. He was much too young for me, and that was slightly embarrassing in itself. There was also the fact that I had a fiancé back home.

On the stoop, he waited. "Let me give you my mobile. If you fancy trying a tour another day, you can ring me."

It was entirely businesslike. I typed the password into my smartphone and opened my contacts list. Matter-of-factly, he typed his name and number in, then handed it back.

"Thanks," I said, but he was already heading for the truck, moving in that loose-limbed way some tall men have, as if there were no actual bones, only muscles and grace.

Jet lag was about to make a fool of me. Time for a nap.

The rain began again in earnest in the late afternoon. Exhausted and emotional, I ate in my room for a second evening, curled up by the fire in a blanket, sipping tea and pulling up everything I could find on the internet about the estate. Wikipedia had a solid entry, much to my surprise.

The photo was one from an earlier era, on a sunny day. The house shone bright gold against a bucolic sky, with poplars leafed out around it.

Rosemere Priory dates back to the eleventh century, when it was a monastery and famous medicinal garden. When the monasteries were dissolved by Henry VIII, the land was awarded to Thomas Shaw, and the title of Earl of Rosemere was created. The earl built a grand Elizabethan house on the site, which still stands. The holdings, with orchards, farmland, a lake, and a river, were extremely well positioned, and the family thrived for over a hundred years, when the estate was lost to Parliamentarians in the civil war.

After the war, Lady Clarise Shaw, a great beauty who was rumored to be a mistress of Charles II, petitioned the king for the restoration of the estate. The king agreed, provided she married a man of his choosing, and she countered with the caveat that the estate could always pass to a woman if there was no immediate male issue. It has stayed in the family ever since, for four hundred years, until it was mysteriously abandoned in the 1970s.

These paragraphs were followed by a genealogy of the earls—and in some cases, the female heirs of the place—from 1555. Their accomplishments and additions to the house were noted. The medicinal gardens of the monks, which Samir had mentioned earlier, had been maintained throughout the centuries, and I made a mental note to explore them. Another ancestor, the sixth Earl of Rosemere, created the Georgian-era gardens and began to fill the conservatory with plants from his explorations.

It pained me that both were now in shambles.

The modern entries in the genealogy were George Shaw, twelfth Earl of Rosemere, 1865–1914. Probably died in the war, I guessed. Next was Alexander Shaw, 1892–1941, maybe another war death.

The final three were Violet Shaw, Countess of Rosemere, 1917–1973; and Roger Shaw, fourteenth Earl of Rosemere, 1938–disappeared 1975. Presumed dead.

The last entry was Caroline Shaw, Countess of Rosemere, 1951–present day. Whereabouts unknown.

For a long time, I sat with the tablet in my lap, staring at those bald, strange facts. I could edit them. Add my mother's death. My own name, Olivia Shaw, Countess of Rosemere.

Instead, I went to Google and typed in "Caroline Shaw, Countess of Rosemere." The first entry was Wikipedia, the same one I'd been on for the house. Not much else, but a line of images marched across the top of the page, and I raised my finger, hesitated, and clicked the images link.

And there she was, my mother, younger than I'd ever known her. A delicately built teenager in a pencil skirt, laughing with a crowd of other teens. In a party dress with her hair swept up, almost certainly on the steps of the house, with that cathedral window behind her, a suave-looking man on her arm. In another, this one close-up, she looked coy and knowing at the camera, her eyes lined in a cat eye that was so recently back in fashion.

I didn't even realize tears were pouring down my face until they splashed on my wrist. How could she have left all of this behind and never told me a single thing about it?

Overwhelmed, I shut the tablet and flung off the blanket. What I needed was a bath and a novel that would take me away.

My cell rang. I glanced at the clock, which showed nearly ten, and considered letting it go to voice mail, but when I glanced at the number, I saw that it was my Realtor in San Francisco. "Hi, Nancy."

"Olivia! I'm sorry to call so late. Is this all right? I just have a bunch of news and wanted to talk to you as soon as possible."

I sat back down. "No, it's fine. What's up?"

"I have an amazing offer on the house."

"But it's not for sale yet."

"No, not technically. But this buyer has had her eye on the house for more than three years, and she would really like to settle with you before it goes to market."

I closed my eyes, thinking of the kitchen where I'd eaten my breakfasts as a child, where my mother had made her endless pots of tea. "What's the offer?"

"Three point two."

The number pinged around my brain, impossible and ridiculous for a breathless moment. When I found my voice, I croaked, "That's *insane*."

"It is a lot of money, but in this market, it's not at all uncommon. This neighborhood is highly prized."

"You think I should take it."

"No, actually. This makes me more eager than ever to take it to market. It might go for even more."

"What about all of my mother's things?"

"Look, Olivia," she said gently, "we can leave everything in place when we show it, because you know it will be torn down the minute the sale goes through. But wouldn't you rather everything be safely tucked away in a nice, climate-controlled storage unit? Then it will be safe, and you can go through it at your leisure."

I felt airless, exhausted. "Maybe."

"It's your call. I do not want to rush you, and honestly, this lot is going to sell for a great price no matter when we put it up for sale."

Three *million* dollars. Three million, two hundred thousand dollars. That was life-changing money. Winning-the-lottery money.

In my mind, I heard my mother's sensible voice say, "Be practical, darling." She said it so often it was engraved on my brain. She would want me to make the deal, give myself the possibilities the money would offer.

"Put it on the market," I said, "but you're going to have to give my mother's gallery a few days to get over there and get the paintings and drawings out. Not taking any chances on that."

"Done. Do you want me to handle it?"

"No. I will."

"All right, I'll await your direction."

"And, Nancy, I don't want you to talk to Grant about this. Communicate with me directly."

"No problem. You're the boss."

I hung up and looked up the other numbers I needed. Within twenty minutes, I had arranged for the removal, packing, and storage of all of my mother's work at the gallery warehouse, safely away from . . .

Hmm. From Grant. He'd always been so avid for her paintings, dreaming of hanging them in our apartment. Some of them were quite valuable, and I would probably sell a few. But not yet.

Suddenly, I thought of the triptych she'd done, three gigantic paintings in a mysterious wood, so layered with detail that much was hidden until you looked deeply. I wondered if there might be secrets hidden in those paintings. I called the gallery back and asked for prints of them to be sent to me here, along with her oldest sketchbooks. It was a hunch. Maybe I could piece together her secrets if I looked at that material through the lens of all this new information.

I looked out the window at the edge of a thatched roof illuminated by a streetlamp, my head spinning. What next?

Chapter Four

Three days later, I finally had an appointment with Jonathan Haver. The time in between had been quiet, which turned out to be good for me. I wrote two essays for *Egg and Hen*, one an ode to M. F. K. Fisher and eating some simple food alone, the other, more researched and nuanced, on the venison stew.

I also sent my publisher, the man in charge of my fate, a note.

> Dear David,
>
> You will not believe the twilight zone I've fallen into—it turns out that my mother was heir to an estate in England, and I've traveled here to see what I can do to settle everything. Hope to be finished in a couple of weeks. In the meantime, I've been thinking there might be some benefit to the magazine—maybe a series of essays on English food and cooking, keying in to the Anglophilia that's all the rage. I've attached a couple of essays I've written this week as examples of what I have in mind. Maybe an entire English (British?) issue? The idea is still shaping up, but maybe follow the seasons or the various cultural influences . . . ? Would love to discuss when you have a moment.

You've been very patient with this long, strange trip I've been on (cue the Grateful Dead), and I promise I'm working on ways to make it up to you.

Olivia

The rest of the time, I lazed around reading novels I found in the hotel common room, forcing myself not to dig into more about the house or the family. After the previous hard months, my soul and body were tired.

The weather was still horrible, either rainy, wet from the rain, threatening to rain, or foggy. That morning, it was the last, so I bundled up in a pink wool sweater that was one of my favorites, with fleece-lined leggings beneath my jeans and wellies, which were the only practical shoe in such conditions, then headed for the bakery I'd been meaning to visit since my arrival.

The street was empty. Fog eddied around lampposts, drifted down alleyways, obscured and revealed a shop front here, now gone. The butter cross loomed like an ancient pagan monolith, and I glimpsed a car making its slow, careful way down the street. The idea of driving in such weather made me shudder.

A scent of coffee and fresh cinnamon rolls hung heavily in that thick air, a nearly visible lure to the bakery. I followed it into the shop with a growling stomach. A bell rang over the door as I entered.

Within, the place was bustling, most of the tables were occupied, and a line snaked around a glass case filled with pastries and breads. A woman behind the counter called out, "Hello! It looks like a long line, but it goes fast."

"I'm not in any rush," I said, and the woman in front of me turned around.

"American." She wore a brushed wool coat and expensive leather boots, obviously on her way to work. I wondered where. Surely not in this village.

"Guilty," I said, smiling.

"Leave her alone, Alice," the woman said behind the counter.

"I wasn't going to—"

"Yes, you were. Next!" The baker was tall, with rangy limbs and raggedly cropped gray hair. A capable sort, my mother would have said. When I made my way to the front of the line, she said, "Hello, love. What sweet thing would you like for breakfast this morning?"

"A pot of tea," I said, "and whatever that is." I pointed to a beautiful dark-glazed pastry.

"A chelsea bun." She called out the order over her shoulder, then leaned over the counter toward me. "I'll bring it out to you in a trice. We're nearly done with the commuter rush."

"Thank you." I paid, then turned toward the room, looking for a seat, and realized that several patrons were staring at me. Openly. I flushed, feeling alternately alarmed and shy. Keeping my head down, I made my way to a two top next to the wall and looked out toward the window. The murmur of conversation stuttered back to life, then rolled into a predictable, comforting rise and fall. When I glanced around surreptitiously, they'd all gone back to their phones or companions or even a newspaper or two. My shoulders eased.

The baker brought a tray with my tea and pastry, along with a mug of coffee. "Do you mind if I join you for a moment?"

An odd request from a stranger, a thought that must have showed on my face, because she said, "I knew your mother, long ago."

"Oh!" I gestured. "Join me."

"I'm being cheeky because I can," she said, sliding into the open seat. "I'm Helen Richmond, and I own the bakery. You are Olivia Shaw, the new Countess of Rosemere."

"Yes."

She inclined her head. "You have your mother's grace."

A sharp sting of tears burned the back of my eyes. I swallowed. "Thank you. How did you know her?"

"We took painting classes together."

"You're a painter too?"

"I dabble now and then. Never like Caroline. Did she end up doing anything with it?"

"Yes." Emotion made it hard to speak for a moment. I had not ever met anyone who'd known her as a young woman. Focusing on my tea, stirring in sugar, then milk, I found calm and had to smile at the power of tea. "She did very well, actually. Illustrated children's books as well as painting her own work."

"Children's books! Lovely." Her eyes were a clear, light blue. "Was she happy in America?"

Happy? She had always been so private, so utterly practical about things, that happiness would have been superfluous. "She seemed to be. Her paintings were very successful, and she had her friends and me."

"Your father?" She sat straight up. "Sorry. Too far?"

"No. I'm glad to talk about her." I sipped the hot, strong tea. "He died when I was a child. I don't really remember him."

"More tragedy. I'm so sorry." Her face showed genuine regret, a bowed head. "She didn't have the happiest childhood, you know."

I was tired of saying all the things I didn't know about my own mother, but no one would flee a happy life. I nodded.

"Helen!" a girl called from the counter. "Problem!"

"There's my cue," Helen said. "Come see me, love. I'd love to talk more about your mother. I adored her."

"Thank you," I said. "I will."

I sipped my hot, sweet, milky tea, feeling myself settle, center. I couldn't possibly stay in a state of high emotion, and there was a lot to get through in the next few days or weeks. Right this minute, I could enjoy this table in a bakery in a small English village. The place was clearing out, and the chelsea bun beckoned. It was a coil of pastry laced with currants and a hint of lemon zest, quite sweet. I gave it the attention it deserved, since a person couldn't be pigging out on pastries and eggs and bacon all the time. Not me, anyway. Unlike my slender mother, I was built of rounder stuff, and I hadn't been able to walk as much as was my habit.

In the meantime, the tea was excellent, served in a sturdy silver pot with a mug that didn't seem to match any other mug on the tables. The room smelled of yeast and coffee and cinnamon and the perfume of a woman who had walked by. Light classical music played quietly. From the kitchen came voices engaged in the production of all the goods in the case. A rich sense of well-being spread through me, and I realized that my leg didn't hurt at all.

As I stirred sugar into my second cup, a woman with dark hair came over. "I'm sorry to intrude," she said, "but I am so excited to meet you, and Sam said you wouldn't mind if I introduced myself if I saw you in town."

"Sam?"

"I'm sorry—my brother. I'm Pavi Malakar." Now that she said it, I could see the resemblance. Her hair was heavy and thick, though hers was straight, swinging in a bob that swept her shoulders. It was the same intense black, and she had the same enormous liquid eyes. "He said you were the editor of *Egg and Hen* magazine until recently. I am *such* a fan."

"Wow." I grinned, taking her hand. "I am so happy to meet someone who wants to talk to me about *that* world—I can't even tell you."

She grinned, and it gave her eyes a tilt. "I love your columns when you write about just one ingredient. The one about yams was amazing."

"Thank you. That was one of my favorites, too, honestly."

"I've always thought you should write one on coriander."

For a moment, I let the idea settle, then deflected. "Ah, that's right—you have a restaurant, don't you?"

"I do." She settled her second hand over mine. "You should come, let me cook for you."

"I would love that."

"How about Tuesday? It's a slow night for us, usually."

"Sure."

"That's great!" There was a musical lilt to the British accent that I hadn't heard in Sam's, and I wondered what made the difference. "Come at seven, yes? Do you know where it is?"

"Yes."

"Wonderful. I can't wait." She swirled away to the counter, sending me a wave.

As I pulled on my coat, I wondered if Sam would be there. Samir, which he said he liked better.

At any rate, it would be great to get out, have a glass of wine, eat some non-pub-style food. It had been a while since I'd had a social evening of any ilk.

Haver's office was located down a narrow alley that angled into an even narrower passageway. The pathways underfoot were cobblestones, uneven and slippery in the fog, and I kept a hand on the wall to be sure I didn't lose my footing. It would be irritating to start feeling better and then reinjure the traumatized leg.

Anyway.

Haver's office was at the dark end of the passage. The door was painted bright blue, as if to ward off the gloom. An older woman in a tidy, pale-yellow shirtwaist let me into the office and showed me to the two chairs tucked against a wall in the tiny room. "He'll be right out. It's been such a palaver getting caught up from the storm!"

"I can imagine. Thank you." I pulled out my phone for something to do, but there was no Wi-Fi, and data would cost a fortune, so I tucked it back in my purse. Maybe it would be wise to look into a local phone if I planned to stay any length of time. "Can you tell me if there's an electronics store close by?"

"Not in the village. You'll have to go to Letchworth for that."

"How far is that?"

"Only a few miles. Half hour, perhaps."

I waited. Mulled over the information about the estate that I'd found online. Wondered how long it would take the prints of the paintings to arrive. I had an email that they'd been packed and readied for shipping. Nancy had arranged for a moving company to pack everything else in the house and settle it in a storage facility. The open house would be next weekend, Sunday. A week, then, to give myself a chance to figure out my next steps. I didn't want to stay in the hotel forever—

"Lady Shaw?"

In my imagination, Jonathan Haver was a slight graying man with glasses. This guy was an athlete, no more than forty, with broad shoulders straining the fabric of his tastefully striped shirt and a foppish mustache. My intuition waved a flag of wariness. I adjusted my behavior accordingly.

"Good to meet you at last," he said.

"You too," I said and took his outstretched hand. A firm regulation grip.

"Come in. You must be completely overwhelmed by all of this."

"That's the understatement of the year." His office was cold, without windows, the walls a thin blue color. It didn't seem like the office of a successful lawyer, but maybe I was judging by San Francisco standards. He was, after all, a small-town solicitor. "I'm looking forward to actual details."

"Well, the happy news is we have a very good offer on the estate."

I raised a hand. "Whoa. Can we start somewhere else? I need some background here."

"Oh, of course." He folded his hands. "What would you like to know?"

"Everything. I don't know anything. My mother never breathed a word of this to me. I gather there is an uncle?"

"We assume he's dead, I'm afraid."

"Where did he go?"

"Unknown." He reached for a pair of reading glasses, which only slightly humanized him, and opened a thick file. "My father managed her affairs until his death seven years ago, but he never gave any particular instructions about them. I sent your mother reports every quarter, but that's the extent of it."

"Did she receive payments?"

"Of course. We sent distributions each quarter. We retained her accounting firm, and they oversee the actual financials."

"I'd like that information, please." I was typing into my phone quickly, making notes of his comments.

"Absolutely."

I dropped my hands into my lap. "Tell me about the estate."

"Have you done any reading on the place?"

"Some. I know the general history."

"Right." He consulted the paper. "Rosemere is an estate of seventeen hundred and ten hectares, of which there are three hundred and fifty hectares of wood, eight hundred and ninety of farmland, and the rest allocated to gardens, lawns, et cetera."

"What crops on the farmland? Rebecca mentioned rapeseed and barley."

"Yes. I believe there has been some rotation, and I can assemble that information if you like, though I assume you're not a farmer." He glanced at me over the top of his glasses.

"Well, no, but I'd like a clear picture."

"There is sheep, mainly lamb, for market. But you Americans don't really eat much lamb, do you?"

I thought of a long-form article I'd written a couple of years ago on the burgeoning lamb market in the US. My favorite recipe of that lot had been for a leg of lamb roasted with garlic and rosemary. When I had served it to my mother out on the deck of my apartment on a warm May evening, she'd practically swooned and eaten more in a sitting than I'd ever seen her eat. Ever.

"More than we used to," I said. "Who does the actual farming? I saw the cottages."

"Yes, those belong to the estate, but the tenants rent the land and the cottages and offer a boon to the estate on successful crops. Most of the families have been on the land for generations."

"Do you have the paperwork for that income?"

"Of course. I'll be happy to prepare a report." He scribbled something on a notepad. "I'll have Mrs. Wells pull it all together so you can go over it."

"Thank you." I made a mental note to see about finding another lawyer to take a look at the assembled material. Maybe an accountant as well. "And what about the house?"

"You saw it."

"I did. I'd like to go through it, see what's there. What can be done with it."

"I'm sure that can be arranged."

I let that sit between us for a moment, then said calmly, "It's mine, isn't it?"

"Yes, of course. You can do whatever you like."

"Good." I made another note on my phone and then checked the list I'd made this morning. "Tell me more about it. How many rooms, how long has it been abandoned? All of it."

"All right, then." He settled the glasses back on his nose and consulted another sheet of paper. "Rosemere Priory is, let's see . . . thirty-seven rooms, with additional space in the converted carriage house, which has three apartments for staff. The caretakers live in one now, though I believe they're on holiday at the moment."

"What are they caretaking, Mr. Haver? The house is falling down."

"They oversee the rest of the property—the ruin of the abbey, the gardens attached to it, and whatever issues or concerns might come up with the tenants."

I took that in, thinking about how vast the responsibilities were, how many moving pieces. It winded me. But again my mother's practicality righted itself. "Why did they leave the house alone?"

"I believe they expected someone would be coming back to give them instructions. Your mother let all the staff in the house go, so—"

"No one knew what to do."

"Exactly." He bent his head, flicked a thumb over the edge of the paper. "The history of that house is quite dark, Ms. Shaw. I believe your grandmother wanted it to fall down." He paused. "A feeling a great many of us share."

I thought about the soaring center hall with its magnificent woodwork, the neglected rooms, the vine growing through the window with a rose blooming inside.

"Why?"

"It's said to be cursed, and although I'm a practical man, the evidence seems to support that idea."

"I'm not a superstitious person," I said and realized that I'd already formulated a plan while I'd been reading and supposedly resting. "I'd like to call in a contractor and see what they have to say about the house. It seems to have good bones, and maybe it's sentimental of me, but I want to know what's there before I let it fall down."

"Oh, dear." He pursed his lips, and the mustache looked like a little animal, perched and prissy. "I don't mean to pierce your romantic dream, but the costs of saving that house would be truly extravagant. The rents won't pay for it, and once you pay the inheritance taxes, the funds will be thin indeed."

Ah, the infamous inheritance taxes. "What's the tax rate?"

"Forty percent."

I didn't imagine the relish with which he imparted this information. "That is substantial. And what's the most current valuation of the estate?"

"I'll include that with the notes, of course. And the offer."

"Thank you. I want the full picture before decisions of any kind are made."

"Understood." For a moment, he took my measure. "These great old houses are white elephants in this day and age. Many of them have already collapsed, and the rest stand to bankrupt their owners. The offer we've had is remarkable. Perhaps you will want to consider that as well."

The reporter in me smelled a story. Who would be willing to take on the estate for a "remarkable" sum? What was to be gained? But I said only, "Absolutely. Include those details too."

"Anything else?"

"No," I said and stood. "I'll look forward to those reports."

Chapter Five

When I returned to the hotel, Sarah stopped me as I went by. "Lady Shaw," she said with some excitement. "Something came while you were out."

She was practically vibrating as she handed me a modest square envelope made of heavy linen paper. The handwriting was old-fashioned and very English, with those square formations along the lower edge, as if it had been written along a ruler. It was addressed to Lady Olivia Shaw, Countess of Rosemere.

Inside was a note written in the same hand.

> Dearest Lady Shaw,
> I will be having a small gathering Sunday next, 3:00 to
> 6:00 p.m., in the garden as long as the weather holds.
> It is very short notice, but if you are so inclined, I will
> send a driver to fetch you at 2:30 p.m. I knew your
> mother and grandmother, and it would be my great
> pleasure to welcome you to the neighborhood.
> Sincerely,
> George Barber, Earl of Marswick
> Marswick Hall
> (01632) 960401

Sarah still shimmered behind the counter, as if a fairy godmother might appear any moment and whisk her into another life. As mildly as possible, I said, "It's the Earl of Marswick, which I'm guessing you knew."

She nodded. "It's his crest, there on the back. And his driver brought it in a Bentley." The last word was uttered in a whisper.

"So I should accept his invitation to a gathering next Sunday, then, if only for a ride in that car?"

Her eyes widened. "Oh, yes."

I tucked the card back into his envelope, feeling absurdly shy and panicked. "I have no idea what to wear."

"Oh, it won't matter."

"Thank you, but I'm sure it will." I took a breath. "I doubt I brought anything with me that would be appropriate. Where should I go shopping?"

"London is the only possibility, Ms. Shaw."

"Maybe." I inclined my head. "What do people wear this time of year?"

"Perhaps you should ask Mrs. Poole."

Rebecca. Maybe she would even be attending. I had her number but again felt hobbled by my telephone and the logistics of what I was doing here. "I need to go to Letchworth. Is it Mr. Jenkins who brought me here? I'd like him to drive me over there this afternoon. Will you call him to see if he's available?"

"Of course." She picked up the phone. "I'll send Allen with a pot of tea, shall I?"

"That would be wonderful."

I made my way back to my room, feeling pampered by her solicitousness, and warned myself not to get too comfortable. It would be all too easy to get used to being attended.

With a pot of tea at my elbow and a low fire offering warmth, I opened my laptop and made notes of my conversation with Jonathan Haver, along with a list of questions.

And following Haver's suggestion, I also made notes on the research I needed to do—had anyone saved a manor house like this successfully? What methods were used to keep estates going? I didn't know who I'd meet at the earl's gathering, but there might be some help there. I picked up the phone in my room and dialed the number on the bottom of the note.

A woman answered, her voice high and fluting. "Marswick Hall."

"Hello," I said and suddenly felt my mother beside me, lending me grace. "This is Lady Olivia Shaw. I received a note from the earl just now. I'd love to accept his invitation to the gathering at Marswick Hall next Sunday."

"Very good, my lady. I'll have a car sent to the hotel at two thirty, if that would be acceptable."

"Yes, thank you." I hung up. Staring into the fire, I realized I was starting to feel a little bit more like myself, which made it easier to trust my instincts.

I didn't trust Haver. Or Rebecca, for that matter. Even before Samir had warned me, there had been something a little too friendly about her. She might just be a social climber. Not exactly an attractive trait, but it wasn't criminal.

Now there was the earl and whoever I'd meet at his party. At this point, it would be wise to assume that almost everyone had an agenda and proceed with caution. I'd have to keep my wits, especially considering the challenge of interpreting English culture.

By the time Mr. Jenkins, who insisted I call him Peter, picked me up, the rain was beginning to clear. Fingers of sunlight poked through the clouds, glazing the green fields, the roofs of the odd village in the distance. It always amazed me how empty the countryside of England felt, when in reality it was crowded with people, especially so close to London. "How many people live in Hertfordshire County, Peter? Do you know?"

"Oh, more than a million, I reckon. Going to be twice that if they keep building up housing estates in every field."

"Are there a lot?"

"Too many," he spat. "We get far too much traffic now in Saint Ives, thanks to the one south of town. Have you seen it? Line at the bakery is a mile long of a Monday, everybody stopping before they head out to the train in Letchworth."

"I did see it." I thought of West Menlo Park, where my mother's other house was, the price of a single lot because of location. "Is the village convenient to London?"

"Aye, right down the A1, or by train though Letchworth or Baldock."

Very easy access to the city. I thought of that "remarkable" offer on the estate and the two thousand hectares. How many houses could be built on that much land?

A lot, I guessed.

At Letchworth, Peter took me to a shopping center. "I'll be here waiting, my lady."

"You don't have to sit in the car," I said. "It's going to take me a little while. Get a cup of tea or something. I'll ring you on my new phone when I've got it."

He grinned. "Right, then. Maybe a wee scone."

The phone was easy enough. I bought exactly the same model as my American phone and transferred all the contacts and apps right there in the store. It was amazing how much more grounded I felt, walking out of the store. When I sat down, I checked to be sure Peter's number was there, and right below it was Samir Malakar.

Impulsively, without giving myself a chance to think about it, I texted him, the skin on the back of my neck rustling. Hello, Olivia Shaw here. Maybe go back to the house sometime soon? I want to see what's really there. I sent it. Then I added, This is my new number.

It was the first time I'd been out and about since I had arrived in England, and it was pleasant to take a few minutes to people watch. Setting the phone down face first, I crossed my arms and looked around me, wishing suddenly for a sketchbook. I'd never been an artist like my mother, but as long as I could remember, I'd loved sketching. I hadn't been doing much recently but itched for proper materials now.

On a Friday morning, it was a thin crowd of mothers with toddlers and old women in tidy trousers, the odd business person in a suit.

From my bag, I took out a Moleskine notebook and a pen that I always carried for essay ideas and made notes on the setting. The clothes and attitudes of the passersby, the kind of shops that populated the hallways, the cakes in the case, so different from what I'd see at Starbucks in the US—these heavier slices, richer and smaller, along with an array of little tarts.

I sketched them, finding my lines ragged and unsure at first. Then as I let go a bit, the contours took on more confidence. My pen made the wavy line of a tartlet, the voluptuous rounds of a danish.

The barista, a leggy girl with wispy black hair, came from behind the counter to wipe down tables, and I asked, "Which one of those cakes is your favorite?"

"Carrot," she said without hesitation. "Do you want to try one?"

If I ate cake every time I sat down for coffee, I'd be as big as a castle by the time I went back to skinny San Francisco. "No, thanks. I was just admiring them. What's that one?"

"Apple cake." She brushed hair off her face. "That one is a brandenburg, and that's raspberry oat. You're not English."

56

"No, American."

"Yeah? You don't really have an American accent."

People said this to me all the time. I was never sure if it was because my accent was western or because my mother's accent had influenced me. I gave her a wry smile. "In some places these days, that's not such a bad thing."

She grinned.

On the table, my phone buzzed, and I turned it over to see a text.

Hullo. Samir here. Want to tour today? No work bcuz rain.

I picked it up. Yes! In Letchworth now. Back in hour or 2.

K. Text when you're back.

K.

Perfect. I could get some kind of idea of what a rescue would look like, and he would be a good guide. "Thanks," I said to the girl on my way out.

She waved. "Bye now."

Out in the shopping center, I looked for a clothing shop that might give me ideas of what to wear to the garden party. I only realized I was trying to imagine what my mother would wear when I entered one clothing store and saw the quality of the fabric and turned around and walked right back out. Nice enough, but my mother had had very high standards. She'd always dressed exquisitely, simply, in very good fabrics—wool trousers and crisp blouses, nothing ever slightly stained or ill fitting. Even when she painted, she wore a long smock that kept her clothes tidy.

She had, however, disliked wearing shoes. It was one of the quirks that made her so adorable, her taste for very soft, warm socks that she wore inside all the time. In the summertime, she puttered around her garden in bare feet, singing quietly as she snipped the heads of dead flowers, plucked weeds from the roots. Her skin was fair, so she wore a big straw hat to shade her face, but her hands—her hands were always tanned and stained and entirely unladylike.

I smiled to myself, thinking of that, and rounded a corner. A woman in a good camel hair coat and a jaunty scarf passed me, leaving a trail of her scent. It was my mother's perfume, Joy, but it also held the faint undertone of her hair—something I didn't even realize I associated with my mother until it slammed me, breaking my heart afresh.

I had to sit down on a bench, scrambling in my bag for my sunglasses. And tissues. I bent my head so that my hair would hide my face and tried to discreetly wipe my dripping nose, my watering eyes, all the while trying to breathe through the wave of pain.

Mom, Mom, Mom, Mom, Mom, Mom, Mom, Mom.

After a moment, it eased, as always. I looked around to see if anyone was staring at me, but of course, nobody was. It was England. Everyone would give me my privacy even if I were sobbing loudly in the middle of the place. A relief, really.

I felt her with me, my mother, and took a breath, talking to her softly. "You'd just die if I did this with you, right? Die, haha—get it?"

She would have laughed. I knew it.

Taking in a bracing breath, I righted myself and looked from one end to the other of the center. I would not find what I was looking for here and would likely have to go to London for that kind of clothing. In the meantime, I probably had something that would get me through.

Texting Peter as I walked, I headed for the parking lot. In the car, I had a sudden yen. "Is there an art store in town, Peter?" I could pick up a better sketchbook and a few pens and maybe even a small box of watercolors. It would give me something to do and a way to capture memories.

After lunch, Samir picked me up in a small dark-blue car, and I realized I'd been thinking a guy who worked in the building trades would drive a truck, as Tony did. It was pouring again, so I dashed from the door of the hotel through the door he'd flung open, yelping a little as I landed and tugged the door closed behind me.

He grinned, those black curls tumbling around his arresting face, and I suddenly wished that he were a little older. Flustered, I blurted out, "So wet!" which was ridiculously obvious.

"My mum says England is a cold, wet, miserable country. Which is why"—he swerved easily into a faintly wider spot in the road to let a truck rumble by, approximately two and a half inches from my door, then swerved back onto the road—"she left it."

"Where did she go?"

"Back to India. She was there until she was fourteen, and she has rheumatoid arthritis. The weather here was not good for her."

The way he said it, his face wiped clean of all emotion, spoke volumes. "How long ago?"

"Two years." Short, end of subject. Another car whizzed by a half inch away, and he muttered under his breath a word I couldn't quite catch.

"Where does all this traffic come from? It's such a small village!"

"This is the road to Tesco over in Stevenage and to the railway station in Letchworth. But really, these roads were never meant to carry so much traffic, were they? Built for wagons and"—he swung left beneath a row of trees with branches meeting overhead; in summer it would be a green tunnel, dark and deep—"horses."

The road was paved but barely wider than the car—and again I glimpsed the forest of my mother's paintings, mysterious and dangerous and intriguing. "My mother painted these woods endlessly." I peered out. "Endlessly. Hundreds of times. Maybe thousands, in books and paintings and drawings."

"Did she?" He glanced at me, downshifting so we could climb the steeply rising hill.

"Yeah." Rain swashed overhead, over the windscreen, through the branches, making a humid, close cave of the car. I could smell something in his hair, elusively familiar, and thought of my breakdown at the shopping center this morning. "And never told me that it was a real place! I'm mad at her about that."

"Fair enough." The car rocked a bit, bumping our shoulders together. "Sorry. It's the rough and dirty way to get here. If you want to walk, this is the way you'll come from the village."

"Not on that busy road?"

"No, there's a footpath behind the church. I'll show you if you like."

"I do love to walk. I hope to find places to get some good long walks in, actually, once I get my bearings."

"Do you know about the right-of-ways?"

I shook my head.

"All of Britain is lined with footpaths, everywhere. An old man in the village walks the ones around here in rotation to keep them open. Dr. Mooney. You should meet him."

I smiled.

"What?"

"You seem to know everyone in town."

A one-shoulder shrug, a little shake of his head. "I love Dr. Mooney. He used to be the town doctor, but he retired. Sometimes I walk with him. He tells good stories."

We emerged at the foot of the track that went between farmland and the farmhouses. From this side, I could see chickens pecking away beneath shelters behind the cottages and the starts of home plots. Again, it seemed to me a prosperous place—why let the house go so desperately?

He parked beneath a shed. "Pretty sure we can get in through that door. Wait here, and let me check."

From this angle high on the hill, I could see over the tops of the farmhouses toward the wood and the open fields. The angle of the road hid the town, but I knew it was there, just beyond my view. The whole was blurred beneath the gray rain, but far away on the horizon, impossibly blue, was a swath of cloudless sky.

Samir called out, "We're in!"

I dashed out of the car and splashed through the mud underfoot. In the vestibule, plain and empty except for a single forgotten broom hanging from a hook, I stomped my feet. "Should we take off our shoes?"

He only looked at me.

"No, you're right. I don't know what I was thinking. Lead the way."

He ducked into a narrow passageway, turned a corner, and headed up a set of stairs. The walls were stone, the wooden banister utterly plain. "Servants' stairs," I said.

"Yeah. But this takes us to some less damaged parts of the house, so you can see that it's not all like what we saw last week."

He tried to open a door on the next floor, but even when we both yanked on it, it wouldn't budge. "Swollen. It's all right. We can go up another floor and come back down the other side."

A couple of mullioned windows spaced at intervals as we climbed offered a view of the landscape, the soft greens of emerging spring, arrowed rows of dark pines, and when we climbed above a hedge, a tumble of gray ruins. Maybe the old abbey.

At the next floor, the door was off the upper hinge, sprawling sideways. Samir pulled it upright to give us passage, gesturing for me to go first. I shook my head. "Not a chance. You first."

"Really?" His eyes twinkled. "Afraid of ghosts?"

"And spiders." Afraid of all kinds of nameless things, actually. I touched my chest. "I'm hyperventilating right now."

His grin flashed, and for a moment I forgot what we were doing. It was a wide, beautiful smile, with good strong white teeth, teeth that had been well tended, given braces and routine checkups, but it was the way it changed his face that made me nearly stumble, as if someone had flung open the curtains in a dark room, allowing sunlight to come flooding in. A generous, genuine expression. I couldn't remember the last time someone had given me such an unguarded smile or looked at me so directly.

"My sister, Pavi, and I used to sneak in here all the time." He held out a long-fingered hand, and I took it, letting him draw me forward. "It will be fine."

I stepped over the threshold, and although I wanted to cling to him—my heart was honestly skittering in terror—I forced myself to let go, hovering just beside his arm. In front of us was one long section of the letter *E* that made up all Elizabethan houses. A corridor ran all the way to the other end, where it ended in a room so damaged I could see light coming in from above. To our left was a staircase and—I moved impulsively toward it—the light- and color-soaked grand staircase.

Samir caught my elbow. "Carefully," he said.

I nodded and paid attention to where I was stepping, over a carpet that once must have had a pattern, toward a bannister that overlooked the stairs. The warm golden wood of the walls glowed from the light falling through the stained glass that had been taken long ago from the ruined abbey. As if to show off, a thick shaft of sunlight broke through the clouds and set half the window ablaze, giving the entire great hall an aura of life.

"Oh, wow," Samir murmured.

"Seriously." I looked down toward the littered stairs and across to the shadowy gallery. "How do you get there?"

"Stairs from the ballroom, but that's one part of the house that's very badly damaged." He lifted a hand diagonally toward the back left corner and spread the other arm toward the front right. "Both corners and a lot of the rest of it is fine."

Encouraged by the sunshine, I said, "Show me."

We turned back from the stairs and headed for the corridor. Doors, some open, some closed, broke the line of the hallway, allowing in a few muted swaths of pale light. The old floorboards creaked with our steps.

"Creepy," I said. "Are these all bedrooms?"

"Yeah. I don't remember what's in all of them, but there isn't as much furniture up here. Maybe guest bedrooms or something like that."

"Because who doesn't need seven or ten guest bedrooms?"

"My friends sleep on my sofa when we drink too much."

"In my world, they'd stagger home in an Uber."

"Mine live further away, I think."

At the first open door, we peered in, and for the first time, I forgot to be frightened. Letting go of Samir's arm, I stepped inside the room, drawn by the view through long, mullioned windows. They looked out over farms and fields and undulating hills, the forest crouching on the edge like the border into Fairy Land. Playful beams of light broke through the clouds here and there, fingering a field, a tree, a distant rise.

The sight caught in my throat, as if my ancestors were standing beside me, puffed up with pride. "Lovely," I murmured and forced myself to shake off the fanciful feeling. Everything in the room was coated in decades of dust, but most of it was still intact—the four-poster bed with a blue or faded-purple cover, a large wardrobe, a rug on the floor. The drapes were tattered, rotted. Faintly, I smelled cat urine and mold. "It's really not in terrible condition here, is it?"

He was performing another sort of inspection, stomping a heel down on the floor in various places and slamming the flat of his palm along the walls at intervals. "Seems sound enough." He pointed at a landscape. "Here's one of the paintings—you asked why there weren't any downstairs."

It didn't look notable in any way, but I was hardly an expert in English landscape painting. "I guess I need to have someone come in to appraise anything that's left and clear out the rest."

"Sure." He brushed dust from the top of a bureau. "Are you going to keep it, the house?"

"Oh, I don't think so. Haver certainly seems to think it's a white elephant, but I'm not going to make any decisions until I have more information." Feeling less superstitious, I led the way down the hall, and we looked in all of the rooms on the floor, just to get a feel for them. Most of them were in stages of disrepair—mold on the walls or the fabrics, holes in the curtains, and even some vines growing through openings—but two others were simply as dusty as the first. I imagined a ball, visitors coming in from all over England, or perhaps a house party. Most of my idea of old houses had come from *Downton Abbey*, and I imagined women in delicate Edwardian dresses headed for dinner, ropes of pearls and rubies looped around their thin necks. As if to accommodate my vision, I opened one of the doors to find a peacock-themed room, redolent with the fading colonial era.

The other door hung at a bad angle, and when Samir poked his head in, his hand pushed me backward. "Stay back. The floor's gone."

"Really? Let me see."

He used his body as a protective device, and I peered over his arm to see what must have been a bathroom, half the floor dropping away. Below, the bathtub had landed on its side next to another bathtub below. I laughed. "It's like one of those commercials for impotence," I said without thinking and blushed.

"Sorry?" He looked at me, one side of his mouth curling into an expression I already recognized meant he was going to tease. "One can buy it? Is it expensive?"

"No. You know what I mean. Drugs for . . ." I peered into the mess of the bathroom. "They always show two bathtubs side by side."

"Maybe instead of drugs, they should try getting into the same tub."

I laughed.

He kept his arm out as we moved away, as if I were a small child who might tilt over the edge. "Let me show you the bad part here," he said, "and then we'll go down to the floor below, and I'll show you my favorite room. You'll like it."

"Will I?"

"I'm quite sure."

We walked to the end of the hallway, past a door that opened into a storage area I peeked into. It was immediately darker and cold, and a ripple shimmered down my spine. It was part of the south tower, the walls unfinished stone. Dusty and filled with the detritus of decades. I closed the door and hurried to catch up to Samir. He opened a door at the end of the hall and stepped back. "The floor here is bad, so don't go in."

A wave of rot and bad air spilled out, and I stepped back, covering my face with my arm. "Ugh!"

"Pavi would never come down this corridor."

There had obviously been a fire. Smoke stains ran up the walls, and shreds of fabric were all that remained from the draperies—which, ironically, exposed the view. These were the bay windows to the front of the house. On the floors below, they were covered with vines and roses, but here the vista was unobstructed, a clear picture of the roofs of Saint Ives Cross and the church on the hill.

"The views are absolutely amazing."

"Yeah."

"Where was the fire? We are . . ." I turned my head, narrowed my eyes. "Two floors above the dining room and parlor, right?"

"Right. Floor below is where the fire was. Not sure what happened. It's always been like that. Pavi and I think someone lived in here, like a homeless person, because it's like a campfire right in the center of the room. Maybe it got out of hand."

"Lucky it didn't burn the entire house down."

"Yeah." He tapped a hand on my shoulder. "Let's go see the good room. You'll love it."

We turned left at the end of the tower and took a set of carpeted, littered stairs to the floor below. It was immediately more luxurious. We ended up near the grand staircase, but Samir zigged and zagged around corridors to get to the other side of the house, into the other long arm of the *E*.

Again I had to stop to look over a railing, this one facing a room— a ballroom?—that was profoundly ruined by water damage and falling plaster. Looking up, I could see light through a substantial hole in the roof. The room was long and had once been quite grand, but it was practically empty aside from the rubble. "Again," I said, "it seems like there would be paintings on those walls."

"It does." He tilted his head. "There are some paintings in this room. Come see."

The hallway was a mirror image of the one upstairs, following the length of the *E*, but this floor was more luxurious, with more golden wood on the walls.

"Here," he said and pushed open a creaky door to reveal a room as lush and surprising in all the rot as a blooming bougainvillea in a desert. Time and ruin showed here, too, but even so, the colors were visible— patterns and embroidery and exuberant fabrics. Paintings of a dozen sizes crowded together on the walls, the frames thick with dust and strings of cobwebs, paintings of peacocks and tropical landscapes and portraits of exotic people—a sultan in a harem, a tall dark-skinned woman with dark eyes as mysterious as a deep lake, a tiger lolling on a carpet amid a crowd of beautiful women. More, too. Many, many more, in all sizes.

"It's like another world in here." I turned in a circle, trying to take it in. Then I halted to look at Samir. "Don't tell me—this was my grandmother's room, right?"

He nodded, looking up at the paintings. "She died wishing she was in India."

"How do you know that?"

"My grandmother was her personal maid. What do you call it?"

"You're asking me? I'm American. Lady's maid?"

That slight, almost imperceptible lift of his mouth. "You seem like the kind of girl who'd know those things."

"Woman."

"Of course." He dipped his head, but those dark eyes—deep as lakes—stayed locked on mine. He was way too young for me. I was entangled in a not-ended relationship. But I swore he was flirting with me. "Woman."

Don't get delusional, Shaw, I told myself and moved away.

"My grandmother talked about Lady Violet to my father her whole life. He knew her, I think, before she died, but there were all these things that happened right then—it's sort of confusing."

"What things?"

"Not sure of the order—he could tell you—but my aunt, his sister, disappeared. My grandmother was still alive then, but I don't remember if your grandmother was or not. You'll have to ask my dad."

I narrowed my eyes. "The sister never came back?"

He lifted a shoulder. "No. They never found her. She was only fifteen."

"That's very sad."

"Yes." He wandered around, poking through things.

"He still lives here, your dad?"

"Mmm."

"I'm having dinner with Pavi on Tuesday."

"She said. That's nice of you."

"It's nice of her," I countered. "It was his restaurant first, right? Does your dad still work with her?"

"Sometimes." He waved away a net of ancient spiderwebs and picked up a photo. "This is them, in India. Our grandmothers."

My heart lurched, hard, as I took the photo. It was of two young women, a black-and-white snapshot in an ornate frame. The Indian woman looked directly, unsmiling, at the camera, a long black braid draped over the shoulder of her sari. The white woman, my grandmother, sat in a chair, with her hand resting on the head of a large pale dog. She wore riding pants and boots and a crisp tailored shirt, and I knew her face instantly.

Because it was my face.

"Even our hair is exactly the same," I said, touching my wavy hair. It fell below my shoulders, unruly and streaky, just like my grandmother Violet's.

"My dad has a copy of this photo," Samir said and came behind me to look over my shoulder. "It startled me when I met you. It felt as if you'd traveled forward in time."

I stared right into my own eyes, looking at my too-wide mouth, my own cheekbones and jaw, so much more aggressive than my mother's delicate features. "I don't even know what to think."

"Pavi looks like my grandmother," he said, "but not as much as you look like yours."

His breath rustled the hair on my shoulder, and beneath the strange turmoil the photo stirred up, I was aware of his body along my arm, aware again of that elusively familiar scent.

One thing at a time. I handed the photo back to him and moved away. "I'm feeling very unsettled."

"Understandable."

An inlaid dressing table covered with bottles sat beneath a painting of a lush nude reclining on a fainting couch. I picked up one of the bottles and pulled out the stopper. The perfume was dried up—all that remained were the harsh last notes—but it was unmistakably Shalimar. "This bottle is likely worth a fortune on its own. It might be Lalique." Holding it, I looked around the room and felt the sudden weight of decisions that needed to be made. Paintings and junk and priceless treasures, mysteries and precious keepsakes, tumbledown walls and pristine museums of a lost time. "What am I thinking with this place? There's so much . . . I don't even know where to start."

"It doesn't have to be decided today." He took the bottle out of my hands and settled it back in the spot it had occupied—a perfect oval, empty of dust. "Perhaps that's enough for one day, hmmm?" He nudged my shoulder, turning me toward the door. "One revelation at a time."

I nodded, looking over my shoulder at the extravagant room, then up to him. I wasn't sure I could manage more revelations at the moment. "Do you have any idea which bedroom might have been my mother's?"

"Maybe." He inclined his head, tapped his index finger on his mouth. "Down the hall."

He led the way past several doors. I peeked into the open ones, seeing one that was much the worse for wear, the ceiling lying on the bed, the paper peeling from the walls in great moldy strips. We passed the top of the exquisite staircase, practically glowing in the center of the house. I stood at the top, looking down toward the foot, then up to the gallery. "Can we get there?"

"Sure. But maybe another day."

"Oh, sorry. I'm being greedy and monopolizing you."

His mouth quirked, ever so slightly. In the low light, his nearly black eyes shimmered, reflected, invited me to dive in, find out what might lie there. It had been so long since a man looked at me with such deep attention that it took me a while to realize what it was. "Be as greedy as you like." His hand floated up; fingers brushed my elbow and fell away. "It's more that you're tiring."

"Am I?"

"You've begun to limp a bit."

"Oh." I realized that my leg was actually aching quite a lot. "I guess I am. But I really want to see my mom's room if we can."

"Sure." He offered his elbow again, and I had a swift, strong wish to lean into him, smell his shirt.

I waved my hand with a little laugh. "Lead the way."

"This is the one I'd guess was your mum's," he said and pushed the half-open door wide. A cat dashed off the bed and ran underneath it, and as we came into the room, the creature broke for the hallway, a black-and-white streak. I wondered if there was a feral colony living here and if so, what would happen to them if I actually decided to renovate.

The room was less preserved than my grandmother's and much less furnished. No paintings or perfume bottles. The bed was made, the floor relatively empty. A water leak stained most of the windowed wall, and part of the plaster ceiling hung precariously over the corner. I tried to open a bureau drawer, but it was swollen shut.

Nothing much to see here. Move along. My disappointment was much larger than it should have been, and the same swell of emotion that had caught me in the shopping center earlier pooled in my throat and fell down my face as tears. I turned away, dashing them off my cheeks, embarrassed.

It didn't particularly help. Standing there, I was awash with missing her. Maybe this had been her room. Maybe she'd slept here a thousand times. Samir must have known I was weeping, but he wandered away, giving me space. After a couple of minutes, I took a breath and looked around. An ornate wardrobe stood against the near wall, and I tried the doors, blindly. They opened easily, and the tattered remains of a row of evening dresses hung there, held together by threads. I imagined what we might have talked about if she'd allowed me to know this part of her. The gowns would disintegrate if I touched them, but I spied something behind the clothes and, delicately as possible, moved the hems aside. It was a canvas, the colors unfaded, and I drew it out carefully. One of the dresses collapsed off the hanger, but it didn't matter in the slightest.

It was a small canvas, no more than ten by ten inches, and clearly the work of a young artist who had not yet learned all the techniques that would later mark her painting. The tone was very dark, with little of the whimsy that later showed up in the forest paintings, but it was undeniably the same forest, only malevolent. The trees, the grass, the coalescing shadows, the eyes peering from everywhere.

"This is my mother's work." I handed it to him.

He held it loosely, a frown on his face. "Grim, isn't it?"

"It really is." I peered more closely. "What could be in the forest here? There are no wolves anymore, are there?"

"No. Maybe boars, now and then. Maybe there was something else back then. One of the older people in town will know."

I took the painting back. "All right, I'm taking this with me, but I guess I'm ready to go."

"Right." As we headed down the main stairs, he stopped, his hand on the bannister, and said, "You know what you should do? Call the Restoration Diva."

"Who is that?"

"She has a program on television about restoring old properties. Goes into these old wrecks and figures out ways for them to make money."

"Really? Like a reality show?"

"Yeah. Look her up on YouTube." He stopped at the foot of the stairs, looking up, around the golden woodwork. "I bet she'd love this place. There's a good story, a mystery"—he grinned up at me—"a pretty woman."

I half rolled my eyes. "Flatterer."

"Not at all."

71

Television. All the past revealed. My mother's secrets, whatever they were, whatever had driven her away. Maybe she wouldn't like that.

But maybe it would be a way to save the house. My very practical mother would say, *Do what you must, darling.* "I'll look into it. I can really use all the help I can get." When I had made my way down, I said, "Why do you care what happens to this house?"

He shrugged and looked up, first at the window and the high ceiling, then the paneling. "I dunno. It just seems a shame to let it fall to pieces." He raised a hand, pointed. "Look."

Peering down at us from the gallery was a cat, presumably the same one who'd dashed out from under my mother's bed but a different cat than the one we'd seen the first time, this one nearly all black with white on his face and paws. "Hey, cat," I said.

He didn't move. His long tail swished over the edge. I clutched the painting to my chest, thinking of all the cats peering out of my mother's forests. Again, the tears welled in my eyes, and I had to turn away. "This is all making me kind of emotional."

"It's all right to miss her, you know."

I nodded. "I just wish she was still here."

He touched my arm, gripping it just above the elbow for a moment.

We were quiet on the return trip. Parked back at the hotel, he reached into the back seat and pulled out my mother's painting and then also handed me the framed photo of our grandparents. "You might like having this."

"Thanks. And thanks for showing me around."

"Of course." He was quite close in the small car, his hair tousled from our explorations. Curls fell down over his forehead and touched his eyebrow on one side, where there was a streak of dust. He smelled like twilight and cool dew. For one small second, I indulged the pleasure of looking at his face, that strong nose and wide mouth and silky, very black goatee.

It took me a little longer to realize he was gazing right back at me. On the radio, a woman sang something bluesy, and I knew I should go, gather up my things, but I just hung there, between moments, peering into the fathomless darkness of his eyes. The air around us condensed. Something earthy and green and fertile bloomed between us, twining like the vines through the windows of Rosemere Priory.

It was too close, too intense, and I bolted, nearly flinging open the door before Samir stopped me. "Whoa."

A car whizzed by. From the wrong direction. "Sorry. I'm still not used to it."

"Takes time."

"Yeah. Thanks." The back of my neck burned.

"Listen, this might be a bit . . . er . . . there's a manor house an hour's drive from here that might inspire you. I'd drive you out there if you'd like, Sunday next."

"Sunday next? I'm sorry; I can't—the Earl of Marswick is having some garden party or something."

"The earl." His tone flattened.

"What?" I allowed myself to look back at his face.

"He's one of the richest men in England."

"Oh, great. That makes it easier." I sighed. "Thanks for sharing."

"You really haven't yet grasped all of this, have you?"

"Grasped what?"

He shook his head. "Never mind." He looked though the back window. "You're clear now."

"Thanks again," I said and opened the door.

"Sure," was all he said, and he drove away. I clutched the painting and photo and made my way to my room, aware that I'd stomped very hard on that new green thing.

Intentionally? I didn't know.

Chapter Six

I showered and washed the cobwebs from my hair, suddenly aware that it had been a very long day. My leg was aching, and my emotions were all tangled over the revelations of the house, and—

All of it.

Wrapped in a cozy bathrobe, I opened my laptop. In the search bar, I typed, "Restoration Diva."

Google returned hundreds of related results. At the heart of them all was a dark-haired woman in her fifties, Jocasta Edwards. She was tall, with a direct gaze and an appealing expression, brisk with a helping of whimsy, as if she could get things done but wouldn't be opposed to a good belly laugh. I went through the results, skimmed a couple of her shows and blogs. Her enthusiasm for her subject—saving the old houses of England—was palpable. She also used a set group of experts on architecture, art history, gardens, and restoration, and that could be enormously valuable to me.

After all the feedback about how much money it would take, what white elephants the old houses could be, she offered a wisp of possibility.

It couldn't hurt to reach out. I clicked on the contact link on the BBC page for the show and began typing.

My name is Olivia

I backspaced.

Lady Olivia Shaw, the new Countess of Rosemere. I've only just learned of my inheritance, which includes a wreck of an Elizabethan mansion. I'm not at all sure the place can be saved, but

Suddenly I realized part of what appealed to me.

I feel I'd be letting down the women who've come before me if I don't at least try.

I was skilled in pitching ideas. What would set this property apart?

As you may know, the house has been vacant since the late seventies, when all the members of the family deserted it. My mother went to San Francisco, where she raised me without saying a word about her past. There seems to be no trace of her brother, and it is quite unclear when my grandmother died. The locals seem to think she cursed it because she never wanted to leave India to live in England, but she was forced when she inherited the house.

I am a native Californian, a food writer with no experience in any of this, but Rosemere Priory has a long and storied history, woven with women's lives, which I find compelling, and perhaps you will

too. I'd love to meet with you if you think there
might be potential for your show. My telephone
number is (01632) 961796, or you may contact me
at this email address.

Sincerely, Olivia Shaw, Countess of Rosemere

I pressed send. And as if to reward me, an email popped up from
my publisher.

Dearest Olivia,

Heir to an estate? Whyever would you need us
anymore?

Love both pieces, as well as the idea of a series of
essays on English food and cooking. I'm open to discussing an issue devoted to English food but would
like to involve Lindsey. Let's talk early next week.
Wednesday? Let me know a good time to call.

David

My overwhelming response was relief. If I could convince him
that an entire British edition would make sense, I'd buy myself a fairly
substantial amount of time. Lindsey, the acting editorial director in
my absence, would probably eat raw goat eyes to keep me out of the
city awhile longer, so that would not be a big problem. I flipped my
notebook to a new page and scribbled a few ideas—the cake-shop girl,
the lamb industry (take care with the ick factor), and maybe craft beer.
Thinking of my upcoming meal with Pavi, I added, "British Indian

food?" I sent a quick email back offering a selection of times we could Skype and leaned back, setting pots of possible ideas to simmer on the back burners of my imagination.

On my desk, my phone rang, a quaint British two-note ring, because I hadn't set a new tone. Ring-ring. Ring-ring. I wondered with a quickening of my heart if it might be Samir. Who else would call me on this phone?

But it wasn't a number I knew. "Hello?"

"Hello, Lady Shaw," said a cheery, singsong British voice. "This is Jocasta Edwards. You sent me an email about Rosemere Priory?"

I sat up straight. "Yes! Hello."

"Oh, my dear, I have loved that house since I was a girl. I grew up just outside of Horndon-on-the-Hill, and when I was small, we went to festivals and picnics on the grounds. Rosemere was the very place that gave me my love of old houses. It's just tragic, what's happened to it."

"Does this mean you might be interested?"

"Absolutely. I could drive up from London on Tuesday if that would work for you."

"Wow. Yes! That would be great. I should warn you that I don't have all the figures or any real numbers at all. I'm waiting for that from my solicitor."

"No matter. Not at this early point. Shall we say one p.m. Tuesday, at the house?"

I laughed. "Yes. That would be wonderful."

"You know that we don't pay for renovation? We only offer experts and sometimes help scare up a bit of support."

"Wonderful. That's what I need."

"Do you get my show in America?"

"Not that I know of. Someone here told me I should call you."

"Hmm. Interesting. All right, darling, I'll see you in a few days."

"Okay. Bye."

"Bye-bye now."

I sat with the phone in my lap for a moment, dizzy again at the speed of things. Should I text Samir and tell him? I thought of the chilly stiffness in his car at the end and my own awkwardness.

No. Better leave it alone.

I stood and stretched, trying to decide whether to wander out for dinner or stay here and eat pub food. My stomach protested. I wasn't used to eating such heavy food every day, and it was time to see what else the village had to offer. As I dressed, my grandmother's face gazed at me from the photo on my desk.

I was suddenly filled with a sense of outrage. How could my mother have looked at me, wearing her own mother's face all these years, and not said a word about it? Had she loved her mother? I tugged a sweater over my head. Was my resemblance a blessing, or had she hated it?

Would it have killed her to have shared the secret with me? Surely she'd realized that I'd be in this situation once she died.

Or maybe she hadn't realized it. Maybe she'd believed that someone else would step up or the whole business would just fall into the hands of the government.

My limp was much improved, though I knew I wouldn't wear heels for a bit longer. The cobblestone streets were wet, reflecting lights from shop windows and the flats on the floors above them. In one window, I saw a woman washing dishes and wished with a weird force to be her, to be cooking and cleaning up dinner for myself. It had been ages since my life had felt anything like normal—months since my days had taken on a reliable rhythm of walking, research and writing and editing, cooking and eating. I missed everything about that life, but at the moment, it didn't look as if I'd be returning to it quickly.

Still, maybe I could create some sort of normality for myself. After I spoke with Jocasta on Tuesday, I'd decide whether to find an apartment for a couple of months or continue to stay in the hotel.

Several restaurants were open and serving, and I peered into each one curiously, intrigued to see a fairly upscale crowd, judging by the tidy trousers and crisp bobs. They must come from the housing estates Peter had told me about. Maybe the large number of restaurants had risen in response to that population, rather than the other way around. I made a mental note to do some research. Suburbs populated by commuters to the city had a familiar ring—uncovering how it was different from the US might make an interesting slant on an article.

I came upon Pavi's restaurant before I knew it. The name, Coriander, was painted in gold on the plate glass window. Within, the lights were appealingly low, the tables with candles in cut-brass holders that cast geometric patterns over white tablecloths. Touches of turquoise picked up the peacock colors—napkins in turquoise wood holders, turquoise handkerchiefs in the vest pockets. Servers wore black trousers and vests over white shirts. Classic.

I wished, suddenly, that I didn't have to wait for Tuesday. The aromas drifting from the restaurant were mouthwatering.

But I would wait for Pavi. Wait for the earl. Wait for my life to get moving again. Instead of Coriander, I chose a French-style bistro, quiet and easy, where the server talked me into the braised rabbit, which arrived exquisitely tender in a gravy of such textured depth that I took out my notebook and scribbled a few notes on what I thought the ingredients might be. Thyme, rosemary, carrots, and parsley. Mushrooms and mustard and shallots.

Sublime. The company of such perfection eased my loneliness, and I lingered with a second glass of wine and the small sketchbook I'd purchased in Letchworth. My table was tucked in a dark corner by the window, and I sketched my table setting, the glass, the ingredients in my food, then shifted my attention to the locals moving across the square and down the pavements, the stars rising above the round hills beyond. A pair of teenaged lovers wound tightly together beside the ancient stone butter cross in the middle of the square, their figures illuminated by a streetlamp, and from this distance, they could have been from any time—the Restoration, when Charles II had given the house and lands back to my ancestress; the Victorian era; or perhaps the war years of the forties, when bombs had practically annihilated this small island country.

People had lived and died in this little village for hundreds and hundreds of years. I felt them suddenly, long lines of them reaching back through time, and let my hand capture that emotion in an easy sketch, figures in all manner of dress moving through and around each other, their feet crisscrossing the same paths. The quiet square seemed busy with their ghosts, their stories, and it made me feel peaceful in some arcane way.

Life had washed me here on this strange errand. Maybe the best thing to do was to just let it show me what it had in mind.

Early Tuesday morning, I took the sketchbook and pens with me to the hill by the church. It was, at last, a dry, fine morning, the light a pregnant yellow that angled at a long slant from the east, shimmering over the open fields and glazing the grass on the rolling hills. Rosemere Priory was thrown into shadow, but I sketched it too. The lines were awkward and shaky, but the practice gave me the same sense of quiet that it always did. I'd never been able to get comfortable with sitting meditation, but cooking and sketching and walking gave me the same feeling I'd heard others describe. Wordlessness, focusing on the moment, letting go of the crazy voices all vying for attention.

An email had come from Nancy overnight that she'd had a dozen offers at the open house Sunday, and all we needed now was to pick one—which meant, *Let's go for that big number.* It was staggering how much people were willing to pay for that small plot of land. We'd exceeded the $3.5 million she'd predicted by another $300,000, and even after taxes, that was a serious sum.

Sitting on a low, ancient wall, sketching the graveyard, I let the conflicted emotions over the pending sale move through me, one after the other. I would never sit in my mother's kitchen again. I would have an amazingly fat bank account, which would help get things moving on Rosemere, if that was what I chose, or help me find a new place to live in San Francisco. Or . . . almost anything, really.

The one thing that did not appeal to me was to buy the San Francisco apartment with Grant. A year or two ago, that possibility would have been the best I could have asked from the universe. We were happy.

Except that it had turned out we were not.

On the way back to the hotel, I popped into Haver's office. "Good morning, Lady Shaw," the same secretary said. "I was just about to ring you and let you know this was ready." She handed over a very thick envelope. "Everything you asked for should be there. Just give us a ring if you need clarification or anything at all." She folded her hands on the desk beatifically, and I realized that she was older than Haver by far.

"Thank you," I said, holding the packet close. "Were you also secretary to the previous Mr. Haver?"

"Yes, for nearly forty years."

"So you were here when everyone disappeared or whatever, right?"

"A sad business, that."

"Mmm. I just need to get the order of things straight in my head. My grandmother died, right?"

"Yes. That must have been 1973." She paused, frowning. "Maybe '74."

I was born in 1978, in San Francisco, which gave my mother enough time to emigrate, find a husband, and give birth to me. "So who was the earl when Violet died?"

"Her son, of course. Roger Shaw was the fourteenth Earl of Rosemere."

"That's my mother's brother. My uncle."

"Yes." Her phone rang—ring-ring! Ring-ring!—and she held up a finger to me while she answered it.

I waited while she explained something to a person on the other end, and when she set the handset back in the cradle, I asked, "Where did he go?"

"To India, as far as I know—that's where we've always sent the money, but he's disappeared now too."

"Disappeared?"

"No one has been retrieving the money for quite some time."

"India? Why would he go there?"

"How should I know? He was born there, and some people . . . well, they don't adjust, do they?"

"What do you mean?"

The phone rang again. Mrs. Wells said, "I'm sorry, dear; this phone will keep ringing. Why don't you read the materials, and then we can talk some more, all right?" She picked up the phone without giving me a chance to answer. Dismissed, I headed back.

When I got back to my hotel, there was a package on my neatly made bed, a box that turned out to have a stack of my mother's sketchbooks. Madeline Reed, my mother's manager, had written,

> There are many boxes of these. I tried to find some
> of the earliest ones, as per your request, but they are
> not all dated. I'm judging by style and sophistication—
> these look like they might have been done by a younger
> artist. Let me know what you need. Do be aware that
> they are quite valuable.
> Best, Madeline

The books, all kinds and sizes, were inside. The one on top was square, about ten by ten inches. I flipped open the brown cardboard cover, and there was my mother in the lines of a bird, drawn in dark pencil. The wings were outstretched, falling off the page, and yes, it was without the polish and flair of her later work, but there was still an air of confidence to the shapes of the feathers, the single curved line of the beak, the tilt of the head.

It was so her, already. I wondered how old she'd been when she had drawn this, and I imagined her in the forest, back propped against a tree trunk, sketching. Looking through the page to that day, I longed to be able to travel in time, just to glimpse her for a minute.

What would my mother tell me about all of this? Whom should I trust? What should I do?

Despite her art, she'd been a fiercely practical woman. What she'd want me to do right this minute was to stop gazing backward and dig into the paperwork Haver, more likely Mrs. Wells, had assembled.

That's what I did. I was not the most adroit banking person, but I was able to figure out most of what I needed for the moment— particularly the income and rents, which were, as the earl had predicted, quite substantial. I'd need advisors—multiple advisors, no doubt—but the estate was essentially a large business with several arms, and my task was to become CEO of the concern.

Daunting. But not impossible. With a quiet sense of confidence, I opened my laptop and began making lists. Things I needed to understand. Advisors I'd have to consult. Where I was strong. Where I was weak.

It was a start.

Chapter Seven

The meeting with the Restoration Diva was set for 1:00 p.m. I took the opportunity to walk up the path behind the church to the estate. It wound through the woods, thick and hearty, ripe with the scents of leaves and earth and cool damp. Tiny flowers bloomed in protected spots, and what I thought might be bluebells lay thick in the patches of sunlight. Birds twittered and called, a plethora of them, many calls I had never heard before. Blue jays rocketed overhead, trumpeting my presence, and doves cooed, and some persistent sparrow whistled and sang and whistled again.

I thought of the way my mother had painted the forest, with malevolent eyes looking out from every turn, but try as I might, I could sense nothing threatening here now.

The trail ended near the kitchen door, which made sense if villagers had walked to the manor over time. I walked around to the front, but Jocasta wasn't there, so I ambled to the back and toward the gardens. The weather was gorgeous—still and warming under a cloudless sky— and from the top of the hill, I admired the tumble of cottages, the fields now showing a glaze of green. I walked along the edge of the terraced portion of the gardens toward the ruins of the abbey, which I hadn't yet seen. As I rounded a curve of hedge, it came abruptly into view, gray and somehow sorrowful, most of it in ruins. Only the back wall and most of the southern side still stood, and the window area gaped where the stained glass for the stairs had been taken. A stand of pines sheltered the fallen north side.

A small fist of people worked an orderly garden to one side. This must be the medicinal garden, originally planted by the monks of the abbey. As I approached the group, I called out, "Hello!"

A rotund woman wearing sensible slacks and a big garden hat to shade her pale complexion straightened. She held a trowel in her hand and didn't speak. Some of the others looked over but kept working.

It was a little unnerving to be regarded so silently, but I tried to channel friendliness and openness. She no doubt knew who I was, and despite Samir's claim that witches tended the medicinal gardens, Rebecca had told me it was the local garden. The woman still had not spoken by the time I reached the boxwood border. "Hello," I said again, more pointedly. "You must be part of the Saint Ives Cross garden club—is that right? I'm Olivia Shaw." It hung there, and I hardly knew how to go on. I glanced over my shoulder. "I seem to have inherited this house."

"Yes, yes." She slapped dirt from her gloves and dipped her head backward to see me more clearly from under the brim of her hat. Her spectacles glinted. "Yes, we've been hearing all about you. I'm Hortense Stonebridge, president of the garden club."

"Ah." The formidable Hortense. She had that no-nonsense air so many women of a certain age in England carried with them. Her face was barely lined, but something in the softness of her chin made me guess her age to be more than seventy. "Of course. Mrs. Stonebridge. How nice to meet you. I understand the club has been taking care of the garden here for a long time."

"Yes." She took off her hat, revealing a thick pelt of silver hair I could imagine she was quite vain about. "What you may not know is that I'm also the conservation officer for the local authority, and if you intend to make any changes whatsoever to the house, you'll need permission. Rosemere Priory is the prize of the county, you know. We are very protective."

"Yes, I've been getting an education in listed buildings." I crossed my arms nervously, looked over my shoulder. Wondered if it would be better or worse to let on that the Restoration Diva herself was about to appear. "I'm not sure at all yet what I'll do. It depends on what the consultants say."

"Mmm." Her mouth pinched, exaggerating the faint stain of lipstick in the vertical lines around her lips. "Well, we shall see. I hate to see it a ruin."

"So do I."

Her blue eyes, pale with age, rested with some hostility on my face. "You look like your grandmother."

"I have been hearing that. Did you know her?"

"I did." She fisted a hand on her waist and looked away. Clear enough.

"Would you tell me about the garden? I'm going to meet someone, but she isn't here yet."

Another woman, softer looking and somewhat younger, wearing a dotted red blouse, leapt up. "Oh, I'll show you, Lady Shaw!"

Mrs. Stonebridge nodded. "I've got to get back for a meeting." She dipped her head. "Good day. I'm sure we'll meet again soon."

"Good to meet you," I said and gave her my most dazzling smile.

The other woman introduced herself as Ann Chop, and she gave me a tour. It was a very medieval garden, with yarrow and rue, chamomile and gillyflower, all arranged into tidy geometric shapes by the low-growing boxwood.

"These are not the original plants, I assume."

She said, "Goodness no. They've been replanted many times, but we work from a set of maps the monks made in 1298."

I gaped at her. "1298? That's incredible!"

"It's quite wonderful. We only have copies at the garden club, of course, but the originals are in the Shrewsbury Museum. They have a lovely collection of medieval garden materials, if you're interested."

"Thank you. I might have a few other things to study before I can get to that, but I appreciate it."

She smiled. "I'm sure."

A toot on a horn made us both turn, and up the back road came a cheery red Land Rover, shiny new, with a woman behind the wheel. I waved, certain it must be Jocasta Edwards, and she waved a hand out the window. When she stopped and climbed out, Ann squeaked. "Is that the Restoration Diva?"

"I think it is."

"Do you mind if I meet her? Is she coming to look at the house? Oooh, she's quite tall in person, isn't she?"

At least six feet, I calculated as she came forward, a cameraman at her heels. Her dark hair swung neatly at her shoulders, a rich mink shade, and her clothes were country appropriate but expensive: a simple blouse, a split skirt, and tall boots with low heels. She looked ready to take the dogs out for a ramble.

She was also good-looking in a way that would play well on camera—wide mouth; straight, strong nose; and penetrating dark eyes, which she fixed on me. "Lady Shaw," she said, extending a hand. "Jocasta Edwards. Very happy to meet you."

"Oh, please call me Olivia! This is Ann Chop, who was showing me the medicinal gardens. The garden club in Saint Ives Cross looks after them."

"I'm such a fan," Ann said. "I've watched every episode. My favorite was the season on Turlington Castle."

"Oh, that was a good one. I love it when things work out, don't you?"

"Yes."

"Well, thank you, dear. It breaks my heart when these old piles can't be saved, so I do my best." She shook Ann's hand, then purposefully turned to introduce me to her cameraman, a man in his late twenties with a tousle of blond hair and plenty of hipster facial hair. "This is Ian, and if you don't mind, he'll shoot our meeting so that we can have some footage later if it works out to feature the house on the show. Is that all right?"

For a moment, I wondered if that was a good idea. Secrets might be uncovered here, things I might not want the world to know. But honestly, I was so over my head with this whole thing that the revelation of secrets that were decades or centuries old seemed minor. Jocasta had access to the kind of information I would need, going forward, and I would take what help I could get. "Sure, that's fine."

We did not explore the entire house, but I took her on the same basic journey Samir had taken me on last week, up the back stairs to the third floor, then down to see various highlights. She paused to have Ian film the derelict ballroom, silently assessing it, and made notes on various things along the way. She pointed her cameraman to capture the bathtub that had fallen through the floor, and I held my nose and led them to the ruined room where it looked as if there had been a campfire.

We stopped in Violet's room, and she gasped aloud. "That painting is an Ingres."

I looked over her shoulder. "I thought it seemed familiar."

She stepped into the room, turning in a slow circle to look at the rest of it. "Incredible." In the hallway, she cocked her head. "Where is the rest of the artwork?"

"I have asked the same question. No one seems to know. The library is empty too."

She pursed her lips. "Why take all but the paintings in Violet's room?"

I opened my hands and shrugged in the universal expression of bewilderment. "No idea."

On her notepad, she scribbled for a while. "There's more to this story. Something isn't jibing."

"A lot of things," I agreed.

"It may be that digging into all of this will turn up unsavory or unpleasant family secrets," she said. "It happens quite a lot. Are you prepared for that? That there might be something you'd rather not have known?"

"Well, until a month ago, I had no idea any of this existed, so I'm not attached to a particular version of history."

"Yes, I suppose that's true." She peered over the railing to the ball-room again. "You knew your mother. What if the secrets are about her?"

"I think she must have had some kind of secret, or she wouldn't have left here the way she did, just abandoning it."

Jocasta nodded, moving around the room slowly, looking at things. Standing by the bed, she paused. "This room is just what I might have imagined. When I was a girl, the countess held a ball for all the girls in the county. I suppose it was to give us a taste of life at a different level, what to wear and how to conduct ourselves. I was twelve, and I wore a blue gown, and I'd never felt so beautiful in my life."

"Was my mother there?"

"Of course! By then she must have been twenty or so and as glamorous to all of us as a film star. Princess Grace, perhaps. Sad, a little aloof, very kind."

It was so easy to imagine my mother with a sleek, swinging page-boy, rounding a room full of adolescent girls to engage each one.

"Thank you for that story and for the insight on my grandmother. I keep getting mixed messages about her."

"The countess was a very large personality. You'd love her or hate her. Of course, later in life, she grew more eccentric and extreme—I've always thought she must have had dementia."

"Did you ever meet my uncle?"

"That would be Roger. He must have been around, but I don't remember him."

We continued the tour and ended at the foot of the grand staircase. No cats were in evidence today, or they were more careful than they usually were. The cameraman filmed the entire space, making sounds of awe as he panned over the wood, glowing in the light that fell so luxuriously through the stained glass window. Ruby and sapphire and topaz bars of light spilled over the stairs and the walls, as if we were inside a kaleidoscope. "It's astonishing, isn't it?"

Jocasta nodded. "It's a remarkable property, even more than I remembered from childhood." She eyed the gallery and the abbey window, then leveled a gaze at me. "It's also terribly damaged. It's going to take a fortune to repair and probably years of work. Are you up for that?"

"I honestly don't know." The ghost of my mother walked down the stairs, through red and blue and yellow light, and I watched her descend with my grandmother's eyes. Both of them had hated it. Why would I save it? "But it pains me to imagine it falling down, being lost."

"Me too," she said. "Come on—let's look at the gardens. That might be the first place we could turn around to make money."

"Why?"

"I'll show you."

We left through the back door. "Kitchen is remarkably untouched," she commented as we passed through it again. "This could almost be a flat, if you wanted a base camp."

I imagined myself living there alone, with the house silent and empty around me, and shuddered. "I'd rather check out the carriage house. Someone told me there are some flats there."

"Let's have a look on the way back up the hill." She marched down the road, and I followed, trying to keep pace, but the slope was substantial, and I could feel the irritation starting in my leg.

"Do you mind if we slow down?"

"Of course. I'm so sorry." She gave a shout of laughter. "No one has ever been able to keep up with me."

We stopped at the foot of the hill. "I did a bit of research yesterday, and what I remembered proved to be true. One of your ancestors created these eighteenth-century gardens, with topiary and knot gardens and all that. It was one of the more splendid places in Hertfordshire, and people traveled miles to see it.

"It was damaged in the war, but your grandmother brought it up to snuff, and it brought in tourists like a sighting of the Virgin Mary. It turned a tidy profit." She turned to the cameraman. "Do you have the map?"

From a leather satchel on his shoulder, he tugged out a folded piece of paper and handed it over. She unfolded it, shifted the orientation. "Here we go." She headed down a path, untidy, nearly buried, but still visible.

"These are the terraces," she said, waving a hand. "They're a Georgian invention, part of the craze for everything Italian. The young lords made their grand tours and came back enamored with Italy or the Moors or some new tree." She pointed. "Those are tulip trees, I believe. Beautiful in the spring. And those are daffodils popping up. They'll be blooming in a week or so, I'd say."

I imagined one of my ancestors as a dashing young lord, dazzled by the terraced gardens of Italy. "I'm not an experienced gardener," I admitted. "I've always lived in the city. My mother has—had—a beautiful garden."

"Well, you'll have a chance to learn here if you wish." She gave me a half smile. "We expect our lords and ladies to know these things. And you must buy yourself a good hound."

I laughed but heard the kernel of truth in it. Point taken. I'd have to educate myself if I planned to stay.

The paths wandered through deciduous forest, opening here for a pool, long and still, the water overgrown with algae and muck, and yet it had a powerful spirit. I halted, captured by the moodiness of the spot, the whispering edge of coolness wafting out of the shadows. A bridge crossed over the pool, green with time, and I imagined a lovers' rendezvous. With my camera phone, I shot a photo and then another. "This is a beautiful spot."

"There are several ponds and pools throughout. This one looks to be in fairly decent shape. It only wants a bit of scrubbing and water lilies."

I imagined the water clean, reflecting the sky and trees and clouds. "I'd want a bench here."

"Yes."

Jocasta marched on, and I hurried to follow, but the cameraman, too, was taken by the spot. He lingered until Jocasta called to him.

The gardens meandered along banks of rhododendron—"This will be magnificent in a month"—and what must have once been a knot garden that meandered into a half-walled garden. We paused at the edge of an enormous field of rose bushes just leafing out on their leggy stalks. "How could they have survived so well?" I said in wonder.

"Well, they've gone wild, haven't they?"

"My mother had a rose garden. I suppose I know why now."

Jocasta looked at me. "We'll want to tell this part of the story, that you had no idea you were an heiress. We'll probably do some digging to see what happened to your uncle, too, tell some more of the history of the house."

"I assumed you would."

"Have you heard much of the story—of the house, that is?"

"Some. I love the bit about the mistress of Charles II who convinced him a woman could inherit."

"Else you'd not be here, would you?"

"Right. Nor would my grandmother have had to leave India."

"The twists and turns of history."

"Of life," I added.

The walled garden gave way to another that made use of a ruin from the monastery days. Overgrown beds and pots and shrubs gone amok couldn't hide what had once been a most romantic spot—private and designed for contemplation. A stream ran alongside it. "This comes from the spring at the center of the medicinal garden," Jocasta said, consulting her map. "The building might have been a buttery or the like, since it would have been cooler here by the stream." Fig vines covered the old stone, but everything else was overgrown beyond recognition.

At a hedge, Jocasta stopped. "This is the pièce de résistance. The maze."

"A maze?" My inner seven-year-old perked up. "How do we get in?"

"The problem would be getting out, since it hasn't been tended and we haven't a proper guide." She walked along, however, and came to an opening cut into the hedge like a window. "Oh, this is a delight. Look!"

I peered through the opening and saw that it opened onto another square, just slightly off from the first, which opened onto another so that I could see a long way into the maze, but not all the way. At each window, you'd be able to see just a little further. "Magical!"

"It is." She clapped her hands. "Get this, Ian, and we'll head back up to the top of the hill. Shouldn't be much farther."

As we emerged from the overgrown garden, I saw we had made it to the top of the garden and the ruined conservatory I'd spied the first day with Rebecca. "That'll have to come down, I expect," Jocasta said.

"No, really?" I stood looking at it with my hands at my sides, feeling all the things we'd seen move through me again—the jeweled light in the stairway, the still pool, the magic of the maze—and now this beautiful wreck of a conservatory. Plants grew all through the broken glass, in and out, and it seemed so very sad that such a beautiful thing could have been lost like this. "It couldn't cost that much to restore, could it?"

"You'd be amazed. But it's your call, of course." She gestured toward the carriage house. "Let's take a peek at these flats."

My leg complained, but I did my best not to limp behind her. She noticed my pace and slowed hers to mine, and I assumed that she and Ian had an understanding because he was now filming at his whim, not bothering to keep up with us.

The first two doors of the carriage house flats were locked, but the third opened into a neglected but very sunny space with a view toward the house. The brick had been exposed and the old beams left in the ceiling. A fireplace with a carved mantle took up the far wall, which would be a sitting area and dining room adjoining a kitchen that must have been built in the twenties, judging by the sink. "Quite charming," Jocasta pronounced.

"Agreed." I poked my head around the corner and found a bedroom, small but again faced with that open brick and a row of windows that looked toward the hills. A bathroom that was the same era as the kitchen was far more charming, with a pedestal sink and a claw-footed tub. "No shower, but that would be easily added."

If I'd had any inkling that I'd be returning to my old life, the tide turned in that moment. I saw myself so clearly in this space, writing in that spot by the fire, cooking in that kitchen. Maybe I could get another dog, I thought, and saw her, too, sitting by the fire, a red-coated retriever. "This is perfect," I said.

"Chilly, though. Let's stand in the sunshine and talk."

Outside, I said, "What do you think?"

"It's a wonderful old pile," she said. "That staircase alone is worth the price of entry, as will be the maze." She looked back to the house, then down to the farms and cottages. "According to the public records, the rents and holdings bring in approximately two hundred thousand pounds a year, which will be enough to support you in the cottage, even give you some funds to do the upgrades it needs."

I nodded.

"But it won't be anywhere near enough to do the repairs that are necessary for the house."

"Okay. So . . . ?"

"I believe the gardens will generate a healthy income if you start there."

"How?" I asked.

"Tours. The madness for garden tours grows every year—great busloads of tourists from all over the world." She propped one hand on her hip, gestured with the other arm toward the garden. "We'll bring in a landscape architect and a historian, get some estimates, get that going, and then in a few years, maybe start to tackle the house. There are also treasures in the house that should be examined and might generate some revenue."

"I love the idea of starting with the gardens. But I don't want to just leave the house as it is. I think I told you that I have some funds of my own."

"That would change the game a bit. Tell me."

"I've sold my mother's home in San Francisco for more than three million dollars. Not sure what the conversion rate is at the moment or what my tax obligation will be, but I'm guessing I'd have a pool of at least a million pounds to start."

Jocasta blinked. Then she laughed, tossing back that magnificent hair and laughing with her whole body. It made me think of Julia

Child, the way she seemed to always be standing in a river of pure enjoyment. "Well, that is a delightful surprise, Lady Shaw. Wonderful." She flung an arm around me and turned me toward the house. "It won't be enough to finish, but it is certainly enough to begin."

We stopped in the circular drive in front of the house. "I do love this old wreck," she said quietly, leaning back to take in the top floor. Then she looked at me levelly. "I do not have full autonomy in my choice of material, but I'm going to lobby hard for this. In the meantime, we can get a better picture of what's going on."

We mapped out a plan of visits from various contractors, historians, architects, garden experts, and art experts. She made an appointment to come back in a month, once the others had made their reports, and the first segment would be filmed. "I'll send the various permission forms, and you can see to them. If you have strong feelings about any of the people I bring in, I'm not attached. Just efficient. I know the networks of people in the business, and because of my profile, it goes more quickly."

"That's great."

"I can probably have a contractor out here to look at the place by the end of the week. The landscape historian I'm thinking of is heading to Italy at the end of the school term, so I'd like to get her out here as soon as possible, too, to see if she can unearth some drawings of the terraced gardens and help us make a plan for the restoration."

"Great."

"The last thing, my dear, is to think about what you might want to do to support the house once it has been saved. You'll have to do something. These prodigal houses take endless pots of money, and you will need another means of support. Just giving tours is not enough these days—you'll have to think about what else you can do."

"Like what?"

"You said you're an editor—is that right? Is there something with writing or food that comes to mind? Maybe you can—"

"Maybe a fair on Saturdays, to bring people in."

"Good start."

"A cooking school. Or—"

"I suspect you'll think of something."

I suspected I would have to.

Chapter Eight

By the time I returned to the hotel, I had worn out my leg completely. It was the first time in days that it had bothered me at all, but I had given it quite a workout. I was half tempted to call Pavi and reschedule.

But of course I could not. It would be rude to cancel at the last minute, and I did know that she was interested in me, at least in part, because of my position at the magazine. She would have gone to no little trouble to create a beautiful meal.

A small part of my mind wondered if Samir would be there. Why would he? It wasn't his restaurant. I'd hoped we were developing a friendship, but I hadn't heard from him, so maybe not.

Whatever. I had enough to think about without crushing on a hot thatcher. Though I had to admit, as I flipped through the few clothes I had with me, having a crush was a forgotten pleasure. I'd forgotten the rustle of anticipation, the zing of remembering his wide, beautiful mouth, the way he looked at me so intently. Surely, after everything, I'd earned the right to crush right out.

I had been living in jeans and sweaters (jumpers, I reminded myself) since I arrived. From the closet, I pulled out the single dress I'd brought, a simple black jersey with a deep V-neck, long sleeves, and an empire waist. The hem and sleeves were embroidered ever so slightly with turquoise and silver thread. The best part was that I could look halfway decent in it even if I was twenty pounds over the weight I should be—which was probably not far off, considering how long I'd been unable to exercise.

Checking my reflection in the long mirror behind the door, I was happy to see that it still fit. It draped my too-generous behind with some kindness, but the low neck was almost scandalous. I tugged the two sides of the V closer together, and it seemed okay, but just in case, I draped a bright scarf in abstract splashes of turquoise and navy around my neck. Didn't want to stir the gossips my first evening out.

With a swath of bright-red lipstick, I felt ready to meet the world. Standing back from the narrow mirror, I approved my reflection—a countess, I told the woman in the mirror, and she gave me a nod. This was what this countess looked like. It would have to do.

Rain was spitting as I walked to the market square and Coriander. Again, it was quite busy, most of the tables full even on a Tuesday night. Evocative fingers of spice hung in the air, waving me inside.

It was larger than it looked from outside, and the space had been divided into more intimate sections with screens printed with peacocks.

A young woman approached. "Hello. You must be Lady Shaw."

"Yes."

"I'm Amika. Pavi gave specific instructions for your service tonight. If you would follow me."

She led me through the restaurant, and I could feel eyes on me, hear slight whispers as I passed. I channeled my mother and pretended I didn't notice. I did notice the family-style service, the tasteful tableware, the flowers tucked into glass vases.

At the back of the restaurant were three alcoves set on a ledge a foot higher than the rest of the floor. Intimate, for lovers or a small party of friends, which was exactly what two of them held. The last was empty, and of course, it was meant for me. As I settled, pleased to have the view over the restaurant, Amika said, "Pavi will be out momentarily. Can I bring you a glass of wine?"

"Yes, that would be wonderful. Did she tell you what it should be, by any chance?"

She smiled. "Yes, ma'am, she did." With a little bow, she headed for the kitchen.

A second later, Pavi hurried out, dressed in chef's whites with a turquoise apron, her hair caught back from her face beneath a tight scarf. "Hello! I'm so happy to see you!" she cried, taking my hands as she stepped into the booth. "Everything is ready. I just have to slip out of these clothes, and I'll be right with you."

"Wonderful."

Again she squeezed my hands, bringing an aura of warmth and welcome to the space. "I'll be right back."

The wine arrived, and I took a sip—a pretty, pale rosé, ordinarily only served in the summertime in California, but I could immediately understand how it might be brilliant with Indian spices. I swirled and tasted, and it was light and dry and fruity. It was also the first glass of wine I'd had in weeks, and it hit my tongue like a dance troupe, tapping all my taste buds, waking me up.

Pavi appeared, hair smoothed into a bun, wearing a simple floral dress with a floaty skirt and flat shoes. "How is the wine?"

I laughed. "Amazing."

"My father is going to join us, too, if you don't mind. He's been a bit agitated about it all day, so I think he's a little shy." Her eyes glittered, exactly the same way her brother's did, and I felt a pang. "He'll probably be overly formal at first, but he'll warm up."

"It sounds like he knew my mother and grandmother. I'm really excited to talk to him."

"How did you know that?"

"Samir told me."

For the space of a breath, so short a moment that I almost could not say for sure that it happened, she paused. "Have you become friends?" She broke a piece of popadam and swirled it in a tiny crystal dish of mint-coriander chutney.

"Yes, a little." I decided to confront the subtext head-on. "Is there a problem?"

"Oh, no! I'm sorry. He tends to be a bit of a loner—that's all." Her smile was generous. "I'm the more outgoing of the pair of us." She plucked up a small dish of riata and set it down in front of me. "Try this one. I've been perfecting it. Coriander." Her smile flashed. "Naturally."

I smiled and did as I was told. The riata struck my tongue, filled my mouth with crisp and cool, sharp and soft. "Marvelous," I said. "I could eat it by the spoonful."

She nodded.

"Is Samir the oldest?" I dipped another piece of popadam in the mint coriander. "This is always my favorite," I commented. "And this one is delicious."

"Yes, he's my older brother by three years. I've just turned thirty."

A ping like a thorn stuck in my throat. That meant Samir was only thirty-three. I was thirty-nine, forty this summer. Reaching for my wine, I managed a half smile. "Honestly, I thought you were about twenty-three. I'd kill for your skin."

"Genetic." She shrugged. "My mother looks forty, and she's over sixty."

"My mother looked every minute of her years," I said, "but she smoked, always. Never gave it up even when it made her a social pariah in San Francisco."

"How long has she been gone?"

I didn't even have to stop to calculate. "It will be six weeks on Monday."

"Oh, dear!" She covered my hand on the table with her own. The warmth weighted me, kept me from flying away into my grief again. "I'm so sorry."

"Thanks." I turned my hand over and gave her fingers a grateful squeeze, and as I did so, I realized I felt as comfortable in Pavi's presence as I did in Samir's. "And your mom has gone back to India—is that right?"

Again, a slight, startled pause, but she recovered quickly. "Samir told you that too. I'm so surprised. He doesn't talk about her."

"He didn't."

Amika and another young server, this one a boy with the long neck and big hands of a teenager, arrived with a plate of what looked like prawns and vegetables on sticks. "Paneer prawn tikka," the boy said and eyed his boss. "With mango chutney and red onions."

The fragrance wafted over us, spice and heat, and I couldn't wait to try it. "Tell me about your journey," I said as she used tongs to fill my plate. The serving dish was brass with carving on the edges, and I took out my phone. "Do you mind if I post things to Instagram?"

"No." She laughed, nudging the low, flat bowl of chutney my way. "I seriously do not mind if one of the most respected food editors in the US Instagrams my food."

I grinned and shot the prawns, the edge of the dish, and the pot of chutney, then leaned back to get a good shot of Pavi, who easily smiled just enough to look intriguing. I put my phone aside. "Now, tell me."

"Wait—here comes my father. He'll weigh in on this too."

A tall, broad-shouldered man approached the table. His face was timeworn, with deep grooves along his mouth and a definitive stamp of sadness on his brow. He'd given his children his strong nose and wide mouth, but their eyes must have come from their mother. His were slightly hooded beneath thick, heavy brows. "Good evening," he said in a strong British accent. "I am Harshad Malakar, and you are Lady

Shaw. You look so much like your grandmother; it is as if you stepped out of a photograph."

"So I have been hearing," I said and started to half stand, but he waved me back into place. "I'm so happy to meet you, Mr. Malakar."

"Please, call me Harshad."

"Then I insist you must call me Olivia."

"Oh, no. I could not."

I glanced at Pavi, who ever so slightly shook her head. "Will you eat, Dad?"

"Sure, sure." He waved a server over, asked for a place setting and tea. "How do you find us so far, Lady Shaw?"

"The town or you and your family?" I asked, a prawn between my fingers. "The town is bewildering. Somehow, your family is grounding me."

"Ah, very good. That is because our families have known each other for many, many years, a century, perhaps."

"Really, that long?" The prawn was perfectly cooked, the spice a masterpiece of layering. I widened my eyes at Pavi. "This is amazing."

"Thank you." She inclined her head. "Dad, I was just about to tell Lady—"

"Ugh! *Please* call me Olivia!"

She smiled. "I was just going to tell Olivia the story of the restaurant. Do you want to start?"

"No, no. You go ahead." The girl brought his tea, and he gestured for her to bring more of the tikka, for which I was grateful. It was layered with paneer and perfectly seared onions, and I couldn't identify all of the spices but could definitely pick out the coriander and fresh ginger.

"Dad spent his salad days in London, as you do, and met my mother at a wedding. They came back here to start a family, and he took over the takeaway from a friend of his father's."

"Good business," Harshad interjected. "Always busy. People came from all around to eat at the Curry Pot."

"It was," Pavi agreed smoothly. "Sam and I went to university in London. I started with economics"—she gave me an amused lift of a brow—"but halfway through my third year, my roommate was a chef, and she just kept dragging me around to all these restaurants. I fell in love with food and the food scene and restaurants. All of it!"

Her father shook his head, muttering, "Threw away their educations! Both of them!" But it was an old complaint and held no heat.

Pavi gave him a pat on the hand. "My father would have liked going to university."

The plate of tikka was picked clean. Amika arrived to take it away. "Did you drop out of school, Pavi?"

"No. I finished my degree and dutifully went to work at a research firm." She shook her head and, as if the memory caused discomfort still, took a sip of wine. "But I could not bear it and left after three months." She glanced at her father. "The howling! Good lord."

"I wanted to go to art school, and my mother wouldn't allow it. That's how I ended up in magazines. Funny how that goes." I leaned in. "Did you go to culinary school?"

"Yes. Worked in London for nearly four years, and then both Sam and I came home when my mother got sick three years ago. I had a lot of ideas for the restaurant, and my dad listened to my proposal—and voila! Here we are."

As if she'd pressed a button below the table, the two servers arrived with more dishes—meat and fresh green peas topped with chopped mint and served with a bowl of cumin-studded rice.

I bent my head a little to take a deep breath. "This smells fantastic." As ever, I began a deconstruction, picking out ginger and cardamom in the fragrances rising from the dishes, but not which came from which. "Did your brother come home to help with the restaurant too?"

She snorted. "No way."

But she didn't offer anything more. Instead, she began dishing up the food onto our heavy plates. "This is one of my experiments, an adaptation of a lamb *kheema* with *jeera* rice." She smiled. "What could be more Indian and more English than lamb and peas in the springtime?"

"Wonderful."

Next to me, Harshad nodded almost prayerfully over the dish.

"Is this one of your favorites?"

"Everything she cooks is this good," he said gruffly, taking a hearty bite. "When she first started telling me what she wanted to do, I thought, 'Who would want that? People like Indian food to be familiar, curries and the like.' But she's right." He waved his hand to the full dining room. "We never had such crowds before."

"You must be proud of her."

"Yes. She always has her own ideas, but she has the intelligence to go with them."

"I can see that."

We ate in silence for a time, reverently. The lamb, roasted with spices and garlic, was as tender as butter, the peas only steamed long enough to heat them through. "The timing on the peas must be challenging."

Her eyebrows rose. "Yes! We steam them quickly, then keep them cold and only heat them and add them to the lamb just before serving."

"Kheema is usually ground meat, if I recall."

"Again, right. Fresh-roasted lamb with ginger is much healthier and lighter. The jeera rice, however, is very traditional."

"I love it," I said, taking another careful mix of everything. Cumin kissed ginger; ginger embraced the umami depth of lamb; peas and mint and coriander leaves crowned it all with bright spring. "It's amazing, Pavi. Like, so incredible." I touched my lips. "Thank you."

She laughed and reached over to touch my wrist. "The pleasure is mine, Olivia. I'm so pleased."

When we'd feasted through the lamb and naan and three small vegetable dishes, along with more wine—and laughter, because Harshad liked jokes and told them with a sly eyebrow—we all leaned back. I was slightly tipsy, definitely high on the food and the pleasure of an evening out.

Harshad said, "I knew your mother, you know."

I blinked the sudden well of tears from eyes. "Sorry," I said and looked away to take a breath.

"I'm so sorry," he said. "If it is too emotional to speak of her—"

"No, no, no! Please. I'd love to hear." I swallowed. "I just . . . miss her."

"As a daughter would," Pavi said, and it was not my imagination that she moved a little closer, as if to protect me.

"Did you know my grandmother too?"

"'Know' is not exactly the word."

I nodded. "Here's the thing: I had no idea who my mother was until she died. I didn't know I *had* a grandmother. Or an uncle— wherever he is—or that my mother was English nobility. Nothing. I knew nothing of any of this until a few weeks ago. Anything you know is more than I do."

"My mother and your grandmother were good friends," he said. A certain heaviness weighted his brow. "They spent their lives together in India, and my mother still looked after her, even after they both married. It used to make my father angry, I think, but he didn't stop her." For a moment, he tapped a spot on the table, lost in memories. "We would go to the big house, and my mother would visit with Lady Violet—that's what I always called her, Lady Violet. And while they drank tea, we children played hide-and-seek or duck, duck, goose. Later, we climbed trees or tried to catch fish in the stream."

"You and my mother?"

"And Sanvi, my little sister. She was five years younger than me."

I nodded, aware that I hardly even knew what to ask, where to begin. "Was my mother happy in those days?"

He pushed out his bottom lip, considering. "No. She was never a happy girl. She missed her father."

"Did he die too?"

"He divorced Lady Violet when Caroline was a small girl. I never saw him." He took up his fork and ate a little, and I followed suit, aware of Pavi's alert attention beside me. "Your mother . . . she wasn't unhappy either. We didn't think so much about that in those days, you know." His smile was wry, and I saw Samir in the expression. "We just were."

"Did she draw and paint then?"

"Always."

I would have to stop—it was feeling like an inquisition—but a couple more questions. "And my grandmother? What was she like?"

He shot a glance toward Pavi, who nodded. "It doesn't matter, Dad. She's been dead for more than forty years."

"Mmm. We were a little afraid of her, all of us children, including Caroline. She could be generous and full of laughter, or she could be mean and petty, and you never knew which one it would be. I once saw her slap my mother so hard it left a mark for hours."

"What? Really? And your mother continued to go visit her?"

"They had been quarreling about something, something old, maybe, back in India, and it made my mother angry, but she said that Lady Violet had demons and we weren't to judge."

I thought of the photograph, the unsmiling, straight-on way she looked at the camera. "She didn't want to leave India."

"No. She was freer there, but she inherited the title, so she had to come back."

My mind whirled. "So why did everyone leave, if the inheritance was so important that Violet gave up the life she wanted to come back here?"

"She did her duty. That's what people did then. She stayed until she died, but my mother said she never got over missing India." He pierced a stray pea with the tine of a fork. "She's buried in the churchyard."

"I didn't know that. I'll have to go look."

Something passed between father and daughter, and I rushed to ask one more question. "Were you still friends with my mother when she left?"

"Things were different for us then. We'd grown up, and I was grieving my sister, and it was all . . . just a very dark time."

"Your sister? What happened to her?"

"Disappeared." He wiped his face as if to erase the memory. "She went to the market one day, and we never saw her again. No one ever confessed to killing her or kidnapping her. She just vanished."

"That must be excruciating," I said slowly, "to never know."

"Yes." He carefully tucked his napkin next to his plate. "You must excuse me."

"I'm so sorry. I didn't mean to bring up painful memories . . . I just don't know how to get answers to all of this."

He paused. "Maybe you don't really want the answers. Sometimes it's better to let dead dogs lie."

As he walked away, his shoulders hunched as if under a great weight, I said to Pavi, "I'm sorry. I shouldn't have asked all those questions."

"It's all right. I can't imagine how strange it is to have no answers about who you are, who your people are."

I took a breath, feeling the hollowness in my chest again. "Exactly."

"But now," she said, her voice light, "you must tell me about the *Egg and Hen* and how it feels to write for such a magazine."

I took a breath, glad for the shift in tone. "Yes. Let's talk about that—in a moment." I pointed toward the ladies' room, and she nodded.

"I'm going to check on my father. We'll meet back here in a few minutes. Can you possibly make room for some *gulab jamun*? I make the rose syrup myself."

I laughed, touching my belly. "Maybe in a little while."

In the ladies' room, tastefully appointed with two walls white and one stenciled with an arty peacock, I washed my hands and noticed that my cheeks were quite flushed. A little tipsy. It always showed in my cheeks. My lipstick had lasted remarkably well, but I touched it up a bit, and as I leaned in, I realized the scarf probably wasn't hiding the too-much cleavage as well as I'd hoped. Maybe I'd have to give this dress up until exercise got me back down to my usual, still-not-svelte self. Too bad. It was my favorite.

In the meantime, I adjusted the scarf again and headed back to the table. Pavi wasn't back as I approached the table, but Amika paused. "Would you like anything? Water, perhaps?"

"Yes," I said emphatically. "Please."

As I slid in, I sat on my scarf and pulled it sideways, a winner of an awkward move, and I was chuckling to myself as I tugged it out from beneath my rear end when I sensed Pavi. Laughing, I said, "My friend used to tell me it's hard to be cool when—"

But it wasn't Pavi, because it had to be Samir standing there in going-out clothes, a pale-blue shirt with tiny dark stripes and black jeans that hugged his legs all the way down. "When?" he echoed, one side of his mouth lifting.

I managed to free the scarf and clutched it in my fist, very aware of the "too much" that was on full display in my one and only dress. I could feel him noticing, too, and tried not to look at him as I draped the scarf around my neck and tied it demurely. "When you're a klutz," I said, folding my hands.

"I rather liked it the other way," he said. One hand rested on the tabletop, long and elegant, the nails perfect ovals. The hands of an artist. A lover.

A shiver rippled up the back of my neck, as if those hands had touched me. But he only stood by the table, still as a cat, his eyes capturing me, seeing me. I reminded myself that he was thirty-three. That he could, theoretically, date twenty-five-year-olds.

But his gaze waited for me, and in the end I could only meet it, let that steady regard draw me into something quiet and private, a country of our own creation.

"Samir!"

The country disappeared as Pavi bustled out of the kitchen, her hands full with a wide, shallow bowl. The *gulab jamun*, no doubt. As she settled it on the table, I saw the sprinkles of rose petals. Beautiful.

"I didn't know you were coming by tonight," Pavi said, standing on her toes to kiss his cheek. He had to bend down, and in a flash I saw how close they were.

"I thought I'd see how you'd got on with the famous editor." He grinned, encompassing both of us, and easily slid into the booth beside me. He smelled of night and dew, and his shoulders seemed a mile across. "I knew you would cook this."

So he had known I would be here. A slight shimmer of possibility edged along my arms, down my thighs.

She slapped his hand. "Guests first."

"I'm not sure I can take another bite!"

"Of course you can. Taste the rose syrup at least." She dished out a brown dumpling into a small white bowl and drizzled syrup over it, then topped it with a few rose petals. She did the same for Samir and then for herself. I pulled out my phone and shot an Instagram photo of the dessert, three rose petals cascading down the river of syrup, light shining on the curve of the dumpling.

The siblings dug in, and I watched them for a moment before I picked up my spoon and tasted mine. Like everything else we'd eaten tonight, it took the ordinary to an extraordinary place—I tasted a thousand fluttering roses and a rain of sugar and the soft, spongy texture of the dumpling itself. "It's sublime, Pavi. You'll have to show me how to make it."

"I'd be happy to. We should have an afternoon of cooking—that would be so much fun."

"Where's Dad?" Samir asked. He smoothed his goatee with thumb and forefinger, but I noticed that his hair was still a riot of big curls, untamable.

"We talked about Sanvi and Olivia's mother and that whole mess."

He nodded, gave me a look I couldn't interpret. "Sad stories."

"They are," I agreed and wondered if I might need to take my leave now that Samir had arrived.

But Pavi said, "Now that you've had your dessert, Samir, you can go. We are going to talk about food, and you're getting in the way."

"Am I?" His smile was definitely meant to be slow and flirtatious this time. "Olivia?"

"It is my practice to never have an opinion between two siblings."

"All right." He slapped a hand on the table and made a move to go. "See you around, Countess."

I raised a hand, aware that my face was not behaving, that I was trying to avoid smiling, as if I were fourteen and this was summer camp. And when he met my eyes, I saw that he knew it too. He winked. "Careful with that scarf."

"Are you twelve?" Pavi asked. "Go." As he ambled out, she shook her head. "Don't mind him."

I took a breath. "No. No, I won't."

And finally, we leaned our heads together and began to talk about the industry. Food and restaurants and magazines and recipes and writers. I felt like myself for the first time in months.

Chapter Nine

Sunday afternoon, a black car rolled up in front of the hotel, and a driver in a crisp black suit stepped out. I was waiting, nervous and a little overwrought from a lack of sleep. The lobby smelled of beer and cigarettes that had been consumed just outside the door while laughter and music had spilled out of the club Friday night and Saturday night till very, very late. My room, though it was down the corridor a long way, thrummed with the noise.

I hadn't slept much either night, and it showed on my face today, showed in my nerves. I'd changed clothes three times, finally settling on pair of camel wool slacks and a simple green blouse. I didn't have a coat other than the same one I'd been wearing since I arrived, a lined raincoat that saw me through the winter in San Francisco and had seen me through more than a few. Still, it was a Burberry and would do.

"Good morning," I said.

"Good morning, my lady. I'm Robert, and I'll be driving you to the Earl of Marswick's garden party today." He tipped his cap and opened the door. "It's going to be a fine day, innit?"

In surprise, I looked up. Not only was it not raining, but actual sunlight was leaking through the clouds. In a couple of spots, blue sky peeked through. Where the sun touched the hills around the village, the grass shone gold. "Oh, my. Is it going to clear up?"

"So they say. Sunshine all week." He saw me settled and closed the door. From the front seat, he added, "Right welcome. Rainiest March I can remember. But now it's spring, and those lambs'll be frolicking."

I smiled. "I hope so. It's rained nearly every day since I arrived."

He pulled out, and I remembered I was supposed to notice for Sarah that it was a Bentley. I ran my hand over the leather seat and took notice of the wood appointments. Luxurious, but as I wasn't a big car person, it was hard to know how it differed from other luxury cars. I'd take the description of the leather and wood back to Sarah.

"Is it far?" I asked. "To the estate?"

"An hour, I expect, given that it's Sunday. I brought you a bottle of water there. Anythin' else you need?"

"No. Thank you."

"Music?"

"Yes. That would be great." To my own ear, that sounded obscenely American. *That'd be great.* But I *was* American, and I didn't have to become anyone else. *Just be who you are*, my mother had drilled into me. *Be who you are.*

And yet she hadn't at all, had she?

The looping back roads were relatively empty, the car exquisitely comfortable, and I found myself drifting off, waking with a start only when we bumped over a rutted road into a long drive. The sun had broken through, chasing clouds off to the sea, and entire swaths of bright, clean blue sky showed through. Beneath that splendor sprawled a house made of gold stone, surrounded by open green lawns dotted with painterly trees.

"Here we are," Robert said. "Marswick Hall."

Unlike Rosemere, Marswick had been well tended. A gleaming row of windows marched across the face, end to end for four stories, each row getting smaller until they culminated in a small, ordinary row just under the eaves. Wide stone steps led to a pair of gigantic doors painted dark blue, one of which was open, guarded by another man in a suit, balding and ostentatiously aloof, like a butler from an old movie.

But this was no movie, and he probably was the butler. I smoothed my trousers and took a breath. He came down the steps to greet me. "Lady Rosemere." He bowed a little. "Please follow me."

The house was long but not deep. The marble corridor at the entrance led straight through to a pair of glass doors at the other end, doors open to the garden at the rear. I could hear music and voices, the ring of laughter. I steeled myself to enter the party, but the butler turned right and led me down a corridor to a room that must be a parlor of some kind. A genial-looking black Lab leapt to his feet and trotted over to greet me as the butler announced, "The Countess of Rosemere, Olivia Shaw."

"Very good, Mr. Tims. Thank you." A man stood, lean and fit despite his advanced years. He'd said he'd known my mother and grandmother, and he might well have been a contemporary of my grandmother, so late eighties? Early nineties? "Hello, my dear," he said. His voice was strong, not at all wavery. "Please, come sit with me a moment before we go out into the madness."

"I'd be delighted." Sunlight poured through the long windows to spill over elegantly worn Persian rugs. Thousands of books lined the walls. The contrast with tattered, neglected Rosemere made my heart ache. This is how it would have looked, once upon a time.

The earl waited by his chair, leaning on a magnificent walking stick carved of dark wood into a loose weave of tree branches. I admired it openly. "That's beautiful."

"Oh, yes. My nephew brought it to me from his travels. Can't remember where he was. Ecuador, Argentina. Somewhere like that." He tapped it on the floor, then looked at me. His eyes were a startlingly bright blue, not at all rheumy but direct and clear. "Makes me look dashing rather than old."

I laughed. "Absolutely."

He held out his hand, and I took it. "You are Caroline's daughter, then. Olivia, is that right? May I call you Olivia?"

"Of course."

"And you may call me George."

I narrowed my eyes. "Oh, I'm pretty sure that would not be polite."

"All right. Marswick, then. How's that?"

"Yes."

"Let's sit down, my dear. We haven't much time before they come after us, but I wanted a moment to have you to myself. Welcome you to the neighborhood."

"Thank you."

A woman appeared at the door with a tray, and he waved her over. "Tea? Or a ginger splash?"

"Ginger, please," I replied, intrigued.

He accepted a cloudy ginger, too, served in a tall, narrow glass with a slice of lime floating on top. I sipped it delicately, and the flavor sang through my mouth, sharp and bright. I forced myself not to make a sound over it and politely took just one more sip.

"How are you finding us?" Marswick asked.

"Everyone has been very helpful." I sipped again, trying to trace the flavor profile. Ginger, lime, sparkling water, or maybe tonic?

"Oh, I'm sure, Lady Rosemere, I'm quite sure. They'll all want a piece of that pie that's landed so neatly in your lap."

I thought of Rebecca and the solicitor. "Yes, some of them. Not all, I don't think."

"Humph. In my experience, a woman of your rank will have to watch her back. You've not had much experience, I warrant."

"None at all. My mother never said a thing. I thought she grew up in some forgotten industrial town somewhere."

"But her accent!"

"We don't hear accents the same way in the US as you do here. They all just sound English."

"My word." He sat back, large hands on his thighs. "You must be reeling."

"Yes."

"Well, I'm going to tell you frankly that there are a good number of social climbers who've had their eye on that property for years, and they were just about to snap it up when you arrived out of the blue."

"I've gathered that. They want the land for developments, I'm guessing."

"Perhaps. I suspect others might wish to buy a title."

"Can they do that?"

His mouth turned down at the corners. "They can. I gather it isn't easy, but it has been done often enough in recent years." He folded his hands over his bony knee, and I realized he must have been a very big man, once upon a time. His hands were nearly the length of my forearm. "And a title without responsibility is an abomination, so I'm hoping to convince you to give it a try."

"What do I know of any of it?"

"It's in your bones."

"Mmm. I doubt it." I shook my head. "Have you seen that house? It's a complete wreck."

"Yes. But the lands earn a good income, and with enough time, anything can be fixed."

Maybe it was the lack of sleep, but today, it felt overwhelming. All of it. The mystery, the house, the possibility of not just being here for a visit but leaving my life in San Francisco behind completely. I fell back on my rote response. "I need more information before I can make any kind of decision. I don't know where I'd live or what steps to take or—"

"You'll rent a cottage, won't you, and renovate one of the apartments in the carriage house."

I laughed at his easy answers. Maybe someone else would have been put off by his bossiness, but my gut said he was trustworthy. "Why does it matter to you?"

He fixed those bright-blue eyes on my face with great intent. "Our families have been neighbors for more than four centuries. Four hundred years," he added for weight. "Always, it was the Barbers and the Shaws, side by side. We stood in solidarity over many things and quarreled about others, but I believe our people have always stood for the same ideas—that with great wealth comes responsibility. That responsibility takes on a great deal more weight when it comes to protecting the estates, and the titles, from the greedy." He visibly straightened. "We are charged with looking after the land, too, and none of them care a whit about that."

"Noblesse oblige." With nobility or high rank comes obligation. I thought of the taxi driver the very first day telling me that he remembered picnics on the grounds of Rosemere when he was a child and of the lanes filled with cottages, the lands stretching far into the distance when I looked out the window of the house. "I have no idea what to do, even where to begin, or what it means to have inherited this title. I don't know what to do with it."

"I shall tutor you, Olivia, if you'll allow it."

I bent my head, suddenly overcome. "Thank you." Taking a breath, steadying myself, I looked at him. "If I decide to stay, I will certainly take you up on that kind offer."

"Oh, it isn't kind, my dear. It's an obligation." But his eyes twinkled as he said it. "Come, now. I suppose we have to go mingle. Which is your first lesson. One must speak to everyone at the party and remember something important about each one."

He offered his arm, and I took it, aware that he probably wished for the stability he found in my grip. "Another day, you must tell me all about your mother's life in America," he said when we walked down the corridor to the glass doors. "I was very fond of her, you know."

"I'd be happy to," I said, and then we were walking out the glass doors. It felt as if the entire company raised their eyes to the pair of us.

"Good afternoon!" the earl cried.

The murmuring faded. Women in spring dresses and high-heeled sandals and men in tidy trousers and sport coats waited. A few raised a glass in his direction.

"I know you've all been curious about the latest addition to our local gentry, and I am absolutely delighted to be able to present to you the Countess of Rosemere, Olivia Shaw."

A round of clapping splattered around the knots of people. They looked at me expectantly. My brain emptied entirely, but as the pause grew, I managed to blurt out, "I look forward to meeting each of you."

Oh, well done, you.

"That should get them going," the earl said under his breath.

"Gossiping about my lack of a brain, I'm sure."

He chuckled. "Not at all. Come; I'll introduce you to a few people you should know."

The rest of the afternoon was a blur of faces and floaty dresses and crisp slacks, handshakes and face kisses. It was a relief to find a face in focus when Rebecca swam up to greet me, her husband in her wake. "Olivia!" she cried, kissing my cheeks. "So lovely to see you!" She leaned into the earl, ever so slightly too close, and kissed his cheeks. "You haven't met my husband, Philip."

Philip, too, leaned in to kiss my cheeks and left a waft of leathery cologne behind. The edges of his blond hair blended thinly into his tanned neck. A golfer, no doubt. "So happy to meet you, Olivia! Rebecca told me about your lunch together and the tour of the house. Are you really going to try to save it?"

"I have no idea. Not yet."

"It is something of a white elephant, I suppose."

"Maybe. I'm still gathering facts."

"Never mind. You must come to a proper supper one evening. Next week?"

"Of course."

Rebecca squeezed my arm lightly. "I'll call you."

I nodded.

"Yes, yes. Nice to see you," the earl said and nudged me along. I could tell he was tiring.

"George," I said, realizing I could use his first name after all, as he'd asked, "I'll be fine on my own. Wouldn't you like to sit down for a little while?"

"Are you tiring of an old man's company?" He raised one wild, bushy eyebrow. "You want to find yourself a husband at my garden party, do you?"

I laughed outright and saw by the twinkle in his eye that he was pleased. "No husband for me just now, thanks."

"They'll be after you, though. You'll see. Be wary." He paused, leaning on his walking stick. "A beautiful young heiress—it's a wonder you haven't made the papers."

"As long as it's not page three, I guess I'm all right," I said, referring to a now-defunct feature in a major newspaper that had run photos of topless girls every day.

George laughed loudly, throwing his head back, and I joined in, pleased that I could elicit such a reaction. But after a moment, he started coughing, and I led him to a chair alongside the portico. "Do you want some water?"

"No, no. Just shaking loose the boring days, that's all." He patted my hand. "You're a delight, Olivia Shaw. Very much like your grandmother. You look like her, of course, but you've got her brain and good sense. The estate could use that again. Do you know she tripled the income of Rosemere in the years she ran it?"

"Really? Everyone says she hated it."

"Oh, perhaps she did. It was more England she hated. She wasn't as free here as she'd been in India, of course. Used to doing things her own way, which is why she didn't last with a marriage, even when she gave it a try. I'd have married her, if I hadn't been married myself." He winked, and then another coughing fit overtook him. Worried, I looked around for a place to get water.

A woman in her forties joined us, her manner easy, her voice a melodic murmur. "Are you all right, Uncle George?"

"You can walk me inside in a moment, Claudia, but in the meantime, meet the local heiress, the Countess of Rosemere, Lady Shaw. She's making me feel eighteen and witty."

Claudia was tall like the earl, with dark hair swept away from her face in a rolling twist, her eyes direct. "Is that right? Pleasure to meet you. I'm Claudia Barber. I do my best to look after this rebel. It might be time to go in, mightn't it?"

"It might indeed." He was red-faced with the coughing, and a lock of hair had come loose. However hale he appeared, he was a very old man. He squeezed my hand. "You must come for luncheon next week. I have much to teach you and probably not much time to do it in."

"Name the day." I stood up and gave him a kiss on the cheek. "It was wonderful to meet you, truly."

"Leave your number with Mr. Tims," Claudia said. "Very nice to meet you."

My obligation done, I turned to leave myself, but as I walked up the steps, a couple waylaid me, introducing themselves as Baron Something and wife. We chitchatted about San Francisco and travel and were joined by another trio, and for the better part of two hours, I was engaged by a dizzying whirl of locals. I did my best to remember something about each of them but failed spectacularly.

One very tall man in his forties brought me a drink. "Gin and tonic," he said. "You look parched."

"Do I?" I sipped the drink gratefully. "Thank you. It's perfect."

"They always get me through these things. Properly spaced, of course." He offered his hand. "Alexander Barber, the earl's nephew. You met my sister a bit ago."

I accepted the handshake. He had the same dark hair, thick and unruly, and the wiry body of a long-distance swimmer, which I recognized from a high school boyfriend. "Olivia Shaw."

He grinned, giving his face a boyish expression. "Yes, I gathered. American, is it? What do you do back there?"

Not a single person had asked me this, and it brought into focus how divided I felt mentally. "I'm a magazine editor, a food magazine called *Egg and Hen*."

"Is that right? Are you a writer as well?"

"Yes. Essays, mainly, some reporting. Because I'm over here, we're considering an issue on British food and traditions."

"We've a lot more to offer than most of the world believes."

"I think so too." He was a good-looking man, with rugged features and a deep tan on his face. "As it happens, my work is editing and writing, as well. I'm an editor at large for *Travel and Adventure*. I have a book coming out in the fall on the world's best treks."

"No kidding. That's great." The gin trickled into my blood, easing the tension I'd been holding, and I sipped again. "What's your favorite trek?"

"Depends. If you want something accessible, not too long, it's hard to beat the Coast to Coast in England. A little more active—the Langtang trek in the Himalayas. Not too extreme, not terribly crowded, full of cultural treasures."

"Ah. I'd probably stick with the first one."

A trio of women joined us, introducing themselves to me but clearly interested in talking to Alexander. I lifted a hand in a short wave and extracted myself. The butler called Robert, my driver, and as I waited on the front steps, looking out over the well-tended landscape, I wondered if I might be able to stay here in England. If I might be able to make a place for myself in this new world. Did I want to?

And even if I stayed, what were the visa requirements? I should really look into that.

It all seemed more than a little daunting.

What I hadn't expected to feel was a sense of obligation, but the earl had planted something that tickled the edges of my sense of identity. Did I belong to this estate, to the family seat? Or did I belong back in San Francisco, in my busy, arty world? At the moment, I had no idea.

Chapter Ten

When I returned to the hotel, the pub was bustling, which surprised me considering that it was only four p.m. on a Sunday afternoon. A big sign at the door advertised a Sunday roast with all the trimmings, showing a discolored photo of a plate of roast beef, potatoes, carrots, and yorkshire pudding. It didn't look the slightest bit appealing, and I felt irritable at the sound of all the voices.

Even when I got to my room, I could still hear them. Not like the karaoke crowd, but waves of voices and laughing and screechy female commentary. I thought there might be an athletic event of some kind on TV.

Restless, I changed my clothes back to jeans and a soft long-sleeved T-shirt. My leg ached from all the standing, so I sat with a heating pad I'd picked up at the pharmacy and checked my email.

The first one was from Grant with the subject line "Are You Ghosting Me?"

Crap. I'd forgotten to send him my new number. And maybe, honestly, I *was* subconsciously ghosting him, but that wasn't fair. I opened up the email.

> I've been trying to get ahold of you for days. Is everything all right? Nancy won't share anything with me about the sale of the house, and I tried to

get some information on your mother's paintings
at the gallery, but they wouldn't share either. I'm at
a loss here, Olivia. What the hell is going on with
you? Whatever it is, we can talk it out. I love you,
and I'm here for you.

A sense of guilt burned my gut. Whatever was happening, Grant deserved to know.

If I was honest with myself, I didn't feel anything over his email. He'd already faded to sepia in my emotions, a lover I'd once cared about.

No longer.

Not something I could write in an email. And as I'd learned many, many times, nothing difficult grew easier in the waiting. I made a cup of tea, turned on the fire, calculated that it was early but not hideously so, and dialed his number.

He picked up immediately. "Olivia! I've been worried to death. Is everything okay?"

"Yes. Yes, I'm sorry, Grant. I'm juggling a lot of tasks right now, and I got a new phone, and I forgot to give you the number."

"Forgot?"

"I know. I'm sorry."

"Did you lose the old one or something? Why did you get a new phone?"

"There's just a lot to do here, and it's going to take a little while. It was cheaper to get a new phone rather than trying to use the old one."

"What are you talking about? You can't stay there! We have to sell your mom's house. Bill and Joaquin want an answer over this apartment—whether we can buy it or not—so they can put it up for sale. I've been out here scrambling, and you've been totally out of touch. What the hell is going on? Why can't I get any info from the gallery or Nancy?" Exasperated, he took a breath, and I saw him in my imagination—slapping one big, paint-stained hand on his leg. "You can't just be tra-la-la-ing in England right now."

"Well, it turns out I can. I'm here." His tone, his bossiness, hardened what I'd realized only the past few weeks. There was no point to continuing the charade any longer. "Grant, I don't know how to say this except straight out. You can't access information because I told them I don't want them to communicate with anyone but me." I took a breath. "I don't want to be with you anymore."

A deep hush greeted my words. Then, "Oh, sweetheart, you're just grieving your mom. It makes life look stupid, makes everything look ridiculous, but we're a team, me and you."

"Are we, Grant? We weren't much of a team when I spent nine days in the hospital and you breezed in for an hour a day, maybe, if I was lucky. We weren't a team when I ended up going to my frail mother's house to stay instead of coming home because you couldn't be bothered to get things ready for me at our apartment."

"That's not fair! I was finishing work for an exhibit when all of that happened. You know that! I was doing my best."

"No. Your best would have been being there for me," I said without rancor. "I nearly died, Grant. I could have."

"I know. I let you down. I was scared."

"And how do you think I felt?"

"I'm sorry. I love you, Olivia. You know I do." He was silent for a moment, but I didn't have anything to place in the silence. "Look, maybe this isn't grief, but don't they say you shouldn't make any major decisions for a year after a big death? Why don't we just wait until you get home, talk it all out then?"

For one cold, terrifying moment, I wondered if he was right. Was I only reacting to everything that had happened?

But again I thought of my loneliness at the hospital, my sense of being marooned at my mother's house, and shook my head. "We were broken before the accident. I just didn't want to give up the life we had. I didn't want to admit it, but it's over."

"Wait! What about the apartment? All your things?"

"I don't care. I want my mom's paintings, but there's nothing else there that I can't do without."

"You're serious."

"Yeah, I am. I'm sorry."

"This is just crazy. Olivia, we've been together for eight years! Eight!"

"I know. Better now than after we get married."

"But we've worked so hard to get to this point, where things might get a little easier. Your mom's house, the apartment. You love this life. You'll regret giving it up once you get over all this drama."

"Drama? My mother is *dead*, Grant."

"You know what I mean. The situation is making you question everything, but you love me, love our life. You know you do!"

"I did. Now I don't." I donned my magazine voice, clear and direct. "I'm breaking up with you, and it's not negotiable. Let's just be adults about this, can we?"

"Oh, now that you'll have your mom's house money, you're going to walk away, right? After all that—"

"Not going to listen to this," I said. "I want my mother's paintings. You can call the gallery."

"I'm keeping those paintings. They'll be my settlement, since you're going to cut me out of the house."

"Grant! Can we please not do this? It's my mother's work. It doesn't belong to you."

"Well, I guess you'll have to take me to court."

"Court? That escalated pretty fast."

"This happened pretty fast. We've lived together six years. What we've collected together will be ruled common property."

"That's ridiculous. Grant—"

"I don't want to talk any longer," he said and hung up.

Stunned, I stared at the phone for a long moment, then started to punch the redial button and halted.

My breath was coming in hard pants, and I stood up to relieve the anger surging through me. What a jerk! I would get the paintings back, of course. No one would award him such personal property—but it infuriated me that he would make such a claim. I needed to call my mother's agent and find out what the legalities were. What if he tried to sell the paintings? It made me feel vaguely panicky.

On the upside, I realized that I was deeply relieved that I hadn't told him anything about the rest of it: the manor, the estate, my title.

I was also relieved to be free of him. Until I had spoken the words this afternoon, I hadn't realized how furious I was over his desertion, how betrayed I'd felt, lying in that hospital bed. I rubbed my knee, feeling echoes of that deep, painful loneliness.

What had taken me so long?

Filled with a restless, half-furious, half-buoyant exuberance, I tugged on a sweater and a hat and headed out into the still-sunny afternoon. The sun hung high enough over the hills that I would have a solid couple of hours of daylight yet. The tip toward summer felt hopeful after the long dark winter, and I set out down the high street.

The foot traffic surprised me. When I had first started traveling to England, largely for work, it had been impossible to find anything open on a Sunday at all, and nothing after five p.m. on weekdays either. Few shops were open today, but the cafés and restaurants nearly all were. I wandered by each one to read the menus and peer inside. I wanted a good walk first, but maybe I'd have supper out tonight. At Coriander, I paused, but it was closed, the tables neatly set for next time. The card in the window informed me that the restaurant was closed Sunday and Monday. Sensible.

Wandering on, I looped up around the church and looked for a path that might lead to Rosemere, as Samir had said. I found one that meandered through a field, past a small pond, and along a bank of tall bushes I thought might be rhododendrons. I followed it all the way around; crossed a stream over a tiny, ancient bridge; and paused to admire a thicket that was so still it might have been medieval. The path leading out only led me upward to the top of the village. I paused and looked back, wondering where I'd missed the switch, but clearly I'd gone the wrong direction entirely. In the distance, Rosemere stood in mute beauty, flaws hidden at such a distance.

For one moment, I imagined how she could look with light streaming in clean windows, the hallway and stairs brought to life again with feet running up and down and the voices of humans ringing through the rooms.

I walked the rest of the way to the top of the hill and found myself in a grassy clearing that offered views of the wood and a small lake—that must be the "mere" in "Rosemere"—and the quaint tumble of the village with roads leading into the central square from all directions. They would have been tracks, once upon a time, roads worn into the earth by farmer's carts and the hooves of animals.

Again that sense of history and endless time struck me. I stood here on this hill, and how many had stood here before me? How many would after me?

It almost made me dizzy. Made me feel both too small and oddly comforted. My life mattered, but in a way, it was just a blip.

Sweating lightly, buoyed by the fresh air and exercise, I wandered back down the lane. It was lined with a mishmash of houses, here a couple of old cottages with thatched roofs, there a narrow Victorian, three stories high, next door to a modern cube with the utilitarian tone of the fifties, and then a couple of ordinary cottages, no thatch. No matter what the style, the front gardens burst with the offerings of spring—tulips in a dizzying array of varieties, red and pink and variegated; spills of hyacinth; a spectacular dogwood tree. A stout woman bent over at the waist plucking weeds, singing breathily.

I wondered what would be blooming in the gardens at Rosemere Priory. I'd never had a chance to garden seriously. Would I even like it? My mother had been passionate, but that didn't mean it would suit me.

A man came around the side of a cottage with a wheelbarrow full of seedlings. For a moment, I could not place him out of context—not until he looked up, and an expression of pure, unsullied cheeriness crossed his face. "Olivia! Have you come to see me?"

Samir, wearing gardening gloves on his big hands, his hair even more out of control than usual, dirt all over his jeans. "No, I mean, I might have but—I didn't know. I was out for a walk." I paused to admire the garden, which burst with the tulips and daffodils and hyacinths that grew in other gardens but boasted many more as well— something that trailed and another with soft little leaves and bright trumpet flowers. "Is this yours?"

"Yeah." He rested his knuckles on his hip as he looked over his shoulder. "I must admit I didn't plant it, but I'm sworn to maintain it under the terms of my lease. Beautiful, isn't it?"

I nodded. "Lucky you."

"Want a cup of tea? Coffee?" He inclined his head toward the door. His jaw showed a Sunday brush of whiskers around the glossy goatee, and the angle of neck to throat caught me somewhere in my ribs. I wanted to see how he lived. To sit with him.

"Yes," I said and let myself in the gate. Slightly flustered, I pointed to the plants along the fence. "What are those?"

"Primroses."

"They're so friendly."

He grinned. "They are. And tulips are a bit haughty. They think they're better than everyone else."

"Well, they're pretty spectacular. It's like Tulip Lane, coming down this road."

"Gardening is a competitive sport around here."

"So I heard. Jocasta told me that I would have to learn my garden techniques."

"Did you call her, then?"

"I did! We had a meeting on Tuesday, and she's very confident she'll want to feature the house."

"That's great!" He tossed his head to fling curls out of his face, then slipped his gloves off and threw them in the wheelbarrow. "Come in."

He held the door, and I brushed by him, willing myself to just be normal. Inside, sunlight tumbled through the wide picture window, revealing a room that was both masculine and comfortable. A tweedy sofa sat beneath the window, with brightly colored throws flung on the arm. Books filled every available shelf, and stacks sat on chairs and along the wall. A giant Siamese cat reclined in the sunshine and lifted his head as we came in, meowing in greeting. "What a cutie!" I said, reaching out to rub his back, creamy with tan stripes.

Samir leaned over and scratched the cat's belly. "Billi. He's a rag doll. The only thing of any value to come out of my marriage."

"Marriage?" My ears roared a little. "You seem too young to have been married and divorced already."

"It was unfortunate," he said, "but I'm not so young, really." His long fingers nudged the cat's chin upward. "And I'm told I'm an old soul."

"Are you?" I petted the cat, feeling a low, warm purr beneath my fingers. "I sometimes think I'm a brand-new one."

He shook his head. "No. You're an ancient one. Clear-eyed."

"Ha. Thanks." That green bloom filled the air between us again, rustling beneath my skin, making me want to look closely at his mouth.

Instead, I looked at the books. "You're a big reader." So inane, and I knew it the second it was out of my mouth. "Sorry; that was stupid. I just feel all thumbs."

He laughed softly. "It's all right. Come through here. Let's have tea. Tea's always good for that."

For what, I wondered? Giving me back my dignity? My brain?

The kitchen was tiny, but a door stood open to a back garden, and he pointed toward it. "Have a look at the back, and I'll put the kettle on."

"Thanks." I managed to get myself outside without being an idiot again, and once out there, I took a breath, inhaling the fragrant coolness lurking in the barely green shadows. The back garden was as splendid as the front, the borders bursting with color and coordinated height. A small greenhouse stood in the far corner, and beyond the fence the hillside dropped away to show fields on one side and an ugly clutter of rooftops, all made of the same red tiles, on the other.

As I sat down at the small table, the cat sauntered out and meowed at me. I patted my lap. "Come on; I don't mind."

He leapt up, all fifteen pounds of elegantly soft fur, and lolled across my legs. "Thank you," I said quietly, rubbing his belly. "I could use a little unconditional love today." He flicked his tail against my arm. "Everything is just a little topsy-turvy, and I haven't had my dog to talk to or my mom, and I'm feeling a little adrift."

A low, deep purr rumbled into my belly, and he turned his head to look up at me, the blue eyes at half-mast, which someone had told me was an expression of trust. "You're a sweetie, aren't you?"

He blinked, and I blinked back, cat shorthand for love. Something at the back of my neck eased. In a tree nearby, a bird twittered, and far in the distance was the sound of a mower. A bee bumped along a row of some small white flowers I didn't recognize, and I stroked the cat and let go of a long-held breath.

"He has that effect on people," Samir said, carrying a brass tray with a pot of tea and accompaniments, including a little plate of cookies. "I only had digestives, I'm afraid. I don't get many passersby."

"I love them. English cookies are one of the best things about this country."

His grin flashed, and he poured tea into two mugs. "Do you not have them in America?"

"Not like this."

He chuckled. "What does that mean?"

"English biscuits are so . . . restrained."

"As we are," he said, smiling. "Sugar? Milk?"

"Both, please."

He stirred them in and set the cup close to my right hand, then gave me a pair of digestives on a paper napkin. "We wouldn't want to disturb Billi, would we?"

"No." I stroked his fur, down his belly, finding quiet in the movement. Again, I found my breath easing. Life had been completely insane for months now. "How old is he?"

"Don't know, really. He showed up in the back garden one day, as if it were his home, and never left again."

"Someone must have missed a cat like this!"

"I searched for an owner, went to the veterinarians in the area, the rescue centers, all the things you're meant to do, but never found one."

I looked up. "He must have been meant for you, then."

He nodded, a little sadly, I thought. "He came to see me through the breakup." He tugged Billi's ear, and the cat meowed softly, pleased. "Do you have pets?"

"I did. A dog. He died a few months ago."

He didn't look away as people so often did when you confessed a grief. Just kept looking at me directly for a moment, then said, "So you've broken your leg and lost your dog and your mother and inherited a title you knew nothing about in just a few months?"

I raised my eyebrows. "It sounds like a lot when you say it like that."

"It does. It is."

"The leg and the dog happened the same night." I took another sip of tea, finding it did somehow fortify me. "He was very old for a shepherd mix, nearly sixteen, but it happened kind of suddenly—he just couldn't breathe one night, and I rushed him to the vet, but they couldn't do anything." I cleared my throat. "It was a rainy night, and I was not in the greatest shape on the drive back, and I just wrecked the car." A whispering memory of breaking glass, flashing lights, the look of worry on the doctor's face as she examined me. "It's mostly a blur, but I shattered my right tibia, punctured a lung, and was in the hospital for nine days."

"Olivia!" He leaned forward and circled one hand around my forearm, almost exactly the same gesture of comfort his sister had used. "Perhaps you need some brandy in your tea."

I laughed. "The cat will do. And biscuits." I looked away from the kindness of his gaze, feeling embarrassed and revealed and somehow relieved, as if offering the story took a little weight out of the bag of awfulness I'd been carrying around with me.

When the quiet stretched, I looked over at him. "Sorry—that was probably too much."

His hand lingered, fingertips against my inner wrist. "Not at all. I was trying to think of a way to say how sorry I am that all those things happened in a way that wouldn't be dismissive."

That river of emotion that was traveling so close to the surface of my skin nearly overflowed again, and I nodded. "Thanks."

As if he sensed that, he straightened. "Let me tell you about those books."

"Please."

"I've always been a reader, but when I returned to the village, I did nothing but read for an entire year. I had failed at everything I'd tried and couldn't bear to talk to people, so I rented this cottage from a friend of my mother, and Billi and I holed up here, and I read."

"That was the end of your marriage?"

He nodded, with a wry twist of his mouth. "She's an architect in London. She wanted me to be—" He sighed. "Something I couldn't be."

I wanted to prompt him with questions, but it seemed the wrong thing in this quiet afternoon. I nibbled the digestive and waited. He brushed curls out of his face, then held them away for a long moment as he stared into the near past. "It didn't last very long, only two years."

"Oh, ow!" I covered my heart with a hand. "I'm sorry."

"I knew better. I should never have begun, and I knew it, but—" He sighed again, lifted one side of his mouth. "She was the corollary of that beast women like—only men are simpler than women. Drama," he said and shook his head. "So much drama."

A Taylor Swift song popped into my head, and I sang a line.

Samir laughed. "Yes."

"Pavi told me you both went to London for school. Did you drop out to become a thatcher?"

"No. At university, I read literature. I became a professor." He plucked a broken piece of biscuit off the plate. "A writer."

"Really? What kind of writing?"

"Novels. Nothing you've read, I'm sure. They never particularly did anything out in the world."

"Wait. You've written actual novels? More than one?"

I saw the tension in his shoulders. "Three. All but the first complete failures, and I learned my lesson."

For a minute, I held the knowledge in my mouth, rolling it around like a hard candy, sweet and lingering. It brought certain things about him into focus—his attention to detail, his long memory, his encyclopedic knowledge of the house and village and land. His intelligence.

"Huh," I said and sipped my tea. The cat leapt down, and I settled a little more. "I don't actually believe that."

"Believe what?"

"That you learned your lesson, by which I guess you probably mean you gave up. Books fail for lots of reasons that have nothing to do with the writer, but you know that too." I paused. "Did you write the wrong books?"

He raised one thick brow, so like his father's. "I don't know. When I look back, it's all this crazy blur—dinner parties and literary gigs and the students and the writing. That's when I met Tapasi, at a party for the first book." He shook his head and repeated, "A blur."

"Believe me: I know the feeling." I let go of a humorless laugh and swung my body forward, elbows on the table. "I broke up with my boyfriend today."

"Today," he repeated, pointing at the ground, at this moment in time.

"Yeah. That's why I was out walking. We were together for eight years. *Eight.*"

"Are you all right?"

"It was way past time." I shook my head. "When I needed to take Arrow, my dog, to the vet because he couldn't breathe, he couldn't go because he was fucking *painting*." I glanced at him. "Sorry."

He smiled a little. "I've heard it before."

My anger, as hot and liquid as magma, pushed deep into the center of my body for months and months and months, geysered upward. "When I was in intensive care, he came to see me once a day, for like five minutes, and then he couldn't be bothered to get the apartment ready for me to come home with my crutches and cast, and I had to go stay with my mother. Which ended up being a good thing, because she died, but still"—I looked at Samir, and I hadn't lost him; he was listening intently—"why didn't I break up with him *months* ago? How could I not have seen him more clearly? He's a jerk. A big fat jerk."

"You've done it now, though." He held up a fist. We bumped.

I picked up my cup to toast. "To the end of bad relationships."

"The end." He drank and picked up the pot to pour more in both of our cups. "Did you enjoy your visit with the earl?"

"You know what? I actually did. The party itself was kind of weird, all those people and I didn't really know what to say to them. But the earl is wonderful. He's a great old man, and he knew my mom and grandmother."

"I'm glad. You seemed nervous about it."

"And you seemed a little hostile." It popped out before I could stop it.

For a moment, he regarded me. Took a sip of his tea, then leaned back. "I suppose I was. This is a very classist country, and no one ever forgets it for a moment." He steepled his fingers, and in the gesture, I could see the professor he'd been. "It's just always there, judging everything."

"Right, the class thing here is strange. I mean, I'm American. We don't do class."

"You don't really believe that, do you?"

Startled, I looked at him. He only looked back with his liquid black eyes. I said, "It's not like here."

"Perhaps not. But you can't possibly think it doesn't exist."

"I guess." I thought of those dinners I'd eaten, the very privilege of living in San Francisco at all, the homeless people down on Treat Avenue, the neighborhood where my mother's house had sold for millions, the stories of people riding the train for two hours to get to work from places as distant as Stockton, people being taxed out of the homes they'd lived in for decades. "I mean, yeah, of course it does." Thinking more, I felt a little ashamed—the country had been under siege over class for several years now. "But it's different, don't you think? America is essentially a meritocracy, in that you can earn your way up the ranks via education and money."

"But can you, really? University is wildly expensive, is it not? Not everyone can afford the cost."

I nodded. "That's true. But we don't really judge people on accents."

His mouth lifted on one side. "Don't you?"

And again, I realized I was wrong. Dialect and regionalities did influence the perception of class. "Huh. Right again."

He smiled. "Class does exist in America. You're just more subtle."

"And we don't have the nobility."

"Exactly."

"It does appear that the British Indian population is very upwardly mobile, or at least some segments are."

He shrugged. "Yeah, that's true. But it's also true that there are no great British Indian estates that are centuries old. Like yours."

I searched his face. Was that bitterness I heard or only observation? "I hardly know what to think of it."

"You will."

"Yes. And anyway, I'm told you can buy titles these days. That's what I think a lot of the people at that party want. To buy Rosemere to get themselves a title."

"Almost certainly. And they want to make a fortune creating housing estates." He gestured toward the uniform, ugly red roofs. "What a shame that would be, to see your land turned into that."

My gut ached a little as I imagined those rolling fields all turned to houses. "There used to be picnics on the estate. Did you know that?"

"I might have heard my dad talk about them." His phone buzzed, moving a little on the table, and he glanced at the face. "Ack. Forgot. I'm sorry. I'm going to have to get cleaned up. I have dinner plans."

I practically leapt to my feet. "Of course. I'm sorry to keep you."

He caught my arm. "I invited you in, remember?" He dropped his hand but stood there in the dappled sunlight slanting down from the tree overhead. Light danced on the crown of his head and along his brow, spilling into the hollow of his throat. He was like something the forest conjured. "I enjoy your company, Olivia. That's been rare in my life recently."

I swallowed. "Me too. Thanks for letting me spill my guts today."

"Anytime."

He walked me through the house, past all the books, and I paused. "Which of your books would you tell me to read?"

"None of them," he said with a small smile.

I faced him. "You know I'll just go to my room and look you up, right?"

"I would rather you did not." He crossed his arms. Such a defensive posture.

"Why?"

He sighed. "They're all products of that big disaster of a time in my life—that's all. It has no bearing on now."

"Even the first one?"

A shrug, and he looked over my head to some nameless place in the past.

Inclining my head, I said, "Okay. I'll leave it alone for now, then. But not forever."

He smiled. "Thank you, Olivia."

"You're welcome."

On the stoop he said, "Text me after you speak with the Restoration woman. It's meant to be a week of fine weather, so we'll be working late, but I'd love to know what she says."

"Sure." I raised a hand and let myself out the gate, feeling his gaze on my back as I headed down the hill. Or maybe I only hoped he was watching me go.

Dinner plans surely meant a woman. And of course a man like that would have tons of women in his life. I thought about him sitting alone in that bookish room with his cat nearby, reading and reading to cure a broken heart, and it gave me a pang.

Stop it.

Firmly, I focused my attention on the reminder from my stomach that it was time for dinner, and it had been a long day of nibbles and snacks. Time for something robust. I thought of the Sunday roast at the pub—why not? I could write about it. What could be more English than that?

Chapter Eleven

It took some doing to find an evening when Rebecca's husband would be home for a dinner, but we worked out a time, and she picked me up in the Range Rover, smelling wonderfully of some spicy cologne.

"We're going to have to get you out of there," she said as I climbed in the vehicle. "It must be hellish on the weekend. Don't they have karaoke?"

I laughed. "They certainly do. And football or something on weeknights."

"Maybe cricket."

Bernard sat in the back seat neatly and huffed a soft greeting. I turned and said hello. Would I want a Saint Bernard? I tested the idea. No. Too big. "I really miss having a dog."

"They're good company," she agreed.

"My old dog died six months ago. He was a rescue, a shepherd-husky mix."

"He must have shed bushels."

I chuckled. "I could have made blankets for the world every spring."

"The world is divided into those who love animals and those who do not," she said. "I can never quite imagine what people who don't have pets do when they have a bad day."

"I know." It made me like her better. "How did the thatching turn out?"

"Beautiful. We're going to have them back to do the stable." She turned smoothly into her drive, and I thought of Samir standing high on the roof that first day.

Philip waited within, a bibbed apron around his body. "Hello, Olivia!" he said in a hearty way. He had a genial face, which I had not particularly noticed at the garden party. "We're so happy you're here tonight! I'm making chicken shawarma."

"It smells heavenly," I said and meant it.

"Philip is a fantastic cook," Rebecca said, taking my coat. "It was one of the things that captured me."

"You're a great cook too," I said. "I wrote an article on venison stew after tasting that one you made."

"Really? That's wonderful! I'm so flattered!"

We settled in over steamed rice and shawarma and Israeli salad with a beautiful, nuanced white burgundy. It still startled me a little to see the French labels, which were so unusual in California, but of course, French was the local great wine, while Californian was the import.

As Rebecca poured a generous second helping of the wine for Philip and me, she asked, "So have you come up with a plan for the estate?"

"A plan?"

"Will you sell or renovate?" she clarified, taking a sip of water.

"Still not at all sure, one way or the other. I've been doing heaps of research and consulting with various experts, including Mr. Haver, but there are just so many unanswered questions."

Philip nodded. "It's a big decision, but of course, it would be worse if you had an actual tie to the house, if you'd grown up there or something."

"If I'd grown up there, it wouldn't be a wreck, would it?"

"I suppose not," he said mildly. "But it is now. I think the feeling is that it would be best left to fall down. These old piles are a terrible drain on estates."

The wording was so close to something Haver had said to me that I smiled slightly and used an echoing technique that worked brilliantly in interviews. "A drain?"

"Oh, yes." He patted his lips and rested his forearms neatly on the edge of the table, hands in soft fists as he warmed to his topic. "You've just no idea how many of my clients have lost everything over a doddering estate. Sentimentality is never a way to move into the future."

"You must forgive my husband," Rebecca said smoothly. "He finds history inconvenient."

He laughed lightly. "It's true. I'm a cretin when it comes to these things. You're much better about this in America—if it doesn't work, knock it down!"

I laughed with him. "It's true, but even there, we have the historic register, and if something makes it onto that list, woe be unto you." I scooped up more salad, let the sharp, fresh flavors roll through my mouth. Then, "That's what everyone's been saying here. Just as you said, Rebecca, the process for getting things by the committee that oversees listed houses is just grueling."

"That was certainly our experience," Philip said. "Rebecca had her heart set on the old farmhouse authentically restored, so we jumped through the hoops the old battle-ax set for us." He glanced fondly at his wife, and I thought suddenly of Tony, the strapping thatcher.

"Philip charmed her, mostly. She didn't want much to do with me."

"I've had a couple of conversations with Jocasta Edwards, the Restoration Diva, and I'm hoping that she'll have some good suggestions."

"What?" Rebecca asked. "She's helping you?"

"Not yet," I said honestly, "but I think she might take on the project for her show."

"That would be marvelous!" Philip cried. "She has resources you couldn't hope to access on your own, no matter what your title."

Rebecca held her hands in her lap. "But isn't that a bit crass, putting your whole life on the BBC?"

"I don't know about the crass aspect. If there's any chance at all of saving Rosemere, I need all the help I can get."

"But what if they discover terrible family secrets?"

"That could very well happen. I mean, who runs away from a happy life?"

She looked at me with a disappointment I couldn't quite translate. In defense, I said, "Both George and Samir seem to think it's worth saving. Maybe I do too."

"George?" Philip asked.

"Samir?" Rebecca said at the same moment. "You mean Sam, the thatcher?"

"Yes," I said. "And George is the Earl of Marswick."

"Oh, oh! Yes, of course," he said, shaking his head. "I'm not sure I've ever known his Christian name."

"I can see the earl's taken you under his wing," Rebecca said. "But what does Sam have to do with anything?" She seemed genuinely bewildered.

"He's been very helpful, actually. He's the one who suggested Jocasta."

"Okay, I'm sorry I'm not following." Rebecca scowled prettily. "Who is Jocasta?"

"My fault. She's the Restoration Diva."

"Right, right." She gave a little laugh and examined her wineglass as if it were to blame for the lapse.

Philip said, "You mean Samir Malakar, the writer who lives in Saint Ives Cross?"

"Yes," I said, more emphatically. "Our families have been connected for over a hundred years, according to Samir's father."

"Is that so?" Rebecca eyed me, then looked at her husband. "Sam is a writer? How did you know that and I didn't?"

His eyes shimmered, and I saw the droll set of his mouth before he said lightly, "Because I'm not a snob like my wife." Taking a sip of wine, he added, "And I've read them. At least the first one. Never got around to the second."

"I had no idea," Rebecca said. "He's very attractive, of course, and I knew he'd come back after uni, but—well." She shrugged a shoulder. "Anyway."

Philip stood and smoothly took our plates. "I've dessert, so don't think you can sneak away."

"I wouldn't dream of it," I said.

Jocasta brought an architect, a surveyor, and a landscape historian with her when we met the following week. "I have good news," she said, beaming as we met at the top of the gardens. "We're a go!"

I grabbed her hands in my excitement. "Oh my God. That's great news!"

"It is. I'm delighted, and if you don't mind, I'm going to set these good people to work so we'll know what we're dealing with. Ian and Diana are going to follow them around and film, and you and I are going to sit down and talk everything out. Have you heard about the funding from America?"

"Still in process, but I have no doubt the sum will be plenty to get us started."

"Good. You should have funds from the estate as well, so I'm confident in our ability to get it all moving. The plan is to air an episode every eight weeks as long as we have good material. We'll start with our first walk-through two weeks ago and add whatever we get from today, which will air in April. Is that all right?"

I blinked. I'd imagined filming for ages, then finally, somewhere down the line, a season focused on Rosemere. "That's fast," I said.

"It is," Jocasta said.

"In for a penny, in for a pound," I said with a shrug.

"That's the spirit! We'll film some sort of canned bits today for the credits—all about the house and that—and then one day next week, I'll bring the hair and makeup team out, and we'll film the intro with the two of us that will frame the story. Sound good?"

"Sure."

It was a daunting afternoon, in the end. The historian cited so many facts that my head was spinning, and I resolved to get my notes in order when I got back to the hotel. My head was stuffed with generations of history. Centuries of it.

Dizzying.

The minute the group drove away, I texted Samir. Jocasta says the project is a go!

That's AMAZING. Where are you now?

Still at Rosemere. She just left.

I've just driven back from TK. Still in work clothes, but will come there. 10 min.

Find me by conservatory.

A bank of clouds hung in the distance as I walked back down the hill to the wrecked conservatory. More rain later, but this was April in England. What else should a person expect? On one of the hills, a scattering of white balls littered the velvety green grass, a flock of sheep, and the fields that had been empty upon my arrival now clearly showed a glaze of green. Rapeseed, for canola oil. Rebecca had told me that the fields were beautiful when it bloomed.

I didn't yet feel a sense of ownership as I headed down the hill, but something in my heart ached to preserve the land as it was, maybe save the house for generations to come. For my sake? My mother's? I didn't know.

The longer light of late afternoon angled through the broken panes of glass in the conservatory, giving sharp shadows and edgings of gold to the blue glass. The iron framework had oxidized unevenly, coloring the scrollwork and curlicues of the roof with uneven splashes of orange. Somewhere in the distance, a bird cried loudly, a call I thought I should recognize but couldn't quite pull in—loud and screechy. A little creepy, honestly, as I poked my head into the door of the conservatory.

I caught my breath, drawn forward by wonder into the ruined landscape of a plant extravaganza. Vines and shrubs grew wild, and some of them were covered with flowers I didn't recognize. Within, it was warmer than outside, and a breeze whistled through a giant gap near the roof. My footsteps alerted a pair of pigeons, who flew out of their hidden nest to pump with muscular wings toward that giant hole, cooing in protest.

I took out my phone and started shooting photos of the panes of glass and the oxidized iron and the crazy growth of plants. Some of the trunks of the vines were as thick as my arm. I recognized bright-magenta geraniums in one corner and a spill of white petunias.

Everywhere I'd been feeling my mother at Rosemere, but here I felt my grandmother. And as if to conjure her fully, a peacock suddenly trotted into the space from nowhere, as if he were a ghost. His bright black eyes fastened on me with curiosity and no fear, and I remembered that they were bold creatures, sometimes aggressive. This one seemed only curious as he strode toward me, blue head and neck shimmering in the strange watery light, his jeweled tail feathers swishing behind him like the train of a gown. "Hello, bird," I said.

He walked a wide half circle around me, made a low gargling noise, then disappeared through an opening beneath a long table. I laughed. Of course that had been the bird call I hadn't quite recognized—the call of a peacock.

Such Indian birds. Had my grandmother brought them home with her? And what else was in her untouched bedroom? Journals, letters, accounts?

Add it to the list, I told myself.

"Hello?" Samir's voice came through the door. "Olivia, are you there?"

"In the conservatory," I said. "I'm coming out."

He waited at the end of the walk and pointed as I emerged. "Did you see the peacock?"

"He was just inside, like he owned the joint."

"He probably does. I've heard there is a flock of them in the woods, but I've never seen one. Seems very auspicious, doesn't it?"

I smiled. "A party of peacocks."

"Is that the name for a group of them?" He looked down at me, and the heavy black curls fell forward. As ever, he flung them back with one hand, impatiently. I wondered why he didn't cut it all off if it so bothered him, but I hoped he never would.

"Yes."

"One of my favorites is a congregation of alligators."

"A murder of crows," I said.

"Too easy. Everyone knows that one."

"Oh, well, I see, sir. Surprise me, then."

He narrowed his eyes in thought. "A parliament of owls." In his accent, it sounded noble and elegant, the soft swallowed *r*, lingering *l*.

"Nice." The party of peacocks had just popped into my mind. Now I had to really think about it. "A cauldron of bats."

He held up a hand to high-five me. "Good one." When our palms slapped and dropped, he said, "So you're staying then. In England, that is."

"For a while, anyway."

The slightest smile touched his lips. "Good."

"We'll see. It might be the most ridiculous thing I've ever done in my life."

"I don't think so. I have faith in you." Looking back over his shoulder toward the house, he gestured across the landscape. "Imagine what it could be like if Rosemere was grand again."

For a moment, I could see it, the rooms bustling, filled with light and rare, lovely things. "I hope so." I pointed down the hill. "Do you want to see the garden?"

"I don't mean to be too personal, but I can't help noticing that you're rather limping. We can save it for another day, eh? Let me give you a ride home." He glanced toward the densely gathering clouds. "Fancy a little Indian food?"

"Hmmm. Do you know a good place?"

He grinned. "C'mon. You can tell us all about it over supper."

I almost, *almost* reached out to take his hand. It felt like the most natural thing in the world. And yet . . . no. I had to keep reminding myself that he was seven years younger than me. I'd broken up with my fiancé of eight years only a couple of weeks ago. My mother had died. My life was insane.

And yet he felt like the calm in the center of a storm. "Let's go this way first—to the stables. I'm going to make one of these over into a flat for myself."

"You don't want to live in the house?" His grin said he knew I wouldn't.

I shuddered for effect. "Jocasta suggested that I make over the kitchen and live there, but oh my God, can you imagine?"

He inclined his head. "What are you afraid of?"

"I don't know—everything." I widened my eyes. "It's creepy as it is. Would you spend the night there?"

He shrugged. "Maybe. It likely wouldn't bother me."

"Oh, I double dare you. How many ghosts live in that place?"

"They're all your relatives, though, aren't they?"

"But I've never met them and would rather not make their acquaintances unless they have actual living bodies."

He laughed, and I felt a hundred feet tall.

As I opened the door to the flat, again I thought of a dog by the fire and meals at a big wooden table, and again it felt exactly right. "It's going to take a couple of months, but I think this is it."

"It's fantastic. A little isolated, though, isn't it?"

"No, all the farmers are right down the road. Rebecca's five minutes away."

"Rebecca."

"What?"

"She's a sly one. I don't trust her."

"I had dinner with them last week."

"No doubt there was gossip and gin."

It was my turn to laugh. "Chicken shawarma and white burgundy, actually, and her husband has read your book."

"Mmm. You were talking about me?"

"Well, sort of." Turning my back to him, I wandered toward the far window and peered out. "Just to defend the idea that the house might be worth saving."

"It is worth saving." He came up beside me. "I would guess Rebecca doesn't think so."

"I don't know. They both seemed to think it was a white elephant."

"They want the title, I'd guess. If you give up, they can swoop in and become the earl and the countess." He tapped a wall, looked at the ceiling. "That ceiling will need replacing."

"Why don't you like her?"

"I dunno. Don't mind me. Probably more class baggage I'm carting around."

"But you're *my* friend."

"Yeah." The calm eyes rested on my face, and I would have sworn they touched my lips, my neck. "That's because you look like Kate Winslet."

I laughed. "Yeah, right." Suddenly, maybe because I'd seen *Titanic* with my mom, I was seized by a thought that hadn't gelled before. "Wait." I stopped, utterly still, as the truth washed over me.

"What is it?"

"I've been thinking about this all wrong." I shook my head. "My mother had to have known that once she died, all of this would come out. I thought she'd been hiding it and I just accidentally found out, but she knew better than that. She knew that I'd find all the paperwork in her office and contact Haver."

Samir nodded. "That does make a lot more sense."

"So what am I supposed to be figuring out? Is it some kind of a test?"

"Would she do that?"

I bit my lip, thinking. "She might. She liked hiding things in plain sight. In her paintings." I thought of her in her studio and a key on the back of an easel, hanging there with a note that read "Happy Birthday."

"It's a treasure hunt," I said. "Of course. She loved them. Set them up for my birthday and Christmas and sometimes just an ordinary day. Sometimes they were really hard."

"I love her for that," Samir said. "She sounds like someone I would like."

"You would have liked her. She had a very dry wit and a taste for the absurd. I miss her so much it's like there should be a new word for it, something besides *lonely* or *grieving* or—"

His hand, warm and steady, fell on my shoulder.

I swallowed, blinked away the ready sudden emotion, and brushed hair out of my face. "If it is a treasure hunt, I don't know the first clue. I'll have to figure out what that is."

"You found the first clue already, though, didn't you?"

"Did I?"

"You're here, so you came to the place she wanted you to find."

"Of course." I looked through the window to the manor. "I wonder where the next one is. In the house?"

"Maybe." His hand fell away, leaving a cold spot where it had been.

"I just need more information of all kinds." I paused, frowning. "There are a lot of missing details, and they're all a big jumble at the moment. Until I understand what she was thinking, I can't unravel it."

"We should make lists, a chart, maybe. If you want help, that is."

"Yes, please."

"Good. Now, let's go back to town. I'm famished." One long-fingered hand settled over his belly. "Do you need anything from the hotel?"

"No, thanks." I was so weary of the single room and the sound of karaoke. Closing the door behind me, I said, "I do need to look for a place to stay. I really miss cooking for myself."

"Talk to Helen Richmond. She knows everything."

"The bakery woman?"

"Yes. And have you ever tried her carrot cake?"

"No."

"Trust me: that's a treat you don't want to miss."

We drove to his cottage. It seemed straightforward enough until I sat next to him in the small car, and I found my head filled with the scent of him, grass and twilight and earth. I was unexpectedly overcome, noticing his wrists and the shift of muscles in his forearm as he moved, the shape of his thighs. It made it hard to talk, to think of anything to say that wouldn't be completely idiotic, so I stayed quiet.

I was no innocent. I knew my way around courting and rituals and how to play it cool, but in all my life, I'd never simply breathed the smell of another human being and wanted to scramble out of my clothes instantly. It made him seem dangerous. It made me feel unstable.

"Is everything all right?" he asked.

"Fine," I said brightly.

Inside his cottage, he said, "I won't be a minute. Make yourself at home." From his phone, he swiped an app, and the stereo came on, playing something bluesy, easy. "This okay?"

"Yeah. Great."

The cat came running, stopped a moment to greet me and allow himself to be petted, then dashed into the hallway.

Where Samir was shedding his clothes. Taking a shower. It made me dizzy to think of it.

Enough. I tucked my hands behind my waist and browsed the shelves of books. Some of it was what a student of literature would have collected, classics and modern literary novels, British, Indian, and American writers.

But there were also old genre paperbacks, mostly science fiction and horror; history of various eras; a lot of military history; and many novels. I noticed a lot of magic realism—Salman Rushdie and Gabriel García Márquez and Alice Hoffman. I tugged down Laura Esquivel's *Like Water for Chocolate*, a small book with an art deco cover, and a wave of warmth spread through me—it was one of my favorites, magic realism centered on food and sex. Leafing through the pages, I revisited the pleasure of the reading, feeling myself on a foggy winter day in San Francisco drinking hot chocolate. I loved that he had it on his shelf. I would have to remember to ask him about it.

Ah, reading. The best of all things. I tucked the book back in its place.

And there, on the end, were three hardcover novels with paper dust jackets written by Samir Malakar. I kept my hands tucked behind my back. The titles seemed literary. I wondered which one had been first.

From the doorway, he said, "It's all right. Go ahead."

He stood on the threshold, drying his hair. His skin was still damp, and a clean camp shirt clung to his shoulders. His feet were bare, and like his hands, they were long and graceful. I looked away. "Which one was first?"

"*Long Days.*"

I took it off the shelf. The cover was artful and abstract, but instead of a serious tone, it had a cheery sort of art that signaled a comedic novel. Something eased in my shoulders. Of course he would write comedy. Flipping to the jacket copy, I read a summary of the story about a young man running wild in the freedom of London but finding his way back to himself. I looked at the back flap, and there was Samir, much younger, looking back at me with his very cheery smile. His hair was quite short, and he'd not yet grown the goatee, but he was utterly and perfectly beautiful and couldn't have been more than twenty-five.

"Will you let me read it?"

A slight shrug. "If you want to."

Reluctantly but with respect for his actual wishes, I closed the book and set it back on the shelf. "Not until you really don't mind."

A softness between us then. "Thank you."

In time, perhaps he would trust me enough to share. In the meantime, there were plenty of other things to occupy my thoughts.

It started to pour just before we left his cottage, and we both were drenched before we even made it to the car. Laughing, we tumbled in, dripping, and I wiped my face. "Nice to have sunshine while it lasted, I suppose."

"April showers bring May flowers." He started the car. "My father will be glad to see you again. He spoke highly of you."

"Really? I felt like I might have brought up bad memories."

"Well, sure. You did. But that doesn't mean he didn't like you." The windshield wipers—windscreen, I corrected myself—slapped hard against the heavy rain. "He's never stopped wondering what happened to his sister. The loss killed my grandmother."

"It's tragic. I can't imagine how that would feel."

"Nor I." He swung into the back of the restaurant. "Ready to make a run for it?"

"I don't know about running, but I'll hobble as fast as I can."

"Three, two, one!"

We slammed our doors and ran for the building, where a rectangle of light formed a beacon falling from the door of the kitchen. Pavi appeared, dressed in chef's whites, and flung open the screen. "Hurry!"

I ran in first, nearly falling flat on my back when my feet went skidding across the floor. Pavi caught my wrist, and Samir caught my back, and I was upright again before I even really had a chance to register that I had almost fallen. "Whoo! Thanks!" I wiped my dripping hair from my face. "It's raining cows and chickens out there!"

"Where is your umbrella, Samir?"

He shrugged. "Somewhere. We're all right, aren't we, Olivia?"

I laughed. "Fine."

Pavi hugged me. "I'm so happy to see you again. Tonight, I'm experimenting. You'll have to tell me what you think."

Instead of going into the restaurant, she led the way up a narrow, ancient stairway to the second floor, then the third. "We live on the third and fourth floors," she said. "The second has been overtaken by supplies and whatnot."

"Better to use the ground level for table space," I said, understanding instantly. The square footage of the restaurant was not huge, and the kitchens were squeezed into the rest.

"Yes." She entered an open door at the top of the stairs and called out, "Dad? We have a guest."

He set aside his newspaper. "Lady Shaw." He stood and half bowed in a formal way. "So nice to see you again."

"You don't have to be formal with me," I said, helplessly. "Really. Will you please call me Olivia?"

"I will try."

"Over here. Samir, fetch the rice."

Samir said, "The Restoration Diva came to see Rosemere today."

"Jocasta Edwards?" Harshad said. "I love her show! She's very famous."

"So is Olivia, Dad," Pavi said.

"Not at all," I protested. "But she was wonderful. She grew up nearby, I gather. She attended some of the events at Rosemere. You might have met her, Harshad."

"I doubt it."

"Anyway, what did she say, Olivia?" Samir prompted.

"Well, she looked at the house and the gardens and said it's going to cost a fortune to fix all of it."

"No surprise," Pavi said.

I ran down the list of things she'd said about the gardens and the house. "She asked me to think about what might be done to bring in money once the house is restored, and I'm a little flummoxed."

"You could have a safari park, like Longleat," Harshad said.

Samir laughed. "With elephants and giraffes?"

"Why not?"

"A lot of upkeep," Pavi said. "Imagine how much it costs to feed them."

"True," Harshad conceded.

"What about something to do with food?" Pavi asked. "That's your passion—maybe a cooking school or something like that?"

"Definitely a possibility." I tore a tiny bit of naan from my plate. "What other kinds of things do people do? I mean, tours, of course, but I'm not sure Rosemere would bring in that many people."

"You could have a literary festival," Pavi said, and I didn't imagine the sideways glance she shot her brother.

He glared at her. "Or a food festival."

"You should have picnics again. I miss those picnics," Harshad said sadly. "Not that they will bring in money, I suppose."

"How often did they have them?"

"Every fourth Saturday, from May to September."

I thought of the wide green lawn spread between the house and the garden and wondered what it would take to bring the main kitchen into some kind of order. Would the stove work and the sink? That might be enough. In the meantime, maybe food trucks or something like an open-air kitchen.

"Now that might be something to think about. I wonder if local chefs"—I wrapped my palm around Pavi's arm—"could be convinced to come and cook?"

"I like it," Samir said.

I warmed to the idea. "I participated in the organization of food fairs several times, and this could be done on a much smaller scale, just for the locals."

"That's brilliant!" Pavi said and leaned forward eagerly. "You said you're doing stories in *Egg and Hen* on English food, right? What if you do stories on each of the chefs who come cook?"

"I love it." I could see the spread of magazine pages in my imagination—the velvety green countryside, an English food truck, some gorgeous crumble on a plate. It felt good to have something I felt competent about, something in my actual world, to focus on.

"We could just use the lawns, set up tents and lavatories." I looked at Harshad. "Every fourth Saturday, huh?"

He beamed at me. "Yes."

"That might be biting off more than I can chew, but I'd love to do it a couple of times this summer, just to see what happens. Will you help me, Pavi? It might be challenging to get it ready by May, but definitely by June."

"I'm in."

I allowed myself to look at Samir, who regarded me with a reserved expression. "What do you think?"

"People will love it. It's a great idea."

I raised a brow. "And maybe one day we will have a literary festival too."

Overhead, a gigantic clap of thunder rattled the roof, and we all laughed. "Nix that idea, I guess."

After dinner, Pavi headed down to the kitchen, and Samir insisted on taking me to the hotel. I didn't really want to walk in the cold rain. This time, it was he who was quiet, and I let him be. My mind was filled with ideas, plans, hopes for the future.

When we pulled up in front of the hotel, I said, "Thanks for everything, Samir. I don't know what I would have done here without you and Pavi."

"You are quite welcome." He worked his hands on the steering wheel. "Listen, do you want to have a beer or something?"

"Like at the pub?"

"Not there. Everyone will talk too much."

"Talk too much?"

"Gossip. About us."

"Does it matter?"

He nodded, staring out into the rain. "I think it might. There's another pub down the road a bit."

"The rain is awful."

"Yeah, you're right. Never mind." He tossed his hair out of his face. "I just—"

"Why don't you come in? We could go down the hall. There's a little room down there, and we could have Allen bring—"

"Same trouble. Everyone will start gossiping. The last thing you need right now." He moved his hands back and forth on the steering wheel. "The thing is, I just want to explain about the book. Books."

Inside the car, we were enveloped in the sound of the pouring rain, our breaths making the air moist and warm. His arm rested against my shoulder, and I had to shift a little, putting my back to the door, to look at him properly. "You don't have to explain anything."

Our eyes met. We were at such close quarters, and that waft of his skin filled my head, and I wanted to touch his curls, his jaw. I thought of his bare feet.

"That's not really why," he said softly and shifted, sliding a hand around my neck to pull me closer. A rush of both wild yearning and abject terror wound through me, and then my hands were on his shoulders, and his other hand cupped my face. His fingertips touched the line of my cheekbone. For an endless, charged moment, he only looked down at me. Then he tilted his head, closed the gap.

Kissed me.

My head whirled, and I had to hold on to him, or I would have spun right out of the car into the night and the rain. His lips were pillowy soft yet firm, warm and lush, and I could not help but open my mouth, wanting to drink him in as if he were a potion, a potion that tasted of candied fennel from the dish on the table, the brushes of his mustache tickling my lip. The sensation made me giddy, and I wanted to laugh, but I only touched his face, the lines of that facial hair, moving closer, then closer still, both of us leaning in harder, going deeper, tiny noises escaping me and him and me again. I lifted my hands to his hair, and a curl embraced my finger, glossy and cool and silky. His thumb moved on my throat, up, down, settled in the hollow between my collarbones.

And then suddenly, I was thinking of that picture of him at twenty-five, looking so young, and the fact that I would be forty at the end of the summer—and the town and the gossip and the weirdness of the situation. I panicked, wondering if I would lose his friendship, his company, and I pulled away inelegantly. Sharply. "I don't know if—"

"Don't think." He bent and caught my mouth again. His thumbs tilted my chin upward. "Come back with me to my house."

My palms fit themselves to his shoulders, and as we kissed, I shuddered to imagine him in bed naked. All of him and all of me and—

I pushed away, pushed away again, hands on his chest. "Samir. Stop. Think. This is craziness."

"Why?"

"You're so much younger than me!"

He laughed softly. "Five years is nothing."

"Seven."

"Still nothing." He leaned closer, brushed his lips over my chin, traced my shoulder.

"But . . . everything is so chaotic. I don't know what's going to happen or . . . anything."

Abruptly, he straightened. "You're serious."

My heart raced, squeezed, and I wanted him desperately, but just now . . . could I bear it? "It feels a little overwhelming."

He looked out the window. Placed his hands precisely on the steering wheel again. "My apologies. I misjudged . . . things."

"No." I touched my chest, which was still burning. "It's not that."

"Just forget it, Olivia. I made a mistake."

For a moment, I sat there in the cocoon of the car, wanting to climb over to him and sit in his lap and press my body into his. But at what cost? To me, to him? I just wasn't sure I was ready for any more emotion, and my gut told me it could be a lot of emotion in regard to Samir.

Still, for a moment, I hesitated, a little dizzy with the line of his profile, the shape of his hands. My heart thudded in fear, in longing, in—

"Good night," I said. "Thank you."

"Yep."

I opened the door and dashed into the rain, feeling my skin sizzle as the rain hit it.

Summer

Summer afternoon—summer afternoon; to me those have always been the two most beautiful words in the English language.

—Henry James

Chapter Twelve

Almost overnight, full spring exploded across the countryside. Crops grew like Jack's beanstalk in the fields, and bluebells carpeted the forests. The weeks whirled by in a rush of meetings and meals and phone calls with America. Jocasta sent a parade of experts just popping in to check things out, each accompanied by the cameraman, Ian. We filmed the segments that would air at the start and end of each program, and I felt a little nervous, imagining what it would be like to be on television.

The positives outweighed any nerves or negatives, however. Two contractors examined the house from roof (bad) to foundation (good, mostly) and gave me staggeringly enormous bids. I took them into London to an architect I'd hired and asked her to go over them. She was an expert in listed properties, and within a week, she pronounced both bids sound. I hired her to draw up the initial plans, with the understanding that Hortense and her planning committee would have to approve them. "No worries," she said. "A Hortense serves on every local council. She will give you trouble, but I'll do my best to keep it to a minimum."

I hired the second contractor just because I liked his demeanor and the fact that he didn't talk down to me. He gave me a plan for the stages of the work—working south to north, first the roof, then the ground floor, to include the kitchen, dining room, parlors, and servant areas.

While the work on the roof was being addressed, they would restore the flat in the carriage house.

The deposit for the work came from the rents, much to my surprise. Haver had given me a check for the past six months, nearly £100,000, which would be gobbled up quickly by such mammoth tasks, but I only needed it to tide me over until the monies from my mother's Menlo Park house came through.

Walking away from his office, however, I realized that I needed an accountant. Someone not Haver, who was a lawyer anyway. I'd ask the earl to recommend someone.

First up, of course, were the plans we had to submit to the house commissioner, or rather Hortense. While the architect drew up plans for me to look over, I rented a flat over one of the shops on the high street in the village. It wasn't much more than a bedroom/living room and kitchen, but the windows overlooked the hills and a tumble of back gardens, and I was finally able to start cooking for myself, which instantly made me feel more grounded.

The flat also gave me a base of operations. On a gigantic dry-erase board I bought at the stationer's shop, I was able to create a command center to try to keep my life in some kind of order. I divided the board into sections—the articles and columns I was working on, Rosemere tasks (house/garden), Mom mystery, Violet timeline, and last but not least, picnic. When I ran the magazine, we'd used this method to plan each magazine, and I was attached to the visuals.

Life at last began to take on a little bit of a rhythm. Mornings, I rose early and walked the right-of-ways, following a map Dr. Mooney had given me when Samir had introduced us at Helen's bakery. Some days I happened to run into the ragtag little group of right-of-way caretakers on their wanderings, but more often, I had the paths to myself. They gave me the chance to learn the landscape, the relationships of forest to river to field, the divisions of old and new. In one spring-green field, a white horse grazed beneath a single tree, while just beyond the hedge rose a housing estate, all modern brick and conservatory rooms off the back. Upscale and attractive but dull in comparison. I could walk across fields for literally miles, then walk through a copse of trees and find myself in a supermarket parking lot.

I saw the people too. The uneasy mix of villager and suburban dweller; a tangle of teenagers, skinny and ragged, from the local school, smoking cigarettes and snorting over a load of posh kids getting off the bus in their green-and-white uniforms. The diversity wasn't as broad as I was used to—mainly white, with a large helping of South Asians, some clearly from the city in their suits and high heels, some locals who'd come, as Pavi told me, with the enormous wave of immigrants from India to rebuild England after World War II. A handful of refugees from the Middle East kept mostly to themselves, though their numbers were growing, and I'd walked into a nearby village to see a shop selling Middle Eastern groceries on the main square. Last, my flat was one building over from the Chinese fish-and-chips shop, where lines ran down the street on Friday nights, and the lane grew clogged with cars of commuters stopping on their way home from a busy week. The woman who ran the place, a slip of white blouse and black trousers, ran a tai chi studio above her shop. I saw the participants trailing in and out on Saturday afternoons and Monday evenings.

An easy place to live for the time being. And I was always more productive when I kept to routines.

After my walk, I would write for a while or sometimes go to the library to read old newspapers on microfiche, trying to find clues about my mother, my grandmother, the mysterious Roger, anything at all. The old papers also proved to be a great source of understanding of the village itself, the ebb and flow of events, births and deaths, names repeated over the generations, rituals of importance, historical notes. I accidentally stumbled on the wedding announcement of Hortense and her husband, which led to reading about Violet and her second husband, a good-looking man who'd distinguished himself in the war. My grandfather, I thought, but I felt no connection to the photo.

Afternoons and evenings, I met with a wide variety of people—Pavi and Rebecca and Jocasta, the garden club and the landscape historian. Every Wednesday, I met with the earl for luncheon on the protected portico, where roses grew up the posts and bees lazed over the flowers. He had taken on my education and took it very seriously. He was an excellent raconteur and loved having a captive audience.

Every week, I left with homework and reading to do. One week, I was charged with the task of meeting all the tenant farmers, one by one. If any of them asked me to have a meal with them, I had to immediately set it up and put it on my calendar. Which I did, and every single family invited me to a meal—my Sunday luncheons and Wednesday suppers were booked for a month.

Another week, my homework was to attend a parish council meeting so that I could begin to understand the village. It was as boring as I'd feared, and I had to keep pinching my thigh to avoid yawning. It also didn't seem to increase my standing in the eyes of those local politicians at all. They clung to a chilly correctness, and we were all delighted when the meeting ended.

The earl said I would have to return regularly, but I wasn't sure that would happen.

The reading list he gave me included some surprising choices—biographies of local statesmen, of course, but also those of American businessmen like Warren Buffett and Steve Jobs. It was taking me a long time to get through all that reading, but I did my level best. If I was going to do this thing—and I still wasn't exactly sure what this "thing" was—I wanted to do it right.

With Pavi's help, I was making plans for the first picnic for the public, which would be held on the open space of lawn between the house and the gardens. I'd asked the contractors to keep the work trailers and work site on the hidden north side of the house so the lawn would be appealing.

Pavi knew dozens of chefs, and we planned to start small—two food trucks, one offering sandwiches of various kinds and one pies and ice cream. I'd found a local band with a fiddler and a craft brewer to bring in kegs of beer for the adults. Two local moms volunteered to paint children's faces, and when the tenants of the cottages heard, they offered to rope off a strawberry field for the locals to pick berries.

It came together so quickly that we were aiming for the fourth Saturday in May. When I told Peter, my driver, he practically misted up.

That was the other problem I was gnawing on—I desperately needed to learn to drive so I could make my way around the county. But the usual nerves of driving on the wrong side of the road were complicated by the fact that I had not driven since the accident that had nearly killed me. I also didn't actually own a car. Did I buy a car and learn to drive it or learn to drive and then buy a car, and if I did that, what would I drive to learn?

Virtually everything else seemed easier.

The person I had not seen much of was Samir. He pleaded a heavy work schedule, but I noticed that even on the rainiest of days, he was still absent. I'd invited him to have a cup of coffee one Saturday afternoon, but I didn't hear back for hours, and then it was curt.

Sorry. Out of town today.

He did, every few days or so, send me a text with an animal or bird group name. A coalition of cheetahs, one day. A puddle of platypuses. I responded in kind. An exaltation of skylarks. A charm of finches.

I missed him. Aside from Pavi, he was my main friend in the village. I hoped that eventually we could get back to the easy connection we'd had, and to preserve the possibility, I resisted reading anything about Samir Malakar, the writer. Even if we never talked again, I would show that I could be trusted.

So that was that. It made me sad that in trying to preserve the friendship, I'd damaged it instead. Not to mention the fact that I had to shove the memory of that kiss out of my mind a hundred times a day. An hour. It haunted me when I slept. *Come back to my house.*

But there was too much on my plate to brood about any one thing. One afternoon, I took my mother's sketchbooks to Helen Richmond, the bakery owner. We met in her garden, a sunny place with wind chimes tinkling from every corner. A bird feeder ten feet tall nourished the birds away from the pair of black cats who swished their tails in the shade beneath the table. "I made lemonade," Helen said. "Will you have some?"

"Of course." It wasn't lemonade made from a packet or a concentrate. She'd squeezed the lemons, and slices floated in the glass pitcher. When I took a sip, it was icy cold, sweet, and tart. "Perfect."

She nudged a bowl of strawberries my way. "I didn't bring anything from the bakery. One doesn't like sweets so much on warm days."

Around the garden were abstract mosaic pieces, copper shapes filled with stained glass. "Your work?"

"Yes. It turned out I was a much better glassworker and sculptor than painter. Your mother was always the best painter among us."

From the satchel I'd brought with me, I took out a children's book. It was a story about a band of animals, rabbits and wrens and a plucky fox, who had appeared in many of her paintings. "I thought you'd like this. It's one of the books my mother illustrated. She won a prestigious prize for it, and I think it really captures what she did so well. The writer drew the story from the paintings rather than the other way around."

Helen picked it up, ran her hand over the cover. "Glorious. So like her." With a reverence I found touching, she opened the cover and leafed through the pages, pausing here and there. "Oh, look at that! Do you recognize the conservatory?"

"What?"

She held up the page, and there it was, the conservatory that had so captured me, whole and flourishing, with a peacock strutting through it.

"Oh my God. Let me see!"

I took it from her urgently, and yes, that was the conservatory. If I leafed back a page, there were the hills in the distance, and forward a page, then two, and there was the corner of the house. "It's all Rosemere, isn't it? I wonder if all of her work is. I mean, I've read this book a hundred times, and I didn't know anything about the estate, but now I recognize it. Now"—I touched my breastbone, that place that ached so much lately—"it was probably because I subconsciously recognized the conservatory that I want so much to restore it, even though Jocasta thinks it is a poor use of funds."

"May I?" She held out her hand for the book, a patient smile lighting her eyes. "You've seen it all, but I have not."

"Yes, of course. I'm so sorry." I handed it over and flopped back in my chair. "I wish I could figure out what was in her mind. I can't understand why she never told me about all of this. Clearly, she loved it. She painted it for fifty years, over and over and over, and the grounds all around it. The animals, the flowers, the woods."

"Never the house?"

"No." I leafed through a catalog of her paintings and drawings in my imagination. "Not many buildings at all. A cottage once in a while."

"This one?" She held up the book to show a picture of a cozy square cottage with a thatched roof—of course—in a grove of trees. Lights burned within, casting yellow light into the dark forest. It looked like the happily-ever-after cottage in every fairy tale ever written, but now I could see the local influence, the weaving of the thatch, the local preference for beams over the windows.

"Yes," I said. "It's a friendly place, isn't it? A refuge. Do you know where it is?"

"I don't recognize it. I'm sorry. It might not even exist anymore. A lot of those old cottages were demolished when the housing estates came in."

Paved paradise, Joni Mitchell sang in my mind.

Helen flipped to the end of the book. "I'm so glad she was able to make a life with her painting. She had to fight very hard for it."

"Really? Her mother's room is filled with paintings. You'd think she'd be proud of her daughter's talent."

Helen lifted a shoulder. "It didn't seem that way. But of course, by the time I knew the countess, she was—a bit mad."

"Someone else said that she was volatile: wonderful or terrible. Did she get dementia or something?"

"That's a good description, but no, I don't know if it was dementia. She wasn't that old—only fifties, maybe."

"I need to make a chart with everything in one place." I rubbed a spot on my temple. "If it wasn't dementia, do you think she was mentally ill?"

"She drank, love. Heavily."

"Oh!" I laughed. "That explains a lot."

"Even though she was erratic, I adored her," Helen said and meditatively took a sip of her lemonade. "It's hard to explain to women your age how different things were for women then. Women were just . . . not that free to be themselves. People weren't, honestly.

"But your grandmother was. She wore these amazing clothes, all these Indian silks she made into the most beautiful dresses—red and turquoise, with a thousand bracelets, just like an Indian, and she had a spectacular figure, this great head of hair." She cocked her head. "Like yours. Thick and wavy. You really look like her."

"Yeah, not the body. I've seen her slim self. Just like my mother." I picked up a strawberry, eyed it, and sadly set it back down on a napkin. "I seem to have inherited all these curves from my father's side of the family."

"You're built like a classic English girl. Luscious."

I gave her a wry smile. "Thanks. I made peace with it a long time ago, but it pains a fourteen-year-old when her mother's clothes are too small for her instead of the other way around."

"I'm sure." She pointed to the berry. "Strawberries, however, will not make you fat."

I picked it up again, admiring the quilting of the seeds, the shimmery crimson color. "How did they get along, my mother and grandmother?"

"Not at all well. Caroline was introverted—maybe she changed later, but—"

"No, she was a lone wolf, for sure."

"That's a good way to put it. She liked things her own way, and she didn't like parties or any of that. She just wanted to draw and paint and read a book. And of course, the countess was that enormous personality, so it was easy to hide in the shadows."

I imagined my mother and her mother in that ruin of a dining room, over breakfast perhaps. Light streaming in the ceiling-high mullioned windows, paintings on the walls, the antique table gleaming. My mother young and beautiful, my eccentric grandmother in her silks, each of them disapproving of the other.

It made me sad.

"I'm glad I had a better relationship with my mother."

"You must have been a great joy to her. I can tell you loved her very much."

"I did." Lifting the strawberry to my mouth, I took a bite. All strawberryness in all the universe filled my mouth, my brain, my entire being. It was exactly the right depth of juiciness, not too sloppy, not too dry, and if I had ever tasted a sweeter berry, I couldn't remember. I closed my eyes. "Wow." Took another bite. "Mmm."

Helen chuckled.

I opened my eyes and plucked another berry from the bowl. "I feel like I've never tasted a strawberry before." Still trying to savor rather than devour, I ate the second and then a third. "They're amazing."

"English strawberries," she said. "And I think you're more like your grandmother than your mother."

"She liked strawberries?"

"I don't know. I meant your sensuality."

I very nearly blushed and then thought, *Oh, why*. I *was* a sensualist—no one became a foodie without that essential thing. And I couldn't help who I was. "I wonder if I reminded my mother of Violet."

"Oh, surely you did. It must have felt like Violet was following her."

Stricken, I held a new strawberry by its stem. "How awful!"

"I'm sorry. That's not what I meant. Don't pay me any attention."

She meant well. "Where did you buy these?"

"Farm stand over by Haughton."

Of course, because everything was going to keep reminding me that I needed to learn to drive. "Too bad."

"They'll be good everywhere, though. Fresh cream, a little cake."

"No, just the berries. Did I tell you that I'm an editor for a food magazine? And I write a regular column about a single ingredient. I've never done one on strawberries, and I'm very glad right now."

"You'll have to share that with me."

"Yes." I took a breath, sucked juice off my finger. A breeze wove through the chimes, one after another. "What I can't figure out is what happened. Why did she leave?"

"I was abroad when it all happened, but I do know that she'd been seeing someone just before I left. She was keeping it a secret because her brother wouldn't have approved, but I saw them in London together, and she took me into her confidence."

"Her mom was dead by then?"

Helen nodded, frowning. "You'd have to look it up, but Violet must have died in the early seventies."

"So she wasn't that old."

"No."

I wanted to get it straight in my head. "And at that point, Caroline's brother inherited the title. Roger? No one talks about him. It's kind of strange."

"He was a very unpleasant man. Something was just wrong with him. He was cruel to Caroline but sly about it. She really hated him."

"But she kept living in the house after her mother died."

"Where would she go? He held the purse strings."

That one thing had never occurred to me. Because I was operating on the assumption of a certain privilege women enjoyed in the modern world. I looked down at the sketchbooks, touched the cover of the one on top. "That's really sad."

"At least she did get out eventually."

"Right. But why then, after a couple of years? When did you see her in London?"

"I was in Greece in '75, so it must have been—'76, '77? Somewhere in there. She'd met a man. She didn't say that much about him."

I brushed my hand in a circle over the sketchbooks, thinking.

Helen said, "Any possibility that her lover was your father?"

I flinched. "No. My dad was American. I was born in San Francisco."

"Just curious. I wondered if maybe they fled together, perhaps."

"Oh, but that would be the worst, wouldn't it? If she'd been happy and then lost him so young?"

She touched my hand. "I'm sorry. I was only speculating aloud. What else did you bring?"

"Some of her old sketchbooks, but now I don't really know what I'm hoping to find out."

"Let's have a look, shall we?"

One by one, I piled the sketchbooks on the table. It was a motley collection of several eras, I thought. "This seems to be the earliest," I said, offering her the square one that contained a sketch of a bird, so gracefully rendered. The rest of the book was studies of the same sort—other birds, singing and sitting, flying and grooming. One even in a birdbath. She'd also sketched squirrels, a ladybug, and many other creatures.

"She must have been much younger when she did these," Helen said. "It's a very simple form of the kind of detail work she did later."

We went through them, not every single page, but getting a feeling for each one and what my mother had been working on with each. Here were fields, trees, clouds. This one continued the study of birds and squirrels, going into much more detail. Another held eyes of all sorts—human and animal. Here was where the study of the black-and-white cats had begun, I thought. Their eyes looked out from page after page, often with a whimsical expression. I wondered how she'd captured that and studied one for a long moment before turning the page.

And there were my own eyes, looking up at me. I cried out, startled, but of course they weren't mine. They were my grandmother's, penetrating, direct, and yet guarded. Eyes that hid secrets, I thought.

"Why did Violet divorce her second husband?"

"It's no secret. They were extremely incompatible. The fights were legendary. He finally grew weary of her and divorced her."

"I wonder if he's still alive."

"Doubtful. He was older than Violet, and she'd be . . . almost a hundred by now." She sucked in her breath. "Look at this." She held up the sketchbook to show a densely drawn page of a dark forest—alive with eyes. Eyes in the leaves. Eyes in the trunks. Eyes in the very rocks on the ground.

It was terrifying.

What was in the forest?

On my way back to the flat, I walked over to the small local supermarket that served the village. It was always busy, at its worst late in the afternoon when everyone crowded in on the way home from work and school runs to pick up milk and bananas and cereal for breakfast. All I wanted today was strawberries, and there they were—the same robust beauties Helen had served. I filled two bags with them and lugged them to the counter. The woman in front of me eyed them but didn't say anything.

As I carted the berries down the street to Coriander, dark clouds gathered over the soft green hills behind the main street. I'd walked there several times now along the grassy crest, with views of the surrounding countryside for miles. It amazed me how empty the area appeared from there—I knew well there were thousands and thousands of people, but the topography and the trees hid them from view, offering instead the illusion of nothing but farmland and sheep.

The back door of Coriander was propped open to the breeze, as I'd learned. In the kitchen, the radio was tuned to an alt-rock station. A prep cook skinned garlic cloves, and a dishwasher stacked plates. "Upstairs," the prep cook said, pointing with his knife.

"I'm here," Pavi said, appearing from the stairway. "Oooh, what did you bring me?"

"Strawberries." I settled one of the bags on the counter. "I'm not sure these will be as great as the ones Helen picked up from the farm stand, but holy cow, they are amazing." I plucked one out and tasted it. Closed my eyes. "Yep." I gave her one. "Taste."

Her eyes shone with laughter as she complied. As she tasted it, she nodded. "It is a good strawberry."

"But?"

"It tastes like a strawberry to me. Am I missing something?"

"No! I think it's me who has been missing something. Forever. This, these." I held one up. "I'm going to eat nothing but strawberries until the season is over."

She laughed. "Give me those. I'll make some lassi for my dad." Tying a yellow apron around her body, she said, "Have you learned to drive yet?"

"Nope. Which means I have to beat the rain. Bye."

"Bye."

On the way out the door, I saw Samir strolling toward the door in his loose-limbed way. I lifted a hand and turned abruptly left, heading away so that he didn't feel cornered.

In my pocket, my phone buzzed. I took it out and read, A quiver of cobras.

I turned around. He had his phone in his hand. A breeze rustled his hair, tumbling the curls this way and that. Holding his phone one hand, he thumbed a text.

It popped up on my screen. A lamentation of swans.

Something about that plucked my heart, and I held the phone in my hand, looking at him across the space. Both of us frozen. Confused, probably. I typed, I'm lamenting your absence.

Me too. Your friendship.

I looked at him. Stop being mad at me.

He typed back, I'm over it.

Good, I typed. I really need someone to come inside that big creepy house with me.

He laughed, and I could hear it across the parking lot, the sound as welcome as a song. It broke the freeze, and at the same moment we walked toward each other, meeting in the middle. My stomach ached a little with looking at him, and I couldn't help flashing back to the way I had sunk into his mouth, how my blood had changed with that kiss. Against my throat, I felt the ghostly imprint of his thumb.

I said, "A leap of leopards."

His eyes crinkled at the corners. "Have you been saving that?"

"Yes." The wind blew my hair in my face, his hair in his face, and we both reached for the offending locks and pushed them away. "I've also been ever so casually dropping by the restaurant most days, hoping I would run into you."

"You did? You could have texted me. Called me."

"I tried that. Took a person a long time to respond."

He looked down. "Sorry."

"Really, I'm the one who is sorry. I just——"

He held up a hand. "You can't be mad at me for making a pass at a beautiful woman."

I snorted, looked away, thinking of how much faster my skin would wrinkle than his, how much older I would look in ten years. It stung a little and seemed so foolish and roiled up my emotions all over again. Thunder rolled across the hills. "Can you teach me to drive?"

"Sure. We can start this weekend."

"Really?" I caught my hair in my hand, twisting it to keep it from blowing. "Thank you."

"You can tell me what's going on with the house." Wind pressed his shirt to his body, outlining his shoulders, his flat belly.

"Yes, of course." Giddy, a little off-center, I spun toward my flat. "I have to beat the rain home. See you!"

I dashed home then, heart much lighter. The problem of the driving was finally going to be addressed. And Samir would teach me. We would sit together in a car, and he would teach me to drive.

Chapter Thirteen

When I got back to the flat, the remaining strawberries in hand, my mood tumbled quickly. Waiting in the inbox were two emails from my Realtor and one from my mother's agent.

CALL ME. URGENT.

Glancing at the clock to be sure it was an agreeable time back in the Bay Area, I dialed Nancy first. "Hi, it's Olivia Shaw. There's a problem?"

"I take it that you've not yet received any legal notifications in the past twenty-four hours?"

My stomach dropped. "Notifications?"

"Yes. Your boyfriend filed a lawsuit to take half the money of the sale of the house."

"What? How can he do that?"

"Anyone can do anything. It's just a matter of what the courts will see as a nuisance and what will be seen as legitimate."

"How can it possibly be legitimate?" Overhead, a crack of thunder practically split the house in two, and I jumped, glaring upward. "It's my mother's house. We are not together."

"He's making the claim that it's community property, that he has a right to it under palimony laws."

"Like common-law marriage or something?"

"Similar. California doesn't recognize common-law marriage, but there is precedent for awarding a live-in partner settlements under a different set of laws." She paused. "I suggest you get a lawyer immediately."

"How? I'm thousands of miles away!" Blistering anger rose behind my eyes. "How dare he!"

"It's a rotten move. If I were you, I'd be sure I was doing whatever I could to protect myself. We have a little time before closing, but don't wait."

"How much time?"

"It's set for June 15."

Just under a month. "All right. Thanks for the heads-up, Nancy."

"You're welcome. I'm sure you'll get the official notification soon enough." She sighed. "Keep me posted."

"Will do." I hung up and immediately called my mother's agent. "Mary, what's up?"

"I've received an injunction to forbid the movement or sale of any of your mother's work. What the hell is going on?"

"I've broken it off with my boyfriend, Grant, and he's going after my assets."

"That loser. This is why I tell my women clients to never get involved with other artists. They're always so damned self-centered." The bitterness burned across the miles. Personal. "And Grant Kazlauskas is a piece of work."

"I have to make some phone calls, find a lawyer to represent my interests there while I'm trying to figure things out here. I'll give you a call as soon as I know what's going on." I thought of the triptych in my apartment, my mother's best work, and it was mine. Tears stung the back of my eyes. "That bastard."

"If it's up to me, he won't get another show anywhere in this town."

"I'll be sure and relay that information," I said. "I'll call you as soon as I can find someone to represent me."

"A good divorce lawyer is William Veracruz. He handled the Bellingham divorce. She's one of my clients, and he managed to work out a very favorable settlement. You can tell the office that I referred you."

"Thanks."

When we hung up, I fired up my laptop and ran a Google search for the lawyer's name. The web page named an upscale office building, and I called immediately. The office assistant would not put me through, of course, so I left a message.

And then I called Grant, who answered on the second ring. As if he'd been waiting. "Hello, Olivia. I guess you're not calling to reconcile."

"Not in your wildest dreams. What are you doing? You know very well that this is wrong. My mother's estate belongs to *me*. And I want my damned paintings. They're important—" I broke off, biting my lip to keep the sudden recognition in. The triptych almost certainly held clues. I needed to get it back.

Instead, I said, "You know how upset I've been over her death, Grant. You didn't love her. You're only being mercenary."

"So let's talk about a settlement. The house sold for three point four million. Give me a third, and I'll give you the paintings and walk away."

"Why should I?" The lavalike anger rose through my esophagus, choked me. "You *deserted* me."

"You're being dramatic. All I want is the apartment, Olivia, and you know I am not as successful as you or your mom."

"That's not my problem. That's yours." My hands were shaking with emotion. "And if you don't back off, Mary has promised you will not sell your work in any gallery in the Bay Area."

"It's not the only market in the world."

And, I realized, if he had the settlement, it wouldn't matter. He could paint and travel and show if he felt like it—at least until he ran through the money. "Whatever. You'll hear from my lawyer."

"You could just settle, Olivia. Let's just hammer out an agreement between the two of us and leave all the lawyers out. You'll get your money, and I'm off your back. What's the big deal?"

"The big deal is that it's mine, Grant. The apartment was mine, and you're living there. The paintings are mine. The house is mine. Just hanging out with me for a few years doesn't give you any rights."

"We'll see."

I hung up, too angry to speak.

Alone in my village flat, I paced to the window and back to the tiny kitchen, then back to the window, trying to pull my emotions under control. I felt betrayed and furious and like a complete idiot. I never could have predicted this vindictiveness.

Rain was pouring by the buckets over the landscape, obscuring my view across the empty street. What if I just let him have the settlement? How much would be left? Was it worth it to make him go away?

Ugh. No. The very idea made me want to punch him in the face. What a leech! And what a fool I'd been for letting him get away with it for years and years. In sudden humiliation, I realized it had always been this way—that he'd always encroached, slowly, so slowly that I hardly noticed. First the rush to move in, where he painted on the upstairs deck, and then the inexorable move into the best room in the apartment for his studio. Our meals out had often been the result of my job—an interview I was conducting, a new hot restaurant who'd offered free passes.

Before the accident, that tension had become a point of conflict between us. He was painting, but not as much as he was holding forth at arty gatherings, and he wasn't bringing in much money at all. Last year, I'd taken a research trip to Spain and left him at home. He'd been furious, of course, but I hadn't budged. When I'd returned, he had been contrite, changed his attitudes, and I had thought we might be on a better track.

And then I'd wrecked the car.

Resting my forehead against the cool glass window, I wondered how long the money Haver had freed would last. I wondered where I'd get more if this dragged on. How could I keep going on the restoration if there was no money?

Tomorrow was my weekly luncheon with the earl. Perhaps it was time I asked for some help.

The earl's driver swung around the circular drive in front of Marswick Hall, and the butler hurried out with a giant industrial-strength umbrella. The rain had briefly paused once or twice, but it was still pouring.

"Watch your step, my lady," Robert said, steering me around a network of puddles at the foot of the steps and on the steps, places where the footsteps of centuries had worn away the stone. Even inside, there were several buckets in the grand foyer, two beneath the skylight in the center, another in a far corner. I looked up to see the old-fashioned skylight dripping a steady stream. Along the french doors at the rear lay a thick roll of cloth pressed against the base, and I gathered it was to keep out the rain. "Goodness."

"The old girl needs repairs faster than we can address them," the earl said, wheeling himself out in his chair. I'd learned that he used a wheelchair most of the time, but not if there were many guests about. He liked to appear strong, but his health was not particularly good. I'd figured out it was mostly heart, with a few side issues tossed in for good measure. Not a giant surprise when you were eighty-five.

"The rain is like Armageddon," I said, bending to kiss his cheek. "I can't imagine it rains like this all the time."

"No," he agreed, wheeling around to lead me down the hallway, where a woman mopped another spot. "My nephew says it's global warming. I expect he's correct."

We entered his study, the same room where I'd first met him. Here we would have a pot of tea; then we'd be summoned to lunch in a bright alcove I loved, with a view of the estate. I poured, as he expected, and I didn't mind the small sexism in it. He liked one sugar and lots of milk, while I preferred two sugars and just a swirl of milk.

"How are things going at Rosemere this week?" he asked.

"The most exciting thing is that the first episode of *Restoration Diva* will air next week. Wednesday night at seven."

"Oh, my. That is exciting."

I sipped hot tea delicately, glad of the warmth in the drafty room. "The actual work is progressing very well. They've cleared most of the debris from the south end of the first floor; they'll be starting on the north side later this week. I was planning to take a trip over there to see how it looks, but . . ." I gestured toward the window.

"I see. The south would be the parlor and dining room; is that right?"

"Yes. And I've talked to the garden club about doing some of the work in the rose garden. They're absolutely delighted."

One of my lessons had been to enlist the village and tenants in the process as much as possible to give them ownership. "Good girl. What's the reward?"

"It seems they want to be able to volunteer once the gardens are open to the public. And I suspect a couple of them want to be employed."

"Good. Plenty of work for them."

"I'm sure." I gave a report on the homework for the week, another set of meetings, and meals with the tenants of the farm. One wanted to discuss the possibility of pig farming, which I felt would be too much just this minute, and the other, a young family, had some excellent ideas for pasturing chickens, the eggs and meat of which brought in a much higher price.

Claudia, the niece who took care of him, popped in at one point. "How are you, Olivia?" she asked, then touched her uncle's shoulder. "And you, Uncle?"

He waved her away, annoyed. His cheeks were a little flushed, his color beneath it wan, but he was as well-groomed as ever—his thick hair brushed away from his face, his shirt crisp. "Leave me alone," he growled. "I'll call you if you're wanted."

She met my eyes, and I read the message clearly. This was one of his bad days. I gave a barely perceptible nod. I'd keep an eye on him and leave early, pleading weather.

"Lunch is ready," she said. "Shall I wheel you?"

"Yes, yes."

The usually charming alcove was as dreary as the rest of the world, though there were fresh flowers to brighten the table and snowy linens and the china that had been in the family for generations. As we settled in our places, I said, "I would like your opinion on a few things, George, if you wouldn't mind."

"Of course, girl, of course. That's why I'm here."

The soup course was a clear lemony broth dotted with parsley and scrolls of spring onion. It filled the air with a sunny fragrance, and I thought the cook was a genius to make such a dish on so dark a day. The flavor held as much sunshine as the scent. "This is remarkable," I said and wished I could snap a photo on my phone, but I always left the phone in my purse, and the earl wasn't exactly an Instagrammer.

"Mmmm." He took his cook and fabulous food for granted. "Tell me what I can help you with."

"The first thing I need is a reliable accountant who can look over the books at Rosemere and tell me what's going on."

"Easily done. I know just the man. I'll ring him when we are finished with our luncheon."

"I had a feeling you might know the right person," I said with a smile.

"Are there problems?"

"I'm not sure. The reports I received from Haver are complicated, and it's not always easy to trace the money. There's an account in India that received funds for decades, but there's no explanation for what it is or where that money is now."

"Hmm. Could it be to support a love child or cover something up, perhaps?"

"Good question. I assume that's where my uncle went, but no one can find him."

"It would be logical." He touched his chin delicately with a napkin. "I gather he was dragged out of India kicking and screaming."

"That's odd that both Violet and Roger wanted to stay there, even though they'd inherited Rosemere."

"Is it odd, though?" George asked with customary wisdom. "Did you want to come here when you inherited?"

"Well . . . I didn't *mind*. I didn't really think I'd stay, though. I thought I'd come and get things settled and then go back to my life." I lifted a shoulder.

"India had been their home their entire lives. What use was England? Violet was widowed by cholera shortly after Roger was born, so she had the run of the place—heady freedom for a woman in those days."

"But wasn't everything getting unstable in India then?"

He wiggled his nose. "Perhaps excitement is preferable to boredom. I would say Violet always felt that way."

"She was a woman in charge when she returned to England too."

"Oh, but English society would never offer a woman like your grandmother the same power as India would have in those days."

"I suppose that's true." The woman who served all the meals, named Janet, cleared away our soup, piled the dishes on a rolling cart, and served a steaming portion of white rice and fish dotted elegantly with fresh green peas.

"Kedgeree," Janet said. "One of your favorites, my lord."

"How marvelous. We've been talking about India, and here we have an Indian dish for luncheon. Thank you, Janet."

She nodded and gave me a wink. They cooked his favorites so that he would eat. For dessert—pudding, I supposed—there would be rhubarb crumble, a child's dish, but he loved it covered in thick custard. Rhubarb soup, I teased.

"What else is on your mind, Olivia? The shine is not as bright today."

"Isn't it?" I didn't want to share the news of Grant suing me. Instead, I said, "I just can't figure out what my mother was thinking—I told you that I think she had to have known I would discover the business of the house. I mean, everything was right in plain sight in her office. So why not tell me ahead of time, help me get a handle on what she wanted me to do?"

"My guess is that she wished for you to decide for yourself."

"That would be like her. But I can't help thinking she's set up a last treasure hunt."

He peered at me. "D'you think so?"

"Yes, I do. It was something she did for my birthdays and special occasions. She loved the anticipation of me solving the puzzle."

His hands were still. "Poor, dear Caroline. I'm glad to know her childhood didn't ruin her."

"What do you know about it?"

"Not very much. I'm not a man for gossip"—he cocked one wild eyebrow my way as he reached for his glass of water—"but it was plain things were not right in that house."

"The way I've heard it, from people who *do* gossip," I said with a wink, "is that Roger was a cruel man, and Violet drank heavily, which made her mean and erratic."

He nodded. A single pea occupied his fork, and I watched him eat it, chewing with the thoroughness of a cat.

I said, "I hate to think of my mother living that way. One of her old friends said that my mother was stuck with Roger when her mother died—she had no money of her own." I frowned. "And that doesn't actually make sense to me either. Why wouldn't Violet provide for her daughter, give her the independence she valued herself?"

"Violet was erratic at the end. Alcoholic. Ruined her looks."

It felt like something was right on the edge of my brain, a fact I'd overlooked, something that—

"Oh!" I sat forward in my chair. "Maybe my mother left something in Violet's room. All of the books and paintings in the house are gone, except for those in her old bedroom and everything in Violet's room." I slapped a palm down on the table. "That's where it is, whatever the clue is."

He gave me a thumbs-up. "Start there, then."

"One more question, George, if I might."

"Ten more, a hundred more."

"Jocasta said none of these estates survive on the rents and crops anymore. How do you keep Marswick Hall so well?"

"Ha! Not so well, girl. You saw the puddles in the entryway. It's threatening to fall down at every turn. The plumbing knocks and screams. The windows are drafty. Everything drips and leaks. In the winter, it's freezing."

"But?"

"We allow weddings on the grounds and tours every third Sunday, which I hate, but it had to be done. But the main thing is a camp for children down on the shores of the lake." He pointed toward the west. "Eight weeks, full every year. Science camp, I gather."

"I see." I looked toward the blurry view of fields, thinking. "One of the tenants suggested a local farm market, and one of the others keeps chickens and pastures them. Obviously, there is lamb. Wonder if there'd be any value in going organic or something like that."

"It does seem to make a certain sense, with your background." He coughed, the sound rattly and unproductive. "Crops and livestock are not always the most lucrative."

"Right," I said, "but maybe we'd take it up a notch." I was thinking maybe I could become the Alice Waters of Hertfordshire, something very high-end for all those discerning commuters in their gigantic kitchens.

"Perhaps. Janet," he called over his shoulder, "let's adjourn to the study, have our crumble there."

I wheeled him back down the drafty, drippy hallway. It was a place that should have been alive with dozens and dozens of people, not just one old man and his niece and their servants. It seemed sad somehow. If I were to make a go of the estate, I'd want Rosemere to have lots of people in it somehow—a school, perhaps, or something along those lines. People would bring it back to life, chase away the ghosts.

When we arrived in the study, my phone was buzzing in my purse. I ignored it, but a moment later, it came again. "Sorry," I said. "I just need to make sure this isn't an emergency." As he laboriously moved his body from the wheelchair to the armchair by the fire, I glanced at my screen. It was the contractor's number. "Hello?"

"Good afternoon, Lady Shaw. Do you have a moment?"

"Sure. What's up?"

"I'm afraid I have some bad news. Two bits of bad news, actually, both related to the rain."

I sank into the other chair. "Tell me."

"We've lost a part of the roof on the main house. It's on the north end, which was the worst part of the house anyway, but the collapse hit one of the walls, and I'm afraid we've got a bit of a mess on our hands."

For one long minute, I let the information sink in. Not that I knew what "a bit of a mess" meant in real time or how much more money it would cost, but the understatement wasn't understated enough for my tastes. I thought of the hold on the money from my mother's house, and anxiety squeezed its way up the back of my neck, landing at the base of my skull with a fist. "What else?"

"There was also a substantial collapse in the ruins. The abbey."

"Oh. Well, that's not as bad, right?"

"Unfortunately, a skeleton was revealed, and we've had to call the authorities out to take a look, so all work is at a standstill until they sort it out."

"Did they bury people in the abbey? Was it a grave?"

"There is"—he cleared his throat—"some concern that it might be the body of a girl who disappeared in the seventies."

"Oh." I took a breath, blew it out like a puffer fish. "I see. All right. I'll be there as soon as I can. It will be an hour or so, I'm afraid."

"No worries. We'll be here."

I hung up and held the phone loosely in my palm, hands in my lap. "They've found a skeleton at Rosemere, at the abbey. They think it might be the girl who disappeared in the seventies." Her name came to me, Sanvi. "That would have been my friends Pavi and Samir's aunt."

He nodded, eyes clear as they ever had been. "What else?"

I rubbed a hand around my neck. "Part of the ballroom roof collapsed and took down a wall. I don't know which one." I shook my head. "I am in so far over my head. What made me think I could do this, tackle such a huge job? I just don't have the resources or the knowledge or—"

He held up one large hand. "No point worrying until you have the facts. I'll have Robert take you over there. Ring me later, and let me know what you've learned."

"Right. I will. And I also need the accountant's name."

"Done." He stood, and I crossed over to him so that he wouldn't have to walk on his aching feet. "You needn't fret, Olivia. You've a fine mind and plenty of friends. The estate is your legacy, and you've stepped up to the challenge brilliantly."

I touched my heart. "Thank you."

"You know," he said, raising his chin ever so slightly, "what might help in the long run is an advantageous marriage."

I half smiled. "You're teasing me, right?"

"A little," he conceded. "Only a little. The wealthy have always married for reasons of dynasty, my dear. You'll want the right sort of person when the time comes, and a brilliant marriage could be of help."

On one level, I understood his intentions and the reality of the world he had occupied for the whole of his life. Given my "love" connection with the man who was now suing me, maybe it couldn't get much worse. On another level, the American one, it was completely absurd. "Thank you," I said. "I'll keep that in mind."

"Go now. See to your home."

My home. Fat chance.

Chapter Fourteen

On the way to the house, in the insanely pouring rain, we passed a brutal smashup on the A1, and as Robert was holding forth on the overcrowding of the roads, my phone blipped with a text.

Samir wrote, Is it true they found bones at Rosemere?

Yes, I texted back. Not the house but the abbey. I'm headed there now. Roof down in ballroom, wall down, all rain related. Terrible day!

Want moral support?

I closed my eyes momentarily. YES please. It's been one thing after another. Tell you more later.

All right. I'll see you soon.

You use complete sentences in texting.

Can't help it. Reading background. What's your excuse?

Editor.

I like it.

:)

For the first time since I'd heard the news about the lawsuit last night, some of the tension eased in the back of my neck. I desperately wanted to talk this all out—the problems with the house, the challenge of the eventual purpose, how to support it, and how to get it into shape in the short term. Was I out of my mind?

Maybe. Real doubt plagued me, carried by the dark weather and the new challenges.

But I couldn't leave until I figured out what my mother wanted me to know, and I had to start with exploring the things in my mother's and grandmother's rooms. She'd left those for me, and I needed to explore them, but the thought of being in the house alone unnerved me. Even having construction workers in some parts wouldn't be enough.

I needed help.

The road into Rosemere was sloshy with rain, puddles and potholes making the journey from the main road through the trees slow and jolting. All the heavy trucks and equipment, coupled with the abundant rain, had made a mess of it. Mentally, I added another task to the endless list in my head—the roads needed to be graded and filled or whatever one did to make the potholes go away. The task fluttered in my imagination, leading off into the faraway distance, unconquerable.

The rain also made it difficult to navigate to a position where I could see the damage to the back of the house. Looking up meant a face full of water, and the mud was deep. I was glad of my wellies as I gathered my coat and umbrella. "You can let me out here, Robert. I'll walk up to the abbey."

"In this mess, my lady? I'd be happy to wait and carry you up there."

I shook my head. "The road is going to be a mud pit. Easier for me to walk than you to drive. Thank you so much."

Opening my own industrial-strength umbrella, I stepped out of the car and into its shelter and sloshed my way across the back garden to the base of a great old oak. It didn't stop the rain entirely, but at least it was enough to give me a chance to look up—

To the gaping hole now scarring the entire northwest corner. The roof had collapsed inward, leaving only the beams, and stonework had crumbled beneath it, taking down most of the third story wall and some of the second story. Rain poured through the hole. I imagined a pool of muck forming in the ballroom.

What was I *thinking* with this place? How could a woman who had never even owned an ordinary house even *consider* taking on the renovation of a six-hundred-year-old manor house with thirty-seven bloody rooms? Standing in the rain, staring up at the house my mother had fled, I felt like a fool. I'd let myself be seduced by a vision of myself as lady of the manor, lady savior. Vanquisher of darkness.

Ridiculous. Suddenly, I wanted nothing more than to be back in my office at the *Egg and Hen*, going over copy and photos; planning a big, beautiful issue; or drinking handcrafted cocktails in some self-consciously hip bar where the gay server had a man bun or a beard or both.

What the hell was I doing here on this quixotic journey? What did I think I would find?

The gnawing hollowness in my lungs expanded and expanded until I wanted to scream, expanding until—finally—I recognized what it was.

In taking on this quest, I was somehow expecting to get my mother back. Not the idea of her, but the *actual* her—a flesh-and-blood being who would walk through some portal in the perfectly restored house wearing her favorite wool slacks and say, "I had every faith in you, my dear."

What a fool I was!

"Madam?"

I turned toward the polite voice to find a policeman in a black uniform. He was middle-aged, with a heavy jowl born of too many pints on late nights at the pub. "Yes?"

"I'm going to have to ask you to run along. We've a police investigation going. I know there ain't much excitement round these parts, but you'll have to wait on official word like everyone else."

"I'm Olivia Shaw," I said, and when his face remained blank, I added—hating myself for it—"the Countess of Rosemere."

"Ah." He covered his surprise, took a step back. "Well, then. I expect you'll want to follow me. We've found something."

I considered asking questions, but better to wait until we weren't huffing and puffing all the way across the muddy fields. He didn't seem to feel the need to make small talk, and I was relieved. My boots splatted and sank and made sucking sounds as I yanked them out. "Cold, wet, miserable England," my mother had often said, but I hadn't understood how San Francisco with its fogs and rainy seasons could be much different.

This was different.

Even in the rain, a crowd gathered at the abbey ruins, their array of umbrellas blooming against the deluge. I saw police and some of the construction workers and even a couple of faces from the garden club. The rest were tenants and villagers drawn by the commotion.

The policeman led me to a man in a suit who stood beneath the shelter of one of the large pines surrounding the abbey. A crew had erected a tarp over a portion of the interior of the abbey, and I could see the scar of fresh dirt around it.

"Sir, I've found the countess."

"Ah. Hello, Lady Shaw," the man said in a blurry northern accent. "Inspector Greg. Quite a day for you."

"You found a skeleton, I hear. Do you think it's the girl who disappeared in the seventies?"

"Hard to say just now. We've not found all the remains just yet, and it'll all have to be dated and photographed and examined before anyone will say anything." He had very sharp features, as if they'd been carved from a tree and never sanded into kinder angles. "Given the location, the probability is that it's much older."

"How long will all of this take? You might not have heard that part of the roof came down. I'm anxious to get the crew on it, cover it up."

"The local historical council will have my head if I don't follow archeological protocols."

I nodded.

In the pocket of my coat, my phone buzzed with a text. "Sorry," I said and pulled it out, hoping for a ride home.

It was Samir. Where are you?

Up by the abbey, I typed. "Someone has come to give me a ride," I said to the detective. "I was planning to go inside the house and collect some things before the crews start the next rounds of gutting. Is that all right?"

"I'd wait if I were you. Too much chaos, and if the body is more recent, the house will be part of the investigation."

For one moment, I looked at him in disbelief. "Of course," I finally said. "Because it's that kind of a day."

Unexpectedly, he smiled. "You've taken on quite the Herculean task, Lady Shaw. Surely the gods will smile."

"Or smite me," I said, narrowing my eyes at the abbey, wondering if such things as curses really held any truth. And if this was the girl who had cursed the place, did her discovery nullify it, or would she rise like a zombie to punish the new generation?

Samir pulled up in his small blue car. "There's my ride. Let me know what you discover."

"Isn't that Tony Willow's apprentice?" He rolled a mint around in his mouth. "He your boyfriend?"

"A, yes, and B, none of your business."

"Bit young is all."

"He's not my boyfriend," I said with a sigh. "He's my friend. Of which I have very few around these parts."

"Fair enough." He gave me a tip of an imaginary hat. "You ever want a grown-up"—the *r* rolled elegantly—"friend, I'd be delighted to buy you a scotch."

It was said without any rancor at all, and I gave him a smile. "I'll keep that in mind." I dashed over to the car and managed to get inside mostly dry, holding the umbrella out to shake it.

Samir chuckled. "Not sure how much water you're getting out if you shake it in the rain. Just throw it in the back."

"You're right." I did and flung myself against the seat. "Oh my God, what a day. Did you see the roof?"

"I did." He didn't drive away and instead peered toward the crowd at the abbey. "Is it her? Sanvi?"

"They don't know. The detective is pretty sure it's older than that, but they have to follow the rules." I buckled my seat belt. "Will you drive back by the house so I can see it from this side?"

"Sure."

He bumped down the hill, and I said aloud, "I have to get the roads done. They're terrible."

"Maybe you can cross that bridge when you come to it."

I nodded, suddenly so tired I could barely turn my head. He guided the car around a giant tree, and there above us loomed the cave-in. A profane swear word came to mind, but I only said, "Damn. What am I *doing*, Samir?"

"It's not as terrible as it looks. That part of the roof was destroyed anyway. The stonework—" he shrugged. "You'll no doubt be doing a lot of that too." He looked down at me. "I wouldn't fret."

In my rag doll state, I only turned my head toward him. Repeated his words back to him, in his accent. "I wouldn't fret."

He smiled very slightly. The moment hung suspended, filled with his scent and his eyelashes and the shape of his nostrils. His mouth.

But he only shook his head and put the car in gear, and we bumped all the way down the road to town without saying a word. I kept hearing the detective say, "Bit young, isn't he?" But in that moment, did I even care? I wanted some comfort, some warm arms around me.

Wrong attitude. Redirect. "I've been trying to work out the clues my mother left. If it's a treasure hunt, the first clue was the paperwork, all the stuff she could have burned or shredded. She left it all out on her desk."

"Right." He drove around the church, and I thought about my grandmother's grave, which I'd still not visited.

"Most of the paintings are missing, but everything in Violet's room is untouched. Why? That doesn't make sense. Maybe we should go there first. Explore. Maybe there's a clue."

"Yeah." He looked upward through the windscreen. "Let's do it tomorrow. The minute the rain breaks, I'll be back to work."

"I really appreciate it. I'm afraid to be alone in there."

He flashed a smile. "I know. Ancestors who mightn't have bodies."

"Exactly."

"What else happened today? You said you'd tell me about it later."

"Oh, yeah. I forgot this part—my old boyfriend is suing me. So there's a hold on the closing, which means there's a hold on the money."

He whistled. "Will he win?"

"I don't think so. But it's a lot in a day." Again that sense of being overwhelmed, the pressure of a boulder bearing down, came over me. "I'm a fool."

"No. You're mighty, Olivia. You can do anything."

"Am I?" I looked at him. "Mighty?"

He looked back. "Yes."

We drove a little farther in silence, and I realized that I was enjoying the sexual tension between us, the push and pull, the pleasure of his face and long, lean body. "Don't you have a girlfriend?"

"I did have one. Not a very serious one."

"What happened to her?"

"I broke up with her," he said without looking at me. "That day you were at my house the first time."

"Your dinner date."

"Yeah."

"That's the same day I broke up with Grant."

"I know." He pulled up in front of my flat. "See you in the morning."

It took every bit of my remaining will to simply open the door and step out. "Bye."

As I set the kettle to boil, the earl's accountant called, quite polite. He gathered an overview of the situation and then asked if I could fax the files to his office, along with a form he would email to me, giving him permission to contact Haver. "You'll also need to contact their offices and let them know what we're going to do. I expect they will not be pleased."

"No, I'm sure." I glanced at the clock—how could it only be three thirty? "I should be able to get that all done this afternoon." It wouldn't be fun, but if I was to free money from somewhere, I had to do whatever I could. "I'll find a place to fax it all this afternoon."

"You're in Saint Ives Cross?"

"Yes."

"The library will have a machine."

"Thanks."

Reluctantly, I turned off the kettle and stomped my feet back into my boots, gathered up all the material I needed, then trudged back out into the miserable day. The high street was quiet, of course, and I splashed mostly by myself to Haver's office. The alley was so narrow that I had to close the umbrella, and by the time I arrived at the door, my hair was a soggy mess.

Mrs. Wells was just coming around the corner. "Well, hello, Lady Shaw! What brings you out on such a terrible day?"

Rain dripped from my hair down my nose. "I just wanted to let you know that I've hired an accountant on the advice of the Earl of Marswick, and their office will be contacting this office for information."

"Is that right?" Her tone was frosty.

"Yes. Is that a problem?" I could match frosty.

"No, my lady, of course not."

"Thank you."

In the library, I stood by the fax machine feeding in papers, one after the other, for what seemed like a year. I hoped they would be able to make some sense of it all.

When I was finished, I checked the time. A half hour until the building closed, so I headed for my familiar spot, the microfiche machine. The librarian on duty recognized me, of course, and greeted me by name. "What can I help you with today?"

"I need all the papers from the summer of 1975."

"Ah. The girl? We heard there'd been a discovery."

"We don't know if it's her yet, but yes. I'd like to acquaint myself with the details."

I already knew Sanvi had gone missing in late July, so I concentrated my reading there, late July and early August. Because it was a weekly, it didn't take long to find the first mention on August 6, 1975.

GIRL MISSING

The parents of Sanvi Malakar, age fifteen, have reported their daughter missing. The girl, a student at Saint Ives Cross Secondary School, was last seen when she left for the market Saturday afternoon. According to her parents, she was a good student and did not have a boyfriend.

I looked through the next three papers, and there was not a single other mention—I read stories about dinner parties and a lost dog and the best methods for canning peaches, but not another word about a missing fifteen-year-old girl. Would it have been different if it had been a white child instead of a brown one? It made me sad to think so, but I suspected that was at the heart of it.

I wondered how Samir's father was taking the possibility that his sister's remains might have been found. It couldn't help but reopen old wounds. I hoped that her story would someday come to light.

Chapter Fifteen

On the day my mother fell ill, we woke up the way we always did. I made coffee in her drip pot, which I could not convince her to change no matter how many times I illustrated the virtues of a french press. Through the kitchen window, I saw a neighborhood cat perched on the patio table, tail switching in the rare October sunshine. I heard my mother get up, coughing, which was what a person who had smoked for five decades did. I thought nothing of it. She let herself out to the patio to have a cigarette, wearing her pale-pink bathrobe and a pair of white slippers. She had always been thin but had grown more so over the past year or so, making her look as if she might just fade away. I poked my head out the window. "Do you want some oatmeal for breakfast? I bought some blueberries yesterday."

"That would be lovely, dear," she said, smiling at me. "It's always a pleasure to eat whatever you cook."

I didn't know then that our ordinary daily moment would be the last we'd share. Not until twelve or fifteen moments later did I realize she had collapsed outside, and by the time I rushed to her side, she was unconscious. I didn't know that I'd think of it every single time I made oatmeal for the next six months—maybe always.

Today opened in an ordinary way too.

I made oatmeal for my breakfast, trying to warm myself up in the damp. The rain had slowed, but it was still drizzly and cold for May, and I tugged on one of my favorite sweaters, soft turquoise with a loose, open weave and flecks of gold. It was silly to wear such a thing to explore Violet's dusty bedroom, but it felt right. Part of me wanted to show up in the ways that were like her, to show her spirit, should it be lingering, that I was cut from the same cloth.

Which also made me feel guilty. My mother would not want me to be like her, would she? In a way, I was lucky to have been spared the wild dynamic of wanting to please both my mother and my grandmother.

Although, really, I wished I'd had the chance.

Samir knocked, and when I opened the door, he was carrying a paper cup with a lid. His hair was damp, as if he'd just come from the shower, and he smelled of orange zest and patchouli and a thousand other notes that wafted in with him. I inhaled. "You smell really good."

He lifted his sleeve, offered it. "That?"

"Yes," I said emphatically. "Wow. What is it?"

"Cologne. Someone gave it to me a while back, and Billi knocked it off the bureau this morning."

Someone, I thought. "Did it break?"

"No." He blinked, slowly. "But if you like it, I'll be sure to get it into rotation."

"You don't strike me as a cologne kind of guy."

"Not usually. Anyway"—he held out the paper cup—"special delivery from Pavi. She wants you to try her new smoothie." His mouth tilted sideways. "Which I would just call a posh lassi, but it sells better as a smoothie. She said you went mad for strawberries the other day."

"I may have been a bit crazy. They're better here." I took a sip of the concoction. "Oooh. She added fresh coriander! That's amazing. Did you taste it?" I held it out to him. He shook his head, held up a hand, and walked over to the dry-erase board. Touched one finger to Violet's time line, then Caroline's. "You've got practically nothing on Roger."

"That's because practically nothing exists." I carried the cup over to the board. "Seriously. I've looked in all the newspapers around here, looked for records of any kind, and there's just nothing. It's like he wasn't even real."

"How old was he when they came to England?"

"Maybe in his midteens, I think."

"Where was his father?"

"Died of cholera in India, which is probably why Violet stayed. She was mistress of the plantation there. She was a good businesswoman. The earl said she turned the fortunes of Rosemere around, made it profitable."

"All of them coming to England changed the course of my family's life too."

"Yeah. I'd like to see that plantation, honestly. It seemed to mean a lot to her."

He nodded, touching one note on the board and another, frowning. "India, India, England, England. Is the secret with your grandmother or your mother?"

"I don't know. There must be something with my grandmother, or my mother would never have fled."

He frowned. "Maybe."

"Have you ever been to India?"

"No. Seems a bit challenging, doesn't it? People and chaos and heat." He offered me a rueful half smile. "I'm an English country lad, I'm afraid."

"I never thought about it until now," I admitted, "although I have a lot of Indian friends in San Francisco. It seems like someone is always going back and forth. They have long visits, like three months at a time."

"I might visit my mum there one of these days. She comes back here every summer, so it hasn't come up yet."

"Where does she live?"

"Mumbai. And she is a snob about it too. No other part of India is as good as Maharashtra."

It was almost summer. "Is she coming this year?"

In a gesture he used quite often, he ran thumb and index finger down the goatee on either side of his mouth, down and around the bottom, smoothing the hair. "Usually she comes in June."

"Hmm."

He cocked his head. "Why does that make you nervous?"

"Um. How did you know I was nervous?"

"You twist a bit of your hair."

I realized I was doing exactly that, twisting a lock of hair around and around my index finger, a habit I'd had since childhood. I dropped it. "I don't know why I'd be nervous. I guess I'd want her to like me."

"Why?"

I shrugged. "I don't know. I like your family and you, and . . ." I rolled my eyes. "Let's get out of here."

He gestured, palm up. "After you."

As I passed, I punched him in the arm.

"Ow," he said, but he laughed.

We didn't need umbrellas, so we sloshed through the mud to the side of the house where the roof had collapsed to get a better view. "I guess I was hoping it wouldn't be so daunting today," I said. "It looks just as bad as yesterday."

"That's only because you're not used to buildings in transition. The crew will get tarps over the holes in the roof, and that's going to make it feel like it's under construction, not falling down."

"I hope so." Rocks that had tumbled from the wall were scattered over the ground, and Samir knelt to run a hand over one of them. "Beautiful stone. The color is remarkable."

"What makes it remarkable?" I asked, kneeling next to him.

"The rose and gold together. That's why it looks as if it's glowing when you see it from the village." He brushed his hands together, stood. "Let's see what we can find, shall we?"

We went in through the back door, as ever, but Samir had not been there since the work had started, and he made a long, low whistle as we entered. The kitchen was the same but much cleaner. The boxes had all been moved out to a storage facility at Jocasta's order so that the historians and valuation specialists could take a look at everything. It was a giant room, made for serving a household of dozens. "Given this space, I'm giving very serious thought to the cooking-school idea. Plenty of room."

He nodded. "Or industrial kitchens for a hotel or some other kind of school."

"Hotel?"

"Why not?"

"But what's here? Like, why would people come stay?"

"A lot of reasons. It's quiet. You could create value any number of ways. Wedding parties, family gatherings. Any number of things."

"Hmm. I hadn't considered a hotel." I touched the center of my chest, which didn't seem to like the idea. "I'll add it to the list."

This time, I could lead, taking him through the butler's pantry into the gutted dining room and parlor. I hadn't been inside in a week or so, and in the meantime, the vines had been cut away from the windows. Even on such a dark day, light poured in through the long windows and offered a view of the forest on one side and the open fields on the other, with the town of Saint Ives Cross nestled into a tuck of the valley.

"It's much less oppressive now, isn't it?" Samir said, looking around.

"They filmed in here a couple of days ago and in the ballroom. I guess they'll have to come back and show the mess."

"You see, more drama for the show. That's all."

I smiled. "It is exciting, actually. To see what we might be able to do here, how to restore it."

"Has Hortense seen the plans?"

"The first round, but nothing else yet."

He grinned.

"I know. She's kind of scary too."

"You're frightened a lot."

"No, I'm not!"

"Yes, you are. Hortense, being in the house alone, my mother. You were afraid to go see the earl."

"It's just that everything is so . . . unreliable lately."

"You can't cross the sea merely by standing and staring at the water," he said.

"Is that a quote?"

He nodded. "Rabindranath Tagore. He's a great writer. You should read him."

"You'll have to tell me where to start."

"I will." He cocked his head. "He's one of India's best writers, an amazing character writer."

I nodded. Took a breath as I looked toward the second story. "Let's go up the main stairs, as your mother would have."

Things had not changed on the stairway, though it was cleaner. "I wonder where the cats are now that the construction has started."

"They're clever. Likely hiding when people are here."

"Probably."

At the top of the stairs, we turned toward Violet's room. "Wait," I said. "I want to see how the damage looks from the inside."

He followed me down the hall to the gallery, and we peered over the edge into the ballroom. It had been so bad before that it was honestly hard to tell any difference, but debris was piled up on the floor.

"Where are the construction crews today?" Samir asked.

"They can't work until the autopsy is released."

"Ah. Should we be mucking about in here, then?"

"I'm just looking for my grandmother's stuff," I said, knowing I probably shouldn't be. "Lost heirlooms, hatpins to sell on eBay."

He chuckled. "If you're sure."

We made our way down the hall. It seemed lighter, somehow. "How was your dad last night over the skeleton news?"

"Stoic, but I can tell he's bothered. He's always felt he should have protected her, his little sister."

"That's sad."

I pushed open the door to Violet's room, and a puff of cool air washed over us. "Is there a window open?"

Samir crossed to the wall and pulled back the heavy drapes. It wasn't open—it was shattered. Shards of glass were scattered over the floor. "Must have been someone with a pretty good arm," he said, picking up the hefty rock. "Probably kids."

I thought of the teenagers hanging out by the grocery store, smoking. "It's not like there's much for them to do around here."

"True enough." With his foot, he scraped the glass toward the wall. "You'll need to have someone come in and get all of this catalogued, get the paintings to a safer location. I'm pretty sure a couple of these are worth a fair bit."

"Jocasta said that one is an Ingres."

"So how do you want to start?"

I pressed my lips together and turned in a circle. "When my mother set up these treasure hunts, she was mostly visual, and she liked puns, jokes, riddles." I looked around slowly at the paintings, the drawings, the bed.

Wandering to the dressing table, I picked up the empty perfume bottles and smelled them, set them back down. "I want to take the Lalique bottles back with me," I said. "We should have brought something to carry things in."

"I would imagine there is some sort of bag or something in here." He opened a closet, and there, mostly in shreds, were the remains of

Violet's wardrobe, the bright India silks Helen had told me about, the embroidery. The remnants stung me, hanging there for so long unnoticed.

"She died at least a few years before my mother left, and this room is just as it was when Violet was here. Why?" I frowned, moved back into the room, looked at the paintings, one by one. "Mom, what did you want me to see?"

Nothing leapt out at me—if any of these paintings had influenced my mother's work, I couldn't trace it. The exotic landscapes and portraits, some tiny, some enormous, were nothing like her work. In one, a white Persian cat sat in the lap of a fat sultan wearing shoes with turned-up toes. I lingered on the harem painting and the one of a tiger that I'd seen before, and I stepped close to what I thought might be the plantation where my grandmother had been born, the place she had been forced to leave. "I wonder why she didn't just let Rosemere go if she loved India so much," I said aloud. The painting made it appealing, blue-green hills rising in mysterious distance behind the house, the scroll-like shapes of tea plants etched across them.

"Duty?" Samir answered. "Or maybe she saw the writing on the wall with Indian independence. When did she leave?"

"I can't remember exactly. The forties, but it must have been after the war—it would have been difficult to travel anywhere while the war was raging."

"Partition was 1947." He shook out a length of fabric, riddled with holes but mainly intact. "She probably knew it was time to leave." He separated relatively good fabric from the crumbling, destroyed things, each in their own pile on the floor.

The name of the place was tacked to the frame on a tiny brass tag. "Have you ever seen photos of the plantation? Is this it?"

"It was called Sundar Hills."

"This is it." I took the painting off the wall. "I'm going to take this with me too." I looked on the back of the painting for a clue from my mother, but there was nothing more, and I laid it on the bed next to the Lalique perfume bottles.

Next, I moved to the dressing table, opening drawers to find the usual accouterments—a brush, a manicure set made of bone, bobby pins, a loose button. A line of carved wooden elephants, all sorts of them, some decorated with bits of mirror or beads and, shockingly, bits of ivory fitted into their tusks, marched across the back of the table, their reflections murky in the spotted mirror. The elephants, too, I wanted to bring with me, and I gathered them up, frowning again over the idea that no one had cleared the room after Violet's death. Had it been too painful? Had my mother been angry? Why hadn't her son done it either?

What happened here?

I brushed off my hands and looked at the pasha again.

A line from a book ran through my head: "White Persian cats lay limply on the lawn," from *One Last Look*, by Susannah Moore, a book my mother and I had read as one of our choices for our book club of two. It was a novel about a woman being seduced by India, resisting, then falling in love with it. I'd loved it more than she had, and now I wondered if it was because the woman had reminded her of her mother. I crossed the room and tipped the painting upward to see if there was anything obviously behind it, but it was very heavy, and only dust and cobwebs were visible. "Samir, will you help me with this?"

"Sure." We lifted it together and leaned it against the bed. Dust and mildew stained the wall behind.

But there, taped to the wooden frame, was a key. I let go of a chortle. It was an old-fashioned brass key, with curlicues and a flag at the end, tied to the wood with red string. I yanked it, and the string gave way easily. "I was right. It's a treasure hunt." Holding it in my hand, I said, "Now what could this unlock?"

Samir touched my arm and pointed me to a heavy wardrobe. Sure enough, the key fit, and although it took some doing to open the swollen door, with enough yanking it did at last give way.

I don't know what I was expecting, but it was not paintings, two shelves' worth, all carefully wrapped in tissue paper, then sandwiched between appropriately sized cardboard. None were large, and there were probably fifteen or sixteen of them. They'd been so carefully wrapped that I had no idea what they were, but my gut said this mattered.

Except, why leave them here, where they might have been stolen, plundered, destroyed by time? "We can't leave these here," I said. I took one out, wondering if I should take a peek before I—

"Olivia, you'll want to see this." Samir sat on the floor with a low, flat box.

"Okay. Just a second." I chose a smaller painting and began to gently release the tissue paper wrapping.

"Olivia," he said in a quiet voice.

Drawn by his tone, I nested the painting back in its place and sat down beside him. "What is it?"

He handed over a sheaf of pictures. Most were black-and-white photos, faded, some so faded they were hard to decipher. India, clearly, often the plantation in the painting. "Was the box in the wardrobe too?"

"Yes."

I leafed through the photos slowly. A meal at a long table with a dozen guests, men and women; a badminton match with two unknown women making a gesture of conquest. A house with a wide porch—a portico. A handful of letters were tucked into the mix and ephemera of all kinds—a program from a play in India from 1943, a receipt so faded it was impossible to read, a scrap of a note with colors in a list.

"Look. This must be your uncle," Samir said, handing over a dozen snapshots of a blond child at several ages—a thin, tired-looking toddler; a still-skinny but smirking twelve-year-old; a shot of a group of children with the same boy standing on a chair with a sword over them.

"Oh, he looks just swell," I said drily.

"It would have been a surprise if you'd discovered all the rumors of his nastiness were inflated."

"Are there journals or anything? That would really, really help."

"I haven't seen any yet."

We both dug through the box, picking out this and that, looking for clues, anything we could understand. Near the bottom of the box, however, was a surprise—a stash of pornographic photos of women. "What's this?"

Samir sifted through another stack of papers and didn't look up. "What is it?"

"Naked women."

No, not women. A woman, singular. An Indian woman with astonishing black hair she smoothed down over her naked body, looking at the camera in a coy way, sprawling over a patterned bedspread completely naked, her breasts lush and young. "She's so beautiful," I breathed, and then, electrified, I grabbed his arm. "Oh my God, Samir! Did my grandmother like *women*?"

"What are you talking about?" He leaned in as I flipped to the next photo, this one larger and more beautiful than the last, the sloe-eyed woman in her twenties, looking straight at the camera with a small smile, her shoulders elegant, her waist tiny—

"Ack!" Samir reared back and covered his eyes with his hands. "That's my grandmother." He laughed. "Oh, my eyes are burned forever."

"This is your grandmother?" I shuffled through the pictures, and there were dozens and dozens of them, not all fully naked but all suggestive. Some when she was only a teen, maybe fourteen or fifteen, her breasts high and still small. Another was of the same woman in her thirties, her arms rounder, her hips wide, her face mature. Some in India, some clearly here in this room.

"This is—" The implications were tragic. "They were lovers."

He lowered his hands from his eyes and leaned over my shoulder again, covering the top photo with his open palm. His eyes met mine, full of sorrow. "Think of it," he said quietly. "All those years." His voice was raw. "It's so sad."

His eyes were so close I could count individual eyelashes, see the barely visible line where his iris met the pupil. I looked at his mouth, which I knew from kissing him was soft and full. The lingering, intense connection between us flared again, and I looked away. "What was her name?"

"Nandini."

"Nandini." I whispered it, and to my amazement, a tear welled over and fell down my face.

"What's this?"

I closed my eyes, trying to identify the ache. "I don't know. It's just heartbreaking."

"It is." He brushed the tear away. "Now they would just marry and be done."

"Instead they married men. And Violet became a drunk."

His hand, heavy and long fingered, rested across the sheaf of photos on my lap. His nails were clipped short, tidy, efficient, and even so they were beautiful. Like his tapered fingers, his broad thumb, the angle of his wrist. I pressed the tip of my index finger to the tip of his. "Neither of us would exist if they'd married."

"Would you mind?" He lifted his hand, and our palms met, sizzling, as if the combination created a shimmering electric field. "If I did not exist?"

"Yes. I would hate that world." Impulsively, I reached up and cupped his jaw, moved his hair away from his cheekbone, wondering how I'd missed the fact that this face, this singular face, was impossibly precious. I held it between my hands, peering down into his eyes, eyes like a night sky, eyes had that enchanted me the first time I'd seen him and enchanted me again, over and over. I brushed my thumbs down his goatee, as he so often did, and this time, it was me who angled my head and paused, looking for permission, then leaned in and kissed him.

Kissed his mouth, those soft, full lips. I fell into them, into him, and then his arms were around me, hauling me half into his lap, the photos scattering, and he was kissing me back, hard, one hand on the back of my head, the other on my lower back. We were kissing each other, plunging, exploring, hungry. I buried my hands in his hair, and he hauled my body into his chest. I ran my hands over his shoulders, powerful and broad, and he slid his hands beneath my sweater to touch my back, my sides.

Abruptly, he stopped, captured my hands. "Wait." He swallowed. "Not here, with them watching."

"Oh." I laughed. "No, that would be weird. You're right."

He brushed my hair away from my mouth, his eyes following the path of his fingers. "We need to get things right here, too, before we leave."

"I know." I touched his nose, feathered my fingers over his heavy eyebrow. An ache made of equal parts lusty hunger and a piquant yearning filled my body, heart and throat and mind and fingers. Now that we were touching, I didn't want to stop. "I feel like an iron shaving stuck to a magnet."

He smiled, ran his hands down the outside of my legs. "Believe me, I know the feeling."

I glanced at the box, then back to him. "You won't change your mind?"

"No." He caught my face in his hands, fiercely, and kissed me again. Hard and deep. His eyes opened, and they were close, close, close. "No. Will you?"

I couldn't speak. Only shook my head.

Gently, he pulled away. "All right, then. Let's get this business done."

I opened one of the paintings, expecting it to be one of my mother's early paintings, but instead, it was an exquisite portrait of a young woman in sixteenth-century dress, her hair curled on one shoulder, her breasts pressed into the square bodice of her blue gown. The painter had captured a sense of mischief about her, and his command of light—cascading over her skin, tangling in her hair—was magnificent. "This looks important," I said. "Do you know artists?"

"Not really, but I agree that it is very high quality. Is it an ancestor?"

"I don't know, but she could be." I looked at the wrapped paintings and made a decision. "I don't want to leave them, but I also don't want to look at every single one of them. Will these fit in your car?"

"Not all at once." He gestured to the bed, where other things were waiting transport as well. "I can call someone, perhaps."

"No, no. I know who to call." I scrolled through my favorites on my phone and found Peter's number. He was available. "He'll meet us in front in an hour. We can drop the paintings and the box at my flat."

One side of his mouth faintly, faintly lifted. "And then we can go to my house, if you like."

I nodded, just as faintly. The atoms of my skin whispered the news to each other, *Soon soon soon.* I had to look away from him to break the spell. His hand fell on my shoulder, slid beneath my hair to my neck, then dropped away, as if he, too, had to find a different focus.

We worked in silence, making sure nothing terribly important was left behind in the wardrobe, though it really did appear that the paintings and the box of photos were all that was in there.

Samir poked his head inside and pressed on the back. "Hmm."

"What?"

"Just making sure there's no hidden passageway to Narnia."

"Or the kitchen."

He looked at me, then back at the wardrobe. "The kitchen?"

"A lot of these places have secret passageways."

"Ah, so that's how they would get together without people noticing."

I lifted a shoulder. "Nandini was Violet's lady's maid or whatever. She would have been able to come and go whenever Violet summoned her." I imagined her padding through the hallways in her slippered feet, her sari fluttering behind her, then slipping into Violet's room and bed. "I wonder if she slept overnight."

Samir rubbed his diaphragm, looking back over his shoulder at the bed. "I wonder if they were happy."

"Me too."

"I hope they were."

Finally, finally, we carried the paintings, five or six at a time, through the hallway and down the front stairs.

A faint awkwardness had risen between us, and impulsively, I reached out and took his hand. He smiled softly and shifted his hand so that our fingers could weave together.

At the top of the wide, carved staircase, I halted. "Look!" On the ledge of the gallery, another floor above us, sat the cat, his tail draped in luxurious fat length over the edge. It swished as he looked at us, yellow eyes alert and unafraid.

"Hullo," Samir called. "Won't you come down and visit?"

Swish, swish.

"No, I suppose not."

"I worry about him, now that the construction has started."

"He'll be all right. Ferals are wise."

"Yes, but nature is cruel, isn't it?" I looked back up at him. "If you'll come live with me, I'll give you liver and milk and everything else you can imagine."

He meowed.

"Oh, you like to talk, do you?"

Meow.

"Here kitty, kitty," I called.

He only stared at me.

"We could bring him some food next time, if you like," Samir said, rubbing his thumb over my knuckles.

"I would like."

Samir brought his car around to the front, and we loaded as much as we could into it, then waited just inside the door for Peter. Across the open fields, framed by the trees on either side of the house, was Saint Ives Cross, a blurry tumble of houses in the rain. "There's my house, on the hill."

"Can you really pick it out?"

He laughed gently. "No. But I can in my imagination."

Peter drove up and without a blink helped us load everything left into his trunk. I rode with him to direct him to the new flat.

"I heard you had some excitement up here," he said.

"Yes—a part of the roof collapsed, and a skeleton was discovered, all on the same day."

"Eventually everything comes to light, don't it, milady?"

I thought of my mother. "I hope so, Peter. I really do."

"Ye're not canceling the picnic, now, are you?"

"No, no. Pavi and I—do you know Pavi Malakar, who runs Coriander?"

"Course I do. Known her since she was a wee thing. And her brother too. Got all famous, then just came back to Saint Ives like an ordinary fellow."

"Samir is famous?"

"Ye didn't know? He was in all the papers with that book. They almost made it into a movie!"

"No kidding." Of course the residents of a small village would burst with pride over one of their own making a splash. "Did you read it, the book?"

"Nah. I'm not much of a reader, you know. Just like my football and the garden."

I nodded, patted my belly. "I need a little more gardening, a little less reading, I think."

"Ah, love, ye're a beauty, just as you are. Skinny might be in fashion, but we fellas always appreciate a different kind of woman."

I laughed at the faint praise. "Thank you."

Samir was waiting at the flat, holding an umbrella so that we could each haul a box into the foyer, which smelled of bleach and fried fish and mold. When we'd unloaded them all, Samir said, "Thank you, Mr. Jenkins."

Peter tipped his hat. "No worries."

I handed over a clutch of pound notes. "Thanks for your help. I don't know what I'd do without you."

"If you're staying, you might want to learn to drive."

"Yes. As soon as I get a moment."

It took another twenty minutes to haul everything into my flat and find spots for it, and by then we were both sweaty and hungry. "Do you want something to eat?"

"No." He took my hand and drew me close. "Let's go to my house." His hand moved up my arm, over my shoulder. "I have snacks there."

I touched his waist. Nodded.

Chapter Sixteen

The drive took less than five minutes, and every foot of it raised the heat in the air between us. We didn't speak. I took his hand and pressed my much-smaller one to it. He brought our hands up to his lips, tasted each of my fingers.

It had begun to rain again. He pulled up in front of the cottage, and we dashed for the door. He opened it, and we fell inside, kissing in the living room, madly, as if there would never be another chance, no other lips, ever, until Samir drew me to his bedroom, which smelled of that intense cologne. His bed surprised me, luxurious, covered with pillows and a duvet with a red paisley pattern. The window looked out to the back garden, the rain obscuring everything but the barest smear of color where the border was. I stood there, out of breath, and looked at him.

And this was the moment, the ordinary moment, that I would remember always. Samir, so tall, reaching for the hem of his shirt and pulling it off over his head, and standing there, waiting for me, revealed—his burnished, smooth skin, a scattering of dark hair between dark nipples, rounds of easy muscle from his work.

I pressed my palm to his heart, and that wild, intense emotion rose in me again, and I looked up, stricken, tears running down my face. "What if we hadn't met?" I whispered.

"But we have," he said in a low rumble and reached for me, pulled my head against his chest, his lips on my head. "We have. We're here."

"I'm sorry. I don't know why I'm—"

He tipped up my face. "I don't mind." He kissed me, gently, kissed my cheeks so that then I could taste my tears when he kissed my mouth again. "There is another famous quote from Tagore," he said, holding my face. "'I seem to have loved you in numberless forms, numberless times, in life after life, in age after age forever.' That's what this is, you and me."

"Yes." I bent my head back to his chest and pressed my mouth to his skin. His hands moved on my scalp, over my ears, down my neck. The smell of him made me dizzy, and I suddenly, urgently wanted to feel his skin against mine. I stepped back and flung off my sweater and then the tank beneath it, then my bra, and this time, I paused.

He swallowed, reached up one hand and cupped my breast, bent to kiss my neck, my shoulders. "Beautiful," he whispered. My skin rippled as his hair brushed my arms, my chin, and I pulled him closer, gauging the taut span of his waist. He kissed my breasts, my shoulder, the hollow of my throat, and I swayed with emotion. Desire.

Urgently, I reached for his belt, and he obliged me, lifting his hands so I could unbuckle his belt and the buttons of his jeans, pushing the fabric down muscled hips and rock-hard legs. He stepped out of them, and I took in the sight of him fully nude: long legs and that blackest nest of hair nearly made me faint. "Oh, my," I said. "You're beautiful, Samir."

He smiled, touched his belly, ran a hand down his penis, as men do. "It's all yours."

I hesitated, thinking of my not-so-thin thighs. "I'm not quite so perfect."

"This hair," he said, threading his fingers through it, "is perfect. These lips, these breasts." He brushed my mouth, my breasts. "Let's see the rest, shall we?" He unfastened my jeans, skimmed them downward, and then I was naked too.

He ran those artist's fingers over my squishy bits and down the sides of my thighs. "I can't kiss all those beautiful places"—he touched the curve of my belly, my collarbones—"if we're standing up." I let him take my hand and waited as he flung back the duvet, and then we lay down, and I rolled close to him, and our bodies, our skin, all of it, touched, and I made the softest of sounds, reaching for him.

"God, Olivia," he breathed, his hands on my back, my thighs, his lips brushing my mouth, my chin, my shoulder. "The minute I saw you at Rebecca's house, I knew you." He brushed his nose over my chin. "I haven't stopped thinking about this since."

"Me too," I said and pushed him back to look at his face, kiss his mouth, softly, then more deeply, my hands running down his chest, around his ribs, down his belly and into that thicket of heat. "I just kept thinking I shouldn't."

"I thought I shouldn't." He touched my breasts, kissed one and the other, kissed my belly, and then my mouth again, and I found myself lost in it. In him, in making love, in learning the geography of his body, his throat, his mouth, his hands, and allowing him access to the hills and valleys of mine, open, trusting as he traveled the length and breadth of me. In return, I journeyed along the ridges of his hip bones and down the savanna of his broad, powerful back, tracing the valley of his spine, the forest of his beautiful long curls.

And then it was too much to wait, and we joined—fierce, not gentle in the slightest. It was roaring and wild as we moved and kissed, our limbs tangled, our tongues, our bodies slick and sticky and, then, sated.

He lay over me as our hearts slowed. I ran my hands through his hair, releasing the essence of his scent, and I floated in it, in this moment, this very one. When he tried to move, I gripped him closer. "Not yet."

He braced himself on his elbows, dipped down to brush his mouth over mine. "I don't want to squash you."

"I'm rather liking it."

"Rather liking it?" He grinned and swept hair out of my eyes. "Any moment you'll break out in full British."

"Well, my mother did raise me."

He moved just a little inside of me, causing a rippling echo of orgasm. "I can't believe you're here."

"Me either."

He shifted, then reached for the duvet to pull it up over us in the cool room. With gestures as old as time, we moved into a newly woven shape, my head in the hollow of his shoulder, his hands draped around me.

I said, "But if I spoke British, what class would it be?"

"American."

"Not if it's full Brit."

"Never happen. You'll always sound American."

"That's disappointing."

He laughed. "I'm quite fond of a certain American."

"Hmm." My body felt boneless. "I never want to get up. Like, ever."

His fingers moved in my hair, and I drifted a little, happy. As will happen, a sudden thought bolted through my mind. "Wait!" I said and shifted to look up at him. "We didn't read that book until ten years ago."

"What are you talking about? Who?"

"My mom. We had a book club, just the two of us, and the reason I thought to look behind the painting of the pasha was because my mother and I read a book about India, and there was a paragraph I loved reading aloud, all this alliteration, about a young prince and a white Persian cat and curled shoes."

He tucked one arm behind his head, and I was momentarily distracted by the angle of his biceps, the black hair in his armpit, the—

I shook my head. "She's been here, in England, in the house since then. Like, she set this all up *recently*."

"You knew she'd left you a treasure hunt, so it makes sense, doesn't it?"

"But when did she come here? I didn't know she left the country. I would have noticed—I mean, I saw her a couple of times a week."

"Surely you traveled, for work, for holidays."

I closed my eyes. "Right. She could talk on the phone anywhere, of course."

"What bothers you about this?"

"I don't know." I shook my head, feeling that rise of powerful emotion again. "Maybe I wish she would have just told me. That we could have talked about all of it so I would know what to do now."

He held me closer to his body. Skin to skin, his cheek against my hair. "She must have had a reason."

"I guess." The movements of his naked thigh moving over mine kindled new awareness, and my flesh began to rustle again. I ran my hand over his belly, lower, down his thigh, over his belly button. "Maybe I don't care right now. Maybe I'm tired of thinking about it."

His fingers traced the curve of my breast. Naked fingertips, bare skin coming alive. "I'm happy to help you forget about it."

He convinced me that it didn't matter right then.

And after a time, we tumbled into sleep, tangled together in a way I had never before liked, his arms around me; his damp, spent penis nestled against my buttocks; his strong, solid body a bulwark against the world.

We stirred as the sun was beginning to drop into the earth. My stomach was growling, and as his hand was over that spot, he laughed into my shoulder. "I'm famished as well. Shall we find some food?"

"Yes." I turned. "But only here. I don't want to leave this house."

"No." He leaned on one elbow. "Nor do I." He touched my chin, the side of my neck. "This is not casual for me, Olivia. I hope you know that."

"Not me either," I said. "In case you couldn't tell by the tears." I rolled my eyes. "It's a wonder you didn't run far, far way."

"I only took that to mean you could not believe your good fortune to be with such a man among men."

"Well, there was that."

"I knew it. Come on." He slid out of bed, absolutely unselfconscious, and I followed his movements as he picked up our clothes. "Do you want something to wear?"

"A robe or something would be nice."

"Hmm. None of that, but how about—" He tossed me an oversize T-shirt that smelled of laundry. It said, "Saint John of the Woods Lacrosse." It tumbled down my thighs, and the sleeves reached my elbows, but it was plain that the reason he chose it was for the deep V-neck, which showed off a considerable amount of cleavage. I gave him a wry grin and posed. "Good?"

He winked, pulling on a pair of sweatpants. "Quite."

I found my socks on the floor. "Not sexy, I know, but it's kind of cold in here."

"I'll light the fire."

The cat was spread over the back of the couch as we entered, and he yawned. "Hey, Billi," I said and scratched his head. He grinned, allowing it, and followed us into the kitchen.

"I make a very spicy masala chai. Secret recipe," he said, wiggling his eyebrows. "Would you like to try it?"

"Absolutely." It was a tiny room, and I perched on a stool at the counter.

He settled a pot on the stove and poured water in, then slid a tray of spices over and opened them one at a time, counting out peppercorns and cardamom, star anise and something I didn't quite see. With exaggerated care, he hid the tray when he was finished, mugging at me over his shoulder. "Pavi would kill for my blend."

I laughed. "With her palette she could deconstruct it in three seconds, no matter what you put in it."

"Perhaps. You haven't tasted it yet."

"What can I do?"

"I'll have you chopping in a minute." On his phone, he touched an app, and music wafted out of the speaker in the living room, something low and jazzy. "Good?"

"Yeah." I accepted the glass of water he poured and drank a long swallow. "I'm easy with music. Not much I don't like."

He set me to chopping carrots, onions, and garlic while he washed chicken breasts and broke a generous knob of ginger from a larger hand. "What do you choose when you're alone?"

"Depends on my mood, of course." I sliced a carrot with a very sharp knife and, in surprise, examined the blade. "Messermeister!"

"Restaurant family, remember?"

"Ah, of course." I started on a second carrot. "So, music. I love Leonard Cohen, but he's not the guy you want on in the background when you're working or whatever."

"Brilliant. I've studied his poetry, of course, but never heard him sing."

"My mom loved him. She had a taste for dark themes, sad music— all that regret, you know—and Cohen has this great, deep voice, rumbly, raw, but it's the words that make his songs. He was such an old, old soul, especially about relationships."

He started to peel the ginger, but his hair was in his eyes, and in a gesture that had the stamp of a million repetitions, he reached up and tied it back from his face using just the hair, then washed his hands and picked up the ginger. I smiled.

"What?"

"It seems like your hair drives you crazy."

"A little. But"—he lifted a brow—"the girls like it."

"Mmm." I crunched a bit of carrot. "Not all, surely?"

He minced the skinned ginger expertly, his fingers curled to avoid chopping them off, the ginger moving swiftly, cleanly beneath the knife. He dropped half the slices into the water simmering on the stove. "My ex-wife hated long hair, and I originally let it grow to"—he paused—"infuriate her."

"What happened there, Samir?"

He shook his head. The light came straight down from overhead, skimmed down his strong nose, illuminated his brow. "I was young. She was very polished, very beautiful, from a very wealthy British Indian family. She dazzled me." He scraped the ginger into a small bowl, then crushed a handful of garlic cloves. "Do you mind a lot of garlic?"

I laughed. "You can add an entire head of garlic, and I won't mind."

He smiled that sunny, beautiful smile. "I knew I liked you."

My carrots were finished, and I ran the knife through the top layer of the onion, peeling it away. "You were dazzled, and . . . ?"

"Do you really want to hear this right now?"

Seriously, I said, "Kind of. Before I'm so lost in you that I can't turn around."

"She is not a consideration. Trust me."

"That's not the concern." I settled the onion on the cutting board and sliced off the ends. "Large or small dice?"

"Large." His eyes were sober, deep, as they rested on my face. "Then what?"

"You spent a year reading yourself through your broken heart. Maybe that left a wound. Maybe you won't get around it."

He nodded. "Fair enough." Tossing the meat into a pile on a plate, he said, "She loved me for the book I wrote, not for me. Or maybe she wanted to be connected to the young and upcoming Indian writer—it made her look good to have me on her arm."

"You would look good on anyone's arm." I plucked a carrot wheel from the pile. "Seeing that you are a god among men."

His lips quirked, and he pointed the knife at me. "There's that." He shook his head, and a single curl fell down along his cheekbone. "Anyway. The next two books failed spectacularly, and she lost interest." Pouring oil into a heavy skillet, he added, "I was more humiliated than brokenhearted. We didn't like each other very much by the end."

"I'm sorry," I said.

"But if that had not happened, I would not have been here, and we would not have met." He leaned over the counter, very close. "I would have hated that."

I lifted my chin so that our lips connected, and the kiss was sweet, deep, lingering. "Me too."

Still close, he said, "Did that make you feel better?"

"Yes."

He smiled. "Good."

The pot on the stove sent out an evocative scent, and he bent in and smelled it closely, stirred it, moved it off the burner. I peered around him to catalogue the spices, grinning when he caught me. Deftly, he tossed tea into the pot and glanced at the clock on the wall.

Then, like a dancer humming to the music under his breath, he tossed the ginger and onions in the big skillet and stirred; added garlic, sending the scent into the air; then added the chicken and a handful of frozen peas, stirring, stirring, his mouth pursed in a way that I knew I would think about. Watching him, I felt suddenly breathless with both gratitude and terror. What had I done, allowing myself to fall?

Because fallen I had. Fallen for his beauty and his sunny nature, his sexy bare feet and his brains and the way he made love to me and now the way he cooked.

"I forgot limes!" he cried. "They're in a bowl over there. Cut two into quarters. And we need a cup of milk in the chai."

I followed instructions. Mesmerized, I watched as he strained the chai into mugs. "Secret recipe."

The scent alone would have seduced me, but the flavor was sharp, hot, peppery, very sweet. "Wow," I said.

"I knew you would like it." He took a sip, nodded, then turned to the big skillet, piling plates high with rice he'd heated in the microwave and the chicken and peas and, at the very last minute, a big handful of fresh coriander, all served steaming hot and fragrant and perfect with the limes. We were both so hungry we dove into eating like little kids, completely focused. I even found myself swinging my foot.

At last, I rose for a breath. "Samir, this is so delicious."

"Need to keep your strength up."

I grinned.

He poked at the dish, sobering, then looked up at me. "I keep thinking about our grandmothers, in love all those years. What that meant for them."

"I know. It's the epitome of star-crossed. Not just different classes. Not just different cultures, but same sex at a time it was completely unacceptable," I said. "How's your dad going to feel if he finds out?"

"I don't know." He shook his head. "Maybe we don't tell anybody."

"Okay," I said with a little frown. "I mean, I guess it seems prudent to wait for answers, see if we can piece it together first."

"What if we never tell anyone?"

"Ever? That seems so sad, that their story would never see the light of day. It seems at least part of what my mother wanted me to know."

"Yes, but why?" His hands were still on the table. One was in a fist. "Why did she want you to know that particular thing?"

"I don't know." I covered the fist with my hand. "Not yet."

He turned it over and opened his hand to me. "I just don't want my father to be hurt. Or any of the people who loved my grandmother and wouldn't understand."

"I promise that we'll make the decision together. Let's put all the pieces together before we decide anything."

"Not even Pavi," he said.

"Okay." I crossed my heart. "It's our secret."

I stood up to take the plates to the sink, and on my way back, he caught me by the waist and tugged me between his legs. His big hands moved on the back of my thighs, then under the shirt to my naked bottom. "Maybe this should be our secret too," he said, and I could see by the set of his mouth that he meant it.

"Why?" I pressed my hands into his shoulders. "Are you embarrassed?"

"God, no! Why would you say that?"

"I don't know. I'm older than you. The detective made a comment yesterday about it."

Samir smiled slowly, that sexy, knowing grin. His hands skated upward, following the curve of my waist, then back down again. "He thought we were together?"

"Yes." I leaned in closer. "And commented on the age difference, which means I don't even *kind of* look close to your age."

"You're the one who is embarrassed, not me. I don't care in the slightest." His palms came out and rested on my waist. "When I was a boy, I stole the photo of our grandmothers, a copy of the same one you have now, and hid it in my room." He swallowed, lifting a hand to twine his fingers through my hair. "She was so beautiful, like something I made up. That day I saw you at Rebecca's the first time, I thought I was imagining you."

I pressed my forehead into his, deeply touched. "I'm not embarrassed."

He brushed the tip of his nose over mine. The tenderness nearly buckled my knees. "Good."

I closed my eyes, wishing that I could capture this moment in a bottle and revisit it whenever I wanted. I breathed in the scent of his skin and the sex all over us and this new thing we'd created, the fragrance of us.

"Listen," he said quietly, hand brushing the side of my neck. "You've never lived in a little village like this. The gossip can be murderous."

"Why would they care?"

He raised his eyebrows. "You're not seriously asking that question. You're a countess, Olivia, heir to a family name that the village has held dear for centuries. I'm a thatcher."

"A professor who chooses to be a thatcher. A writer who is waiting for his next book."

"No," he said with more force than I expected. "That's not who I am. This"—he gestured to the cottage around us—"is who I am."

"Okay," I said, a little wounded. "I don't care what you do. I really don't."

"Other people do." He brushed the back of his fingers over my cheek. "They'll want you to marry a lord, someone who knows all the rules. Someone they can brag about seeing in the market."

"I hear you." But I didn't like it. "It's ridiculous, however. It's the twenty-first century!"

"Maybe in America."

The smell of his skin was making me dizzy, and I worked my fingers under the neckline of his shirt to feel the bare skin. "I might want you naked again," I said and pressed into him, then bent to kiss him.

"I like that idea."

Somewhere in the middle of the night, I awakened to moonlight pouring in through a window and Samir all around me, arms draped lightly over my waist, his chest against my back. I shifted, very, very slowly, so that I could look at him. The moonlight touched the crown of his head, the sweep of a cheekbone, his bare shoulder.

It seemed both impossible and fated that he was lying here next to me, and the feeling that rose in me was as vast and deep as anything I'd ever felt. Not a crush. Not something that would be easy to overcome if something came between us.

And yet what could I do?

Quietly, I slipped out of bed and padded down the hall to the bathroom. Moonlight poured in through the back windows of a small second bedroom, one I hadn't paid attention to because it had been dark. Now the light showed a desk and more bookcases and unruly sheaves of loose paper on a window seat. A laptop sat closed on the desk, and next to it was a sheaf of paper in a tidy stack.

A manuscript of some kind, I would swear.

For a moment, I only stood there, desperately curious, deeply tempted to tiptoe into the room and take a peek.

But no. If he was to trust me, he had to reveal things in his own time.

I took care of business in the tiny bathroom and washed my face and hands, looking into my eyes in the mirror. Alongside my eyes, my grandmother's eyes, were the faint beginnings of crow's-feet. My lips were full and swollen with all the kissing, and there was a mark on my shoulder, a little bite mark that made me smile. I backed up a little to look at my breasts, and they looked prettier than they ever had, and my chubby thighs were shaky with so much sex.

I didn't know what gods might be listening or who might be in charge of all this, but I let go of a whisper. "Thank you."

When I awoke, Samir had already showered. He sat on the edge of the bed, wearing only dark-blue boxer briefs, and his hand was in my hair. His expression was unbearably tender, and I pressed my cheek into his palm.

"I am so glad you're here," he said, and his low voice rumbled into my ear.

"Me too."

"But now real life arrives—I'm afraid I have to go to work this morning. The rain has stopped."

"All right." I stirred, stretched, and he made a sound, pulling the sheet off my chest and pressing a kiss to my throat, my breasts.

"I don't want to go," he said.

"Me either." I swung my legs off the bed. "But I have a million things to do today too. I'm meeting Pavi to touch base on layout for the picnic, and I need to figure out what to do with Violet's things."

"That room should be cleared now that the window is broken."

"I'm going to call Jocasta. She'll send someone." I tugged on my underwear, then my tank top and sweater. "I guess I need to take a look at the paintings we took to my flat as well."

"I cannot wait to see them." He stood. "I'm sorry to have to rush. I'll drop you at your flat if you like. I've got to be in Woolhope by eight."

"You have to eat!"

He grinned. "Oh, yes. I will." He climbed into his jeans, buttoned his shirt. "You too."

"Maybe I can cook for you tonight."

His eyes shimmered. "Yes, please."

In the car, he said, "Are we going to keep this to ourselves for now?"

"Us?"

"Yeah. I think it would be better."

I wrapped my hand around his forearm, very lightly. "But what if I'm . . ." It was hard to think of the right way to say it—proud, pleased? "Chuffed? Maybe I want everyone to be a little envious."

"Thank you for that." He had to shift gears. "We just don't want the gossips to go mad just yet."

A little of the sheen fell away from my mood. "Not even Pavi? I might feel bad about that."

"She'll know the minute she sees us."

I shrugged. "All right. If it makes you more comfortable."

"It isn't for me. But thank you." He pulled up in front of the fish-and-chips shop and looked back at the street. No one was around, and he smiled, then bent in and kissed me, lingering and deep and sincere. "I'll text you."

Chapter Seventeen

I let myself into the flat, startled by how much space the paintings took up. Another big job, but it would have to wait. I started a pot of coffee brewing and climbed in the shower.

And there, my body remembered. Everything. I touched my throat and arms and belly, remembering a kiss, a cry, a moment of laughter, his hands on my body, his low laughter in my ear. Happiness.

Adrift in my postsex delirium, I wandered back into the kitchen, trying to find my phone, which I'd not touched since sometime yesterday. It was buried at the bottom of my purse, and when I swiped the screen to bring it to life, there were a dozen missed calls and a handful of voice messages. As I poured a cup of coffee, pleased at the heady scent of it, I listened to the first one, from Jocasta. "Give me a call, love," she said. "I've found something."

The next was from the detective, who informed me that the skeleton they'd found was over six hundred years old if they were to judge, so the house work could continue.

A relief. Stirring sugar into my coffee, flashing back on Samir's long-fingered hands chopping chicken last night, tracing the shape of my body, whispering over my lips, I punched the next one. The accountant. Then:

"Did you think I would never find out, *Countess*?" said Grant's voice.

My gut dropped. I swore aloud, forcefully. Somehow, he'd found out about my status here, and now things would be even harder to negotiate. Carrying the cup of coffee to the table, I opened my laptop to read my email—

And sighed. A forwarded email from my publisher held the subject line, "American Heiress Inherits Ghosts along with Estate."

The story had originally run on some website but had gone viral, and now a search on the story showed over a thousand links, most to small newspapers in the US. Of course—it was a sweet little lifestyle filler. The photo that ran with the story was me at a cocktail party six or seven years ago, my hair in a tousled updo, the dress cut way low in the back. The flash had caught my eyes wrong, so I looked drunk.

And maybe I had been. Who knew. The booze and wine flowed freely at the foodie parties we attended.

The actual text was sensational and short:

> Poor Olivia Shaw, Countess of Rosemere, has her hands full enough with the extensive renovations on her newly inherited manor house in Hertfordshire. This week, she had to grapple with a skeleton, which gave rise to the mysteries haunting the ancient estate. Is the skeleton the body of teenager Sanvi Malakar, who disappeared over forty years ago?
>
> The Countess of Rosemere, until lately the celebrated editor of *Egg and Hen*, a food magazine in the US, landed a hefty inheritance when her mother died three months ago. Rumors say she had no idea. We say, give us a secret inheritance, no matter how devastated the estate or how many skeletons are buried there.

At any rate, the countess has been seen often in the company of the Earl of Marswick, who is mentoring her in the ways of the gentry, along with his very eligible nephew and heir to the Marswick estate, Alexander Barber. Could the two families be planning a dynasty?

David had added,

Thought you'd want to see this. You sound quite glamorous, my dear. I suspect we won't be getting you back, will we?

PS: The strawberry *Ingredients* column was one of your best.

I hit reply. Hesitated, fingers over the keys. Across the center of my palms moved the ghost of Samir's side, his ribs. I closed my eyes.

It was one night. One night.

But in the deepest part of my gut, I knew better. This wasn't a flirtation. I didn't know what it was yet. I didn't know anything about anything, except that maybe I was in love.

Which scared the hell out of me. What if I was only leaping toward him because I was lonely and sad and grieving? What if we woke up six months from now and—

Stop.

I touched the keyboard. Gave it a moment's thought and typed,

I have no answers at the moment, boss. That's the honest truth. I love writing about this place, but there is so much happening, so fast, that I can't make any decisions right now. Just sent Lindsey an article on carrot cake, and I'm going to ask a local to write an *Ingredients* guest column on coriander, if that's all right. If you want to make more formal arrangements on the editorial side, we can talk whenever you like.

xoxo

When I hit send, it felt like taking another step away from my old life, which honestly felt far, far away now. It surprised me, but I'd begun to feel very much at home in this little village. Perhaps it was the pleasure of carrying unearned status or the sense of my ancestors walking the churchyard, but it was undeniable.

A wisp of Samir wove through my memory, his hands on my spine. I blinked, letting it fill me. My body was tired and a little sore. The very best feeling. It chased away the dismay of the article.

Against the wall near the bed was the box of photos we'd found, all those shots of my grandmother and Nandini and the old plantation. Impulsively, I picked up the phone and punched a number.

It wasn't until her voice mail answered, crisp and aloof, that I realized I'd called my mother. "This is Caroline Shaw. Leave a message."

Her voice rocketed through every cell of my body. I hurt everywhere, all at once. But instead of hanging up, as I'd done the other two times I'd made this mistake, I waited for the beep and said, "Hey, Mom. I just had to tell you about all this stuff I found in Violet's room. Did you know about her and Nandini? Crazy and so sad that they had to hide all those years. Decades, I guess." I paused, bending my head more intimately. "I think I met someone, Mom. Wish you could meet him too."

I held the phone in my hand, wondering how long it would take to understand that she was actually dead, how long it would be until my heart wasn't broken anew twenty times a day.

It would help to get all this business with the house settled, and I had no time for grief today. Not that grief ever seemed to care.

I called the accountant back first and left my name and number. Next, I called Jocasta. She answered on the second ring. "Hullo, Olivia! I heard there've been all sorts of things happening. Skeletons, the roof! And I have news from my contacts abroad."

"I have news for you too. I found some paintings in my grandmother's room, all wrapped up very neatly. I think my mother might have left them there."

"Remarkable! Anything interesting? Shall we get them appraised, see what's there?"

"Yes. I brought them to my apartment for safety's sake—there's a window broken in that room. I'll take a look later today, and you can have your person appraise them whenever. She's free in June?"

"We're going to have to move a bit faster than that. I've sent out feelers for someone else."

"All right. I also want to get that room cleared, get it all into storage so that I can go through it. Some of the paintings probably are valuable, but it's the only place in the house that I've found much in the way of personal memorabilia, and I'd like to take my time sorting through it."

"And so you should. Can I send Ian over to film you in the room this afternoon, before we clear it out?"

"Sure. I'll be there doing some other things. He can text me. And I also heard that the skeleton is hundreds of years old, so we're free to continue working. A local archeologist wants to examine the site, but that won't interfere with the renovation." I sipped more coffee, feeling the caffeine start to kick in. My stomach growled. Maybe I had time to get a pastry or two from Helen's bakery before Pavi arrived. "What's your news?"

"A couple of things, actually. We've tracked down your caretakers, who are not nursing a sick mother but enjoying a holiday home on the Black Sea."

"What?"

"I suspect they had no intention of returning. Whatever little gig they were running was over the minute you arrived." Someone murmured to her in the background. "It might be worth following that paper trail."

"Right." I'd talk to the accountant I'd hired about this too. "Thanks."

"The other bit of news is more mystery than answers. My research team has been digging into your uncle's history, and it appears that your uncle never went to India, or he did not return to any of the places he would have been known. He seems to have disappeared the summer of 1977."

A sudden, intense shiver of apprehension zapped the back of my neck. "He must have gone *somewhere*."

"Or he's dead, which would be more likely."

"Dead where, though?"

"That's a very good question." She paused. "I wonder . . . the girl who disappeared. Is it possible they were a love match, and they ran away together?"

I frowned. "It seems unlikely. She was only fifteen."

"Just a thought. We'll keep turning stones over. Maybe he went to America after your mother did."

"If he did, I never met him." The whole thing felt tawdry and depressing.

She must have heard something in my voice, because she said, "Chin up. It'll all be right in the end."

"I hope so. It just feels like one damned thing after another."

Jocasta laughed. "Oh, my dear. It *is*."

Pavi and I mapped out the major placement of the picnic by pacing the lawn, and we made sketches of where the three food trucks would set up. I'd hired a pony for children to ride. Picnic tables would be scattered in the shade of the chestnut trees. There would be booths for face painting and baked goods supplied by the local women's guild. The garden club's plant sale would close the rectangular space: "Looks good," I said. "I'm starting to get excited."

"Me too." She planted her hands on her hips. "You should be proud of yourself, Lady Shaw, for reestablishing an old tradition."

"Let's see how it goes before you congratulate me."

"It will be wonderful—you'll see." She slung a cloth bag over her shoulder diagonally. "Show me the rose gardens, will you? I want to harvest some petals for rosewater."

We walked in the warm sunshine. Steam rose from a field in the distance, and the air was filled with the twittering of dozens of birds hidden in trees and fields. In the pocket of my sundress, my phone buzzed with a text. My heart gave a little jolt, as if I were seventeen, and I tugged it out so eagerly, it got tangled in the fabric of my pocket.

I am useless today, it read. I can only think of your skin.

That very skin flushed as if he were trailing his fingers over it. I swallowed and, slowing to type accurately, wrote, Lips. I can only think of your lips. Kissing you. A thousand times. A million.

Mmm. What would a gathering of kisses be?

A rain of kisses.

There was a long pause. Then, I shall look forward to that rain. I glanced at Pavi. "Sorry." I tucked the phone back in my pocket. "You're blushing," she said.

239

I pressed my hands to my face. "Oh, I think it's just hot."

"Not particularly."

I couldn't look at her and kept walking, not at all sure what exactly I should do. Say.

"So," she said, "you and Samir?"

"Hmm?"

"I have eyes. I saw you in the parking lot the other day. You were both practically on fire."

"We were?"

"Incandescent," she said. "And he didn't come for dinner last night."

We entered the garden, and the smell of roses hung in the warm air, spicy and sweet. One tall white blossom, a little past its peak, offered a perfume of oranges. I touched the delicate petals, plucked one to rub between my fingers, thinking of our fingertips, mine and Samir's, touching in the car. It made me very slightly dizzy.

"He's . . ." A vision of his mouth, his way of teasing me ever so gently, his clarity of thinking, moved through me, and I touched my belly, wordless.

She only reached for my hand and held it for a moment. Her face was so much like her brother's that I loved it just for that, and then I wondered if I loved his face, too, because it made me think of hers. "Just know that people won't like it."

"People?"

"The village. In general." She moved her hand over my knuckles. "The earl in particular." She knew he'd been mentoring me.

"Well, he wants to marry me off to his nephew, so . . ."

Pavi laughed. "Dynasties." She didn't let go. "My mother is going to be here soon."

"Samir said she was coming." I took a breath. "She won't like me?"

"No, not for him."

I bent my head, suddenly embarrassed, seeing myself through a mother's eyes—the older woman. Mrs. Robinson. "I hardly know what to think. It's all brand-new," I whispered.

"Not really," she said. "It's been there since you arrived."

I thought of the very first day, when he'd showed me through the house. Had I known then? "I've never met anyone like him."

She smiled, and in this the siblings were different. Where Samir's grin was wide and open, her smile made of her mouth a pursed heart. "Good response." She patted my hand and released me, then briskly produced a thin net bag and a pair of scissors. "Let's find the very most aromatic of all the roses."

I laughed. "What a luscious task! How do you make the rosewater? And what do you use it for?"

"Haven't you explored it?"

"Not really. I might have come across it in a recipe or two, but I haven't made any study of it yet." I smelled a bright-red bloom and found it disappointingly bland. "This has a pretty color but no scent."

"You'll want to write about rosewater," she said with her customary confidence.

"I'll give it some thought," I said. "But that reminds me—I've been wondering if you would want to write one on coriander? A guest column for the magazine."

She halted, eyes wide. "Are you fucking with me?"

"No! Why would I do that?"

"Oh my God! Yes, yes, yes!" She did a little dance, then halted, frowning. "You're not doing this because of Samir, are you?"

"No!" I touched my heart, held up my right hand. "I swear. I've thought about it several times. I just remembered to ask you."

She lifted one perfectly arched brow. "Okay. I'd love to. Though truthfully, I would have done it even if you were."

"Good. I'll send you an email on word count and tone, though I'm sure you've read plenty of them."

"Every single one."

We ambled through the roses, Pavi a few steps ahead of me. The rows between bushes were overgrown with grass and wildflowers, but many—most—of the roses were healthy enough.

"I can't get over how many of them are still alive. No one has tended this garden for forty years."

"Someone must have taken care of them sometimes. You see they've been pruned now and then, and—oh, look!"

Gliding through the garden was a peacock. It might even have been the same one I'd seen before, with a tall crown and gorgeous deep-blue chest. Arrogantly, he turned his face away from us, as if we were below his notice, and called out to the forest. From the trees came an answer, and he strutted off, king of his domain. "They are so beautiful." Pavi sighed.

"Samir told me there is a flock that lives in the forest."

"Roses and peacocks. It's like the setting for a fairy tale."

I looked around. "It's going to take more than a kiss to save this place." I thought of the single rose blooming into the parlor when Samir and I had first walked through. "But it does feel sometimes like it's under an enchantment."

One tall rose drew my eye, a castle atop a small hill, with tangles of white damask roses around it, as if on guard. The rose was orange and yellow with touches of pink, and I recognized it immediately from a hundred of my mother's paintings. It seemed larger than others of the same type, as haughty as the peacock, and I rounded the overgrown white roses to see if I could find a way in.

Pavi, however, was enchanted by the damasks. "These are prime," she cried, burying her nose in a mass of them. "The perfect flower for rosewater. It will be clear and very, very fragrant."

"Look at the size of that!" I cocked my head at the peach-colored rose. "I always thought she was exaggerating."

"You lost me."

"My mother painted this rose. Over and over. Let me borrow your shears, will you? I want to cut some and take them back with me."

"I'll do it. I have the gloves."

As she cut a passageway through the thicket of white roses, I picked up the branches she'd dropped. When I could get through, carefully, I bent my head to the giant blossoms and reared back. It had a strange, feral scent. "I'm not sure I like this one."

But I found the first bracket of five leaves, as my mother had taught me, and clipped a blossom, then another, reaching back to hand them to Pavi. As I handed her the last one, I caught my arm on a thorn, opening a long scratch that immediately beaded up with bright-red blood.

"Ooh, careful," Pavi teased. "Don't want to fall asleep for a hundred years!"

"No worries." It stung a bit, and I let it bleed a bit to get any bacteria out, and anyway, I wanted to trim a couple of canes away while I had a chance. Reaching down over the white roses, I said, "Don't do anything with it yet. I want to shoot some photos so I can reference the paintings later."

"It's visually very appealing, isn't it?" She held it in her hands, took a big sniff, and said, "That's a strange one. I don't think I like it either."

"Probably bred for size, and that threw something off." I pruned the bush and then straightened, looking around at the view from this slightly higher spot. The house was clearly visible, the back windows that would have once been my mother's room, the tumbledown wall that had just fallen into the ballroom. As I turned, I could see the abbey and the first of the fields. "Gorgeous spot. I should make a note of it and ask for a bench here."

"It reminds me a bit of Sissinghurst. Have you been there?"

"No."

"You might like to visit as you're going through the renovations."

"Which reminds me—the cameraman is coming back to go through Violet's room with me. Do you want to come?"

She shook her head. "I hated that room, even when we were kids."

"Really? There's so much stuff in there!"

"It's sad. The way they just left her things."

I thought of the photos, what we had discovered about Violet and Nandini, pushed it away so she wouldn't see anything on my face. "It's all good. Thanks for your help this morning."

"I'll walk back with you. I have plenty of rose petals." She opened the canvas bag to show me a pillowcase's worth of white petals. "These are very nice. I'll make you some rosewater toner."

"What does it do?"

"It's very good for the complexion."

As we walked back up the road toward the house, a woman carrying a woven basket met us at the junction to the cottages. She was tall and redheaded, wearing jeans and red-flowered wellies. "Hullo, Olivia," she said. "I don't know if you'll remember me—"

Smoothly, I said, "Of course I do, Elizabeth." She was one of the tenants I'd visited on the earl's instruction. "How could I forget your rhubarb crumble?"

"Thank you." She blushed slightly across her freckled cheeks. "I saw you walking to the roses earlier and waited for you to come back. We have a bumper crop of asparagus this year, and you said you'd been pining for your own cooking. I thought you might enjoy some."

I poked my head into the basket and made a low noise of approval. "Pavi, look at these." The spears were thick as my thumb, perfectly pointed. We both sighed. "Pavi runs Coriander, the Indian-fusion restaurant in town."

"Oh, we love it. The mulligatawny is one of my husband's favorite things."

"Thank you." Pavi took an asparagus out of the basket, admiring it, then biting into it. "These are fantastic. Would you sell them?"

Elizabeth's mouth turned down. "Not today, but tomorrow I'll have more. How many could you use?"

"How many will you sell? I'm an asparagus fanatic, and the season—the true season—is very short."

"Would you like a look at the garden? I have to admit I'm quite proud of it. When I married Joseph, it was sorely neglected, and I've brought it back to health."

"Yes! I'd love to!"

"I'm afraid I have to meet the cameraman," I said, holding the basket close. "Thank you, Elizabeth."

As I carried the basket up the hill, I was imagining a dozen ways I might use the asparagus to feed Samir, blissfully unaware of everything that would come between us and those exquisite spears.

Chapter Eighteen

Along with the camera crew—who filmed the site of the abbey where the excavation was ongoing, then joined me in the house—Jocasta had sent movers. I directed them to organize and pack everything in a way that would make it easier for me to review later. The paintings were taken down and carefully wrapped for storage with the other possibly valuable items from the first round of clearing. I looked at each one as it was removed from the wall, but there were no more messages. I hadn't expected there to be.

By two, Ian was finished filming and dropped me off at my flat. Sunshine poured in the back windows, making the rooms stuffy, and I settled everything on the wooden kitchen table and opened the windows to let in the breeze. Below, in the garden, the Chinese woman who ran the fish-and-chips shop was leading a group in tai chi. The sight of them, all dressed in easy clothes, some barefoot, moving with deliberation, calmed something in me, and I actually let go of a breath.

I told myself I needed to get back to yoga, but I was already thinking about the asparagus and what to pair it with. Asparagus and peas and . . . lamb, of course, with fresh herbs and new potatoes. Kicking off my shoes, I started making a list in my head of all the ingredients I'd need to pick up from the market.

The place had come furnished, but I hadn't done much serious cooking yet. The cupboard yielded a heavy skillet and one medium-sized pan, but when I tested to see if they'd both fit on the tiny stove, the answer was no. I'd have to cook in shifts.

And for one moment, I imagined what it would be like to cook on the AGA in the kitchen at Rosemere. What if the kitchen wasn't a commercial kitchen at all but filled with a big wooden table and lots of cupboards, and I opened up the back wall to french doors that looked out over the fields? What if it was my kitchen, and my friends came in to eat there, and we drank wine and watched the sunset? What if I had a family gathered around a big farmhouse table?

The vision pierced me. All at once, I realized maybe it *could* be a home eventually. Maybe not all of it—who wanted to live in thirty-seven rooms?—but some big portions of it. It excited me, and I thought suddenly of my friend Renate, a designer who had moved to New York three years ago, breaking my friendship heart. We were still friends, but coast-to-coast friendships were never the same. She would love the idea of transforming those ancient spaces into a welcoming, comfortable place. I would have to remember to email her.

Suddenly, there were too many things to remember. I was juggling so many ideas that I was getting dizzy with it. It was the way my mind worked—a thousand tasks spinning at once—but when it got to this point, I needed to get lists going. Carrying my dry-erase marker over to the board on the wall, I made a to-do list. I knew people who used digital tools, but I needed to have them in the physical world. The tasks were more manageable when I just looked at them in a tidy row:

- Send Renate an email
- Market: lamb, butter, potatoes, peas, rosemary, good salt
- Next clue in treasure hunt. Paintings?

Smiling, I then added,

- Have wild sex with Samir as often as possible

I surrounded this with spirals and hearts. It turned out that falling in love at thirty-nine was just as heady as it had been at nineteen and twenty-nine. I found myself drawing his face: those heavy brows; the straight, bold nose; his lush mouth; the suggestion of his tumbling hair, all in orange dry-erase marker.

For no reason, for every reason, I laughed, capped the pen, and went off to the market to gather supper.

I did my shopping, then stopped in at Haver's office. Mrs. Wells was there at her desk, and she looked instantly on guard when I came in. Coolly, she said, "I'm afraid he isn't in."

"That's fine. I just wanted to be sure you had all the permissions you need to release the files to the accountant I hired."

"We have the information," she said stiffly, moving a piece of paper on her desk. "Thank you."

She turned her attention to the computer. When I stood there a little longer, she deigned to look at me. "Is there anything else?"

"There's no judgment on the firm, Mrs. Wells. I am just not an expert on any of this, and I need some help understanding what is going on with the estate."

"It's none of my concern," she said, typing something.

"No, it isn't," I said, "but I had hoped we could be polite to one another."

"Of course," she said and dropped her hands on her lap. "What else can I do for you?"

"Do you know when Mr. Haver will be back?"

"He's gone to Mallorca on holiday. It will be a few weeks."

"Weeks," I said. "I assume he left the contact information for the banks?"

"Yes." Wordlessly, she flipped through a file and brought out a single sheaf of paper.

"Thank you." I tucked it into my shoulder bag. "See you soon, I guess."

"Or perhaps you'll find everything you need in the next village over." She pushed up her glasses and focused on the screen.

Ah. A faux pas. I should have found an accountant in Saint Ives Cross. I nodded, creasing the paper. "I'm sure I'll find everything I need right here. Thank you, Mrs. Wells."

Out in the still-warm day, I told myself it was a good lesson. No matter how I felt about Haver, I had nothing against Mrs. Wells, and I was sorry I'd hurt her feelings.

But it was annoying that Haver was out of town. I had a lot of questions, and now it would be that much longer before I could get the answers. In the meantime, I needed to move the accounts to my own control, and I would do that in the morning. Something else to add to my to-do list.

Just now, however, the sun was warm on my arms, and I had a lovely meal I looked forward to cooking. Even the challenges of the tiny stove and limited tools would be fun. A man passed me, and I realized he was a regular at the pub. "Good afternoon," I said.

He tipped his hat with a little bow.

I had planned to pick up some little something for dessert at the bakery, but of course, it closed at 1:00 p.m., or whenever they ran out of goods for the day. No matter.

With my bag on my arm, I slowed to text Samir: I hope you're very hungry. I am so happy to cook! It's been ages.

I thought it might take a while for a response, but it came through almost immediately. Oh, yeah. I'm famished, all right.

I stopped to text more easily, the bag swinging on my wrist. When will you be finished?

I'm just feeding my cat. Do you want me to bring anything?

Kisses. I smiled as I sent the text.

At the doorway to the stairs, I paused to scramble for my keys, always lost in the bottom of my bag no matter how often I tried to create a system of pockets for things. I opened the door and skipped up the stairs to my door. It took a moment to unlock it, as always, because the key was old, but eventually, it turned, and I dropped the bag on the counter.

"Well, hello, Countess."

I practically jumped out of my skin, shaken out of my dreamworld by a voice that was totally out of context. Grant stood like a surly giant on the stairs, his hair greasy and tousled, along with his clothes, which looked as if he'd slept in them. He probably had. It was a long trip from San Francisco to London.

"What are you doing here?"

"Just thought I'd come see for myself what you'd inherited."

I moved to close the door, suddenly aware of the paintings stacked like gold bricks against the wall. He'd know exactly what they were. "I am not going to talk to you without a lawyer."

His flat palm and a carefully placed foot kept the door from closing. "C'mon, Olivia. I never thought you'd be this person, all materialistic and shit. We were good together, and if the situation were reversed, I'd do the right thing."

"I'm doing what's right." I looked up and shrugged. "Which I already told you. I don't know why you came all this way."

He tossed his hair out of his eyes. "Just let me talk to you for five minutes, will you?"

"What is there to talk about? We broke up. I'm finished." I fingered my phone in my pocket, wondering if I should call the police.

"Did you break up because of all this?" He gestured toward the town and consciously or unconsciously toward Rosemere. "I had the driver take me by the estate, and it's a fucking castle! Did you think I wouldn't live up to some class standard?"

"That's ridiculous."

He looked over my shoulder. "More of your mother's paintings?"

"None of your business."

The proprietor of the shop, my landlady, stepped out on the landing, her tiny arms folded over her chest. "Everything okay here?"

"It's fine, Mrs. Su."

"We're old friends," Grant said over his shoulder. "Nothing to worry about."

She stayed put, and I was grateful.

Another foot on the narrow stairs made Grant turn. I peered around the door and saw Samir, freshly showered and wearing a linen shirt the color of new leaves. Despite the tension of the moment, I felt a surge of lust over the glow of his skin, the curve of his mouth. "Sorry to keep you waiting, Olivia," he said in crisp British, the crispest I'd ever heard from him. "Are you ready to go?"

I leapt at the manufactured excuse to escape. "Sure." My hands were shaking a little as I moved to close my door.

Smoothly, Samir said, "Hello. Samir Malakar."

"Samir, this is my ex-boyfriend Grant. I've told you about him."

"Nice, Olivia," Grant spat out. "Jesus Christ."

Had he always been so crude? It had never seemed like it before, but maybe England was changing me.

"You go now," Mrs. Su said to Grant.

He eyed her. "I don't need directions from the landlady."

"Go, Grant. I have nothing to say."

For one more minute, he stood stubbornly on the stairs, looking from me to Samir and back. "This is your boy toy, huh? He gets the money, and you get hot young cock."

My ears went bright red. "You need to leave, or I'm going to call the police."

He laughed in an exaggerated way. "Fine. I'll see you in court."

He headed down the stairs, and Samir stepped sideways into an alcove to allow it. I half expected Grant to throw an elbow, but he only glared.

Samir came up, touched Mrs. Su's arm. "Thank you."

"I don't like him."

I looked up at Samir. "We have to get all the paintings out of here."

"Yeah, we will," he said and closed the door to the apartment. "Are you all right? He was pretty nasty."

"I'm fine." The green shirt was open at the throat, and I swayed forward as if drawn by a magnet to kiss the hollow there.

"I was charged with bringing kisses," he said. Swinging me around to press my back against the wall, he leaned in and kissed me, and I met it eagerly, opening to his tongue, running my hands under his shirt, over his smooth, muscular back. In seconds we were lost.

Over my lips, he said, "All I have thought about all day is this." His hands ran down my sides, pulled up my hem, skimmed my thighs. "I have had so many fantasies about this dress," he said and pressed into me.

"What kind of fantasies?" I breathed.

"This," he said and, with a single movement, pulled the two sides of the V neckline apart, revealing my breasts in a lacy little bra I'd known he would see. "Oh, yeah, this," he said and kissed my throat, my breasts, then my mouth.

I was already on fire, unfastening his jeans, shoving them off, and he was pulling up my skirt, yanking down my panties, and then we were tangled, deep, tongues and hands and legs and everything.

When we were finished, panting, me leaning on the wall, he touched his forehead to mine. "I've lost my mind over you, Olivia."

"Me too." I kissed him again, ran my hands over his lower back.

We didn't get to the lamb chops.

Later, we raided the kitchen for apples and cheese and opened beers. "You think your mother's next clue will be among these paintings?" Samir asked, settling cross-legged on the floor. His feet were bare.

"Maybe. It's my next best guess."

"All right. Let's take a look at what's here. Then we can take them over to the space above Coriander until tomorrow."

I nodded, worrying again about Grant coming back. "The earl warned me that people would be coming after a piece of the pie. I didn't think one of them would be Grant."

Samir said, "You don't believe you have to worry about me, do you?"

I didn't know what he was talking about at first. "Worry?"

"That I'm a fortune hunter."

"Well, it would help if I had a fortune." I wiped my fingers on a napkin. "I suppose I could be worried that you're after my Starbucks card, but then again, you'd have to drive to London to use it."

"Starbuck's card?" He paused. "Is it a credit card?"

"Oh, honey, no. It's a rewards card. You get stars every time you use it to pay or order or whatever. You preload it with money, and then it makes everything go faster."

He tucked his lower lip under his upper. Raised a brow. "That's a thing?"

"Yes," I said very seriously and leaned close to whisper. "You can get *free coffee*."

He shook his head. "Americans."

I grinned. The paper on the painting was loose, and he made an exaggerated examination of his hands, then held one up. I nodded, and he tore the paper away.

We both sucked in our breath at the exact same instant. It was a small, exquisite painting rendered in oils, unmistakably Monet.

Samir said, "Do you think it's real?"

My heart was pounding. I reached for the painting, holding it up. "I have no idea, but it's brilliant, isn't it?"

"Yes. We should see what else there is."

I picked up the plate of cheese and apples. "Let's wash our hands."

"Good idea."

In the end, most of the paintings were clearly important, but I didn't recognize any others as priceless. One other kept nagging me. "This might be Constable," I said. "That's a Constable kind of sky, for sure."

"I don't know that leaving these with Pavi is the best idea," Samir said. "She would take good care of them, but God, what if there was a fire or some such thing?"

"Right. It might be hard to tell the insurance company that we had a painting worth millions in the lot." I stood up, looking at the paintings all in a line. "I don't know what the clue in the bedroom was, though, unless the photos were the clue."

"But why lead us to the paintings?"

I tapped my nose with my index finger, thinking. Looking at them all in a row. "Maybe just for the money they'd bring. Or she wanted them safeguarded."

"So she left them wrapped up in a crumbling manor house for God knows how long?" He scowled. "That makes no sense at all."

"I don't think it was very long," I said. "Maybe only a few months. I'm starting to think she might have had an illness she didn't tell me about." I shifted angles, looking at the assembled artwork from another position. "She smoked for fifty years. Her lungs were crap."

"I'm sorry, Olivia."

"Thank you."

"But even if she was ill, why do it this way?"

"She loved treasure hunts." I shrugged, picked up one painting, and traded it with another without much thought. My hands moved without my brain, until I'd rearranged all of them into a rainbow—which was perfectly filled out.

My throat closed with pain, with the severity of missing her, the sweetness of this gesture. The work it must have taken. "I used to do this in her studio when I was a little girl. Move the paintings into making the colors of a rainbow. It almost never works this perfectly." I pointed: red, orange, yellow, green, blue, indigo, violet. "Roy G. Biv." The red was another of the series from the pasha and the harem girl, and each painting moved through the spectrum in exactly the right hue. The Monet, real or copied, was the violet.

Samir started shooting photos. "There might be something in the artists' names or the subjects." He shot the entire line as a panorama, then each one in turn. "Do you know who all of the artists are?"

"No. We can probably run an image search on Google."

He tucked the phone back in his pocket and stretched his legs out, hands behind him, studying the paintings. I captured the image of him in my memory—the beautiful hands, his long body, his grace. He was utterly comfortable with himself, something that was very rare. It was true of Pavi too—she was exactly herself. It must have been some aspect of the way they had been raised. Mother or father? I would be curious to see.

"They're all exactly the same size," Samir said slowly, "and exactly the right hue. There must have been a lot more paintings to choose from."

The knowledge sank in. "All of them. All of the paintings from the house. She stashed them. But where?" My head was starting to hurt with figuring it out, and I was getting very hungry. "It's too late for the supper I'd planned to cook, but we both need to eat."

He hopped up and flung his arms around me from behind. "I'm so sorry, Olivia. You've been looking forward to cooking, and I ruined it."

I laughed, pointing toward the dry-erase board, where I'd drawn his portrait. "You helped me with another goal, so it's all right." I leaned backward into him. "We do need to eat, and we need to figure out what to do with the paintings. I don't want to leave them."

"You live right next to a fish-and-chips shop. One of the better ones around, actually, which is why there is a line of cars to the motorway every Friday night."

"Well, then, let's have fish-and-chips and figure this out."

Chapter Nineteen

In the end, we hashed out a midway solution—we borrowed Pavi's van, loaded the paintings up, and drove them to Marswick Hall. It was after dark when we arrived, and I assumed we might not see the earl, but he met us by the servant's entrance, using only his cane. "Hello, hello!" He wore a crisp striped shirt and slacks and his usual orthopedic shoes. His color was good.

"Lord Barber, this is Samir Malakar. He's been helping me with just about everything in the house. Samir, Lord Barber, the Earl of Marswick."

"Good to meet you, lad. Olivia has spoken highly of you."

I had? I didn't remember that.

"Let's see this haul, shall we?"

Four young men from the estate carried the paintings inside to a room I'd never visited. It was long and dark, with lamps offering feeble light against the shadows. The walls were hung cheek by jowl with paintings of all eras and sizes.

"They'll be safe here until you get them appraised," George said, gesturing to the carriers to line them up at waist height along a massive sideboard. Most of them fit on the ledge. The others were lined up below, against the footers. "Gerald, see to more light, will you, please?" he said to one of the young men.

As I looked at them side by side like this again, something bothered me. I narrowed my eyes. What was I missing?

When the lights came on, the paintings were more dazzling than they'd seemed in my small rooms. George made an approving noise, limping forward to look at each one closely. "The frames are gone, but these paintings hung in the library and study of Rosemere." With his cane, he pointed to the clouds I had thought were Constable and confirmed it. "Constable, and the Monet. This is an early effort by Wootton. And this is a portrait of your uncle Roger." He shook his head, staring at a light-infused portrait of a very handsome young man, maybe twenty, with piercing eyes and a dissolute mouth. "The women loved him, they did. Fools. Something happened to the lad in India— that's always been my theory." He turned. "Anyway. They're safe here for now."

"Thank you, George."

"Of course. Will you be to luncheon on Wednesday?"

"Wouldn't miss it for the world." I stepped up to give him a kiss on the cheek, as I always did, but he caught my elbow.

"Will you spare a moment for an old man?"

"Of course." I glanced over my shoulder to see Samir looking around slowly. Taking it in. I realized that I knew he was cataloguing the paintings, the details of the room—click, click, click—as every writer did in an unfamiliar world.

An image rose in my mind: that stack of pages on his desk, revealed by the bright moon.

"Samir, I'll be right back."

"I'll wait outside."

"That isn't necessary," George said. "It will only be a moment."

I followed his shuffling steps into the study, where he took an envelope out of the desk. "Your mother said if you found the paintings, you were to have this."

My throat tightened. "If I found the paintings?"

He nodded.

The envelope was brown paper, and I could feel something hard inside. Ripping it open, hoping for a letter or note, I found only a plain brass key. It might have gone to anything and had no identifying marks. "This is it? Nothing else?"

"No." He sat down in his chair, hands piled one atop the other on the handle of his cane.

"She came to England," I said, staring at the key.

"Yes. She came to see me last summer."

"So she knew she was dying."

"Yes."

"Did she say what she was dying of?"

"No. Cancer, one gathers."

Of course. She would never have told me she had a terminal disease, and pneumonia often carried off a cancer patient. I nodded, staring at the key. "I don't suppose she told you why she set up this long, crazy treasure hunt rather than just telling me about all of it?"

His smile was bittersweet. "I'm sorry, my dear; she did not. I reckon you'll find out soon enough."

I sighed, suddenly extremely tired. "All right. Thank you." I bent and kissed his cheek. "See you on Wednesday."

As I straightened, he said, "Isn't your young man the one who wrote a novel, from Saint Ives Cross?"

"Yes."

"I read about him. Seems a smart fellow. But you know, you'll need someone to help you with Rosemere."

I smiled fondly. "I know. You want me to marry your nephew, but I'm afraid I'm too American for that plan."

"Very well. Remember your position—that's all."

"I'll do my best." Carrying the key tightly, I headed back to the library.

"You're going to have to tell me about your book," I said when I found Samir. "Everyone knows about it except me."

"Who knows?"

"The earl. Peter, the driver, the other day. He said you were famous."

"Clearly, that is not true."

"Still," I said.

"I noticed something while you were in there." He drew me toward the paintings. "They're all the same size. Exactly."

I closed my eyes, recognizing the truth. "That's what was bothering me too." With a sigh, I crossed the room and picked two of them up, turned them over. The canvases had been aged and weathered, but in an eerily similar fashion. "They're copies."

"All of them?"

"I don't know." We reached for the paintings and turned them over one at a time. Out of the lot of fourteen, three were clearly copies. The rest appeared to be original, but they would have to be evaluated.

"Do you think your mother did the copies?"

I shrugged. "I doubt it very much. She wouldn't do this kind of thing, and anyway, she was pretty feverishly working on a project of her own the past year." Suddenly aware of the butler waiting by the door, I said, "We should go."

We walked out to the van.

He opened my door, quiet. Around us, the night sang its own song, crickets in the shrubs and water running somewhere far away. An owl hooted at the moon.

"You can read it," he said. "I told you that before."

"No. Not until you give it to me." I swung my feet into the van. "I can wait."

He didn't say anything else, just came around and climbed in and started the engine. For a long moment, he sat in the dark with his hands on the steering wheel.

"Is something wrong?"

That same bright moon from the night before poured cold light through the windscreen. "It's just . . . that room. All those paintings. All that time and history. That's your world now."

"Not exactly."

"It is, Olivia. And the fact remains that our social classes are vastly different."

"Don't," I said, and to emphasize my point, I covered his mouth with my fingers. "Let's just be us. Let it be." I took my hand away. "Okay?"

He captured my fingers. "We're tired. Let's go to sleep, shall we?"

"Side by side?"

"Yes." He shifted, pulling out of the drive. "What did the earl want?"

I opened my hand. "My mother left me a key."

I dreamed of roses, thousands and thousands of roses, and one gigantic orange-and-peach beauty tumbling through the air. I woke up, confused about where I was. A cat on my feet padded up to my face when he realized I was awake.

Samir's house. His bed. He was not next to me, so I cuddled Billi, kissing his head, talking to him softly. The image of the roses tumbling through the sky wafted back through my mind. What had that rose represented to my mother? She loved them, all roses, honestly, and now I understood a little more of that piece of her. But that particular rose showed up in her paintings much more often than others. Did it have some special meaning?

The whole crazy day wove in and out of my mind as I dozed, half waiting for Samir to come back. I thought about Grant and about the tenant who had given me asparagus, Pavi telling me her mother would not approve of Samir and me, the roses, the bedroom.

And that key.

I'd shared with Samir everything the earl had said—my mother's illness, her trip to England last summer—as we drove back from Marswick Hall to Saint Ives Cross, enveloped in the night, music playing on the radio. We didn't try to solve any puzzles, just let them be, and I realized we were both exhausted. It had been a very long day.

"You should let me cook tomorrow night," I said. "One of the tenants gave me the most beautiful asparagus, and I bought peas and lamb chops to go with them." As the words tumbled out of my mouth, I worried that they sounded too domestic and started to qualify them. "I mean, it's just—"

But Samir covered my wrist with his hand. "I'm sorry your meal was interrupted by so much. It sounds brilliant." His thumb moved on my inner arm. "Why don't you bring the food to my house? It will be more comfortable to cook there."

"Thank you." I turned my head. "Pavi mentioned that you didn't show up for dinner last night. Will you tell her that I'm cooking?"

"Does she know?" He gave me a quick glance. "About us?"

"She was there when you texted."

He nodded, and I couldn't quite tell if he was displeased.

"Is there something wrong? I thought you said she'd know anyway." I started to take my hand away, adding, "I wouldn't like lying to her. She's my friend."

He caught my hand before I could pull away. "I don't want you to lie."

"Then what?"

"It's just new, this thing between us. Precious." He kept his eyes on the road but lifted my hand to press my palm to his mouth, to his cheek. "I don't want anything to ruin it."

A heady surge of emotion moved in me, in my belly, my chest, my throat. "Me either, Samir. I mean it."

He settled my hand over his heart and, holding it there, looked at me. I nodded.

Now, curled up in his bed with his cat, I wondered what he was doing that kept him out of bed so long, and wearing the T-shirt he'd given me, I padded out of the bedroom and saw the light on in his study. The door was cracked slightly, allowing a bar of light to fall across the wooden floor. "Samir?"

He came to the door wearing sweats and a worn sweater and a pair of horn-rimmed glasses that only made him look more amazing. He said, "So sorry. I didn't mean to wake you. I just couldn't sleep, and—"

"It's all right. I'll go back to bed." I stepped close to give him a kiss. He caught my arm and then turned to push the door open.

"You may as well know that I'm in here writing."

I nodded. "I saw the big stack of paper last night."

"It's not another novel like the ones in the living room." He took off his glasses, tossed them on the desk, and turned to pluck a paperback from the shelf. He placed it in my hands.

The cover showed a starry sky with a trio of moons, two people standing in the foreground, faces upturned. *Moons of Vara*, the title read, by Sam Malak. "You wrote this? You write science fiction now?"

His arms were crossed over his chest. He nodded.

"How many have you written?" I turned the book over to read the copy, and it had a thoughtful, alien discovery tone. "I wonder if my boss has read you. He loves this kind of book."

His defenses were still in place, cloaking his expression. "I've written six, in two different series." He shrugged. "They're . . . somewhat popular."

"Can I read this one?" I held it to my chest.

He smiled slowly. "If you like."

"I want to read all of your books, Samir. I want to see how your mind works."

"It's not embarrassing? That I'm writing genre instead of literary fiction?"

I gave him a look. "I love to read, and honestly, who cares what category it is? A good book is a good book."

He caught my face, kissed me, and then just stood there with his forehead against mine for a moment. "I am so happy we met."

"Me too." I closed my eyes and breathed in his scent. "I'm going to take this back to bed and read it and let you keep working."

"Sure you don't mind? I wouldn't, but I have a deadline, and I've been spending a lot of time with a certain buxom beauty."

"Buxom, is she?"

He cupped a breast. "Indeed."

I stood on my toes and kissed him one more time. "You know where to find me."

In the morning, I walked home across the village green, a carrier bag full of Samir's novels, both the science fiction series and the first three. He said not to give him book reports, and I promised I wouldn't, but I also felt that he was allowing me the history of his literary self.

Aware of my grumbling tummy, I stopped in at the bakery to pick up a loaf of bread for later and a pastry for my breakfast. It was just after the morning commuter rush, and the line was only ten minutes long. I checked my phone as I waited.

There were a lot of emails and voice mails. I would listen to the voice mails at home, but I scrolled through the emails as I stood in line. Another note from Grant, which I didn't open; one from my accountant containing figures I wouldn't be able to read on the phone; and one from my Realtor, asking if there'd been any change.

My mood, so light and airy when I'd left Samir, started to fold in on itself as real-world obligations and problems began shoving their way in. I thought of Grant, threatening me yesterday, and wondered if I ought to just let it go, let him have the money.

The bell rang over the door, and I glanced up idly to see Pavi, wearing a pair of jeans and a bright peasant blouse with embroidery along the neckline. Behind her was a woman in a turquoise kurta, the hem of the tunic embroidered with darker thread and a border of silver. Her hair was cut into a thick, straight pageboy, and she wasn't as old as I'd imagined—maybe late fifties.

Their mother. My stomach dropped.

Pavi caught my eye and gave me a very slight shake of her head. I turned away, glad to step up to the counter and place my order. Helen spied me through the window to the kitchen and gave a vigorous wave but held up her flour-covered hands to illustrate why she could not come out. I shook my head, waved.

Don't look at Pavi, I thought as I took my place in the group waiting for goods. I held my phone in my palm, and my head was directed that way, but out of the corner of my eye, I couldn't stop trying to capture more glimpses of her. She moved stiffly, and her hands were slightly misshapen, and I remembered that she had rheumatoid arthritis. Other than that, she was youthful, her face unlined, no gray in her hair.

When the girl behind the counter called out my order, I picked it up and planned to hurry out, but Pavi caught me. "Olivia! I didn't see you there. Come, meet my mother, here from India for her summer visit."

"Oh, hello. How nice to see you," I said, coming over.

I held out my hand as Pavi said, "Ma, this is Olivia Shaw, the Countess of Rosemere. Olivia, this is my mother, Mrs. Malakar."

She grasped my hand with a firm grip despite the twisting fingers. "How do you do."

"It's wonderful to meet you," I said. "Your family has been very kind to me since my arrival."

Her face showed little expression, as if she were wearing a mother-shaped mask with a shimmer for eyes. I felt my skin was marked with

Samir's touch, covering me over with fluorescent streaks, his scent imprinted over my own. How could a mother avoid knowing? Feeling slightly panicked, I turned to Pavi. "How were the asparagus, Pavi?"

"I'll get them today."

"That's right."

"Did you cook yours?"

"No, so many things happened. I'll have to tell you later." I touched her arm, gave it a squeeze, and started to split off.

"Are you a fan of Samir's work?" Mrs. Malakar asked.

I flushed, even as I tried to keep my cool, and glanced at the open top of my bag, where the books showed all too plainly.

Game on. I took a breath. Met her eyes. "I don't know, but I'm looking forward to finding out."

This time, I could read the expression just fine. It was disdain.

I had too many phone calls to return and emails to answer to spend much time brooding over Samir's mother. I called the accountant, who returned my phone call within minutes. Not a great sign. "Lady Shaw," he said formally. "I'm afraid I have a bit of bad news."

I sat down, legal pad in front of me. "Go ahead."

"We've reviewed the accounts you gave us access to, and unfortunately, aside from the current income from the rents and whatever the estate generates, there's not so much as a farthing in any of them."

Farthing, I thought, my brain frozen. Who used a word like *farthing*? "I don't understand. Money has been fed into those accounts for nearly forty years. I had a feeling the India monies were gone, but what about all the rents for all those years? What about the investments and—"

"Gone." He cleared his throat. "It has been slowly stolen for more than a decade. It's unclear who was in charge, but I rather suspect that your caretakers and Mr. Haver were in collusion."

I moved my head, trying to loosen my neck. "Haver's gone. I went by his office yesterday, and he's supposedly on vacation in Mallorca."

"Skipped town, more like."

For a long moment, I said nothing, trying desperately to gather my thoughts. I'd had my suspicions, of course, but the realization that he'd out and out cheated me landed in my gut like a hot coal. That bastard! "What are my options, then? I'd like to recoup the money, but failing that, what are my prosecution options? Can I just call the police?"

"Of course. But I'll handle that on your behalf, as your accountant of record. No need for you to involve yourself in all the messy details." He paused. "I most sincerely doubt you'll recoup any of the money. Best to plan on simply moving forward from here."

"Move forward," I echoed.

"You've still got the rents, which appear to average between five and seven thousand pounds per month, a quite tidy sum, and I gather you've other income. I'm happy to help you in any way I can."

"Thank you. I really am so grateful. Please do what you can to bring the thieves to justice. In the meantime, I'll see what I can do from my end."

I hung up, my gut burning with this new betrayal.

And loss. If the accounts here had been drained, I would have to find money somewhere else. It was possible the copied paintings could lead to something, but I couldn't count on it.

In the meantime, I was left only with the money from the sale of my mother's house in West Menlo Park. I stood up and paced to the window, looking down at the high street, which was coming to life in the sunny morning, women out in flowered dresses, men in their shirtsleeves.

Impulsively, I dialed the hotel. Sarah answered, and I said, "Hello, Sarah. Olivia Shaw here. Do you have a guest by the name of Grant Kazlauskas by any chance?"

"We do. Is he a friend of yours?"

"Not exactly."

"I'm relieved. He's not a particularly nice man, is he?"

"No," I said, wondering how I'd missed that fact for so long. Or maybe he once had been nice and now had soured. "Thanks, Sarah."

I took a moment to email my mother's agent, asking for digital copies of her entire body of work, or as much as she had, then jumped in the shower and dressed in an outfit I knew Grant particularly liked, a thin white linen blouse from Anthropologie over a lacy chemise and a pair of jeans that were just slightly too tight, although they hadn't been when I'd worn them last.

That particular recognition didn't do a lot for my confidence. And as I looked in the speckled bathroom mirror of the sad little flat I'd rented, what I saw was a nearly forty-year-old woman with emerging crow's-feet and an expanding ass who'd bitten off more than she could chew.

But my mother had wanted me here. Of all the humans in all the world, my mother had loved me most unconditionally. Everything she'd done on the trip her last summer she'd done to help me in some way.

Today, I would be true to that quest no matter who disapproved of me.

It was amazing how much more attractive I looked in the mirror after thinking that, as if I were looking at myself through the eyes of my mother—which made it possible to remember Samir and the way he kissed me, as if kissing were a secret potion and the touch of lips were the only way to capture it. I thought of his reverent adoration of my body. I thought of how I felt when I was with him.

His mother's disdain tried to creep in, but I pushed it away. I was in love with him, and he was—I was quite sure—smitten with me too. That was what I needed to carry with me, a fire lending light to my face as I confronted a man who was now my enemy.

Grant sat in the breakfast room with his phone and a full English breakfast. He'd showered and pulled himself together, so it was easier to remember what I'd once seen in him. His hair was thick and brown, his face square, strong, intelligent.

The girl on duty recognized me. "Hullo, Lady Shaw. Pot of tea?"

"Not today, thanks." I pulled out a chair at Grant's table. "Do you mind if I join you?"

He waved a hand toward the chair. "I don't know what we have to say to each other after yesterday."

"Just listen. I thought about what you said—that you'd be fair in these circumstances. Maybe I've been caught in my own grief and just haven't been thinking clearly."

He spread strawberry jam over a generous slice of toast. "Is that guy the reason you broke up with me?"

"No." I said it as clearly and firmly as I could. "I told you the reasons, and I meant them."

"What is he, like, twenty-five?" His gold-green eyes, once so lionlike and intriguing, met mine coldly over the toast. "The benefits of being a rich bitch, I guess."

"Please, Grant, let's not do this." I kept my voice low, glancing over my shoulder at the others in the room. "Why don't we take a walk?"

He tossed the toast down on the plate. "Fine."

Outside, I led us, walking in stiff silence, to the churchyard with its view of Rosemere. In the bright summery sun, it was stunning, all gleaming stone surrounded with forest and fields of yellow rapeseed, so bright it looked as if cans of paint had been spilled across the landscape. I sat down on a bench. "Please join me."

With a slight huff, he did, but the artist in him couldn't resist the view. "God, I'd love to paint this."

"You should."

"Yeah, maybe." He leaned back, weary. I felt him watching me. His fingers touched my arm. "Jesus, Olivia, I really miss you. I might have blown it, but I didn't mean to. I still love you. We've been good together for a long time."

"We were good," I said. "I didn't mean to blindside you, honestly. But it's been over for a while. I thought you knew it, too, but maybe I was wrong about that."

He nodded, brought his hands together, and laced them between his knees. "So why'd you come see me?"

"Let's settle all of this. Nancy has sold the house. We just have to come to an understanding, and we'll both have the money we want."

"We?"

"Yeah. Let's figure out something that's fair to us both. I have repairs to do on that white elephant of a house." I gestured toward it. "It looks so beautiful from here, but it's a mess from top to bottom."

"What do you have in mind?"

"I'm offering a third of the West Menlo Park house, after taxes."

He straightened, shaking his head. "Half."

"You were willing to settle for a third the last time we talked!"

"Changed my mind. I'm going for the full half."

I pinched my nose, trying to stay calm. "Grant, I need that money. And you know it's technically mine."

"Is it, though?" He made it sound so reasonable. "If we'd been married all this time, would you feel the same way?"

I took a moment to think about that. "Yes. I think I would. The house belonged to my mother, and I inherit whatever she leaves behind, and I'm offering you a third of that."

"No, you're offering a third of the house. That doesn't come anywhere close to the estate. Not including *this* estate, which has to be worth a pretty penny."

"It's not. There's no money left. It's a wreck of a house."

"On land that's—what? A half hour from central London on the train?"

"Only if I sell it will there be any money in it."

"So sell it."

"I'm not doing that," I said and realized that I meant it. Fiercely.

"Still, how much are your mother's paintings worth? Another mil, easy."

"I don't want to sell them."

"You're gonna have to make some choices, Olivia. You don't get to have everything your way."

"You have no right to any of this!" I cried, slapping a hand on my thigh. "You practically deserted me, and now, only when there's something in it for you do you want to make things right." I stood. "I'm offering you a third of the house in West Menlo Park. Take it or leave it."

As I started to walk away, he said, "Olivia."

I turned, hopeful.

He smirked. "I'll leave it and see you in court."

"Fine."

I walked blindly, but my feet were on the path to Rosemere. I followed it through the forest my mother had painted as such a malevolent place, walking furiously at first, but at some point the exercise kicked in, and I felt the tension drain away.

There had to be some kind of answer to all of this. Something. The Monet and the Constable were clearly copies, but maybe some of the others were worth something, and they were small enough to transport to London. What if I called Peter to drive me in? It would feel better than sitting around waiting for the sky to fall.

In the back of my mind, Mrs. Malakar's face rose, that glance of disdain and knowledge that had seared me. Were they close? He didn't like to talk about her, which made me wonder. Had she disapproved of his marriage? Or more far more likely, his divorce?

In my pocket, my phone buzzed with an incoming call. Surprised, I stopped to take it, leaning against an oak tree that had been a sapling when bombs were dropping in the Blitz.

"Bad news," Samir said.

"I bet I already know. Your mother is here."

"Yes."

"It's not bad news—I'm sure you're glad to see her."

"I will, but it means we have to change our plans this evening."

It stung, but I made sure that didn't show in my voice. "Of course. Do whatever you need to do."

"Don't waste the asparagus. Eat them."

"I'm sure I can get some more from Elizabeth. She's been working on that bed for years. It's prolific."

A little pause fell between us, and I realized we'd rarely spoken on the phone.

"I'm so sorry to cancel, Olivia," he said.

"Don't be silly. Let me know when you're free."

"Is everything all right? You sound a bit . . . pinched."

"It's not you or your mom. I just had more bad news this morning. Looks like Haver and the caretakers have drained all the accounts."

"All of them?"

"Looks like it." I toed the earth, scraping away leaves to reveal the rich topsoil below. "So I'm trying to figure out the logistics of the repairs, and Grant won't back off, and I just . . . maybe I'll take some of the paintings into London and have them evaluated."

"If they're real, you'll have no worries at all. Wouldn't there be someone in your mother's circle who could give you advice without all that trouble?"

"Ah. Yes, that's probably a lot easier. Will you send me the photos you took?"

"I'll do it at lunch."

"That would be helpful. I'll send them to my mother's manager."

"Text me if you find out anything. I'll call you later. After dinner."

"Okay." Overhead, a pair of starlings flew across a sky that was growing cloudy. "I ran into Pavi and your mom at the bakery this morning. Your mother saw the books in my bag."

"Pavi told me."

I thought about the look on her face. "She's really not going to like me at all, is she?"

"It doesn't matter, Olivia. I'm the one who needs to like you, and I more than like you."

"Thanks. I more than like you too." Straightening, I headed up the hill. "Text me if you need distraction."

"Will you sext me if I ask very nicely?"

"Oh, sure!" I laughed. "What could possibly go wrong?"

A little pause. "I don't want to hang up. What are you doing?"

"Walking through the forest up to Rosemere. It suddenly occurred to me that if the caretakers are gone, their flat is available. I'm going to take a look at it."

"But you don't drive."

"Yet. And anyway, the walk to the village is less than a mile. I just need . . . a home. That's not going to be in Rosemere for a long while, although I did have a flash of what it might be like down the road. Maybe french doors along the back of the kitchen."

"I like it." In the background, I heard thunder. "Argh. Gotta go. Looks like a thunderstorm is on the way. We have to cover the thatch."

"Bye!"

I hung up and started walking back toward the top of hill. A text came in, buzzing against my palm. I feel like I've always known you.

I typed, Me too.

As I mounted the hill, seeing the great house looming over everything and the ruins of the conservatory in the distance, it occurred to me that I was setting myself up for the world's most devastating broken heart. It was idiotic to fling myself into this with such abandon when I knew better. Things always seemed amazing at the start. That chemical flare, that heady obsession.

But what could I possibly do? A vision of his profile, that strong nose and the goatee, rose in my mind. The sound of his sigh wafted down my spine. I flashed on his hand moving over my belly, the brush of his hair across my shoulder.

Good God. I was lost, lost in him, in us, and I hoped no one would lead the way out for at least a little while longer.

Chapter Twenty

At one point, Haver had given me a ring of keys, some of which were labeled and some not. When I arrived at the carriage house, I peeked in at the progress they'd made on the space I'd claimed, and it was barely started—which was good if I changed my mind.

The caretaker's flat had a fine modern lock on the door, and I found a correspondingly shiny key for it. It opened on the first try.

The rooms were empty, down to bare wooden floors, which confirmed that they would not be hurrying back anytime soon to make things right.

But the space was wonderful—five big rooms with polished wood floors and exposed beams. The sitting room faced a large hearth, and new windows had been installed, three of them, side by side, to let in the light. The bathroom was modern, with a proper English bathtub, and what I presumed was a bedroom had a wardrobe that must have been built five hundred years before. I opened it. Empty.

The kitchen was the killer. It had been recently updated, as recently as three or four years, I guessed by the finishes. The AGA, which I'd looked up out of curiosity after admiring the one in the main house, was a $16,000 appliance, and this one was in British racing green, a color I knew because a friend had a MINI Cooper. Tiny lights hung down over a generous granite counter furnished with stools.

Beautiful. At least they'd had good taste, all weathered wood and natural finishes and the open beams. Yes, this would be a great flat for now. Maybe for a long time. I could knock out the walls between the other two bedrooms and live in more space than I'd ever had in my life. Again, I caressed the AGA. What would it be like to cook on it?

"Okay, Mom," I said aloud. "This is not so terrible."

But I still had to figure out how to pay for everything. Maybe I should talk to the earl again, get his advice on what to do about Grant.

In the meantime, I had to figure out what my mother wanted me to find. When I got back to my flat, I'd go through the photos Samir had forwarded to see if I could piece anything together. Today, however, it was time to deal with my fear of Rosemere. I would go to my mother's room and see if I could find any clues. The construction workers were there still, banging around. Their noise would help.

And really, it was just time to begin to actually own this house, become her caretaker in truth. What kind of caretaker couldn't even walk through the place without a friend?

Before I left the carriage house flat, I shot photos from every angle. It would need furniture.

Definitely a dog.

Thunder rumbled distantly as I walked across the stretch of grass between the carriage house and the main house. I let myself in the back door and walked through the kitchen with determination. This room never bothered me. I loved the light and the open spaces and the potential it offered.

From the kitchen I marched through the butler's pantry and into the dining room, which was so much more appealing now that the vines had been cut away from the windows. The walls still showed mildew and grime, but it was possible to see how it would all look later. The parlor was the same—the mullioned windows filled the entire wall, with window seats and picturesque views of the fields. It was easy to imagine a dozen ways to make the room appealing and interesting.

As I moved into the stairway hall, I could hear construction workers barking orders and the banging of tools. All very reassuring, but my feet still halted at the bottom of the staircase. In the darkening day, the colors of the abbey window were muted, and I almost felt as if they judged me. A cold draft poured from the damaged north wing, and I looked up, wondering if it was a ghost I felt or just the approaching storm.

A sudden noise behind me made me whirl, and there was the black-and-white cat, his long fur a bit scruffy but not terrible. "Meow," he said.

"Are you going to talk to me today?" I didn't move for fear he would run away. "I didn't bring anything to eat, but I do keep meaning to do that. What do you like?"

He sauntered toward me, as if he were a house cat and not a feral stray at all, and rubbed against my legs. "Wow. Thanks." I let him circle my ankles for a minute. "Would it be all right if I pet you?"

With great gold eyes, he looked up and mewed.

I bent down and stroked him, and his back rose up against it. "You're friendly. Do you want to help me with this scary thing I have to do?"

As if he knew what that thing was, he started up the stairs. Halfway, he paused and looked back.

"I'm coming." I followed him up the stairs, aware of the house around me, rustling in its stillness. At the landing, I stopped and looked back down, looked up and toward the gallery, feeling it. Time. Lives. Generations. I imagined the first Earl of Rosemere standing here, full of pride at his accomplishment, and then the woman who had championed her cause with King Charles, meaning I could, all these years later, inherit. I made a mental note to find her name and remember it. I imagined Christmases in the 1690s and balls in the Georgian years, days of mourning and days of birth and ordinary days in between. Breakfasts changing styles, dinner parties, servants, pets.

It calmed me. All of them belonged to me in one way or another.

My mother's room and Violet's room were at completely opposite ends of the house, my mother in the southwest corner, Violet in the northeast, along opposite hallways. I made myself walk the corridor down to Violet's room and take a peek inside. The sight of it nearly empty gave me a sad jolt—as if she, my grandmother, had been suddenly buried. For a moment, I stood there, looking at the empty walls. The cat joined me, poking his head in, and then sauntered away, disinterested.

I made my way over to the other wing, and on this side of the house the voices of the construction crew were muted. This hallway contained the worst damage on this floor—the bedroom that had been on fire and the bathroom with a collapsed ceiling. I headed to the room at the back and opened the door, noticing anew that it was very plain in comparison to some of the others.

But of course my mother had taken her things with her, or at least some of them. I opened the wardrobe doors, which were less complaining now that we'd had a few dry days in a row. The tatters of rotted clothing still hung there, and I found moth-eaten handkerchiefs when I opened a drawer. I opened all the drawers, methodically, looking for anything she might have left for me. The bureau had been impossible to open the last time I was here, but when I tried it this time, the drawers were sticky but actually did open. Nothing.

Damn. I looked round the room. The bed was neatly made, and I suddenly realized that it was not a tattered bit of fabric, as it should have been. It was old but not rotted. Crossing the room, I tugged the coverlet back. Placed precisely in the middle was a postcard of the Golden Gate Bridge shimmering beneath a rainbow.

My heart squeezed, hard. With a hand that trembled, I picked it up and turned it over.

On the back, my mother had written in her spidery hand, "Brava, darling! Never forget that there is gold at the end of the rainbow."

I scowled. Did she mean there was gold in the West Menlo Park house? Had she hidden something there too?

"Gah!" I cried aloud, and the cat jumped off the bed and ran away. "Oh, honey, I'm sorry." Carrying the postcard with me, I followed him out. "Kitty, kitty! Come on. Where'd you go?"

But he was nowhere to be seen. Feeling guilty, I turned back to the room and looked around carefully. Was there something I was missing? Could she have hidden something somewhere else in here?

I suddenly thought of Samir knocking the back of the wardrobe to check for a passage to Narnia. Maybe there was a false back or I'd missed something in there. I opened the wardrobe again and tried to shove the clothes aside. When I couldn't really get to the back, I grabbed a big armload of clothes and deposited them on the bed. For one moment, I stared at the skirts, the beading, the rotted silk, and imagined my mother wearing them. One red evening gown peeked out of the pile, and I pulled it out. The neckline was plunging, cut close, and it would have been magnificent on her.

It also didn't appear to be ruined. I set it aside for the moment. Maybe I needed to check the clothes from Violet's room too. Maybe not all of them were rotten. I had no hope whatsoever of wearing my mother's clothes, but everyone said my grandmother had been built more like me. That would be a strange thrill. Smoothing a palm over the red dress, I wondered about Pavi, who was built delicately. Maybe she'd be able to fit into some of these vintage pieces. This dress would look amazing on her.

I headed back to the wardrobe and shoved the rest of the clothing aside so that I could see the back and the floor. Both appeared to be utterly without feature, but I knocked on them anyway, feeling a bit foolish.

Until the back gave way, just slightly. Startled, I pushed it, but it stuck partway, and I couldn't get a grip on the edge to pull it toward me. Stymied, I looked around for a tool. If anyone had used wire coat hangers, I could have taken one apart, but they would probably all have fainted over the idea.

This room was bare, but maybe something had been left behind in Violet's room. Leaving my bag, I crossed the hallway, circled behind the landing, and made my way back to Violet's room. As I opened the door, a gust of cold, rain-soaked air blew through the window, and the curtains fluttered up in their tatters.

I froze for a moment. If anyone would haunt the place, Violet would be a candidate. Maybe she had liked her things where they were—

Don't be absurd. I heard the words in my mother's no-nonsense voice. The window was broken. And, anyway, ghosts didn't exist.

I entered the room and looked around, poking through the debris on the floor for anything I might be able to use to pry away the back of the wardrobe. Amid the scraps of paper and dust and unrecognizable junk, I found a thumbtack. Perfect.

On my way out, I kicked the rest of the debris, just looking for anything that might be better, and my toe sent something sailing across the room to ping off the edge of the door. I picked it up—a single, delicate silver circlet, carved lightly and set with tiny red stones I thought might be garnets.

Nandini. She, too, probably haunted the place. Or maybe she haunted the town itself, looking for her lost daughter. The idea gave me a shiver. What a lot of sad stories had played out here.

Maybe in this generation, I could change that. I slipped the bracelet over my hand as a promise to myself and went back to my mother's room.

But when I pried open the back of the wardrobe, nothing was there. Deflated, I closed the door, and only then did I become aware of the sound of rain pattering against the windows. Time for me to get back, then. Maybe I could hitch a ride with one of the construction crew.

Pondering the puzzle of the key and how to find the answer my mother meant me to find, I walked down the passageway and suddenly saw the cat at the other end, poking his head around the door. "Meow!" he said and dashed away from the door, deeper into the room.

"You stinker," I said and hurried down the hall. "Are you playing chase with me?"

I pushed open the door—and halted as a wave of foul air slammed into me, so noxious I reared back and covered my nose. The floor was rotted here and burned in places, and the cat perched on the end of the bed, which had also been burned.

A wave of intense sadness moved through me. Some of the other rooms had been ruined by time, the ballroom worst of all, but this was the only one that truly felt malevolent. I backed away, my nose still covered, wondering how such an old, old fire could have left such an odor.

Suddenly, I became aware of the silence left behind when the construction halted, and I turned and dashed down the hall, then down the stairs, rushing around the rooms, and through the back door—to see the last of the trucks trundling down the hill toward Saint Ives.

Great.

I was about to call Peter when a horn honked, and I saw Pavi at the wheel of her van. Her mother was in the passenger seat. "Need a ride back to town?" Pavi called through the open window.

"Please!" I dashed through the rain to clamber into the back of the van, sitting on the floor next to a box full of asparagus. "Thank you. I was just about to call Peter."

"Peter Jenkins?" Pavi said. "He's such a nice man. You remember him, Ma?"

"Of course," she said. No more, no less.

I picked up a handful of asparagus from a box on the floor. "They're gorgeous. What are you going to do with them?"

"I'm not quite sure." The van bumped down the hill. "Countess, you need to fix your road."

"It's terrible, right?" I smelled the earthy green scent of the asparagus and put them back in the box, thinking I might steam mine and serve them with soft eggs and toast made from the bread I'd picked up at the bakery this morning.

Then, because I had to make conversation somehow, I asked, "Did you have a pleasant journey over, Mrs. Malakar?"

"It's never particularly nice," she said. "It was as expected."

"That must be about a twenty-four-hour trip from Mumbai to London."

She shook her head. "Oh, not at all. Only about ten, usually."

"Oh, of course." I shook my head. "You would fly west, not east, to London, as I do from San Francisco."

For the first time, she swiveled her head to look at me. "Are you an American, Lady Shaw?"

"Please call me Olivia. Yes, I was born just outside of San Francisco."

"Your accent doesn't sound American."

"My mother was British. Obviously, I guess." Which sounded snotty on some level, and then I was afraid if I fixed it, it would be worse.

"Your mother was Caroline Shaw—is that right?"

"Right. Did you know her?" I leaned forward eagerly.

"No. She was gone long before I arrived. I've always thought she had something to do with poor Sanvi's disappearance. Or knew something."

"Here we are!" Pavi said brightly, and I realized that we were parked in front of the chip shop.

But I couldn't just let the accusation lie there. "Why would you think such a thing?"

Mrs. Malakar turned back to look through the windscreen. She gave the slightest of shrugs.

"No offense, Olivia," Pavi said, "but I've got to run. Get these asparagus in cold water."

"Sure." I climbed out, but before I closed the door, I said, "Mrs. Malakar, my mother wasn't that kind of person."

"No?" Her eyes, large and dark as a night sky, met mine. "She knew something."

Pavi gave me a look over her shoulder. "Gotta go, Liv."

I nodded. "Sorry."

"I'll call you later," she said, giving me a barely perceptible shake of the head, as if to nullify her mother's words.

I closed the door and watched the van disappear, feeling suddenly cold. Left out.

As the rain continued to pour down, I turned on the radio for company and steamed the asparagus, sliced fresh bread to make toast, and set out an egg to top it all. Wrapped in a warm sweater and yoga pants and thick socks, I tried to focus on cooking for myself, instead of feeling bereft that I had really been looking forward to cooking for Samir in his tiny but efficient kitchen. Cooking was my lingua franca, my love language. I hardly felt I could express myself fully, show him what I was feeling, if I couldn't cook.

Instead, while I sat alone in my flat, over my egg and toast—and it had to be said, the beautiful asparagus, which tasted of every moon of winter and the first dawns of spring and the first fertile stirrings of the earth—I imagined all of the Malakars sitting down to their supper above the restaurant. Would Mrs. Malakar have done the cooking tonight, or would Pavi want to dazzle and spoil her mother?

A hollow little echo of loneliness filled my lungs.

Ridiculous. I'd only just met these people!

Trying to get myself in hand, I considered the tasks I could knock out. It was late morning in California, and I could get in touch with several people I'd been needing to talk to.

The first was the lawyer, who called me back within a few minutes. I explained the new situation with Grant and my need to get things settled as soon as possible. He didn't seem to think it was a huge problem— California was not a community property state—but he'd have to check into options for getting the case dismissed. "If your main issue is to get the money from the house sooner, I'd try to find some common ground with your ex, see if you can come up with something you'll both be able to live with."

"Yeah, I tried that," I said.

He promised he'd do his best to expedite the hearing, but I could tell he didn't think it would happen at all fast. In the meantime, the money was in escrow so the sale could move forward from the buyer's end.

I hung up, wondering if he was right, if I should just give in and let Grant have half of the sale of the Menlo house. Make him go away.

I called my mother's art dealer. "I've come across a puzzle," I said and explained the paintings my mother—I assumed it was my mother—had left in the wardrobe. "Any idea why she might have done that?"

"No idea," Madeline said. "Which ones are copies?"

"A Monet, a Constable, and another one by an artist I can't identify. I can send you pictures."

"Do that. I'll see what I can find out. What else was in the group? Anything I might be interested in?"

I parried. "Not sure. I have an appraiser coming in this week"—a lie—"but you'll be my first choice if there's anything interesting."

"Mmm. Just remember, Americans pay a lot more for European paintings than anyone in Europe will."

I laughed. "I'll remember." I took a breath. "In the meantime, I'm wondering if there are any of my mother's paintings that I might be able to sell?"

"Maybe. Do you want to go through them, first? That was what we were waiting for."

"I do, but I'm not sure when I'll be back to the Bay Area. Things are complicated here—and expensive. I'd like to make a sale as soon as possible."

"Still the ex?"

"He won't back off."

"That asshole. I'd like to set the dogs on him for all this."

I let go of a harsh laugh. "You and me both."

"All right. Let me see what I can do. I can also have my assistant email you digital copies of the paintings, at least all of the ones we have in our catalogue."

"Great idea." I paused. "Madeline, do you know what she was working on the last few months before she died? She was working all the time, but I don't remember seeing what she finished."

A soft pause fell, which made me sure she was lying when she said, "I have no idea."

Was this like the earl pretending to know nothing of my mother, when actually he'd seen her? "Thanks, Madeline. I'll look for those digital copies."

"Olivia, I would caution you to be careful. You don't want to make decisions in your grief period that you'll regret later."

I rolled my eyes. "Not making big decisions is a luxury I don't have right now. But thanks. I'll be careful."

"I'm going to talk to a guy I know who specializes in intellectual property and estates. It would infuriate me if Grant were able to get his hands on your mother's money."

"Thanks."

It had been a long day. The air was cold and damp. Maybe a nice fire and a hot bath. A good book. Since Samir's books had caused all this trouble today, I was inclined to avoid them, but I was sure I had something in my bag or on my reader.

From below came the sound of braying laughter, a girl trying too hard. The chip shop was always busy this time of day, and it was the only time I really had a sense of how many people lived in the area, really. The smell of frying food wafted upward, not unpleasant, but it grew wearying after a while. This place was better than the hotel had been, but it still had the feeling of a skin that I'd shed any second.

I imagined again the carriage house flat, what it would be like to cook on that AGA, how much I loved the finishes and the space. I could bring some of my mother's paintings over and hang them on the walls. In my imagination, the vision started to take shape—I would paint the walls a pale celery and add accents in shades of magenta. A giant bed for the generous bedroom, with excellent sheets and big fluffy pillows. I imagined waking up in that room and looking out toward the fields and the distant hills.

Maybe I should go shopping in London. Take a day off from all the madness and see what I could find.

But in the back of my mind, I was still rolling the puzzles around, trying to fit the scrambled pieces into something that made sense. Or at least pointed in a single direction.

From the table, I picked up the key the earl had given me. Nothing at all remarkable about it. A little smaller than a standard house key. Shiny new, as if she'd had it made for me. What did it open?

Samir had sent the photos he'd shot of the paintings, along with a note that said, simply, "Very sorry about our dinner plans tonight. Will call when I've finished with family obligations."

Again that hollow feeling of being on the outside. It would have been unseemly for me to be there, but somehow Pavi and Samir had become my cornerstones in this world. Without them, I was untethered.

Focus.

I opened the paintings one by one, arranging them on my screen so that I could see them clearly. No commonality of subject matter— there were portraits and landscapes and still lifes. Again, I moved them around until they formed the colors of a rainbow and found a sweet, nostalgic pleasure in the exercise, but it didn't seem to point to anything I understood.

Next, I laboriously copied each painting into a Google image search. A few came up with nothing, but I matched several others to minor painters over the centuries: a sixteenth-century portrait painter, Joseph Highmore, who'd also illustrated the original novel *Pamela*; a minor pre-Raphaelite John Wharlton Bunney.

Maybe, I thought, feeling a bit lighter, *some of these would be worth something.*

I almost didn't run an image search on the painting of my uncle. It seemed unlikely the portrait was worth anything. In the end, I fed it in and clicked search and sat back, taking a sip of tea while I waited.

The search populated with a dozen matches. One was to a Dutch portrait of a noble in seventeenth-century dress, and it was startling how close the resemblance was. Another was to the portfolio of the painter, long dead, who had painted many of the English gentry in India. So this painting had been done before they'd left.

All of the others were connected to actual stories of Roger Shaw, Earl of Rosemere. I clicked through to the Wikipedia article I'd already read, which was very sparse, just birth—September 9, 1939, and basic facts. Born in India, immigrated to England when his mother inherited. Then a short paragraph on the disappearance. "In 1977, the house was abandoned and has stood empty ever since."

The search brought up several minor newspaper mentions of Roger, of the same type I'd found of my mother. Social pages, a dance, a ribbon cutting. In the early seventies, he was in his prime, a very good-looking man with his mother's sensuality and a mouth that was somehow cruel.

Or maybe I was just projecting.

I looked at the portrait again, then abruptly stood up and went to the box I'd brought from my grandmother's room. There were hundreds of photos in the box, and it took a little while to find some of Roger. The first I pulled out wasn't one I'd seen before—this one was in England. I recognized the house in the background. It must have been one of the picnics. Violet stood next to a tall, lean man with a craggy face—of an age to have served in the war, which would have made anyone weary. Roger, a little over twenty, held his little sister in his lap. My mother. She looked ready to cry. He smiled into the camera. The camera had caught the exact second that Violet's husband—really, he was my grandfather; why didn't I feel any connection?—had swung his hand toward Caroline, as if to pick her up.

The little girl was reaching for him. Or Violet. Roger clung to her waist.

I swallowed a sick feeling. Here was the evil in the forest. Everyone said Roger was cruel, controlling. Had he abused her? Physically? Sexually? Mentally?

Carefully, I leafed through the photos again, sorting them into piles. Roger; Violet in India, Violet in England; Caroline; Nandini. I tried to blur my eyes respectfully over the nude photos, but again, my heart was captured by her lush beauty and even more so by the knowing, powerful connection she'd made with the person who had snapped the photos. Violet.

Very few of my grandfather. He was the Shaw. I fed his name into Wiki and came up with nothing except the acknowledgment of his once having been married to Violet. He'd died in 2001, married to someone else.

I tapped my fingers on the keys, feeling as if I was missing something, something just in the edges of my peripheral vision. On impulse, I paused and typed into the search engine, "Sanvi Malakar."

Nothing. No match at all, only "Did you mean *Sanjaya* Malakar?" who had, evidently, been a contestant on American Idol.

Frustrated, I closed the program and looked again at the paintings, JPEGs lined up on my screen. I played with last names making words and first names making words. Nothing.

My phone buzzed, and I picked it up. No, I *snatched* it up, which made me feel embarrassed, even more so when I saw that the text was from Samir: Might I stop by on the way home?

Everything in me wanted to say yes. I felt like I hadn't seen him in twenty thousand years. And yet I couldn't shake the way his mother had looked at me. I also had to be honest enough to admit that my feelings were hurt. Not because he hadn't brought me to a family dinner. But maybe the feeling that he was hiding me.

Which was completely ridiculous. We'd been dating for five seconds. It wasn't like me to be so . . . dramatic.

As I considered what to type, a knock sounded on the door. "It's me, Olivia."

I opened the door, and Samir stood there, looking like six feet of dessert. His hair was smoothed a bit, and he wore a dress shirt with tiny blue stripes, open at the throat. He carried a package of food, which he lifted with a wry smile. "Pavi sent a peace offering."

"I already ate dinner."

He grinned. "I assumed you had."

I shrugged a little.

"Was my mother terrible?"

"Yes!" I stood in the doorway, half-torn as I eyed the box. "What is it?"

"You'll have to invite me in to find out."

"Why should I?" I said, and to my horror, there was more emotion in the words than I had meant to show.

Samir flowed over the threshold. "Oh, sweetheart. I'm so sorry." He gathered me close, and I let him, my defenses melted by the smell of his skin and the smell of whatever was in the box he carried. Just the solidness of his chest rocked me, opened me, and I pressed my face into his shoulder. "She hated me on sight. I felt about thirteen."

He kissed my forehead. "I'm sorry. She is sometimes difficult." Against my hair, he said, "It's coconut asparagus. She said you would love it."

"Coconut, really?" I stepped out of his arms and let him come in, closing the door as I took the box of food, spinning around to take a fork out of the drawer. Leaning on the counter, I opened the box to taste the asparagus. "Mmm. That's very fresh!" I could pick out black mustard seed and cumin, garlic, chilies, but the flavor of asparagus was the main event—big and so perfectly itself. "Your sister is . . . an *extraordinary* chef."

"She is." He stood where I'd left him, right inside the door.

I didn't make him comfortable, not yet. Taking another bite of asparagus, I eyed him. "How was dinner?"

"It was good. She's much healthier than she was last year. Being back in India agrees with her."

"How long will she be here?"

One shoulder lifted. "All summer."

I looked at the food. Set it aside. "I think I need to take a hot bath and read a book and go to bed early."

For a moment, he was silent. "Are you all right?"

"I guess. It was a terrible day. Your mother and Grant—and I can't figure out any of this puzzle, and I don't know what the hell I'm doing with any of this."

He inclined his head, his arms still folded. "Mmm."

"What does that mean?"

With a sure, easy gesture, he took my hand and pulled me across the room to sit us both down on the couch, which smelled of years and dust. Our bodies fell close, leg to leg, hip to hip, and my shoulder nested right beneath his armpit. "You are tired," he said, rubbing my arm. "Let me just hold you for a little while, and then I'll go."

I closed my eyes and rested my cheek on his chest. "Just for a little while."

"Okay." He stroked my hair, found the elastic that held my braid together, and tugged it out, releasing my hair to fall around my face. Tenderness swept out from his fingertips, over my head. "My mother does not hate you. She's angry with me. She's afraid I'll create another romantic disaster. I more or less agreed to see if she could find someone for me." His voice rumbled through his chest below my ear, making me sleepy.

"Like matchmaking?"

"Mmm. It's still common enough."

"That doesn't sound like you."

"I was embarrassed by how badly my marriage ended. Everything about it was humiliating." His fingers threaded through my hair. "I thought perhaps it could be worth a try, to meet the women she would find."

I imagined a parade of lovely Indian women, dewy and glowy, with clear eyes and glossy hair. Jealousy stabbed me. "She was going to do that this summer?"

"Yes. So you can see why she might be a bit put out that I've been seeing someone."

"I thought you had a girlfriend when we met."

"Mmm. Not really a girlfriend. Just . . . someone I was seeing a little, here and there."

"Are you still going to meet those women?"

"No!" He moved, bringing me around to face him. "How can you even ask that?"

"Because you are younger than me, and your mother will always hate me, and this whole—"

"Olivia." He said it firmly.

I swallowed, embarrassed by my emotional insanity, and also defiant.

He cupped my face, stroking both sides of my cheeks, running his hands up into my hair, where he clutched handfuls of it. "Do you really believe anything you're saying?"

I met his eyes, the starry, starry eyes, and saw in them what I'd been seeing all along. The tension in my body sluiced away. I shook my head.

"I didn't think so." He kissed my nose, then mouth, and I was so very glad to be with him that I kissed him hard right back. "There you are," he murmured.

And then there was no conversation. Not with words. Only hands, mouths, breath.

Chapter Twenty-One

The rain had half stopped by morning, which meant I had to get to the estate to work with Pavi on picnic prep. She picked me up just minutes after Samir left, but if she'd seen him, she didn't say.

"Hey," I said, slamming the door behind me. "Thanks for the asparagus. They were amazing."

"You're welcome." She drove toward the estate, dodging puddles in the road. "I cannot remember a spring with so much rain! It's insane!"

"I'm worried about the picnic. Even the tarps won't be enough."

"I know. So am I." As if to underscore the concern, it started to patter down again, just enough to obscure the countryside. "What would you think about moving the tables inside?"

"Inside where? The house?"

"Yes, the kitchen is empty enough. And nothing is dangerous in there, is it? Ceilings and floors all sound?"

"I think so." As we bounced up the rutted back road, I hung on to the dashboard. "I have to rope this road off, however. It's not sound enough for a lot of traffic, especially if it keeps raining. Everyone will have to come down the main approach."

"That's good. Let's make sure."

We were silent for a while. Pavi finally said, "I'm sorry my mother was so rude to you."

I shrugged.

"I know it will probably not make it easier, but she does suffer from arthritis terribly. That's why she goes to India during the cold months. This weather is not easy for her."

"I'm sure."

The silence deepened. Pavi looked at me.

"I don't know what you want me to say, Pavi. It's understandable that you defend her, and I would have lived with her disdain for me—"

"She isn't disdainful of you. She's just—"

"Let's not." I held up a hand. "She implied terrible things about my mother."

"Oh. That." She bumped up the driveway to the house. "Yeah, I'm sorry about that. That's a bit of . . . not jealousy, but possessiveness . . . there. My dad always had kind of a thing about your mom—they were good friends, I think—and he always defends her against any negative comments."

"You didn't say it, Pavi. I'm not upset with you."

She parked and turned off the van. Looked at me. "Good. Because I really like you, Olivia Shaw. I haven't made a new friend in a long time, and I will hate it if my family gets in the way of that. My mother *or* my brother."

I reached for her hand. "Me, too, Pavi. I mean it. Who else would get it when I flip out over a strawberry?"

She laughed. "You did flip out a bit." She slapped the steering wheel. "Enough. Let's go see what we can make happen here."

We organized the vendor schedule and the timetables and mapped out the indoor plan, which actually seemed quite doable. If the day was fine on Saturday, we'd set up on the grass. If not, we'd set up inside.

When we were done, it was still only ten, and I asked her to come with me to the carriage house, where I took measurements and paced out what I thought I might do with the space. I'd need everything from pots and pans to furniture to linens, and it was fun to imagine.

"Are you moving soon?" Pavi asked.

"As soon as I can get some furniture, actually. Why not?" I turned in a circle, narrowing my eyes to add the pale celery of my imagination to the walls. "It will be a lot better than the place over the chip shop."

"I can see that." She ran her fingers over the counter. "I'm jealous. My father doesn't want to live alone, but I'd love a place like this, where I could come and go without any bother."

"Why doesn't he go to India with your mother?"

She shook her head. "I don't know. They seem to still have a good marriage, but they're both intractable on this point of location. He's never lived in India, and he isn't sure he would feel at home there. But he's lonely without her all winter." Bending to open the doors of the AGA, she added, "That's why I'm staying single. Marriage is too much trouble."

I realized I'd never heard her say anything about lovers. "Or not," I said.

She rolled her eyes. "Oh, please. Don't. I cannot possibly listen to a woman who is in the new throes of—" She brushed her hands, avoided choosing a word. "You know."

"Yes." My phone buzzed, and I glanced at it. "It's Jocasta." I picked up. "Hey, Jocasta. What's new?"

"Where are you, love? Can you meet me at the gardens in a bit?"

"Sure. I'm at the carriage house, actually. I think I'm going to make over the caretaker's flat, and I was getting some ideas. What time?"

"We're on our way." She sounded oddly buoyant. "I have a surprise for you!"

"Really? I'll walk over there. Meet by the rose garden?"

"How about the pool?"

I shrugged. "Sure."

"See you in ten."

"Great." Hanging up, I looked at Pavi. "She has a surprise. Which she will no doubt film. Am I a big mess?"

"Not really." Pavi brushed at my shoulder. "You just need to comb your hair. Put some lipstick on."

"I don't wear much lipstick."

Her gaze was level. "Put some lipstick on. The camera washes out your face."

I scrambled through my bag and came up with a berryish color. "How do you know something like that?"

"At one time, I was desperate to be on *Master Chef*." Hands on her hips, she looked around the room. "I love this place, but how did they afford the upgrades?"

"*They* couldn't afford it. The estate afforded it."

"Ah." Her phone buzzed, and without answering, she said, "I'd better get back to Coriander. If you decide to go shopping, I'd love to go with you. I can only get away Mondays, but we could make a day of it, go to London. Escape."

"That would be fun."

On the way out, she said, "Everything is good for the picnic, I think, but if you think of anything, let me know."

I saluted her.

"Comb your hair."

"Right." I dug out my comb, ran it through the tangles, and spread my hands. "Good?"

She gave me a thumbs-up and headed out.

But the minute she was gone, I felt the weight of the picnic's expense fall on my shoulders. It was going to be wildly expensive, and while there was enough in the accounts to cover it, I would be virtually broke until the next influx of rent payments, which meant if I wanted to move soon, I'd be in a sleeping bag on the floor.

A team of gardeners, herded about by one of the garden club officers, had been hard at work the past few weeks, or at least whenever the weather had allowed. Not that English gardeners seemed to mind the rain—I'd often seen groups of two or three in their macks and wellies working in the drizzle.

They had accomplished a lot, I noticed as I wound down the path toward the pool. I'd not seen as much progress on the roses because evidently Jocasta had recruited a pair of rose experts from Kent to come in the following week to assess and formulate a plan, but here, weeds had been cleared and some of the shrubbery trimmed, enough that I could get a feeling for what it would be like when it was finished—willows trailing fingers in the winding stream, rhododendrons blooming purple above tufts of primrose. This was the wilder section, quieter, meant for contemplation.

And peacocks, evidently. One strolled ahead of me, stopping now and again to poke at the earth. It didn't seem to care about me in the slightest. Its long feathers swept the ground like a train. Another bird, as plain as the other was showy—a female—bobbed ahead of it.

The path bottomed out at the pool, which had been swampy and green with neglect the last time I'd seen it. Now the little bridge and balustrades around the rectangle were scrubbed clean, showing the pale stone, and the concrete pool held clean water that reflected the sky and tree branches. A few pots had been planted with ferns and geraniums, and those reflections shimmered across the surface. It was extraordinarily peaceful. I walked onto the bridge and leaned on the ledge, peering down. Around me, the trees rustled, and birds twittered and sang out.

Magical.

"Gorgeous, isn't it?" Jocasta said, emerging from the trees in another direction, Ian right behind her, filming. "So far, this is the best payoff."

"I love it." At the far end of the pool, a white peacock emerged from the greenery beyond and strutted toward the pool, where he bent his head to drink. His reflection shimmered across the surface, ghostly. "They aren't afraid of humans at all, are they?"

"Don't seem to be." She took my shoulders and turned me to walk the path upward. "Time for your surprise."

"I'm so excited. But I hope it isn't going to be something that costs another fortune."

"It is not, and anyway, this is my treat." The three of us puffed up the little bricked steps, emerging by the conservatory. "Ta-da!"

A large truck loaded with supplies I couldn't quite figure out was parked near the conservatory. "What's happening?"

"That is a load of glass, my dear. Your heart was so set on doing the conservatory that we decided to give you a little present for showing up for the estate so diligently."

"Oh, wow." I covered my cheeks with the palms of my hands. "This is absolutely wonderful."

She touched my shoulder. "I thought you'd be pleased. Helen and I are friends, you know. She showed me the picture book your mother painted. I was enchanted."

Impulsively, I hugged her tight, and she chuckled, patting my shoulder in a gesture of calm. "You're welcome." She gestured to Ian to film the greenhouse, and when he was engaged, she said, "Everything all set for the picnic Saturday?"

"Yes. I was just with Pavi in the kitchen, figuring out where to put the tables if it rains."

"Wonderful. We'll be here. Might be nice to give the locals a little national coverage. Which trucks will be here?"

I listed the three that were coming. "And of course, Coriander is providing many dishes too. Have you been there, Jocasta?"

"No. I take it I should go."

"Yes, you should. Pavi is one of the most talented cooks I've ever met."

"Mmm. I'll take a look." She waved as she took off, busy as ever, on to her next project. I'd been very lucky to connect with her. It was hard to imagine how I would have been able to do it without her insights. And the earl's, of course.

I watched as materials were unloaded, seeing the conservatory whole in my mind, filled with exotic plants and seedlings for the gardens. Using the greenhouse system, we could propagate plenty of plants to beautify the front of the house, as well. If I used bright-colored flowers in mass plantings, the colors would be visible from the village, a sign of beauty and prosperity. A tiny, tiny sense of pride took root in my heart. Maybe it was going to work out.

In my pocket, my phone vibrated. Expecting the contractor, I answered without looking.

"Olivia," a woman's voice said, "this is Claudia Barber. I'm afraid there's bad news. The earl has had another heart attack. It's quite dire. I thought you'd want to know."

"How dire?"

"Very, but he was still alive last I heard. He's been taken to Watford Hospital. Shall I send the car for you?"

I'd been afraid to ask if I could come, given that we were only friends, and not a very long acquaintance. But somehow, in our limited time, we'd become very close. "Please."

Three of us waited for news together—Claudia; her brother, Alexander; and me. I felt a little awkward, but Claudia sat next to me and held my hand, clearly beside herself. Alexander, who looked as if he'd just come in from a great hike, in battered boots and rip-proof pants, fetched paper cups of tea for all of us.

"How long have you been caring for him?" I asked Claudia.

"Nearly fourteen years now. Ridiculous, isn't it?"

"Not at all."

"He was so kind to me as a girl. Our parents were killed when we were in grammar school, and while Alex is made of stern stuff, I was a wreck over it for months and months. He just let me be. Brought me dolls and games and finally"—she smiled, sniffing—"a horse. That did the trick."

"Do you still ride?"

"When I can. The past five years, he's needed my attention."

"Sounds like you're both very lucky."

"He's been so alive since you arrived, Olivia."

Tears stung the back of my eyes, but I didn't feel I had the right to let them show, and I lowered my lashes to hide the emotion. "He's very dear."

We waited in more silence for another hour until the doctor came out looking grim. I'd already known he would likely not survive, but that expression sealed it. I felt I was again back in that hospital in San Francisco, where my mother had not survived the pneumonia that she'd known, given her cancer, would kill her. "He's conscious," the doctor said. "But he hasn't much time. You can see him, one at a time."

"What bloody difference does it make if he's dying?" Alex blustered, standing to his full six-foot-three.

"Hospital rules," the doctor replied mildly. He gripped Alex's arm just above the elbow, as if bracing him.

"You go," Alex said to Claudia. She hurried away.

We sat down. My phone buzzed, and I glanced at it. Samir had texted. Is he all right?

I texted back: No. I will call in a bit.

I'll fetch you when you're ready, any time. Just ring.

Thank you.

"Boyfriend?" Alex said.

I never liked the word "boyfriend" for grown men, but it was too much trouble to come up with any other description. I nodded.

"The thatcher, is it?"

I raised my eyebrow, suddenly feeling like my grandmother. "None of your business."

He half grinned. "You're right. My uncle's been on about it. 'I like the lad well enough,'" he growled in a fair imitation of the earl, "'but the girl has no idea what she needs in a marriage.'"

I laughed. "I've heard the same."

"The match he wanted is between the two of us." Alex scraped a thumbnail along the seam of his hiking pants. I could see the grizzled shine of unshaved beard along his jaw. "But I'm sure you've already realized that's impossible."

"I had never given it any thought. Are you married already?"

"No, no. Just quite thoroughly gay."

"Ah!" I laughed. "That would be problematic."

Claudia joined us. "He wants you, Olivia."

"Go," Alex said.

"Sure?" I stood, but uncertainly.

He nodded, gestured with one giant hand.

George was connected to nothing, and I realized that he would want it that way. His breath was shallow and uneven, his color quite gray. I took his hand. "Leaving so soon?"

A twitch of his lips, and he squeezed my fingers. "Thank . . . you . . . Olivia," he managed. "Save . . . Rosemere."

"I'll try. I swear."

His grip tightened infinitesimally. "No . . . try. Do."

I grinned. "Okay, Yoda."

"Kiss," he whispered, pointing to his cheek.

With a deep breath against showing my sadness, I gladly kissed him. "Thank you. I'm so grateful you've looked out for me."

His eyes closed. "Alex."

I let go and went to find him.

Chapter Twenty-Two

I left Claudia and Alex and headed out into the street to walk. I didn't call Samir or anyone else. I only walked, up one street and down another, not caring when a light drizzle began to fall, soaking my hair. The rain hid my tears.

As I walked, my mother walked with me. She was in the sensible shoes of the women with their net bags, and in the window of the bookshop where I saw another of our book club selections, I spied her tan raincoat, a thousand years old and still in perfect condition, because she took care of things. The earl was gone, and I would miss him, grieve him, but it was my mother's loss I felt in the cold rain of that English afternoon. I wanted to talk to her just one more time.

When the rain began to fall with more intent, I ducked into a Costa and ordered a latte for the first time since I'd arrived in England. The frothy milk and strong coffee braced me, and when I had finished, I found I could call Samir for a ride. "I don't exactly know where I am," I said apologetically. "Let me ask the barista."

"Are you all right?"

"No," I said and blinked back a new rush of tears. "I'm heartbroken."

"As you should be. I'll be there as soon as I can. Traffic will be heavy."

From my purse, I took my sketchbook and flipped through it. Here was a small record of my time in England. The lemon chicken soup at the earl's, the strawberries I had bought after tasting them at Helen's, a page full of spices tumbling down in a diagonal line, star anise and cardamom pods, cumin seed and coriander.

When I got to a clean page, I started sketching from memory my mother's kitchen. The windows overlooking her garden, the backsplash she'd always hated and never replaced, the curtains. I'd taught myself to cook in that kitchen because my mother was hopeless and had never learned to like it.

On the opposite page, I sketched her face. The pointed chin, the smooth swing of her hair, the big eyes, so full of secrets. Until a new tear splashed on the page, I didn't realize I was weeping again, but I had no way to stop it, so I only turned my back to the room and faced the rainy day through the window and drew, feeling as if I might actually die myself from the weight of my sorrow.

When Samir arrived, I'd had a coffee and a tea and a pastry that was dry and nowhere close to Helen's beauties, but I was calm again, the grief stuffed back into a safe place. I ached over the fresh new cut of losing the earl, but the rawness of my mother was hidden carefully away.

The rain had snarled the heavy commuter traffic, and he looked as if he'd been in traffic jams—his hair was wild from his fingers. He sank down beside me. "I'm sorry it took so long."

"Don't apologize. It's ridiculous that I'm still not driving."

"You've had a bit on your plate."

"Are you hungry? Want a coffee?"

"No, thank you. It would be best if we just get back. The traffic won't be heavy on the way back south." He tucked a lock of my hair behind my ear. "Pavi said to bring you to the apartment. She wants to make sure you're fed."

I looked away. "What about your mom?"

"She'll be all right." He stood, holding out a hand. "Come."

In the car, he turned the radio to the news. "Lay back and rest while I drive."

It didn't take much to convince me. Within moments, I'd fallen asleep, and I didn't awaken until he brushed his fingers over my cheek. "We're here, Olivia."

I straightened, blinking hard to wake myself up. For a moment I stared out at the parking lot, trying to get my bearings. The back door to Pavi's restaurant stood open, light falling from the kitchen through the screen. I could see staff bustling about. "Maybe I should just go home and sleep," I said, and my voice was rough.

"After dinner." He took my hand, raised it to his mouth for a kiss, and I let my head fall backward, seeing him anew. The tenderness in his expression, the mouth that was so generous, the intelligent, starry eyes.

"Okay," I said softly. I felt wide open and raised my hand to his jaw.

He smiled. "Let's find you some food. I think we're eating mulligatawny tonight."

"One of the tenants mentioned that. I'm not sure I've ever had it."

"You're joking."

I shook my head.

"Well, it's quite a common dish here. Pavi has a whole little thing she wrote about it."

The weather was clearing, and a soft, refreshing breeze washed my face as we crossed the lot. He took my hand, tightly, and bumped my shoulder with his. I laughed a little, bumped him back.

The dinner hour was in full swing in the kitchen. Pavi shouted orders to her staff, dressed tonight in an orange chef's coat, her hair tight beneath a matching cotton scarf. She spied us and lifted a hand, and we slid sideways up the stairs to the apartment.

A scent of cumin and pepper came out of the kitchen, and I realized that it was Mrs. Malakar who was cooking. She was in the kitchen, a towel tossed over her shoulder, and she was busy at the stove when we arrived, so she didn't halt, just called out, "Hello, hello. Your father is watching the news." Only then did she glance over and see me. "You brought the countess?"

"Please call me Olivia," I said, and the weariness must have sounded in my voice.

Mrs. Malakar's face softened. "We are eating one of my husband's favorite foods tonight."

"Mulligatawny?" I said. Samir released me, gestured toward the doorway to the kitchen, and gave an almost imperceptible nod. "I've never eaten it. What's in it?"

"Ohh, a lot of things. Chicken, onions, apples, sweet potatoes, many spices."

I inhaled the scent. "Can I help you in some way?"

"No, no. You sit. They told us that your friend the earl died today."

"Oh," I said. That explained why she was being nice, I supposed. "All right, then."

Pavi clattered up the stairs, bringing spices from the kitchen downstairs. "I'm not going to be able to stop tonight—it's so busy!" She gave me a kiss on the cheek. "You all right?"

I nodded.

"You're not, but you need to eat and get a good sleep. Only three days to the picnic!"

"Olivia, come sit with us," Harshad said, gesturing from the living room. I joined them, sinking down into a luxuriously lush sofa. The room was bright with paintings and colorful fabrics at the windows, and along the wall to my right were family photos. With lazy curiosity, I looked at them, easily picking out Harshad as a young man, skinny but quite dashing, with a startlingly beautiful girl at his side. She was slim but womanly, her hair a shiny black curtain over her shoulder and an expression very like her mother's in her bold expression. I didn't want to ask if it was her even more than I wanted to ask, but I made a mental note to ask Samir.

But Mr. Malakar must have noticed my attention. "That's my little Sanvi," he said. "Isn't she beautiful?"

I nodded. "It must have been disappointing that it wasn't her bones at the house."

Mrs. Malakar came into the room. "Come. The food is ready."

Samir stuck by me, sitting down next to me, his knee resting against mine under the table. When I glanced at him, he winked, and I let my face relax.

Mulligatawny turned out to be a soup, or perhaps more of a stew, with chicken and carrots and chunks of apple. The broth was thick, yellow with turmeric, and delicately spiced. I tasted it, taking in the flavors, then took another slow, savoring bite. "This is wonderful," I said. "Does Pavi use the same recipe in the restaurant?"

"Yes," Mrs. Malakar said, reaching for a chapatti. A trio of bracelets rolled down her arm. "She took my recipe and made it more. I use her recipe now. My daughter, as you have seen, is a wondrous cook."

"Wondrous," I echoed. "Yes, that's a good word."

We fell to eating in easy silence. Music played quietly from the kitchen, maybe Indian pop music, though I couldn't make out the words.

Mr. Malakar said, "You asked about the bones."

I raised my head.

"I was relieved that they were not her bones. It appears that I would rather believe she is alive in the world somewhere, and one day . . . she will walk through those doors."

The easy river of tears filled my eyes. "I understand that so completely. I would trade a foot to spend one more hour with my mother." The words were unexpectedly intense, and I flushed. "Sorry." I glanced at each of them. "I didn't mean to be so—"

"My mother died when I was twenty-two," Mrs. Malakar said, "and I have missed her every day since." She touched my hand, and again the bracelets swam down her arm. I was grateful for the kindness, for the possibility that she might not hate me forever.

But something else caught my attention. "Look," I said, raising my right arm to show the bracelet I'd found in Violet's room. "My bracelet matches. Did those belong to Nandini?"

"Yes," Harshad said. "Where did you find that?"

"In my grandmother's room. They cleared it out, and I found this on the floor." I started to take it off, but he waved a hand.

"No, keep it."

"Sure?" I glanced at Samir, and he gave me a very slight nod.

But it was Mrs. Malakar I wanted to please. I took the bracelet off and laid it on the table beside her bowl.

She only looked at me. Shook her head. "It's yours."

"Dad," Samir said, "I've been meaning to ask you if you saw Caroline last summer."

He didn't reply instantly. "Why would you ask me such a thing?"

"She visited the earl," I said, and a pain worked its way between my ribs. "She knew she was dying, and she seems to have set up a . . . treasure hunt."

"Is that right?" He shook his head. "I don't know anything about that."

But again, I had the sense that he knew more than he was saying. "Is there anything about rainbows around here? Legends or stories or a pot of gold?"

"I don't know any," he said, and I could tell he meant it. "Samir?"

"Nor do I."

Rainbows, peacocks, treasure, paintings. The words echoed around and around my head, and I stared down at the bowl of soup with blurry vision, finding myself lost and—

"Olivia," Samir said at my side. "Let's get you home, shall we?"

"I'm so sorry," I said. "Did I fall asleep?"

He chuckled softly. "Yes."

I reached for his hand without thinking, and he took it, helping me up, his other hand at my back. "Sorry," I said to his parents. "It's just been—"

"It's all right," Harshad said.

"Good night, Olivia," Mrs. Malakar said and held up the bracelet. "Don't forget this."

I slipped it on my wrist.

I slept a solid eleven hours, falling far away into the other lands where the sleep spirits knitted me back together. When I awakened, my mind was as clear and sharp as the sunlight of the late-spring day outside my window.

I knew three things—that I wanted to stay and try to save Rosemere, that I wanted to move to the carriage house immediately, and that I needed new clothes. My own clothes, in a size that actually fit me. I needed something for the picnic, and I wanted to furnish the carriage house flat as soon as possible.

Unfortunately, Peter was busy, and on such a sunny day, Samir would be working, but these days, a person didn't need to be anywhere in person. I fired up the laptop, credit card in hand, ready to shop.

But an email from Grant waited. *Call off your hounds*, the subject read. I opened it curiously. *I've dropped the suit*, it read. *Get Madeline off my back.*

Cautious optimism bloomed in my chest, and I scrolled down the list of emails. Sure enough, there was one from Madeline. No subject, but an attachment. I opened it.

Please notice the date of the photos here, she'd written. *I've forwarded them to my lawyer, and he says this is enough to remove all possibility of the common-law suit.*

The photos were from a party, dated last October. In them, Grant was shown in a series of more and more intimate poses with a young woman. I recognized her from the publicity that had surrounded her enormously successful debut last summer, an event I'd attended with my mother and Grant.

She was exactly the kind of creature I could never be—waifish, fragile looking with pale skin and a sexy tumble of wild red hair. She'd made all the papers with her first show, and the second was promising to be gigantic.

The second group of photos showed them in a low-lit restaurant, very intimate, just days after my accident.

All the rage I'd been biting back roared up my spine, into my throat, and I wanted to reach through the screen and tear out his hair by the handfuls. How dared he cheat on me like that? And manipulate me for the apartment? And—

I let go of a growling roar and jumped up out of my chair to pace the room.

The room where Samir had made me chai, naked. And teased me, his eyes glittering with genuine love, and only last night, put me tenderly to bed and loved my curvy self just as it was.

Pfft, my mother had often said over things better left alone.

I called Madeline. "Thank you."

"Oh, sweetheart, you know it was my pleasure. I couldn't stand for him to go after everything your mother worked so hard to give you."

"Have they been together awhile?"

"Do you really care about that affair, Olivia?"

I sighed. "It's kind of humiliating."

"I know. I'm sorry. But life is just going to get better and better from here. I just know it."

"I know. Thank you so much."

"All right then, just go enjoy your freedom."

Buoyed, I did exactly that. With a great deal of cheer, I ordered a summer wardrobe in a size bigger than what I had, as well as almost everything I could think of to furnish the flat. Most of it was due to be delivered Friday, but I couldn't get some of the furniture until next week.

No problem. In the meantime, I spoke with my contractor about getting paint in that celery color I'd envisioned for the walls, and he had it onsite by afternoon, along with drop cloths and paint rollers. "Sure you don't want some man power?"

I refused politely. It felt good to do something so physical, to open the doors to the fresh air and play tunes on my phone and sing along as I painted the walls. Samir texted midafternoon. Feeling better?

YES! Slept the clock around, and I'm over at the estate, painting the walls of my new flat. Want to come over and see?

Can't, I'm afraid. Didn't want to call too early, but we're in Devon on a job. Told Tony I had to be free Saturday afternoon, but I have to be back here Sunday night.

Understood. Glad you'll be here Saturday night. FaceTime later?

Yes, please. I'll text you.

I went back to work on the apartment, excited for the new possibilities arising. Maybe everything would finally just be all right. Flow, like water down a mountain.

By Wednesday night, I had managed to get the cable installed in time to watch the first episode of *The Restoration Diva* focused on Rosemere.

I made a bowl of popcorn on the AGA and poured a glass of wine, and just as I sat down, Samir texted. **Are you ready?**

Maybe. It's nerve-wracking. Do you have it on?

Yes! Wouldn't miss it.

On BBC One, the music of *The Restoration Diva* started. **Eeek! I** texted. **It's on!**

Call me when it's over.

K

To Pavi, I texted another sentiment. **I hope I don't look too FAT.**

Her reply was swift. **Never. My parents watching. I'm dvring. BUSY NITE!**

I set the phone aside and gave myself over to the experience. Jocasta looked much the same on TV as she did in person. I was pleased to see that her makeup and hair people had done wonders for me for the opening segment, the one we'd filmed to talk about the house and the story and how I'd come to be an unsuspecting heiress.

The rest of the program dived into the first month of our work, the discussions the first day we'd met, going through the wreck of the garden and the ruined, littered rooms of the house. As I'd suspected, Ian was a gifted cameraman, lingering over the colors cast by the stained glass in the hallway, that rose blooming indoors in the parlor, the sad shimmer of the neglected pool. I wasn't unhappy with the way he filmed me, either, though I did think it was time to get rid of some of that butt.

A task for another day.

What I had not expected was the piercing history woven in to the current-day narrative. Jocasta had focused on two characters this time, the dashing lover of King Charles II who'd won back the house after it had been seized by Parliamentarians and the earl who'd built the gardens and conservatory. I loved hearing a fuller version of each of their stories, and I thought my mother quite looked like her ancestress, the king's mistress.

If not for her, I wouldn't be sitting here—that much was sure.

The show ended on a dramatic note, outlining the gargantuan task of saving Rosemere and the experts they hoped to employ. The last shot was me standing with my arms crossed, the stained glass behind me, and I had to admit it was quite thrilling.

I laughed aloud.

The phone rang. "That was amazing," Samir said. "You were smart and thoughtful and very hot."

"I'm really happy with it. This is good for the estate, I think."

"Yes. I wouldn't be at all surprised if you found yourself some donors."

"Really? Do you think that could happen?"

"Yes, I do."

I sighed. It was weird and strange and wonderful, but I thought my mom would be pleased. "I wish you were here," I said.

"Me too." He sighed, and I had the sense of him settling. "Instead, I'm stuck in a faceless motel that smells of old cigars."

"Ew."

"It's all right."

"Do you mind if I ask why you're still doing that job?"

"Billi needs food."

"But you said the books are doing well."

"They are. I'm very pleased. But novels are not reliable. One day you're in; the next day you're out."

I laughed. "Okay, Heidi Klum."

"I won't stay with it forever. But like it. Being outside all day. Minding my own business, making something beautiful."

In my ear, the phone buzzed, then buzzed again. "I have to go. I'm getting calls."

He chuckled. "The life of a famous countess."

"Right. I'll see you soon."

"I'm proud of you, Olivia. Good night."

He hung up before I could reply.

Chapter Twenty-Three

By Saturday morning, I had accomplished enough at the flat to pack up my things and move when Pavi came by to pick me up. It was very early, just after sunrise, and she carried a lassi with her. "Try this," she said. "It's rose. But I think it needs a little something more."

"Rose lassi?" I said and smiled. "That sounds so romantic." The taste was subtle, not as bright as the strawberry but delicious anyway.

We dropped my suitcase at the flat, and Pavi turned in a circle. "You must have worked like a demon. This place looks amazing."

"It's been a very long stretch since I had a place to call home. I was motivated." The bed was made, and I dropped my suitcase there. "I ordered groceries for delivery," I said, swinging open the American-style fridge. "How posh is that?"

"You're going to have to learn to drive," she said.

"I am." I took a breath and spun around in a circle. "Yay! Home!"

We'd left the door open, meaning only to stay for a moment, but a cat—the cat—came sauntering in. Seeing the two of us, he sat down just three steps out of reach and swung his tail in a tidy circle around his feet. "Well, hello, Meow Meow."

"Meow," he said.

"I actually remembered to buy you some food," I said. "Wait right there, and I'll get it for you."

"You're going to feed a stray cat? He'll never leave."

"He's my cat," I said and realized I meant it. "He's been showing up since I arrived."

"Just don't get your heart broken, sweetie. Who knows how old he is or if he's healthy."

I lifted a shoulder, pulling the lid off a can of cat food, which I dumped onto a saucer and put down on the floor. "It's all yours, Meow Meow." I backed away.

For a moment, he eyed me suspiciously, looked at the plate, then back to me. Finally, he seemed to come to a decision and stood, then walked over to the plate as if he did this every day.

And wolfed down the food.

"Oh, look, he's starving!" Pavi cried.

"He's probably not starving, but it's nice to eat cat food." I glanced at my phone. "We should get over to the site. He can stay. I'm going to leave the door ajar."

"Is that safe?"

I gestured around the room, barely furnished. "There's nothing to steal but my good pots, and anyway, it would be awkward for people to come over here."

"Fair enough."

My phone buzzed with a text. "That's Samir," I said. "He's made it to London and will be here when he's had a shower."

"Good." She shook her head, frowning. "I wish Samir would stop it with this whole thatcher thing. I don't like Tony. He's capricious and erratic." She narrowed her eyes. "I also think he's got something going with that Rebecca person."

"Do you think so? I thought that the first time I met them."

"I just don't like him. And anyway, it's dangerous for Sam to be climbing up on those roofs all the time. I worry about it."

I didn't feel I had a right to say anything about that. As we walked up the hill, I did say, "I've been reading his books."

"And?"

"He's a wonderful writer, but he's much better with the science fiction than the literary stuff. The first one is great and funny and real, but—"

"Science fiction?" She halted.

"Damn," I said, quietly, and paused. "Let's just leave this right here, okay? I can't say anything more."

For a moment, she narrowed her eyes at me. Then she smiled, and the dimple appeared in her cheek. "You're right. And I'm so, so glad he's writing again."

Miming a zipper across my lips, I tossed away the key.

"I understand."

By ten the trucks and tables were in place, and although a few clouds scuttled over the sky, it looked to be a beautiful day. Some of the women tenants had gathered flowers into wild bundles they tucked into canning jars of various colors, and crews of moms from the elementary and preschools made sure the tablecloths were secured and that there were plenty of paper plates and cutlery. A bake sale to benefit the local mobile library set up just outside the Rosemere kitchen, and they asked if they could charge a dollar for tours of the kitchen, which had more takers than I would have ever expected.

I changed into a fluttery dress, which made me think of the first day I met the earl and his garden party. It had not been long ago at all, and yet he'd made his way into my heart.

But I felt the part of a countess as I greeted villagers and other locals who made their way to the picnic. The hem of my dress fluttered around my knees, and a soft breeze brushed through my hair. Children tumbled over the grass, and the men—and some of the women—gathered around pints of good brown ale, and the music was exactly right.

Standing there looking at everyone, at all of it, I felt a sense of pride. "Is this what you wanted, Mom?" I said under my breath.

Peter came up to me, dressed in clothes I'd never seen, a pair of khaki trousers and a striped shirt pressed crisply, the sleeves actual points above his elbows. A pretty woman of indeterminate age stood beside him. "You pulled it off, my lady!" he cried. His hair, which had always been under his cap, was a mix of auburn and gray, making his eyes quite spectacularly blue.

"Just for you, Mr. Jenkins," I said and took his hand. "You were the first to tell me about the picnics."

"Ah, now." He turned to include the woman. "This is my wife, Pat. Patricia, that is. She's a teacher, third grade."

"So nice to meet you, Patricia. You must be a brave woman to teach third grade. They're suddenly not little kids anymore, are they?"

"It's true. I'm so honored to meet you. We saw you on *Restoration Diva*. It was thrilling!"

"Jocasta is supposed to be here today, if you want to meet her."

"You don't say!" Peter beamed. "You reckon I could take her picture?"

"I'm sure you can."

Behind them, coming up the path from the village, were Mr. and Mrs. Malakar, and behind them was Samir, loping along with an attitude of peaceful enjoyment. A slight smile played on his lips, and he was dressed beautifully in the green linen shirt I found so lovely and black jeans and the pointy-toed shoes Londoners were wearing this year.

But the best of it was the moment he spied me. I clasped my hands, waiting, and I knew the exact instant he caught sight of me—his entire being lit up. His face brightened. His posture lengthened, and his body turned toward me, breaking away from everything, his focus pure and direct.

He smiled.

And I, standing there in the wavery shade of a chestnut tree, beamed the same bright, hungry light toward him. When he reached me, he took my hand and came very close. "I wish I could kiss you. It feels a thousand years since I've seen you."

"Ditto," I said breathily. "But I can say you are a sight for sore eyes."

"As you are." He let go of my hand, brushing the back of his knuckles over the back of mine. "I'll leave you to it and see if Pavi needs me. Me and you tonight, yes?"

"Yes. I'll introduce you to my cat."

He laughed.

Mr. and Mrs. Malakar came up, and Mr. Malakar bowed slightly. "Lady Shaw, you are the very vision of your grandmother."

"Thank you. Welcome." I turned to Mrs. Malakar, who was a hair taller than her husband. Today she wore a simple, patterned cotton dress, sleeveless, her hair sleek and shiny. On her wrist was a carved silver cuff. "I'm glad to see you again, Mrs. Malakar. I hope you forgive my strangeness the other day."

"Nothing to forgive. I'm sorry for your loss."

"I am going to find a beer," Mr. Malakar said.

She nodded and stood there, waiting for him to depart. Nervousness shimmied up my spine.

When we were alone, just the two of us beneath the tall, elegant tree, she fixed her sober gaze on me. "You seem like a very nice woman, Lady Shaw."

"Please," I said, "call me Olivia."

"I'm sorry; I can't. You are Lady Shaw, whether you are comfortable with it or not." She turned toward the picnic, all the villagers and the food trucks. With a hand as long and graceful as her son's, she gestured toward the fields, the house. "You are the daughter of a long line, and despite your lack of training, you are, by all accounts, stepping up admirably to learn what you must do to honor your family. I respect that."

"Thank you." I squared my shoulders. "But?"

"Samir has already had a disaster of a marriage with a woman of a social class far above him. I would not like to see him repeat it."

"With all due respect, Mrs. Malakar, he's a grown man. He can make his own decisions."

As if to illuminate our conversation, Samir appeared with two little girls, one on each hip. They had adorned their faces with paint, and ribbons rippled away from their hair. Mrs. Malakar said, "He's going to be a very good father one day. As his father was. Is."

One little girl patted his cheek, and he laughed. "He's a kind man," I agreed.

Mrs. Malakar folded her hands. "I will speak frankly. You are too old for him, Lady Shaw. Even if you were to marry immediately, you will only have, what . . . a year, two, maybe even five to have children?"

The words stung, and I felt color flood my cheeks. "It's ridiculous to even think like that. We've only just met."

"I think you know that is not true. Please don't be selfish. I understand quite well why you care for him. He's a good man and wise beyond his years. But true love is unselfish."

I didn't look at her as the heat spread from my cheeks to my ears and down to my throat, bringing with it a small roar that blocked out all sound. I willed myself to be dignified as she walked away, my eyes on Samir, playing with the two girls and a little cadre of boys who joined in.

Love is unselfish.

But I didn't feel unselfish. I felt greedy and hungry. I wanted my hands on him, but I also wanted his voice in my ear, his thoughts tumbling into and tangling with my own. I wanted to walk the fields with him in the early morning and listen to his fingers on the keys as he wrote his stories. I wanted the tenderness of his breath and yes—a child with his face, his ready smile. All those things. I didn't feel faint and accommodating. I felt Amazonian, empowered by the fierceness of my feelings.

Shake it off, I thought, and I dove back into the whirl of the picnic, trying to greet each and every person there. Jocasta arrived and created a stir, but so many of the locals remembered her as a girl that it settled down fairly quickly.

Pavi rushed over at one point, taking my arm urgently. "Jocasta is going to film the restaurant Monday as part of the village segment for Rosemere!"

"That's amazing! You'll be famous."

"I'm so excited and so terrified. She warned me to get ready. I'm going to have to do a ton of work, so I'm probably going to cut out a little early. Will you be all right?"

"Yes, yes, yes. Do whatever you need to do."

She squeezed my hands, made a little squeak of sound, and dashed off.

A shadow fell across the landscape, and I started.

"Are you all right?" It was Alexander Barber with a slim, tall man in a beautifully tailored suit.

"Yes. Wool gathering, I'm afraid." I reached for his hands, stood on my toes to give his cheek a kiss. "How are you? I wasn't sure I would see you today."

"We're doing all right. Poor Claudia has the worst of it. She sends her regrets, but she's really quite broken up."

"I'll make a point of going to see her next week if you don't think it's too soon."

"No, that would be lovely." He turned, drawing forward his companion. "I'd like you to meet my partner, Joshua Gains. He's an art dealer in the city."

"It's a pleasure, Lady Shaw," the man said. He had large, pale eyes, and his hair was fading backward from his forehead, but there was a solid clarity in his gaze, and I immediately liked him.

"My mother was an artist, you know."

"Yes, I've seen some of her work. Extraordinary. And tortured."

I nodded. "Please, both of you enjoy yourselves. We've hired some of the best new chefs in the area, and they're getting rave reviews."

Alexander said, "If you wouldn't mind, I'd like a moment, Olivia. Can we walk?"

"Of course."

He gave his partner a nod, and we headed away from the crowd.

"We're renovating the gardens," I said. "Would you like to see them?"

"Yes, of course."

I led the way. "It really is the most remarkable day. We've been worried all week that it would pour."

"It's lovely. I haven't been to the estate before. It lies in quite a pretty spot."

"What's on your mind, Alex?"

He stopped at the top of the garden and withdrew two envelopes. "I've done some footwork, and it appears there has been quite a lot of surveying and plotting going on over your land here."

I accepted the envelopes. "Shall I open them now?"

"It would be better to wait." He tucked his hands behind his back. The sun struck his eyelashes and teased out the gold in his hair, and I recognized again that he was a very handsome, virile man. The ladies of the country would be crushed to discover he had no intention of marrying, at least not one of them. "That information and the parties behind it are in one envelope. In the other is my offer for the estate."

Startled, I looked up. "Offer?"

"I know you've given this your best, and you've been so much more successful than anyone expected, but I humbly suggest that it takes a lot of skill and balance to run an estate of this size."

"I see. And you're going save me from myself?"

He met my eyes. "It wasn't meant like that."

"Well, I'm only a woman. What could I know of what you mean?"

"Olivia."

"I have no intention of selling. Not to you; not to the silent investors who made an offer on the land via Haver, who seems to have run off with a rather enormous sum; and not to whoever this is"—I waved the envelopes—"who wants to build yet another ugly housing estate."

"You have my word that I would not build housing estates," he said. "My goal is to protect and keep the land."

"That's good to know. I guess you can just make me a promise, cross your heart and hope to die, and I'll believe you." He started to speak, and I raised my hand. "No. It's your turn to listen."

His mouth set.

"I am over my head: there's no question. I may very well fail. But I'm not going to just roll over and let you whisk my inheritance away from me."

"Very well. I admire your grit." He nodded. "The offer stands, and if you change your mind, you know where to find me."

I smiled. "I do."

With a jaunty salute, he started back to his partner. Standing on the hillock, looking down at the gathering, I felt my skirt rustling around my legs and the breeze dancing in my hair as I watched the gathered number weave together and apart, celebrating new life. New purpose.

No, I would not sell to anyone.

By the time all the stragglers and the food trucks had departed, I was exhausted both from the effort of smiling and trying to remember names and the very physical work of the day. Pavi had packed up by two to return to town, and I stayed to supervise the cleanup.

The one person I'd not seen and had expected to was Rebecca. All afternoon, I'd half waited for her arrival, but she never showed, nor had her husband. Odd, considering how solicitous they'd been. I wondered what had happened.

As the last truck bumped down the road, the sun played peekaboo with a bank of lavender clouds. Samir had driven his parents home and now returned with a pack over his shoulder. "I haven't had a chance to tell you how lovely you look," he said and bent to kiss me.

I met his kiss, twining my fingers more tightly around his. "So do you. I love that color on you."

"I'll wear it every day if you like." He raised his head and touched his nose to the tip of mine. "God, it feels like a year since we had time together."

"I know." I tugged his hand. "Let me show you my new flat."

"That went very well, I thought," he said as we walked hand in hand over the path to the carriage house.

"It was a great success, and Jocasta raved about Pavi's food, so that will be good for her when the show airs." The shadow of his mother's comments rippled over my pleasure, but I brushed them away. "I've been reading your books."

"More than one at once?"

"Dipping through them to see what I see."

"Mmm." Against the gold-and-lavender sky, his profile was still. "You needn't give me reports. Everyone always feels they must prove they have read them, but I don't need that."

"You're very funny, but not in a mean way, which I love, and there's a tenderness in your approach to the world that I find very touching."

"Tender? I don't know that I've heard that before. What do you mean?" He paused, and I had to smile—what writer could resist hearing more about the perception of his work? I myself could never resist.

"You really see things as they are. The beauty—or maybe the particularity—of everything, and you're fond of it all. Awe is in all of it." I inclined my head. "There's a lot of wisdom in that, being so present."

"Awe," he said quietly, brushing hair away from my face. "Thank you."

"I'm awed by you," I said. "I feel like I made you up, that you can't possibly be the man you seem to be."

"I'm as flawed as any," he said.

"I know. I see you, you know."

He swallowed. "And I see you."

"What do you see?"

"Intelligence and curiosity and open-mindedness. A certain delicacy, a little brokenness."

"My mother."

He nodded. "And your dog and the loss of your health and your work. You became unmoored when all those things happened."

"I did."

"You're afraid too. Afraid you won't find your place, that if you do, it might be taken."

The words cut a bit too close, and I scowled at him. "That's enough, sir."

He grinned, but then his attention was caught by something behind me. "Oh, look!" He turned me gently by my shoulders, and there in front of us was Rosemere, the sun striking the windows with gold, setting the stones afire with rose.

"It's beautiful," I breathed. He stood behind me, his hands on my shoulders, and I covered one of his hands with my own.

"It's been standing here for six hundred years," he said quietly, "those very windows looking out to those very same fields. It's hard to even imagine what that means, six hundred years."

"I know. All those lives, the mornings and the evenings, the dinners and the disasters and the Christmas mornings. So many of them."

"And there will be more, because of you." He kissed my head, and I leaned into him.

"Thank you, Samir," I said.

"For what?"

"For just . . . you."

He wrapped his arms around my shoulders. "Thank you for the very same thing."

Later, after we'd reunited properly after four entire days apart, we puttered into the kitchen. "I have everything you need for chai," I said proudly, opening a cupboard. "Will you make some? I'll make my very special broiled cinnamon toast."

"Done."

My phone rang, and when I glanced at the screen, I saw that it was the constable. "Hmm," I said and answered. "Hello?"

"Hello, Lady Shaw. I'm calling with some news. Is this a good time?"

"Of course." I widened my eyes at Samir, who plucked a banana out of a bowl and peeled it. "What's up?"

"We've been coordinating with the Turkish government and local officials, and we've made several arrests in your case."

"My case?"

"The serious fraud case? Regarding Haver and various others?"

"Oh!" I realized that my solicitor had actually undertaken the work of getting the police on the case. "That's great. Who was arrested?"

"Jonathan Haver was picked up in Rome, Rebecca Poole and Tony Willow in London, and"—he paused—"Judith and Rick Vickers, your former caretakers, en route to England."

My mouth dropped open, and I looked at Samir with wide eyes. "Wow. That's incredible. Do you need me to do something?"

"Eventually, you'll be called upon, but nothing for now. I just wanted to give you the good news personally."

"Thank you. So much."

"You're quite welcome, my lady. Thank you for all you're doing for us."

I hung up and told Samir. "I doubt if I'll get any money back, but at least they don't get away with it."

He high-fived me. "That's great."

"Now, about that chai?"

He picked up the packets and spice boxes. "How did you know the right things to buy?"

"It's chai," I said with a shrug, smiling over my shoulder.

"But this is my special blend, my very own. You can't have known that."

My sketchbooks were on the counter, and I opened one to a watercolor-and-pen sketch of his chai. "Water. Cinnamon stick, star anise, whole allspice"—I held my place with one finger—"which is a very nice touch, by the way. Whole peppercorns, cloves, cardamom pods, coriander, ginger, black tea."

He smiled. "Well done. Where are the pots and pans?"

"Below, in that cupboard."

As he measured spices, I was aware of a sense of deep contentment. He wore a loose shirt and sweats, his feet bare, his hair loose and tumbling. I watched him count out peppercorns and cardamom pods. "What's the difference between black and green cardamom?" I asked.

"One is ripe?" he offered.

I laughed. "Okay, I guess I need to ask Pavi."

"Better choice. Or look it up on Google."

"More fun to ask Pavi. She always weaves a story around food. Did I tell you she's writing an article for *Egg and Hen*?"

"No! That's fantastic. She must be thrilled."

"I knew she'd be a great writer, just from reading her menu. And now I see her brother has the same touch with words. Which of your parents taught you that?"

"Both of them, really, but my mother is a poet."

The facts of her rearranged themselves. "Is she published?"

"In India. She writes in Marathi."

"Hmm. What does she write about?"

"Nature, rain, and skies and cows."

"Cows?"

A slight tilt of his head. "She's fond of cows. Animals."

As the spices simmered, he reached for my book. "This is your sketchbook?"

"It's nothing," I said, closing it. "My mother was the artist. I just play around."

"May I?"

My hand covered it for a moment, while I measured my fear that he would find them primitive. "You can't laugh."

"I would never laugh at you. With you, but never at you."

I lifted my hand, let him take the book and open it.

"Food! Of course." He looked through the pages slowly. "You are not your mother," he said easily.

"No." I laughed and stood up to begin making the toast. I'd bought a good hearty loaf from Helen's bakery and fresh butter from a farm stand. Slicing the bread as evenly as I could, I arranged the slices on a cookie sheet.

"You do share a sense of whimsy with her," he commented, turning the page to show me the sketch I'd made of cakes and slices of pie in a case, with the ghostly reflection of my own face in the glass, eyes big and greedy. "I love it."

"Thank you." Spreading butter over the bread, I asked, "You see whimsy in my mother's work?"

"Yes, don't you?"

"More threat. It always seems there is something lurking. Some dark danger."

He held my sketchbook open in his palms. "Her brother, I would guess."

"What did he do, I wonder?"

"We'll probably never know. And maybe that's better."

"Is it, though? Secrets just fester." I opened a small box of brown sugar and sprinkled it over the butter. "I do hope you'll feel comfortable letting out Violet and Nandini's secret at some point."

He looked away, ostensibly leafing through more pages. "I'm sure I will."

"Does it embarrass you?"

His eyes flew open to meet my gaze. "No! Not even a little. I just worry about my father. He's sixty-five years old. It might hurt him."

"Maybe he would surprise you." I sprinkled ground cinnamon over the bread, then opened the roasting oven and slid the tray in. "I had to Google how to do this in the AGA."

"It's quite the thing, isn't it?"

"It is. For a cook, this is a dream machine. I will have to make more friends so I can have parties."

He came over to stir the spices and bent his head to smell the brew. "Ready," he said, and he took the pot off the burner and measured tea into it to steep. "I have friends. I'll share them."

Leaning on the counter, I narrowed my eyes. "Do you? I've never seen any evidence of that."

"That's because," he said in his low voice, the smooth, seductive rumble, "I never want to see them anymore." He settled his arms on either side of me, leaning in, pressing our bodies together. "I only want rains of kisses." He dropped them on my forehead, my nose, my cheeks, my mouth. "I'm greedy for you."

I caught his face. "Me too," I whispered. "Greedy for everything about you."

"The whole time we were in Devon, I wanted to come back here. I thought about just leaving a hundred times."

"You did?"

He nodded and ran his hands through my hair, under it, through it, pulling it away from my face. I tipped my head back into his hands, luxuriating. "I would rather be here, right now, with you, than anywhere."

"It's lucky, then, isn't it, that we're here? So greedy." He unbuttoned my top button, then the next. I kept my hands where they were and let him.

"Our food will be ruined."

"Does it matter?" He opened the shirt, exposing my chest, ran his fingers over my torso, my belly. Bent down and kissed my throat.

"Well, we don't really want it to burn."

"No." He pushed the shirt off my shoulders. "We could eat naked."

"I will if you will."

He tugged off his shirt, shimmied out of his sweats, and stood there with his arms out. "Done."

I swallowed. "Your body is amazing."

"You are not naked yet."

I stepped out of my yoga pants. "Better?"

"You'd better get the toast."

I gave him a look.

He laughed. "Carefully."

So I carefully did, and then there wasn't any talking for a while; there was only our greed, our devouring, hands and limbs and joining. As we lay in a tangle afterward, he said quietly, "I am in love with you, Olivia Shaw. You may as well know it."

I turned in his arms, skimming up his naked torso to kiss his beautiful mouth and look directly into his dark and starry eyes. I took a breath. "Your mother told me I should let you go because love is unselfish and you need to have children."

"She said that?"

I lowered my eyes, feeling again the heat of embarrassment and rejection that had washed over me at that moment. "Yes."

"And what do you think?"

"In a way, she's right." I traced the shape of his goatee, then the lower edge of his mouth. "If you want children, I'm getting a bit too old."

He waited.

"But I am in love with you, too, Samir Malakar."

"That is the right answer," he murmured and tumbled me sideways, kissing my mouth. "All the rest . . . will work out."

As we kissed again, and I breathed him in, I suddenly smelled smoke. "Did you take the chai off the burner?"

He raised his head, frowning. "I did. But that's definitely smoke."

We bolted to our feet, scrambling into our clothes. I ran to the kitchen, but it was as serene as when we left it. The smell of smoke was stronger, and I noticed an odd patch of pink light on the floor and went to the window.

"Oh my God," I said. "It's the house."

Chapter Twenty-Four

By the time we reached the house, feet in whatever we could pull on the fastest, the fire was burning hard enough to make a roaring noise, and it flickered out the back of the kitchen, through the big window I had always admired so much. In the distance, a siren sounded, but there wasn't time to wait. I ran down the hill to the tenants, knocking on doors, crying for help.

Samir ran around the far end of the house to see if there was any water for the construction workers and found a hose he turned on full. By then, the tenants were gathering, running up the hill with buckets, and in just a few minutes, a bucket brigade was organized. I stood between two people I didn't know, transferring water forward, buckets back, over and over. Shouts rang out, and orders were issued, and the fire truck attached itself to a water source near the tenant cottages.

The fire roared and cast hellish light over our sweaty faces. It seemed to hardly be dented, and I kept glancing up at the flames in despair as they lasciviously licked the one part of the house that was in decent condition, that kitchen I had come to admire and the rooms above it. My mother's room.

A bolt of lightning was nearly lost in the chaos, but it was impossible to miss the rain that exploded from the sky just after, rain so cold and heavy that we were all drenched and shivering in moments. We kept working, bucket after bucket after bucket, until my arms ached and felt like noodles, so weak I could barely lift them.

The rain did the work, in the end, splashing out the flames, giving us more water to throw with our buckets and hoses. It was nearly dawn before it was entirely out, a dawn we greeted with sooty faces, drinking tea from paper cups—the efforts of a trio of the tenants—and eating donuts Helen had brought to the scene. Every face looked as shell-shocked as I felt, but I doubted any of them held the ballast of despair that threatened to sink me right through the ground.

Beyond the shelter of the trees, rain continued to pour, making of the grounds a mud field. Firemen crisscrossed the yard, conferring with each other. One by one, the tenants came to me, offered a kind word, touched my arm, drifted back home. "Thank you," I said to each one. "Thank you."

Samir brought me a sweater from the flat and a fresh cup of his chai. "You should eat," he said.

I shook my head. "I want to know what they find out."

"They're not going to have answers today."

"How bad do you think it is?"

"I don't know," he said heavily, looking upward, but the dark was thick enough to hide any real evidence. "Bad."

My vision of the kitchen with its big farmhouse table and family and friends gathered around it floated over my imagination, and I felt the loss of it in a kick. "Why did it have to be at this end, not the other?"

He shook his head. "Random fate."

"Do you believe that?"

"What? In fate? I don't know. I don't know why things happen, Olivia, but I know it's up to us to make sense of them. Just"—he slid an arm around my shoulders—"don't try tonight. Let's go back to your flat and get some rest. It will be easier to manage in the morning."

"Everyone is going to know we're together after this," I said.

"Yes."

"You don't mind now?"

"Olivia," he said firmly. "You've suffered a blow, and you're exhausted. I don't want to fight with you. Let's go back and get some rest."

Irrationally, his calm only made me want to fight the more, but I had no energy or words left in me. More loss. "Fine," I said churlishly and let him lead me back to the flat.

The sound of knocking hauled me from sleep. I had no idea what time it was or how long I'd been asleep, but there was muted light in the room, maybe afternoon-rain light. In the other room, I heard Samir and another man talking, and after a moment, Samir appeared at the door. "Olivia, you'll want to hear this."

I flung back the covers and made sure I was relatively decent, pulling a brush through my hair and slipping into a bra before I padded out into the other room. An official in a police uniform stood there, and when he turned, I saw that it was Inspector Greg, who'd been at the dig. "Inspector," I said, frowning in confusion. "Have you already found criminal intent in the fire?"

"I'm afraid this is unrelated, Lady Shaw. The garden club was in the rose garden this morning, and one whole section of the garden washed into the stream. Bones washed up."

"I'm sorry. I don't understand. Bones?"

"Bodies," he clarified. "This time, we're fairly sure it's the girl who disappeared."

"Sanvi?"

He looked at his notes. "Yes. Sanvi Malakar."

"My aunt," Samir said.

"We recovered some personal effects," he said. "I believe your father has been contacted for identification."

He nodded. "And the other body?"

"It's not quite as clear, but there is some speculation that it could be the Earl of Rosemere, Roger Shaw. Your uncle."

I sank onto a stool, mind reeling. "They were buried together?"

"It appears that might be the case."

"Any signs that suggest the cause of death?" I asked.

"Both bodies show signs of fire damage," he said. "That's all we know."

"Fire?" I said and looked at Samir, who had the same thought I did. The bedroom that was so damaged. My heart skittered at the implications. The possibilities.

My mother.

"What do you need from me?" I asked the detective.

"Nothing for now."

"Where were the bodies found—do you know? What part of the garden?"

"All I know is that it was nearby a wall and a stream. The landslide knocked the wall down."

I nodded. I knew exactly where it was. The hill where the giant orange rose bloomed. The rose that my mother had painted over and over and over, for decades.

When the detective left, Samir said, "Are you all right for a little while? I should go see how my father is doing."

"Of course. I'm fine."

He lifted one heavy brow.

I shook my head. "Not fine as in 'all is well' but fine in the sense that you don't have to worry about me. I have some things to do. Some things to think about."

"Such as?"

"Everything. What I'm doing here."

"You're just tired. Don't give up."

335

"My mother did have something to do with Sanvi's disappearance," I said heavily. "You mother said so, and I was deeply offended. But she was right."

"Don't jump to conclusions, Olivia," he said, a gentle hand on my shoulder. "You're overwhelmed—the earl and the fire and now this. You can't make any decisions right now."

"I made the decision to come here when I was overwhelmed."

"And?"

"Maybe I've been making one terrible decision after another. Maybe I'm still doing that. Alexander said yesterday that I'm in over my head, and he's totally right. He offered me a huge sum for the estate." I looked up at him. "Maybe I should take it."

"You're not seriously considering selling? He'll never give the house what you will."

"The house is not salvageable!" I cried. "Not now. All that progress we made is just—poof!" I snapped my fingers. "Gone." I peered up at him in despair. "Don't you see? It just can't be saved."

"No, I don't see," he said, taking my wrist in hand. "You're not a quitter, Olivia. You're not going to give up like that. Did you see all those people here yesterday? How happy they were? Rosemere is a symbol for the village, a piece of history. There's been a surge of interest through the television show. You mustn't give up."

"He said he wouldn't develop the land."

"You're serious." He straightened, frowning. "You're really thinking of selling?"

I took a breath. "I don't know what else to do. There isn't enough money to fix it."

"So it will take longer. You can live here and go inch by inch."

I shrugged. "Go see your dad. I'll be fine."

For one long moment, he measured me.

"Honestly," I cried. "Would it be so terrible to just let go? I would be very wealthy. Life would be so much easier."

"Is that what you want? Really? To have an easy life? Jet set around, maybe?"

"Would that be so bad? We could do anything, go anywhere." A sense of lightness filled my chest. "It would be fun."

"That isn't who you are. You're afraid. And you cannot have a life of great meaning if you make decisions out of fear."

"Haven't you ever been afraid, Samir?"

"Of course I have! And I've fallen on my face, in public, with the entire world waiting for me to do it." He spread his hands in the air, like a prophet. "Nothing happened! It all blew by."

"But you've been afraid to let people know about us."

"Not because I don't want them to know," he cried. "Because I don't want anyone interfering before we understand ourselves what we are, where we are going." He swallowed, touched his chest. "This . . . thing between us feels so important, and I didn't want anyone else in it until we solidified it."

I flung myself at him then, let him wrap me close, my cheek against his heart, his hands in my hair. I held on tight. "This scares me too," I whispered. "I'm afraid I'll be broken into a million pieces."

"But what if we soar? What if we—what if this—is the way the gods rectify some terrible wrong?" He pulled back, held my face. "What if we can make things right for those who lost? Our grandmothers? What if"—he pressed his hands more tightly to my head—"this our test?"

I wanted to believe in his vision of the world, in his hope, but my soul felt as if it were made of lead, some dull, dead thing I was hauling around. I looked into his beautiful eyes, seeing the world in them, the heavens, and I still couldn't find my way to say anything at all. I could only think of my mother. What she'd done.

What had she done?

He closed his eyes. Pressed a kiss to my forehead. "Rest. I'm going to see my father. I will call you later."

When he left, I dressed in a warm sweater and green wellies with my jeans, my hair pulled out of my face into a ponytail, and walked out to the rose garden. Police tape guarded the site, but I could see my guess was correct—the orange flower was the one that had collapsed under the landslide, along with the damask roses. A young man stood by the landslide, looking stoic in the continuing drizzle. "Good afternoon," I said. "I'm Lady Shaw."

He touched his hat.

"This is where the bodies were buried?" I asked the policeman standing by.

"Aye. They've removed the bones to the coroner's."

The multicolored rose had tumbled sideways, and its roots stuck up in the air. "Can we move that so that the rose doesn't die? It was important to my mother."

"I dunno. You have to ask the inspector. I don't think you're allowed to touch it."

"Hmm," I said and reached for it, pulling it lower into the mud that surrounded it. "There, that'll keep it from dying." I slapped my muddy hands together. "When will they make an identification?"

"I believe relatives have identified some of the girl's belongings. It'll take a bit to identify dental records and such."

"All right." My hands were cold in the drizzle, and I shook them off. "Carry on."

As I walked back to the flat, I thought of the roses in my mother's paintings. The eyes peering out so malevolently from her sketchbook. The little animals in all the paintings. The cabin of safety.

Urgently, I opened my laptop and called up the digital images Madeline had sent me of my mother's work. Nearly all of her paintings were here, and I went through them in the order they'd been painted.

And the story was all there. Innocent creatures in a malevolent forest. A wolf panting in the shadows, teeth long. Roses growing through, over, around everything. The giant orange-and-pink rose often glowing in the distance.

Something was still missing after I searched them all. It was a simple story, but I didn't have the end. I needed to see the children's book I'd given Helen.

The rain had gone again, leaving behind heavy clouds, and I walked through the forest to the village and to Helen's place. She opened the door and cried out, "Olivia! I saw the fire. Are you all right? Is the house all right? Are you—"

"It's a mess right now. I don't know." I crossed my arms over my chest. "I need to look at the book my mother illustrated. If you wouldn't mind."

"Of course. Come in. Can I get you a cup of tea?"

"Please. And . . . I'm sorry; do you have any biscuits or anything? I've just realized I haven't eaten since yesterday sometime."

"Oh, my dear, my dear." She hugged me, sat me at the table in a room cheery with plants and paintings. Before I even really settled, she produced a plate of nut breads and scones and a pot of creamy butter. "Don't wait. I'll just go find the book, but you must eat."

I slathered the bread with butter and devoured it so fast that I got the hiccups, which made me laugh even in my current mood. Waiting for them to subside, I leaned against the wall and took a long, slow, deep breath. My phone buzzed with a text, and I glanced at it. Samir said, My father wants to speak with you as soon as he can.

I'm at Helen's. Will come by soon.

Helen returned with a tray and the book under her arm. "I'll pour," she said. "You can have a look."

I opened the book and leafed through it slowly, looking at every frame, in all the details, for anything I might have missed. In the border was a second story, something she was known to do, and I followed that intently. A little rabbit, down in a hole, covered with a tiny checkered blanket, while aboveground, a monster stomped by, bellowing, while a girl hid behind a tree. The rabbit in a forest, shivering as the wolf grabbed the girl and held her high in the air. More of that, fear and stalking, and the last scene, a dead monster by a pool and a girl with an ax in her hand nearby. The rabbit shivered at her foot.

Helen placed a mug of tea before me. "Is it true they found the girl's body?"

I nodded, touching the girl with the ax. "And probably my uncle's body too."

"Oh, dear. I hadn't heard that part."

"Why did she come back here? What does she want me to understand? Why didn't she just let this whole thing go?"

"I can't answer those questions. They're yours to understand." She patted my hand. "Drink your tea, and have a scone. That will help."

In spite of my frustration, I smiled. "I'm going to leave England just to avoid becoming as big as a house."

"Really? I was thinking you looked well, as if you've trimmed up a bit."

I raised my eyebrows and sank my teeth into the perfectly crumbly, exquisitely slathered scone. "It won't last."

I left the book with Helen, knowing I could get another if I needed it, and walked to the apartment above Coriander. The sky was lightening, and I looked back to see if I could glimpse Rosemere, to see if I could discern the damage at this distance, but the angle was wrong.

The kitchen was quiet—and I knocked at the bottom of the stairs. "Hello?"

Samir appeared. "Come up. He's quite anxious to talk to you."

"Is he all right?"

"I can't tell." He looked at me closely. "How are you?"

I shrugged. "No idea." I paused. "I'm almost certain that my mother must have killed her brother."

His expression did not change. He only nodded, touching the small of my back as I passed into the apartment.

Harshad sat at the table near the kitchen, a cup of tea before him. A window was open slightly to the breeze, which rustled a light curtain. The air smelled of ginger. "Olivia," he said. The sorrow that lived on his brow had fallen to circles below his eyes, turned down the corners of his mouth. He looked ten years older. "I'm glad you could come. Please, sit down. Would you like tea? My wife makes a lovely chai."

"Yes, please," I said and glanced toward the kitchen. "Hello, Mrs. Malakar."

"Hello." She did not look at me, only busied herself with the cup and pot.

"Are you all right, Mr. Malakar?"

"Well, it is no surprise, is it?" He sighed. "We have always known she was dead."

"Knowing and having actual proof are very different."

"Yes," he said.

Mrs. Malakar gave me a cup of milky tea, and I sipped it. Peppery, gingery, sweet. Not quite the same as Samir's and I shot him a glance. "Bracing," I said.

He winked.

"Olivia," Harshad said, touching my arm across the wrist, as each of his children had done at moments of crisis. "Your mother did not come to see me when she was here this summer, though I knew she was here."

My body leaned forward.

"She came to me before she left here, when she was young. When we were young." His hands rested heavily in his lap, and his shoulders were bent with a heavy burden.

I spoke quietly. "You don't have to say, if you don't want to."

"I do." He looked at his hands, wiped one palm against the other. "We always knew there was something wrong with Roger. He did terrible things for no reason—caught a bird and locked it in a shed so that it died."

I flinched.

"Yes." His face showed the pain such a thing roused in him. "Things like that."

"Did he abuse my mother?"

"He was cruel to her in a hundred ways. A thousand, but I don't know about . . . the other. I hope that was not true. She was a very unhappy girl as it was."

"She was very afraid of him. It's all over her paintings."

"If he hurt her, that makes sense," Mrs. Malakar said, sitting down next to her husband.

My throat grew tight, and I had to look away to stop the visions of my artistic, eccentric, kind mother being hurt in any way. I swallowed and met his gaze, prompting, "She came to you?"

Harshad took a breath, looked at his wife, who gave him a slight nod. He nodded. "She found Roger trying to burn poor Sanvi's dead body, and she killed him. Stabbed him with gardening shears." His eyes filled with tears. "Many times." He shifted, cleared his throat. "She came to me for help. There was no one else she could ask."

A place in my throat tightened, choking any words I might have thought to utter. The scene played itself in my mind. The fire, the man who'd gone over the edge, my mother's long-suffering fury suddenly snapping. I covered my mouth, afraid of what I would say.

"You've known Sanvi was dead, all this time?" Samir asked, his voice shocked.

"It was not a choice I made lightly." The grief of his long-ago loss weighed on his shoulders. "I loved my sister, and I wanted to kill him myself."

Again, he wiped one hand against the other, Lady Macbeth. "But Caroline had already done it for that crime and all the others she suffered. If I had told the police where Sanvi was, they would have found Roger, and Caroline would have gone to prison. That didn't seem right to me."

I hated to ask the question, but I suddenly knew it was true. "She was pregnant, wasn't she? With me."

"Yes."

Behind me, Samir stepped close and settled his hands on my shoulders. I asked, "Was Roger my father?"

"No. But I don't know who it was. She never told me that."

I briefly closed my eyes, both relieved and weary. If Roger was not my father, who was? Could I find him?

But I also realized that if my mother had been pregnant with me before she'd left England, I was a full year or more older than I thought I was. Already forty.

I carefully did not look at Mrs. Malakar.

Gently, Samir said, "Finish the story, Dad. She needs to hear it all."

"We buried the bodies in the garden and moved roses to cover them. I came back and told my mother, and she agreed that Caroline should not be punished. We never told my father. He would have wanted anyone, everyone punished for Sanvi's death. He didn't . . . know all of it."

"All of what?" I asked, but it was hard to speak.

"My mother and your grandmother. Their love affair."

I glanced up at Samir. "You knew, all this time? We found some photos—they're very explicit."

"When I was a child, I saw them kissing. I was only six or seven, maybe, but I knew that women didn't kiss that way." He shook his

343

head. "All of their lives, they hid." As if he came back from a very, very faraway place, he raised his head. "It was Roger's discovery of their . . . affair . . . that caused so much pain. He blackmailed your grandmother into marriage, and my mother was furious and married too. And then your mother and I were born, and—" He spread his hands. "They were so lonely, the two of them, without each other."

It seemed I'd been weeping for months, and there could be no more tears in me, but this brought a fresh onslaught, an ocean's worth of emotion, rendering me speechless. The tears flowed down my face, and Mr. Malakar nodded, pushing a box of tissues my way.

"I know," he said.

"Dad, I've been so worried you would be upset if you knew," Samir said.

"Your generation did not invent the world, son."

Emotions continued to pour through my eyes, through my nose, and I bent my head at last, hiding. "Give me a minute. I'll be better soon."

My poor mother, lost and locked and caught in the middle of so many currents. She'd even left behind her lover, for my sake. "My mother," I said and wept the more.

"Leave us alone," Mrs. Malakar said.

I was aware of them leaving, but I couldn't raise my head, couldn't stop crying. It was as if all the happiness in the world had been sucked out, and I heard a wail escape my lips. Mrs. Malakar's hand fell on my back.

"I miss her so much."

"She's always with you. A mother never leaves."

I kept my head down, unable to stop my hiccupping, ridiculous outpouring. "I'm sorry," I said. "I don't know . . . why . . . I just can't . . . stop."

"It was time to weep," she said calmly. Her hand moved in a slow, easy circle between my shoulder blades.

So I let it be time. I cried for my grandmother and Nandini; for Sanvi, stolen and lost so young; and for my mother, who had carried this burden with her for all of her life and never breathed a word of it.

At last, I lifted my head. "She went to America, and she was happy," I said. "She left it all and became someone else."

She gave me a cup towel, and I mopped my face. "It was brave. I didn't know this story. I only sensed there was something between my husband and your mother. I thought they might have been lovers." She shook her head, brushed hair from my wet face. "Women have ever had to pay for the crimes of men."

"I'm even older than I thought I was," I said.

She folded her hands in her lap. Nodded. "You will need to tell him, but I don't think it will matter. He's as arrogant as a lord." She touched the bracelet on my wrist, Nandini's bracelet. "Perhaps, in the light of things, it isn't so important."

I nodded. "Thank you for everything," I said, dragging in a long breath. "There's something I need to do."

Samir and Harshad were waiting downstairs in the closed restaurant. "I'm so sorry about your sister and your mother," I said.

"Thank you. I am sorry about your mother."

I nodded, then realized the kitchen was entirely quiet. "Where is Pavi?"

"She closed the restaurant. I don't know where she went."

"Will you ask her to call me when she returns?" When he nodded, I turned to his son. "Samir, will you drive me home? I have some things I need to do."

His expression was sober, and all the words of the morning filled the space between us. "Of course."

In the car, he said, "We need to get you driving. If you stay, that is."

I was buzzing with emotion and exhaustion. I could only nod and lean my head back. "I need things to just stop for a couple days. I'm so tired."

"If you're tired," he said in a reasonable tone, "perhaps the best answer is to sleep."

"Mmm." I was half-asleep before we left the parking lot. When we reached the flat, he helped me inside. "Don't do anything hard," he said. "Just go to sleep."

I nodded and staggered off into the new bedroom.

Enough.

Chapter Twenty-Five

It was morning when I awakened, dry mouthed and slightly dizzy with lack of eating, but as I hurried to the bathroom, I realized my head was clear. The fuzziness was just gone. I showered and washed my hair vigorously, then made myself a massive breakfast of eggs and bacon and toast and coffee made in a brand-new french press, with whole cream and real sugar. Just the way I liked it.

For all my righteous indignation, I couldn't help looking over the offer from Alexander again, and it was truly substantial. It would be like winning the lottery. I'd never have to work again. I could buy a big house on the sea and take up painting and travel whenever I wished.

It wouldn't be the worst life of all time.

On the other hand was the house. The estate. The lands and people. My mother had gone through a lot of trouble to get me out of here and then to get me back, and I still didn't fully understand why. Why bring me back? Why not just let the old wreck fall into ruin?

It might have taken one more step in that direction with the fire. Before I could do anything else, I had to reckon with Rosemere, with whatever had happened last night, two weeks ago, decades, centuries ago. The only way to do that was to gather up the courage Samir had so accurately named missing and face the actual rooms. By myself.

Entry was blocked from the kitchen, though I peered at it through the window. Smoke stains made it difficult to see anything, but certainly there was damage to the ceilings and walls.

Rounding the house, I touched the stones that made the house glow, crunched over pine needles and leaves, releasing a fragrance of spice and decay. The windows of the first floor were above my head, and I looked up to see if they were fire damaged, but from this angle they appeared whole.

Until I came to the front. The main floor was fine, but the second floor windows gaped across the front, and the third floor windows were buckled too. I frowned. Had the room that burned before been the epicenter of the fire this time too? It had seemed, last night, to have been in the kitchen.

In the quiet, I shivered, thinking of that room.

A cat dashed out of the cover of shrubs and meowed. "Meow Meow," I cried. "Are you okay?"

He looked fine, if a little grimier than usual, and when I bent down to pick him up, he let me, nestling his head on my shoulder and purring under my ear. "I'm so sorry. That must have been terrible. Were you very afraid?"

"Meow," he said, hoarsely. I stroked his fur, long and staticky.

"Let's get this over with," I said, carrying him with me. His body felt like a shield, something protective, so when he leapt down as I approached the front door, I was disappointed. "Do you want to come with me?" I asked, opening the door.

He sat down, curled his tail around his feet.

The rain had stopped, I realized, and I looked back toward the village. It shimmered with distance, the thatched roofs cozy against a slate sky. Did I owe the village my allegiance? Did they really need the estate at all in the modern world?

The door stuck a bit, but when I pushed, it gave way, and I tumbled into the main hallway. The magnificent Elizabethan stairway. The wood had smears of soot, but it didn't appear to be damaged, and I didn't realize how I'd been holding my breath over that. The window, too, appeared to be undamaged.

When I peeked into the parlor, however, the damage was more apparent—the ceiling gaping, blackened supports hanging down. Too dangerous to navigate that direction, so I headed around the other side of the stairs and poked my head into the library, adjacent to the ballroom that had been so damaged by time and then the collapsing roof. Work had been focused here, and I could see the progress. It smelled of fresh lumber, and the floors had been cleared. New shelves waited for new books, or maybe old ones, and the old window seat was stripped, awaiting new wood and fabric. The little girl in me longed to take a book to that spot and look out toward the village—I could almost see a figure there against the glass.

Mom, I thought. *Did you sit there to read?*

And it was only my imagination offering my grieving heart a wish, but it felt as if she were with me after that, when I pushed as far as I could into the servant's quarters, stopping short of the pantry, which was fire damaged, the servants' stairs closed off. She accompanied me up the main stairs and down the long hall to Violet's room, which had never frightened me at all. I stood there in the silence and closed my eyes. If I lived here, this would be my bedroom.

After a moment, I forced myself to explore the rest of the rooms, the ones I'd never entered, the ones that scared me or gave off a creepy vibe. I was careful with anything that seemed to be dangerous structurally, but so much work had been done to the north-side rooms that I didn't have to worry until I crossed the third story.

Again, I entered every room I could. Carefully looked at the ones I could not. I greeted my ancestors and the disembodied spirits of dogs and children and servants. I listened to the quiet and let it tell me its tragedies, entered the minstrel's gallery and made peace with the girl who'd flung herself over the edge for love. I climbed into the tower and looked out at the land.

The land. So much of it. Fertile and productive and exquisitely beautiful.

And protected.

By me.

My heart expanded, as if to encompass everything I saw—hills and sheep and cottages and trees. The conservatory poked up, old glass removed, panels awaiting the new. A pair of peacocks strutted up the path toward the garden. Overhead, a trio of birds flew across the clearing sky.

And there, as if benevolently arranged by my mother, was a rainbow, its end planted in a field of gold rapeseed.

Rainbows. Rainbows. Rainbows.

I knew where the answer was.

Samir and I drove to an address just north of London, in an industrial section of land. I'd found the last clue in the treasure hunt when I finally put together the rainbow imperatives—she'd painted a rainbow for me as a child, a painting that had hung in my bedroom my entire life. It had been moved with the other paintings when the Menlo Park house had been cleared out, so it took some time for Madeline to find it, but on the back was the address.

Now we entered the building and found the proper hallway. It was not an open-air facility but had several security checkpoints for entry, and we finally stood before the door. I fitted the key the earl had given me into the lock, and it turned.

The room was quite full—boxes and boxes of what turned out to be books, all the books from the library, in pristine condition. Samir made a sound that was half hunger, half laughter. "God, this is amazing."

The paintings were stacked neatly against the walls and lined up on shelves—dozens of them, all sizes. "The gold at the end of the rainbow," I said and spied the last painting. The one this had all been about.

Her last painting.

It was massive, as large as her *Forest #5*, but it showed the cottage of her earlier paintings sitting in the middle of a forest clearing. The light was dawnlike, soft, and the animals were all facing the cottage, squirrels and foxes, birds and owls, and three little black-and-white cats with long fur. Through the window, gold lit and warm, were a mother and a child in a rocking chair. My mother and I.

"You were her sanctuary," Samir said, his hand on my shoulder.

"Do you see what a beautiful person she was?" My hand covered my heart.

"I do."

I laughed, suddenly. "And she set all of this up, the treasure hunt, so that I would have something to do other than fall apart over her death. She knew I would be lost, so she gave me a place to find her."

"It's an extraordinary story," he said.

"Another chapter in the Rosemere family history." I looked around. "Even if none of the paintings is at the level of Monet or Constable, there are plenty here to keep the renovations going." I thought of the damage from the fire, which had completely destroyed two rooms. The kitchen had stood up to the fire remarkably well, but the parlor and the bedroom that had belonged to Roger were gone. No sign of arson. The fire chief had said simply there was no evidence of foul play. Sometimes old houses caught fire. I imagined, superstitiously, that it was the house ridding itself of the old evil. "At least for a little while."

"So you're not going to sell it off to the Earl of Marswick and fly off to Saint-Tropez?"

"No." I turned. "I've been thinking about this, and the answer is right under my nose. My area of expertise is food and restaurants. The tenants want an organic concern, with meat and produce, and we can turn that into both a market and a restaurant, a destination restaurant. Maybe turn a few rooms into hotel rooms for overnight guests."

"I like it."

"You realize that if my mother was pregnant when she left England, I'm older than I thought. It might not be that easy for me to have children. Ever."

"Olivia." He took my face in his hands, his long, lovely hands. "I want you. If there are children, there will be children. If not— God knows there are children in the world who need parents to love them."

My heart stilled. "You would adopt children?"

"Yes."

I imagined my farmhouse table, in that big kitchen, filled with children. And family. And friends. The house alive again, the land thriving. "Maybe twelve?"

He laughed. "Let's start with a dog."

"We'll have two cats and a dog!"

"They'll be all right."

"Are we doing this, then? Me and you?"

He gave me his wide, inclusive, benevolent smile. "Has there ever been any doubt?"

As he kissed me amid the treasures my mother had spirited away, I felt her in the room, smoking and cheerful. I felt Violet and Nandini, swirling together, at last, in us, in our blood.

"Let's be happy," he said.

For all of them, for ourselves. "Yes," I said.

Acknowledgments

Sometimes, a book simply arrives, practically whole, and this one did exactly that, flying into my life on a dark Thursday morning when almost everything in the world seemed upside down. I'm so grateful to the people who helped me bring it into the world, including my agent, Meg Ruley, and the publishing team at Lake Union. My fellow G, Kaumudi Marathe, was very generous with her expertise in helping me develop the idea of Coriander and the fresh, beautiful food that would be served there, as well as the vast differences in foods across various regions in India. I learned more than I could have imagined from her books, including her cookbook, *The Essential Marathi*. I am also deeply grateful to Sonali Dev and Monica Pradhan Caltabiano, who made room in their busy schedules to read the manuscript and sometimes had conflicting comments, which emphasized even more that India is indeed vast, not One Thing but many, many, many. Thank you for helping me sort through it.

Finally, I'm grateful to the Writer Unboxed gang who were gathered in Salem, Massachusetts, that week and Sarah Ramsey, who shared it too.

About the Author

Photo © 2009 Blue Fox Photography

Barbara O'Neal is the author of eleven novels of women's fiction, including *How to Bake a Perfect Life* and *The Lost Recipe for Happiness.* Her award-winning books have been published in a dozen countries, including France, England, Poland, Australia, Turkey, Italy, Germany, and Brazil.

Barbara lives in the stunningly beautiful city of Colorado Springs with her beloved, a British endurance athlete who vows he'll never lose his accent.